T0267631

GHOST ISLAND

BERKLEY TITLES BY MAX SEECK

THE WITCH HUNTER

THE ICE COVEN

THE LAST GRUDGE

GHOST ISLAND

GHOST ISLAND

A GHOSTS OF THE PAST NOVEL

MAX SEECK

TRANSLATION BY
Kristian London

BERKLEY
New York

BERKLEY
An imprint of Penguin Random House LLC
penguinrandomhouse.com

Originally published in Finnish as *Loukko* by Tammi Publishers, Helsinki, 2022.

Library of Congress Cataloging-in-Publication Data

Names: Seeck, Max, 1985- author. | London, Kristian, translator.
Title: Ghost island / Max Seeck, Kristian London.
Other titles: Loukko. English
Description: First U.S. edition. | New York : Berkley, 2024. |
Series: A ghosts of the past novel
Identifiers: LCCN 2023026671 (print) | LCCN 2023026672 (ebook) |
ISBN 9780593438862 (trade paperback) | ISBN 9780593438879 (ebook)
Subjects: LCGFT: Detective and mystery fiction. | Ghost stories. | Novels.
Classification: LCC PH356.S44 L6813 2024 (print) |
LCC PH356.S44 (ebook) |
DDC 894/.54134--dc23/eng/20220708
LC record available at https://lccn.loc.gov/2023026671
LC ebook record available at https://lccn.loc.gov/2023026672

First U.S. Edition: February 2024

Printed in the United States of America
1st Printing

Book design by Katy Riegel

For Grandma Sinikka

(1935–2022)

GHOST ISLAND

Prologue

MARTIN HEDBLOM FOLDS the newspaper on the desk and yawns. He has browsed through the sports pages twice but, once again, the *Nya Åland* has not exactly been a stimulating read. The local paper, launched the previous spring, is more to Martin's taste than its competitor, *Tidningen*, but it's no *New York Times*. Martin traces with his fingernail the ring his coffee cup left on the front page, then kicks his feet up onto the desk. He glances at the clock on the wall: in no time at all, the minute hand will nudge ahead to the twelve and it will be two o'clock, which means his night shift is only halfway over. He glances at the man reflected in the glass wall of his cubicle, then quickly shifts his gaze back to the newspaper, as if seeing his own image repulsed him. The reflection does not, of course, show the Martin who started as the night watchman at the orphanage nearly four decades before. His face has swollen like rising dough, not to mention his waistline. And although the sideburns bleeding into the stubble are still thick and lush, the crown of his head has not sprouted a hair in years.

Martin is fifty-five years old, an unambitious, comfort-seeking bachelor who has lived in the same little corner of Ahvenanmaa his whole life, aside from a brief stint when he tested his wings as a professional drummer and played on the cruise boats that sail between Finland and Sweden. But ultimately he returned to the job that was familiar and—most important—easy and undemanding enough for a lazy bastard like Martin. That was how his professor father, without putting too fine a point on it, had summarized the matter, and in the case of his only son, he was regrettably right.

Martin reaches for his gray canteen and takes a swig of vodka cut with orange soda as he eyes the empty corridors. The children are sound asleep in their rooms, and it's unlikely he will be called on to do anything during the night. He rarely is, if ever. As a matter of fact, he could drink himself silly at his desk or, alternatively, sleep through the night and still take home his paycheck with a clear conscience if those assholes from local social services didn't perform their random checks. Martin has been caught dozing twice, and the next time might prove the last. It's a risk simply not worth taking so close to retirement.

Martin glances at the desk drawer, where a porn magazine lies beneath a stack of folders. Jerking off during the night shift always feels a little suspect, but one of the children got special permission to spend the night at the Nordins' tonight, and the other three are asleep in their rooms, so no one can catch him off guard. The intimate moment does not involve hopes of being caught in the act or anything else perverted or questionable, or at least that's what Martin tells himself. He just wants to kill a little time in the company of Desiree West and Laura Sands.

Martin undoes his belt and reaches for the drawer handle. The very thought of the centerfold girls has set his blood pumping. He's going to give them a real ride tonight, at least in his imagination. He even has a tissue in his pocket . . .

But just as he takes hold of the magazine, the black telephone on the desk starts to ring. Martin abandons his magazine and quickly lifts the receiver so that none of the children are awoken by the ringing, especially now that he's sitting at the desk with his fly undone.

"Smörregård Children's Home," Martin says in a raspy voice, and swallows to clear his throat. The fingers of his free hand urgently buckle up his belt, as if the caller has miraculous powers of perception.

But there's no voice on the line, only steady breathing.

"Hello?" Martin says.

Now he hears a voice that seems to be humming something. It's a melancholy tune that sounds vaguely familiar. *Damn it.* Martin is filled with annoyance: some prick has decided to make a prank call to the orphanage in the middle of the night. It's none of the children, of course, because there are only two functioning phones in the building: the one he's holding in his sweaty hand and the one behind Director Boman's locked office door. Besides, none of the children have so much as gone to the bathroom since lights-out.

"Who is this?" Martin asks, on the verge of slamming the receiver down. But the soft melody hummed by the caller gives him pause. He hasn't heard it in decades yet remembers it vividly. "The Birds Fly Back in the Spring."

The humming abruptly stops. Martin's hand clenches the plastic receiver against his cheek harder and harder. The mouthpiece smells of dried saliva.

"Are you ready?" the voice says. It's soft and could belong to a woman or a man, or why not a girl or a boy?

"Ready? For what?" Martin growls, but he can hear the fear in his voice. "Who is this?"

For a moment, Martin hears nothing but steady breathing.

"It's two o'clock," the whispering voice then says.

Martin instinctively glances at the clock on the wall. "What the hell is this?"

"I'm waiting out here. In my blue coat. Come and get me," the voice says, then starts humming the same melody again. A few seconds later, the call ends in a mechanical click, and Martin can no longer hear anything but persistent beeps that ring in his ears even after he has returned the phone to its cradle.

He closes the desk drawer. If just a moment ago he was preoccupied with thoughts of a redheaded centerfold with seductive eyes, arched back, and perky tits, thoughts of a very different nature have now insinuated their way into his mind. Shivers run down his spine as he allows his gaze to slide past the empty hall and closed doors, behind which the children are sleeping. Or at least ought to be.

It's two o'clock . . . In my blue coat.

Martin grits his teeth; it takes all the will he can muster to resist the urge to slam his fist into the desk. Kick every door in this dump open and order the children to line up in the hall. That's what the director would do. One of the children must be behind this, one way or another. A low-down trick. Low-down but devilishly creepy, he must admit. Whoever the little shit is, Martin is going to show them who's afraid of whom.

He lowers his fingers to the phone. A minute passes, but nothing happens. The phone rests on the desk, as mute as if its cord has been pulled out of the wall.

I'm waiting . . .

Martin mentally replays to himself the words he just heard and finds his arm hairs standing on end. The song the caller hummed has remained smoldering in his consciousness.

There's no way. It's impossible.

Someone's just trying to scare me, Martin thinks. *And they succeeded, goddamn it.*

Even so, he has to check it out, go down to the dock and have a look, because otherwise he won't be able to get it out of his head. The possibility that it was . . .

Martin grabs the keys from the desk and stands, steps out of his cubicle. All the doors in the long corridor are closed, including the kitchen door at the far end. The only sound to break the silence is that of his heart hammering in his ears.

His footfalls echo hollowly in the empty hallway. Martin glances to the side and steps onto the stairs. The short flight leads to a stout door. Beyond it, a lawn opens up, and farther to the left loom the red boathouses and the T-shaped dock. As he descends the few stairs, it occurs to him that he could have looked in on the children and made sure all three were actually asleep in their beds. It wouldn't be the first time one of his charges climbed out a window and temporarily ran off. But the fugitive would have had to find a phone to pull off that prank, and there aren't many on the island: maybe one at the Nordin residence two kilometers away on the southern shore, and . . . *Is that little shit who's spending the night at the Nordins' behind this . . . ?*

Martin opens the door and steps out. In the September night the drizzle-dampened lawn glistens, illuminated jointly by the yard lights and by the half-moon shining brightly in the sky. The tarp spread over the rowboats flipped over near the boathouses flaps in the wind, blocking his view of the dock. Martin wipes his moist nostrils and starts striding purposefully toward the water.

And a moment later, a cold chill washes over him. A silhouetted child standing on the dock forms a shadow against the moonlit water.

What the hell . . . ?

Martin has the urge to turn on his heel, run back inside, and lock the door. Call someone and . . . But whom? A child shivering in a thin coat at the end of the dock is not a matter for the police but for social services. And now that he thinks about it, the figure facing the sea has to be one of the four children he's responsible for when he's on the clock. He has to do his job and bring the child to safety— even if the situation is eerily reminiscent of the story Martin knows better than well, the story that everyone who lives in the vicinity has heard or witnessed with their own eyes. Martin remembers it all as if it were yesterday.

"Hello?" Martin says.

But the figure doesn't stir. The hem of the blue coat flutters in the wind. It must be one of the girls . . .

"Milla, is that you?"

Martin holds his breath, takes a step forward, and surprises himself with his determination. The girl's golden-brown hair has been pulled into a ponytail that swings in the breeze. It's a girl; it has to be. One of them, Milla or Laura.

The contours of the diminutive figure come into sharper relief with every step he takes. The neck is a little crooked, the head tilted a bit to the right—stiffly so, like that of a corpse with rigor mortis.

"Laura?"

The child doesn't react to his call.

Martin steps onto the dock, feels it bounce on its long pontoons. He raises his voice, hears it quivering.

"Hey! Knock it off! This isn't funny." Martin realizes he has stopped. Why isn't the girl turning around? Can't she hear him calling to her? The rowboats' tarp pops in the wind, setting Martin's heart pounding.

He advances tentatively toward the girl. The dock is rickety and rocks underfoot like a rolling log, ready to spit him into the frigid water.

This can't be happening, he thinks, and once again he considers the possibility of turning around and running. Because even though a child is involved—and it clearly is a child—the situation is somehow creepy. Not least because long ago he used to see a little girl stand in the exact same spot. Night after night. And eventually she disappeared without a trace.

Martin continues onward, approaches the figure, and reaches out to take hold of the girl.

And just as he lowers his hand to her shoulder, senses the bony body in his fingertips, he feels a sharp pain in his neck and falls to

his knees. Martin doesn't have time to shout, and not a single resi-
dent of Smörregård Children's Home appears at any of the windows.
As he lies there on the dock, he sees tawny hair fluttering in the
wind, and a pale face devoid of emotion. Then the nocturnal seascape with its bridge to the moon is replaced by absolute darkness.

1

2020

THE HUM IS so soft that it isn't really disturbing. Even so, Jessica can't help but notice it.

The other woman is waiting for her to speak, has been for almost a minute now. The thought in Jessica's head is unusually clear, but uttering it requires effort.

"I guess I'm trying to say . . . I'd anchored my life in another person's presence," she begins, and is caught off guard by the confident note in her voice. "Saw it from someone else's perspective. Does that make any sense?"

The woman sitting across from Jessica in a beige armchair doesn't immediately respond, uses the silence to encourage Jessica to continue thinking out loud. She is skilled at leading; the session seems to be progressing according to a predetermined choreography instead of there being two equals sitting there in armchairs, conversing without an agenda. Everything is clinical and coordinated, but Jessica doesn't let it bother her. She knew what she was getting into when she started her psychotherapy sessions a month ago.

"Before I met Erne . . . I was lost. I didn't understand it at the time . . . And now—"

Suddenly Jessica's voice thickens as if she is forbidden from continuing. As if someone else is forbidding her.

The therapist doesn't rush Jessica; she sits in her seat, adjusts her grip on her ballpoint pen. Retracts the tip, then clicks it back out. Under some circumstances, the intermittently repeated mannerism would make a restless impression, but the psychiatrist repeats it in a controlled fashion.

Jessica looks at the woman's angular knuckles and light blue fingernails. They're surprisingly glossy, and for this reason it is somehow brazen for them to be the fingernails of a doctor specializing in psychiatry: a client opening up her heart might have the right to expect something more conservative. More empathetic. Something that shows her therapist isn't above the situation.

"Jessica?"

Jessica looks up at her therapist's face. "What?"

There's a break in her train of thought; perhaps her brain was trying to scan for visual stimuli as an excuse for her to stop talking.

A tender look creeps across the therapist's suntanned face. "Please go on. You were saying that you were lost, and now . . ."

It takes Jessica a moment to reorder her thoughts. She doesn't actually want to reveal her insight to this woman—or to anyone else, for that matter—but at the same time she is burning with a desire to hear the conclusion articulated out loud, to let the words spill out for a professional to assess. She wants to know whether her demons are capable of dodging the psychiatrist's sharp eye, of hiding skillfully, or might they nakedly expose themselves as a result of this sudden insight?

"I guess I've never really liked my life. Or myself, actually. Then suddenly there was someone who admired me in his own way. Loved me. The way a father loves a daughter. And it gave life meaning." Jessica sits there listening to the words she just uttered, as if they echoed in the emptiness. And suddenly she is overcome with shame. "I'm not totally sure whether this is about losing Erne or about losing a perspective that was important to me. About the fact that I didn't just love Erne. More like I loved myself the way he saw me," she continues, despite her rational mind's insistence that she stop.

The psychiatrist lowers her notepad to the armrest and presses her fingertips together.

She looks serious.

"I think we are possibly now on the cusp of something major."

Jessica cannot help but hear the massive cliché in this sentiment. Is this supposed to be the breakthrough they're always talking about on TV series?

"But . . . ?" she asks.

The therapist smiles, as if to reward Jessica for her insightful question. "But at the same time, I'm a little worried."

Jessica shakes her head because she isn't totally sure what the other woman is referring to. Not totally, although she has an enlightened guess.

"Do you feel as if your life hasn't had a purpose since Erne died?" the therapist asks, raising her head slightly. "Did that die along with Erne?"

Jessica looks at the other woman, whose face looks concerned. Perhaps it's purely professional concern, but it's concern nonetheless.

And when Jessica doesn't respond, the other woman continues: "Do you feel like at some point in your life you began to live for Erne alone?"

Jessica frowns; a rising nausea sears her throat. She reaches for her glass, takes a swig of room-temperature water, and turns toward the window. The leafless branches of the large oak sway in the wind; they crook like bony fingers stripped of flesh. The ceiling lights dim, casting the room in gloom. The hum grows louder, as if the electromagnetic potential in it is increasing.

"It's typical for people to want to please others, for instance their parents, and when the people on whose behalf we have made these efforts—which at times are in profound conflict with our own self-image—depart from our lives for good . . . the death can leave an enormous void. This void entails not only longing but also meaninglessness. The person no longer knows how to or even if they want to live solely for themselves. Am I on the right track?"

Jessica doesn't reply. She watches the branches that continue to dance outside, sees them penetrate the room through the seams of the white window frames without shattering the panes of glass. They slither across the floor and wrap around her ankles like gleaming black snakes. Gradually they tighten their grip, probe warily. "Because if that's the situation we're dealing with," the therapist says, "we need to approach it with the requisite seriousness."

Jessica blinks several times, and the lighting in the room returns to normal.

The snakes retreat, withdraw to the other side of the window frame, and freeze into trees again, as if in reverse entropy. For a moment, the yellow light in the room feels blinding.

The psychiatrist reaches for her pad and starts making notes. Jessica sees the woman's wrist move the pen but isn't sure what she's writing. Has she just jotted down the words "depressed" and possibly "self-destructive" in her leather-bound book? That would be a pretty apt description of Jessica's state, which means the headshrinker has earned her hourly fee, she supposes.

"Who does?" Jessica says, lowering her glass to the table. The nausea has overtaken her entire body; her stomach is roiling and her esophagus is burning. She has the urge to dash into the bathroom to vomit, but she restrains herself, swallows a few times.

"What do you mean?"

"You said we have to approach it seriously."

"You and I," the therapist clarifies, and adjusts her thin-framed glasses. "We've gone over a lot of things this past month and made some important observations, but today is the first time I've heard something we absolutely must address. I'd call it a hopelessness of sorts. It's important to pull ourselves out of such mental states, even if it's not necessarily easy."

Out in the freezing air, the branches stop moving until a powerful, howling gust brings them back to life. This time they don't cause Jessica to lose her focus.

"Tuula?" Jessica says, hearing how strange the name sounds when spoken out loud. It's probably the first time over the course of their brief patient–therapist relationship that Jessica has called the psychiatrist by her first name.

"Yes?"

"Over the last couple years alone I've investigated a dozen manslaughters or murders . . ." Jessica chuckles without smiling. "When you break through a brick wall and find a beautiful young woman inside . . . or see a man who has been stoned to death, his bashed-in skull covered by a still-bloody headful of hair . . . or when you smell the flesh of someone who's been burned alive . . . which in turn makes you think that somewhere in the world dogs are cooked alive, because the adrenaline produced by the terror and pain makes the meat tender . . ."

The psychiatrist looks ill at ease and would presumably like to ask Jessica to stop in order for her to define clearer boundaries for their conversations, but she cannot interrupt her patient, not now that Jessica is giving more of herself than ever before.

"Do you understand what I'm getting at?" Jessica says, then continues before the psychiatrist has time to react: "I've never had any hope. None of us do. But in the past I guess I knew how to deal with it better. I'd accepted the meaninglessness of my own existence."

The psychiatrist shuts her notebook and presses it into her lap, under her palms. "Jessica. We need to consider the alternative that—"

A wave of nausea washes over Jessica's body, and she springs out of the chair in the middle of the psychiatrist's sentence. The nausea that began on her way here has been churning inside her for the entire session and is growing less bearable with every passing instant.

"I have to go."

"But it's only half past," the psychiatrist says in confusion, craning her neck to see the wall clock behind Jessica.

"Sorry. I'll pay for the full hour."

"That's not what I—"

"Thank you, Tuula."

The other woman looks dumbfounded but quickly pulls herself together: "Shall we book the next session?"

Jessica doesn't reply. The branches of the oak tree scratch the window, and she shoots them a quick glance.

I don't think we're going to be seeing each other again. Good-bye.

2

OVER THE WAIL of the wind, Jessica hears the heavy wooden door shut behind her. The sky beyond the apartment buildings peering over Kruunuvuorenkatu is a pale gray. The wet rails splitting the narrow street carry the clank of the approaching streetcar.

Watery snowflakes glue themselves to Jessica's face as she adjusts her scarf to cover her cheeks. The vomit rising from her throat compels her to lower her head. She tries to draw in fresh air through her nostrils, hopes this will deter the swelling nausea, but the cold wind only intensifies the burn she's been feeling in her nose since sitting down in the psychiatrist's armchair.

Jessica knows she won't make it home. She glances at the building portico; the ornamental iron gate is open. There's not a soul in the long, vaulted passage leading to the inner courtyard. The courtyard is her only hope; she won't make it any farther than that. Jessica takes a few unsteady steps, passes through the gate, and is glancing back a final time when the stomach acid gushes up and out of her esophagus and splatters to the asphalt.

She wipes her mouth, bends over, and retches again.

Out on the street, the streetcar clatters past. Jessica swears to herself, raises her head, and gives herself a minute. She hawks up the dregs of vomit from her throat and spits the bile-saturated clumps to the ground.

Then she hears squelching footfalls carrying from the courtyard. Someone's coming.

She quickly pulls herself up to standing and leans with her hand against the wall, but the bearded man in the neon yellow safety coveralls who has trudged out from behind the rug-beating rack has already seen too much.

"What's going on here?" he asks, standing at a safe distance with his hands on his hips. There's no concern in his voice, more rebuke: he's like a teacher who has just ambushed ninth graders at their smoking spot.

"What does it look like?" Jessica says, wiping her mouth on her coat sleeve.

"How dare you?"

"Sorry. But it's not like I asked to feel sick."

The man sneers in disgust; his face darkens. "Do you even live here?" he says, grabbing a snow shovel leaning against the building. "I don't remember ever having seen—"

Jessica doesn't answer, just turns to continue on her way.

"Hey, answer me! Are you drunk? You're going to clean up after yourself, damn it!"

Jessica pauses at the iron gate and looks back. She doesn't have any reason to behave threateningly; just the opposite: she should act in accordance with her values, apologize and explain that she simply isn't feeling well. That's the truth, after all. She would, of course, pay for the cleaning, including an extra fee for the repulsiveness of the task, if doing so would get this courtyard tyrant guarding his little kingdom to calm down.

"You're fucking drunk," he says, looking Jessica up and down.

But the building super—judging by his eagerness to call Jessica to account, that's who he must be—has through his own behavior laid a weak foundation for this encounter's dynamics.

"What if I were?" Jessica says.

The man laughs. The mouth between the pockmarked cheeks

turns up in a gleeful smirk. "You can be as drunk as you want, but you're not going to make a mess of my yard, goddamn it."

"I'm sorry. I don't feel well," Jessica says, and is about to continue on her way again.

But the man won't relent. "Hey, little miss," he says, his voice a meter closer than it was before.

Little miss. Something inside Jessica blazes up.

She turns around to feel the man's thick fingers clenching her wrist.

"Let go," Jessica says quietly, but the fingers' grip just tightens.

The man brings his face closer, as if sniffing for alcohol on Jessica's breath. Apparently he's not a germophobe, considering she just puked. The jeering smile oozes with a condescending lust Jessica learned to identify long ago but would never learn to tolerate.

"Let go," Jessica says, trying to yank her arm free.

The man shakes his head and raises the shovel. "You're not going anywhere until you've cleaned up this mess. Or should I call the police?"

"Let go of me."

The man tightens his grip. Of course Jessica could tell him she's a police officer herself; an ID confirming the matter is in her wallet. But she doesn't want this guy to know any more about her than necessary. His eyes bore deeply into Jessica's, which are no doubt red after many sleepless nights. He probably thinks she's some sort of street trash, and Jessica's old sneakers, gray sweats, and black lived-in parka don't help matters.

"Goddamn junkie whore. I know your type . . . ," he says, and for a few silent moments something ignites in his eyes: maybe it's the sensation of power; maybe it's the titillation of the unexpected encounter and the situation. Maybe it's a desire to punish, to give a drunk girl some fatherly discipline. Jessica tastes the vomit in her mouth, takes in the fifty-year-old man's fat cheeks and coarse stubble. The jubilant look on his face.

"And I know yours," Jessica says.

With her free hand, she grabs the man by the wrist and twists, using her full body weight. No, Jessica isn't drunk, but she is fully capable of executing the justified-use-of-force moves she learned at the police academy.

The man roars, drops to his knees, and lets go of Jessica's wrist. She releases his wrist and knees him in the chest. The super collapses on his back in the wet snow and curses.

"Whore . . . ," he groans, gasping for breath. He tries to stand, but Jessica kicks him in the ribs. Once, a second time. Her vision blurs; she looks at the man in berserk fury.

"Call me a whore again . . . ," Jessica says, no longer sure whether she wants him to keep denigrating her. Because if he gives her one more reason to kick him, she will do so gladly, perhaps breaking a few of the asshole's ribs in the process.

Just then, out of the corner of her eye Jessica catches movement on one of the courtyard balconies. She thinks she sees two people, whom her blurred vision has distorted into a single figure. *I have to get out of here.* A car speeds past the portico. Jessica struggles to restrain her nausea, lunges out of the gate into the wan daylight, and starts striding quickly down the sidewalk. The red towers, copper roofs, and gold onion domes of Uspenski Cathedral rise above the park at the end of the street.

She hears an intensifying buzz in her head and the super's distant shouts beneath it.

Suddenly her right foot feels cold, and she realizes the sneaker it was in just a moment ago has fallen to the wayside, in all likelihood with the last kick she directed at the man in the portico. An elderly couple walking past ogles Jessica's uneven gait and the dripping sock on her foot. *Walk. Keep walking. Forget the shoe.*

She pulls her phone from her pocket to call a taxi, but it slips from her trembling fingers and crashes onto a manhole cover.

"*That's her! Stop her!*"

Jessica stoops to grab the phone and raises it to her ear. She tries to unlock it, but the screen is wet from the snow. Her fingers feel stiff. Nothing happens.

A streetcar breezes past, followed by a line of vehicles, a police van gliding past last of all. *How convenient.*

Jessica picks up the pace. Coarse sand prickles beneath her wet sock. If she could only slip into the little park, she might be able to shake her shadow.

"*Police!*"

The voice is faint, but when she reaches the corner of Satamakatu, she sees the blue lights of the police van stopped at the portico flash on. Snowflakes drift into Jessica's open mouth. Her jaw feels heavy, her breathing labored. Her head aches, and her vision is still blurred.

I've never had any hope. None of us do.

Jessica crosses the street, then stops under the trees rising at the edge of Tove Jansson Park. She rests a hand against one of the trunks and feels the urgent need to retch again.

And as she's puking there, she hears the siren of the approaching police van and sees the blue lights lick the snow-skimmed lawn and the low-hanging branches. Then the branches drop, lose their shape, and arch over her, as supple as willow branches.

3

HELENA LAPPI, SUPERINTENDENT of the Helsinki Police Violent Crimes Unit, follows the coveralled officer, yellow plastic bag in her hand. She white-knuckled the steering wheel all the way to police headquarters and tried to calm herself by doing the breathing exercises her wife taught her. If ever there's a time it's important to keep her cool, that time is now, even though she's got plenty on her plate as it is without infernal messes like this.

The police officer unlocks the door to the jail cell, and Hellu stops at the threshold. She sees a woman sitting on a mattress, and a tiny window and a toilet. She feels a sharp twinge of repugnance at the claustrophobic sight.

"Let's go." Hellu's voice is flat and surges forth like the cold from a just-opened freezer chest.

"Why? I'm having a great time here," Jessica says.

Hellu sighs soundlessly, then slowly steps into the cell. The police officer disappears in the direction she came from, leaving Hellu and Jessica alone.

"Niemi, what the hell is it this time?" Hellu leans against the wall opposite Jessica. Surprisingly, the cramped cell doesn't smell of urine but of ice flower toilet freshener. "I came as soon as I heard what had happened, but you could have told the arresting officers who you are. I presume you would have avoided a jail trip, and I wouldn't have had to dip out of my meeting with the National Bureau of Investigation to come get you."

Jessica sweeps her hair from her face and looks up. Tired eyes stare above flushed, mascara-flecked cheeks. Hellu has never seen Jessica like this, so seemingly unmoored and unpredictable. She looks like a wild woman dragged from the jungle to be put on display in the city, confined to a cage against her will.

"Have you been drinking?" Hellu says, even though she doesn't want to, and for some reason it doesn't seem likely. Jessica has ninety-nine problems, no doubt, but as far as Hellu is aware, substance abuse is not one of them.

Hellu glances at her subordinate's feet, one of which is bare and the other covered by a wet sock. In accordance with protocol, the shoes—or, in this case, presumably, the shoe—were taken from Jessica hours before, when she was booked.

"No . . . ," Jessica eventually says. "I mean, no, I haven't been drinking. Anything. Or at least not alcohol."

Hellu raises her left hand and eyes the nails she filed the night before. Despite her reservations, the electric nail file her wife bought has proven quite practical.

"The burly manager of a Katajanokka building cooperative claims you trashed his courtyard and attacked him without warning. Doesn't exactly sound like the house-trained, analytical Jessica Niemi I work with at the VCU."

"I was there visiting a friend."

"Who?"

Jessica frowns and looks as if she means to hawk a loogie on the floor. "Does it matter?"

Hellu shrugs—*Maybe not*—and Jessica continues: "And I started feeling nauseous when I left."

"There in the courtyard?"

Jessica nods.

"So how did the super—"

"Let's just say he wasn't completely innocent of escalating the situation."

Hellu sighs and shakes her head.

"Was he badly hurt?" Jessica asks, and now there's regret in her tone.

Hellu shakes her head. "I spoke with the officer who brought you in and got the sense any permanent problems came from his attitude. When referring to you, he used terms like 'junkie whore' and so on. What I'm trying to say is, under normal circumstances you and I wouldn't even be needing to have this conversation."

"But now we do?"

"There were a couple eyewitnesses who said you kicked him when he was already down. And when you refused to provide your identity or details of the incident to the patrol that happened to be driving past, they didn't have any choice but to—"

"Yeah, I know." Jessica lowers her hands to her stomach. "It was a stupid move. I wasn't thinking clearly."

Hellu glances to the side to make sure no one is standing in the open doorway, then lowers her voice to a near whisper. "What's going on with you, Niemi? I'm really damn worried."

"Things would be fine if I'd just been allowed to puke in that goddamned portico in peace."

"I'm getting the sense there's something else going on here too. Normally I'd find it hard to believe that you'd allow yourself to get so provoked—"

"He was holding on to me, Hellu," Jessica says, now sharply, and rolls up her sleeve. But there's no sign of bruising at the wrist, which seems to vex her. Maybe she hoped he'd left proper marks, the sort that wouldn't leave any room for guesswork.

"I understand. But I'm still getting the sense this is the tip of the iceberg. You've been sort of lost in your own world since the Zetterborg case. I need to know that you're not going to start—"

"Start what?"

"You know what I'm talking about, and I have every right to be concerned."

Jessica shoots a fiery glance at the surveillance camera overhead.

"Let's go somewhere else to chat." Hellu tosses the plastic bag to the floor next to the mattress. "I brought you some shoes, so you don't have to hop around on one foot out there."

4

JESSICA LOOKS UP from the mug gripped in her fingers. The bright glow from inside the glass counter makes her squint. It's a unique spot for Helsinki: an American diner–type neon light flashes in the window, the red tables are surrounded by screaming yellow chairs, and the speakers are blasting bumping music with unintelligible lyrics that could just as well be Chinese or Rhaeto-Romance as Finnish. Considering the hectic milieu, it feels ironic that the only thing Hellu is looking at suspiciously is Jessica's steaming, murky beverage, which gives off a whiff of spinach.

"What is that?"

"A matcha latte."

Hellu rolls her eyes. Jessica has never developed a taste for coffee and has spent the entirety of her adult life drinking rose hip tea while others down their java, but a spontaneous trial a few weeks ago immediately hooked her on the green Japanese tea that is rarely served in traditional downtown cafés.

For a moment, both sip their drinks in silence. Eventually Hellu clears her throat, more to break the silence than to strengthen her voice.

"I'm not trying to pretend we're best friends, Niemi. You don't have to confide in me. But the thing we discussed back during the Yamamoto case . . . The fact that I intentionally buried certain things about your past to ensure matters wouldn't become pointlessly complicated . . ."

"Not very deep."

"Excuse me?"

"You dug everything up pretty fast when there was a little blowback."

Hellu looks hurt. She slips off her glasses with the thick blue frames and wipes the lenses with a chamois. Then she returns the glasses to her nose, folds the chamois into its holder, and leans in. "If that guy decides to raise a stink about this incident, we're going to have to seriously consider whether it might not be best for you to step aside for a little while. This is about the unit's credibility. Without it, none of us can do our work properly. You do understand that, don't you?"

Jessica eyes Hellu at length. She has the urge to argue, but she understands perfectly well what Hellu means, and she knows she screwed up. "Misdemeanor assault isn't a crime that involves the prosecutor," she says regardless, and can tell from the look on Hellu's face that the information isn't relevant.

"But it will become one if the guy has so much as a single broken rib. In that case, it can be viewed as normal or even felony assault, and charges will be pressed even if the victim doesn't demand it."

Jessica suddenly feels a lump in her throat: the possible consequences of the altercation are only now starting to become real for her.

"And if that happens, there's no way I can keep you in the field investigating serious crimes. No matter how badly I want to."

"But—"

"And we'll get through that, at least over time . . . But I cannot get past this bigger, more fundamental issue: something in your demeanor has fundamentally changed. You've been behaving really oddly lately. And I'm not referring to your wiseass and occasionally asocial behavior—as a matter of fact, I miss it a little—but something darker. And I can't help thinking it's related to—"

"My illness?"

Hellu nods reluctantly.

A brief cease-fire follows, during which both women finger their mugs nervously.

"When we last talked about this, in December, I asked if you had difficulty distinguishing what's real from what isn't."

"And I answered that I don't."

"But you have these—"

"Hallucinations? Visions? Sometimes," Jessica says, despite knowing things were clearly better a couple months ago than they are now. Something truly has changed. It's been a long time since she's seen her dead mother, who has followed Jessica her entire life. But something else has appeared in her place. The craziness—that's what Jessica herself calls it—has, unexpectedly and for the first time, arrived in completely uncontrollable form. This is exactly what Jessica has always feared most: that the delusions would become unpredictable; that they would turn against her, pull out the foundations of her entire world.

"I've started seeing someone," Jessica says quickly. But Hellu doesn't seem to immediately catch her meaning. "A psychiatrist," she clarifies.

"Good," Hellu says after digesting this information, but she doesn't seem relieved. "That probably can't hurt."

"That's where I was coming from today," Jessica continues, unsure whether the information might not make things worse.

"Did the therapy trigger a physical reaction in you, the nausea?"

Jessica looks at Hellu. She's starting to feel as if this discussion is some sort of therapy too—as if from here on out she's going to have to somehow prove to anyone she's conversing with that she isn't in need of being involuntarily committed.

Jessica turns to the window. She doesn't have the slightest intention of opening up to her superintendent about the mechanisms that determine the functions of her body and mind, the coordinates of her psychological and physical pressure points—even if understanding them could be beneficial for everyone. The truth is, Jessica can't explain to Hellu what's going on in her head right now because she doesn't understand it herself.

Hellu sips her coffee and shoots a pointed glance over her mug. "Go home, Niemi."

"Why?"

Hellu lowers her mug to the table, glances at her wristwatch, and then folds her hands on the table. "There's nothing important going on at HQ at the moment."

Jessica chuckles. "What? So I can't come back to work until there's a serial killer on the loose?"

Hellu crinkles her nose, then scratches the dark roots of her bleached hair and nods. "We'll have a look again then."

Jessica feels something flare up in her breast. She takes a swig of her matcha latte, stands, and pulls her coat over her gray hoodie.

"Thanks for the shoes. I'll mail them to the station," she says, stepping out the door.

5

IT'S SIX THIRTY, and the sun dipped below the horizon just a few minutes ago, leaving the city at the mercy of artificial lighting. A plow clatters down the street, even though no more than a dusting of snow fell during the afternoon. Jessica mutes the television, rises from her couch, and flicks on the living room lights. For a split second, the large room appears alien: the imposing paintings in their gilded frames remind her of a museum. The expensive, sparsely situated armchairs, couch, and glass coffee table look like they're straight out of an Italian interior design magazine. Every last detail, down to the placement of objects, the wood used in the flooring, and the colors of the walls, has been carefully considered. Jessica looks around and tries to fathom how she has ever felt at ease in her immense, luxurious home, which right now feels incredibly lifeless and bleak.

The doorbell rings. When she steps into the entryway, Jessica sees the friendly face of her colleague Yusuf Pepple on the wall monitor. She buzzes him in and leaves the front door ajar, then returns to the living room and collapses onto her back on the sofa. A moment later, she hears the clatter of the elevator from the stairwell, then echoing footfalls, and then Yusuf steps in, calling out in feigned lightheartedness.

"Hi," Yusuf says again, less eagerly now that he's made it under the arch separating the entryway from the living room. Jessica sees he's holding a white paper bag. A pleasant smell Jessica can't immediately identify wafts through the room.

"You brought your own snacks?"

"No, this is for you," Yusuf says, striding into the kitchen without further explanation.

Jessica hears the bag rustle as Yusuf loads food into the fridge. She knows Yusuf means well, but even so, going grocery shopping on her behalf feels really damn patronizing right now.

A moment later, the fridge door clicks shut, and Yusuf reappears in the living room, a thoughtful look on his face.

"Thanks," Jessica says reluctantly, turning off the muted television with the remote.

"I was going to the store anyway and—"

"Right. I'm sure you were," Jessica grunts, pinching her lips into a thin line.

Yusuf looks around as if he can never get enough of Jessica's sumptuous abode: the high-ceilinged rooms, the art on the walls, the rooftop view across Helsinki. Jessica has grown blind to her surroundings over the years, but the two-story apartment taking up three hundred square meters is undeniably magnificent. She has been so wealthy since she came of age that she has long taken its opulence for granted. Admitting it makes her feel disdain for herself. Most of all, she feels guilty that she has felt so poorly for so long despite her wealth. The millions she inherited from her mother haven't solved her problems; just the opposite. The sense of loneliness that has been her constant, lifelong companion must well up from the fact that she's not like other people, no matter how well she plays the role of an ordinary detective who has to work for a living. She is self-deception personified.

"That was fucked up, what happened this morning." Yusuf takes a few steps, then drops into the sofa-set armchair across from Jessica. His expression is one of wary concern, but even so, the inner glow that has turned into some sort of trademark over the past month radiates through his exterior. With his broad smile, Yusuf has always been a chipper, energetic presence, but now he seems to be taking it to the next level. Especially since it was preceded by a long gloomier stage resulting from his breakup with his long-term girlfriend. During that period, Yusuf chain-smoked cigarettes and trained at the gym with near-maniacal intensity. Now the roles have changed: at that time, Jessica was the one who was worried.

"You look like you're in love," Jessica says.

Yusuf glances at his feet like a teenager embarrassed by attention.

"Right," he grunts.

"Maybe I should."

"Maybe you should what?"

"Fall in love."

Yusuf looks as if he's at a loss for words. His smile fades as quickly as it appeared on his face. Jessica sits up and can still smell the spicy scent, although the shopping has been put away. Then she realizes: Yusuf has a new cologne. Of course. Jessica can clearly make out the fragrance of orange blossom, honey, and geranium, a combination she has certainly come across before, but never on Yusuf's skin.

"You'll find someone if you want to," Yusuf says, tapping his fingers against the armrests.

"It was a joke, Yusuf. I don't need anything or anyone new in my life right now," Jessica says, then realizes she's lying not only to Yusuf but to herself as well.

Yusuf strokes his eyebrow with his forefinger. "Yeah, I wasn't thinking you meant—"

"Did you come here just to bring me food?"

Yusuf's expression immediately darkens, as if he suddenly remembered something unpleasant. He reluctantly pulls his phone from his pocket and unlocks it.

"You talked to Hellu," Jessica says.

Yusuf nods, eyes glued to his phone.

Now Jessica understands that the unfamiliar scent that wafted into the apartment along with Yusuf consists of more than a new cologne: there's no pungent whiff of just-smoked tobacco. Jessica is burning with the desire to ask about this, ask if Yusuf has decided to stamp out his cigarettes for good, but then realizes she'd have to ask what prompted him to make such a decision. And that's something she doesn't want to talk about. Not right now. Maybe never. She already knows the answer. The change in lifestyle means Yusuf is serious about Tanja.

"Did she call?" Yusuf asks. "Did you talk to her again?"

"She tried, but I didn't answer."

"So you don't know yet?"

"So I don't know what yet?" Jessica can tell from her colleague's body language bad news is coming. "What, Yusuf?"

Yusuf slowly passes his phone to Jessica, as if he wanted to put off the inevitable for as long as possible. Jessica's fingertips graze Yusuf's wrist.

Jessica sees the YouTube logo there on the screen. Her heart skips a beat.

"Fuck me." Jessica curses so softly that Yusuf can barely hear. She recognizes the dark green plaster walls in the still, the steel rug-beating rack and the open iron gate. The man in the neon yellow coveralls. The woman in sweats and a parka bent toward the glistening cobblestones. The caption under the video reads: *Detective's Day Off*.

"Someone shot it from one of the balconies," Yusuf says.

Jessica hands the phone back. She doesn't want to see the video because she's already agonizingly aware of what takes place in it. "Detective's day off? How did they know—"

"Shitty luck. One of the eyewitnesses is a freelance reporter for *Iltalehti*. She must have recognized you and made a couple of phone calls to confirm it," Yusuf says, locking his phone with a click.

"Goddamn it." Jessica buries her face in her hands. Her heart is hammering, and her fingertips are tingling like crazy. A series of coincidences and bad decisions has made her out to be a lunatic who is trending virally, a national psychopath who's about to be not only dragged through an erupting social media storm but also shelved from her job.

"What happens now?" Jessica asks, rubbing her forehead.

"Things like this blow over pretty fast," Yusuf says. "Apparently the guy wasn't hurt, and it's clear in the video that he provoked you. Grabbed your wrist and—"

"It's also clear in the video how I puked in his backyard in the middle of the day. Plus probably how I let fly, kicking him three times . . . including once when he was already down." Jessica sighs. "And I doubt you can hear him calling me a whore."

"Nope," Yusuf says. "That's why we have to wait a second for the dust to settle."

Jessica slowly raises her face from her hands and looks at Yusuf as if this is all his fault. And so it is, she supposes, if indirectly and completely unwittingly. Now that Jessica thinks about it, her downhill slide began the moment the Zetterborg case was solved and Yusuf went on a date with the cute technician from Forensics. As she stood alone in her empty apartment, Jessica understood something that had never crossed her mind before: Yusuf was not only a trusted friend and colleague but much more. She'd just never seen it: in her mind, they were the *X-Files'* Fox Mulder and Dana Scully, a pair that had neither the need nor the slightest desire to cross the boundaries of a platonic relationship. But she suddenly realized she'd always subconsciously thought something might happen someday, even back when Yusuf was in his previous relationship. But now that Yusuf was head over heels in love with a woman who scours crime scenes, the idea that something might happen seemed unlikely in the extreme. And if the possibility of the relationship deepening no longer existed, would their camaraderie survive unchanged? Had a certain tension always been a requisite for the friendship, a back door to romance?

The evening following the arrest of Zetterborg's murderer triggered some sort of absolute loneliness in Jessica. She felt like she was an ice floe adrift on open water, gradually melting until it vanished without anyone noticing. Maybe it was that sensation that had begun to feed her hallucinations, to lead her deeper and deeper to the other side, where reality gradually warped.

"You're probably going to be mad at me for saying this, Jessie . . . ," Yusuf begins, and Jessica has no reason to doubt him. "But I think you should go away for a little while. Somewhere, anywhere. You could travel around the world, go surfing in Bali, stay in the biggest suite at the Burj Al Arab for a month or two." Yusuf laughs. "You could finally try and enjoy your financial independence. No one has to know. You can do whatever you want—"

"I feel a little sick," Jessica says, rising from the couch as Yusuf looks on in dismay. "I'm going to go lie down for a while if you don't mind." She walks into the kitchen and flicks on the electric kettle. The paper bag lolls on the counter, empty.

Suddenly she's incredibly annoyed. She opens a cupboard and takes out a porcelain mug. Yusuf appears behind her in the kitchen and continues talking as if Jessica had never cut him off.

"Seriously, Jessie. What the hell are you doing with that money if you're not going to put it to good use? Do you realize the sky is the limit for you—"

"Yusuf!" Jessica slams her hand to the granite countertop so hard that it aches. She turns to look at Yusuf. The hands that were gesticulating so animatedly a moment ago have frozen in place, as if they've been paused with a TV remote. "You don't know shit about my skies and limits!"

A bewildered look spreads across Yusuf's face. "Calm down. All I'm trying to say is—"

Jessica hurls the mug at the wall opposite, sending shards scattering across the room. Yusuf raises his hands to protect his face and swears loudly.

"Why can't you just leave?" Jessica shouts. She takes a step closer, grabs Yusuf by the neck, and kisses him; presses her forehead against his, breathes heavily.

Yusuf puts an end to the fleeting seconds by releasing himself from her grip and taking a step backward. "Jessica, what are you . . . ?"

Jessica feels a tear roll down to the corner of her mouth. She has never seen Yusuf this confused; the kiss has left him utterly speechless. For once. "I'm sorry," she whispers, and wipes her eyes on the collar of her oversized T-shirt. "Please go."

"Jessica . . ."

"Go!" Jessica snaps, shoving Yusuf in the chest, not to hurt him but to hasten the end of the intolerable situation. To get the smell of that perfect cologne out of her apartment.

Yusuf raises his arms, clearly wants to say something, to come up with a reason to stay or to take Jessica with him.

But Jessica's implacable body language leaves no room for negotiation. Her finger is pointed at the front door. "Go, please," she whispers.

Yusuf casts one final glance at her, a glance that contains a lifetime's worth of untold stories. Then he wipes his lip with his finger and turns around. And when Jessica hears the front door close, she opens the cupboard and fumbles for a new mug. She leans against the counter, listens to hear if the doorbell might ring. If Yusuf might be stubborn enough to come back.

And when nothing happens, she lets the tears fall.

6

YESTERDAY I FOUND at the base of a tree a bird's nest with a tiny crossbill chick next to it. He'd survived the fall in one piece, but for some reason his parents hadn't lingered to see how their offspring would manage alone in the cold, let alone the terrain teeming with perils. The helpless, flightless creature had been sentenced to a solitary fight for survival on this remote island, where a long time will pass before the spring sun penetrates the dense forests. I knew the bird wouldn't survive without my help, so I took him somewhere where he'd be safe and hidden from the eyes of hostile animals.

He has been in the toolshed for less than a day now, but I think he has gotten some of his strength back. I'm going to feed and care for him until he regains enough strength for his wings to carry him. Maybe once he has flown away, he'll come back to me from time to time, grateful for my care. For having saved him from certain death. I named him Hope. Unlike the little girl who lived on the other side of the island long ago, one day Hope will fly from here and find himself a new home.

7

THE DEAFENING BLAST of a foghorn infiltrates Jessica's dreams. The disquieting events and obscure human figures from her dream gradually dissipate as reality takes over. Jessica opens her eyes, looks out her east-facing window, and sees that the sun has risen: in the pale sky it shines low, as wan as a weak light bulb glowing behind parchment paper. Frowning, Jessica looks around—just as she has done every morning she has awoken in this bed. Today is no exception. It takes her a fleeting moment to register the compact, cozy room and remember where she is: far from home, away from the city stained with grimy snow, where the crimes never end, no matter how many are solved. She is separated from the capital's pulse by a thousand little islands and a sea dotted with ever-melting ice floes. She crossed over a few days before by ferry to Maarianhamina, and from there by smaller vessel to the southeasternmost edge of the Ahvenanmaa archipelago, to the island of Smörregård. A place where the idyllic archipelago meets the harsh open sea.

Jessica shuts her eyelids; she doesn't want to wake up to a new day yet.

Wake up, Jessica. As long as you're here, you're going to have to get up.

Jessica's eyes pop open as the buzz of a chain saw carries in from outside. She rises to sitting in the bed. There's a sharp, acrid taste in her mouth. Her head feels heavy, as if it is full of fluid.

The old, albeit recently remodeled, room smells of tar and aged wood. The sun casts its light through the veil of clouds onto the floral rococo sofa in front of the light blue wall opposite. An open book, a half-empty water bottle, and an uncapped prescription vial rest on the ornate wooden coffee table.

Jessica lowers her hand to her clammy, sweaty forehead.

Three pills. Only three.

The evening before, she'd considered taking more. A fistful, say. Then maybe she wouldn't have been woken by that damn horn that seems to blare out at exactly the same time every morning, as if its only mission is to wake the lodgers at the guesthouse at as unpleasant an hour as possible.

Take one a day at first, two later if necessary. Do not increase the dosage without consulting me first.

Her psychiatrist initially offered some new drug for sleeplessness, one that would not result in profound morning fatigue, but then admitted to Jessica that traditional benzodiazepines would presumably be most effective against her problem. First and foremost, Jessica wanted to treat her sleeplessness, but she was also hoping for relief from her ever-mounting anxiety. One has to be particularly careful with benzodiazepines, of course, not least because they are more likely than other sleep aids to cause addiction. Jessica was more than familiar with benzos—as they are affectionately known to many—due to the nature of her work: they are widely abused, and the pills are sold on almost every street corner in Helsinki. But the course Tuula prescribed is Jessica's first encounter with schedule III drugs. How has she survived this long without them?

Jessica hears a door close somewhere, then the faint murmur of speech. She gingerly lowers her feet to the white wool rug that, judging by appearances, is handwoven and at least a hundred years old. The floor creaks as Jessica stands; the sealed planks give under the soles of her feet. The plumbing thrums overhead.

She walks to the window, draws aside the curtains of white lace, and lazily stretches her stiff neck.

The owner of the guesthouse, Astrid Nordin, is crossing the yard, holding a chain saw in her left hand as she strides purposefully toward the rocky shore. For a woman who must be at least eighty, she is incredibly straight backed and surprisingly agile. Astrid's lips are moving nonstop, but Jessica can't make out what she's saying or whom she's talking to. A moment later, a stout man with a lush beard appears carrying a box; upon Jessica's arrival a few days earlier, he had introduced himself as Astrid's son, Åke.

Jessica closes the curtains and sits down on the sofa. Fatigue crashes over her limbs like a tidal wave.

She studies the vial and tries to remember the final hours of the previous night, but all she can recall are the dreams she was having a moment ago. In contrast, everything that happened the night before—the book on Roman philosophy she's been reading, the dinner she presumably ate in the dining room—has vanished.

Jessica shifts her gaze to the framed poster on the wall; it depicts a tall red and white lighthouse. The image is practically an archipelago cliché, but for some inexplicable reason it has a soothing effect on her.

Jessica lets her head slowly fall back against the sofa; her eyes close as if of their own volition. The noises outside fade.

Suddenly there's a knock at the door, and Jessica starts.

"Yes?" she calls out, pressing her hand to her chest to make sure she's still wearing her oversized T-shirt. A few days earlier, Astrid barged in to clean the room just as Jessica was wrapping a towel around her naked body.

"Checking to make sure you're awake," a voice says in Swedish.

"I am."

Annoyed, Jessica stands up and trudges to the door. She is unsteady on her feet; the scare from the sudden knock set her heart hammering in her chest. Jessica twists the handle, cracks the door, and finds herself looking into the eyes of an old woman slightly shorter than she is.

Astrid is wearing a sweater, waders, and knee-high yellow rubber boots. As it has every time so far, Jessica's gaze wanders down to Astrid's wrinkled throat, which is darker than the surrounding skin, like a nasty patch of psoriasis or a severe burn.

"Good morning," Jessica says.

"Good morning," the old woman replies with composed tranquility.

Jessica tries to hide a yawn in her fist. "Did you need something?"

"No, not at all. You asked me—"

"To come knock on my door?"

"To come and wake you if you weren't up by nine," Astrid says with a frown.

Now that Jessica thinks about it, she remembers doing so right after dinner. *Damn pills.*

"I'm sorry," she says. "I'm still a little groggy."

"Would you like me to change the sheets?" Astrid asks, and Jessica can't help but think the old woman just wants to snoop around her room, to check under the bed for needles or empty wine bottles. The fact that she's not at her best these days must be apparent even to complete strangers. Her ragged appearance, makeup-free face, huge eye bags, and irregular jaunts around the island are probably giving the impression of someone whose life isn't exactly under control. Who would want such a fishy character around their establishment, even if that person is paying for the privilege?

"No, thank you." Jessica tries to smile. "Tomorrow. Maybe."

Astrid studies Jessica the way a concerned grandmother might, a grandmother who isn't close but still shares the same blood, someone whose responsibility it is to ask and worry despite parting ways long ago.

"Breakfast is ready," Astrid then says, and turns around.

"Thank you," Jessica calls out as Astrid walks away. It's amazing a woman her age is still strong enough to cut wood. The squeaking soles of the rubber boots leave a trail of sawdust on the black rug. Jessica can't help but smile. A few hours from now, Astrid herself will presumably be the one who vacuums the hallway until it's clean as a whistle, which is a good metaphor for the islander mentality. First you make a mess, and then you scour and scrub until everything is spotless.

Jessica shuts the door and raises her arms into a delicious stretch. Now that she thinks about it, breakfast doesn't sound half bad.

8

THE TWO-STORY WOODEN villa stands only a stone's throw from the converted barn where Jessica is staying, but even so, she has wrapped a parka over her T-shirt. The few days she has spent on the island have provided multiple confirmations that, despite the nonfreezing temperatures, the archipelago is icy cold. The chill penetrates to bone and marrow and harshly punishes those who underestimate it by dressing carelessly.

A flagpole stands in the middle of the lawn, and the brisk wind plucks ominously at the taut cord as if it is a string of an enormous double bass. Beyond the dirt drive bordering the lawn, waves tamed by the dense archipelago lap against the inlet's rocky shore. Red boathouses have been built on the waterline rocks; they rest half on dry land and half over the water, as if doing push-ups on the wooden pilings. For all its austerity, it's a beautiful spot, much like the islands where Jessica recalls spending her childhood summers when her family would fly back to Finland from the United States and spend long stretches sailing the Turku archipelago. Jessica remembers how her father would anchor the boat in some random cove, where she would practice swimming in the shallows as Toffe splashed nearby with his floaties. She remembers the dusk that would paint the sky gold, and her mother sitting on the dock at the guest marina, rehearsing her lines. She would be filming a major movie that autumn, Mom said. The most important and biggest of her career to date. Jessica doesn't know how the movie turned out or if it was even filmed before Mom died.

"God morgon!"

The deep male voice rouses Jessica from her reverie as she comes up to the villa.

Åke Nordin is bending over a pail of fish, transferring them to a Styrofoam box filled with ice. His lips form a gentle smile behind his reddish beard.

Jessica returns the greeting: *"God morgon."*

"Astrid wasn't sure whether to wake you." Åke's accent is strong but not as hard to understand as one from an Ostrobothnian town like Närpiö, where Jessica has a difficult time understanding the locals, and vice versa, despite Swedish being her second language.

"I'm glad she did," Jessica says. The wind picks up and she isn't sure if Åke heard what she said. The flagpole line plays a few eerily monotonous notes, then settles as the gusts relent. Jessica glances up at the sky. According to the paper, the sun that shone so brightly earlier that week will not be seen for a while. As a matter of fact, the spring's most ferocious storm has been predicted to hit the following day.

"It's good to take it easy," Åke says cheerily, as he steps lazily toward Jessica with the box of fish in his hands. "People do OK as long as they're in control of their own schedules."

Jessica scratches her head in amusement. Stout and fiftyish, this heavily bearded man has thick, long arms, but his shoulders are as narrow and sloped as a beer bottle. The expressive face is accentuated by a constantly furrowing brow, and the narrow bright blue eyes pinch into crescents whenever he smiles. Åke reminds Jessica of the much-loved Finnish musician Gösta Sundqvist, who died of a heart attack back in 2003.

Jessica looks up at the gray sky again. "Well, I do my best."

"Enjoy your breakfast," Åke says with a smile, then turns and trudges off toward the boathouses.

Jessica watches him, then reaches into her pocket and pulls out her mobile phone. No texts, no calls. Jessica tries to open a news site, but the network is too weak. As a matter of fact, her phone connects to the 4G network randomly at best, and for some reason most feebly right here in the vicinity of Villa Smörregård, where she needs it most. On the other hand, maybe this is just what the doctor ordered: a complete break from everything. No calls, no internet, no email. Their absence means freedom.

Jessica slips her phone back into her pocket. As she approaches the villa's main door, she notices a dark figure flash past the last window on the second floor. Maybe more guests have checked in, in addition to her and the Swedish couple. The white lace curtain swings from side to side, and for some reason Jessica is overtaken by the strange sensation that someone has been standing at the upstairs window, watching her.

"How's your breakfast?" Astrid has appeared at Jessica's table, tray in hand. The cuckoo clock on the wall sounds a note more reminiscent of a mattress with broken springs than of the bird of children's nursery songs.

"Delicious. Thank you," Jessica says, instinctively pulling back as Astrid wipes the crumbs from the tablecloth and collects the dirty plates onto the tray. The scrambled eggs that made their way from the buffet to Jessica's plate, along with the open-faced herring sandwiches, disappeared in a flash. Jessica takes a sip of coffee. For some reason, the thought of rose hip tea wasn't appealing this morning; just now she needs caffeine to stay on her feet.

Jessica eyes Astrid. She gets the sense that the elderly woman is looking at her differently than before, as if something is wrong. Might something have happened last night she has no recollection of? Did she assault someone again?

"I've been really tired," Jessica says, to break the silence or perhaps to explain her lethargy.

Out of nowhere, Astrid pulls out a chair and seats herself across from Jessica.

Jessica glances around, and she and Astrid are the only two in the dining room. The Swedish couple who had been sitting at the corner table has decamped without Jessica's noticing.

"There's no reason to be ashamed of that. For goodness' sake, you're allowed to sleep when you're on vacation." Astrid gives Jessica an enigmatic look. "Aren't you? You're on vacation, right?"

Jessica fingers her coffee cup uncertainly. Until now, the guesthouse staff has left her to her own devices. Eat; roam the rocky shores; stare at the sea, dreaming of God knows what. Spend half the day sleeping.

"Yes," Jessica says. "I'm on vacation."

"Precisely." Now it's Astrid's turn to peer over her shoulder to confirm that there's no one else in the room. Åke walks past the window in his red beanie and lumberjack coat.

"See, springs are pretty slow here," Astrid says, shaking to the empty plate the crumbs she collected. "The occasional guests come and go, but it's not often someone wants to book a room for a whole month."

Jessica's fingernails dig into the tablecloth. She has taken a conscious risk in choosing a place like this for her time-out from the stresses of life: a remote refuge where she wouldn't bump into anyone she knew and yet would inevitably be under a magnifying glass. She could have just as well taken Yusuf's advice and booked a suite at the Burj Al Arab, disappeared into the faceless masses of Western tourists. Or she could have rented—or bought—a hideout on a deserted island in the middle of nowhere, a place where her only companions would have been seals basking in the spring sun. But Jessica decided on a compromise for her escape: a guesthouse on out-of-the-way Smörregård.

"I don't mean to be nosy," Astrid continues cagily, even though that's probably exactly what she means to be: nosy. Jessica's gaze drops again to the wrinkled skin visible above the old woman's collar. "But may I ask: are you *the* Jessica Niemi? The detective from Helsinki?"

Jessica feels her heart drop, looks the other woman in the eye, and folds her arms across her chest. *Damn it.* The internet truly is one hell of an invention. She ought to have barricaded herself in some wilderness cabin in the hinterlands of Urho Kekkonen National Park in Lapland or fled abroad, somewhere where a viral video starring a violent policewoman is of no interest.

Before Jessica can respond, a cloying smile spreads over Astrid's face. "Oh, how exciting!" She leans across the table to touch Jessica's arm. "Åke realized yesterday."

"From YouTube?" Jessica manages to ask, in spite of her angst.

But Astrid doesn't appear to understand what Jessica is referring to. "Åke loves lighthouses. He collects all sorts of memorabilia about them. You may have noticed." Astrid bursts into a laugh so tinkling that it could belong to a much younger woman. "The lighthouse at Söderskär is magnificent. But I don't think we have any paintings of it."

Jessica looks at Astrid. Her defensive posture eases slightly.

Söderskär. Astrid's talking about the Yamamoto case.

Jessica feels the tension drain from her body, even though she's still unsure where this conversation is going.

"This might not be very tactful of me, but—"

"Yes. I was one of the investigators in the Söderskär incident," Jessica blurts out, then picks up her cup and lifts it to her lips. The final drop of coffee has cooled, but it's actually not half bad this way.

"Wow! Åke was really excited about that case; imagine, a lighthouse played such a key role in such an awful crime spree. It was in the news a lot here in Ahvenanmaa before the New Year, and your picture was in the paper a couple of times. I remembered the case because I'm a die-hard detective novel fan. I can't get enough of murder mysteries. And also because . . ."

Astrid falls silent, laugh wrinkles form around her eyes, and her face blushes barely perceptibly.

"Because . . . ?"

"Excuse me for being so direct . . . but because I thought you were so attractive for a homicide detective," Astrid says, waving the thought away in embarrassment. Her eyes sail around the room for a moment, then settle on Jessica again. Suddenly Jessica feels curiously ill at ease.

She glances discreetly at her watch. It's probably time to thank Astrid for breakfast and head out on her daily ramble. And then maybe pack her bags and get the hell off this island. It's only a matter of time before the real motivation for Jessica's vacation is revealed to Astrid, who for some reason appears to admire Jessica on account of not only her profession but her appearance. "Thanks for breakfast," she says, trying her hardest not to sound unfriendly. "I'd better head out now for some fresh air."

"That's one thing we have plenty of here." Now Astrid twists her face up into an exaggerated expression of apology. "I'm sorry. I hope I wasn't too intrusive. Åke saw your laptop and guessed you'd come here to write a detective novel. You must have a lot of ideas for them."

Jessica is on the verge of denying it out of hand, but then realizes it wouldn't be at all bad if Astrid and her son were left with this harmless misimpression instead of actively pondering the true reason for Jessica's visit. One gossip can often be enough to poison an environment, but two snoops in the same household are a risk of greater scale.

"Åke sounds like quite the detective himself," Jessica says, with intentional vagueness.

A girlish smile spreads across Astrid's face. "Oh, how exciting," she says, fiddling excitedly with the collar of her Norwegian sweater. "Hopefully it's set in Ahvenanmaa. Or even here at Smörregård!"

Jessica shrugs, reaches up for an imaginary zipper, and pulls it across her lips. Astrid giggles and does the same. As Jessica rises from the table, she sees that a small motorboat with a canvas cabin has just pulled in. Åke has rushed out to meet it and now grabs the rope the captain tossed and ties it firmly to a bollard. The boat stops, and aided by Åke, a frail figure steps to the dock.

"You said it's a quiet time of year for you?" Jessica remarks as she pulls on her coat.

Holding the tray, Astrid steps over to the window and looks out at the water before turning to Jessica. "The birds of spring," she says.

"Excuse me?"

"That's what they call themselves," Astrid continues, nodding at the elderly people climbing from the boat onto the dock. "They meet here every year. Ten years ago, they would book almost every room in the place. Now that most of them have passed on, three rooms in the main building are all they need. One for each." Looking a little wistful, she wipes her hands on a white napkin.

"I'd better go help them with their bags," Astrid says, turning her glassy eyes back to the window. Then she seems to come out of a reverie and takes a deep breath.

"All right. It was nice chatting," she says, the smile returning to her narrow face. "And don't worry. We won't tell your secret to anyone."

9

JESSICA CROSSES THE villa's empty entry hall into the cozily furnished, smoke-scented library, where there's a back door next to the fireplace. She has decided not to use the front door, because at least for now she doesn't want to meet the new guests. Jessica has walked across the library on a couple previous occasions, but it's only now that she notices the paintings hanging there. They depict rocky, storm-lashed shores; a lighthouse features in nearly every one. *We all have to get our kicks somehow, I guess.* To the right of the massive stone hearth stands a big bookshelf from which Jessica has randomly borrowed vacation reading.

Jessica descends the frost-cracked stone steps. The brisk wind grabs at her hair, and she quickly pulls on her beanie. As she makes her way to the refurbished barn housing her room, she shoots a surreptitious glance shoreward. The elderly visitors are clustered between the two boathouses to greet Astrid.

For some reason, the trio that has arrived on the island reminds Jessica of her Swedish-speaking family. Her actress mother, who sank into an ever-deeper mania. Her melancholy father, who was ultimately forced to come to terms with his own powerlessness in the face of her mother's illness. Her baby brother, Toffe, who never had the chance to be anything but an innocent little human, a brown-eyed towhead Jessica swore to look after no matter what. Her heavily perfumed aunt Tina, who always said the right thing but when push came to shove did nothing for Jessica.

Since putting some distance between herself and her work in Helsinki, Jessica has done a lot of thinking about her mother, started to see her mother's life and death in a totally new light. She has only recently begun to understand that the illness was always present in her mother: it made her a superb actor, just as it later made Jessica a superb detective. Jessica has realized that they both acknowledged their issues, kept an eye on them, and yet intentionally left them untreated. Instead of trying to alter their brain chemistries through medication, they both harnessed their illness as a source of strength, each in her own way. It's almost ironic that Camilla Adlerkreutz tried to benefit from their condition by harnessing that power for herself—power that wasn't hers in the first place.

But one fundamental problem exists in this equation: untreated schizophrenia might be a good servant when it comes to creativity, but it's also an incredibly bad master. The fact that her mother's illness was allowed to smolder and worsen proved fateful for her entire family when her mother, in a fit of mania, drove the car into the oncoming lane. That instant the passenger vehicle was crushed under a semi on the highway near Marina del Rey, the whole family ceased to exist.

But Jessica's mother had accompanied Jessica up until a few weeks ago. Jessica still yearns for the nocturnal awakenings, her mother's touch on her shoulder. Not the living, drop-dead gorgeous, magnetic movie star, but the badly mangled remnants of the human corpse that firefighters had sawed out of the wreckage on Lincoln Boulevard on that beautiful morning, May 4, 1993. The face destroyed by the car's crumpled hood, the mess of muscle, tissue, and bone. Jessica carried her mother's ghost with her for so long that in the end its sudden disappearance felt like a stinging betrayal. Maybe something similar had happened to her mother: maybe her mother had abruptly lost something that had made her insanity to some degree tolerable.

At the time of her death, Jessica's mother was thirty-seven years old. Jessica should have, she supposes, understood that by the time she reached that same age, everything would irrevocably approach its end. That she wouldn't be able to control her illness forever. That she'd simply have to decide on everything in good time before anyone else was forced to suffer. She is going to have to be wiser than her mother.

As she walks across the lawn, Jessica feels strangely calm. Her mind is at ease in a way she hasn't felt for a long time; she has, she supposes, made her decision. She reaches for the door handle and casts a final glance at the shore. One of the old people has turned to look at her. And even from this distance, Jessica can see her eyes smolder with hatred.

10

JESSICA PUTS ON a coat over her sweater and pulls waterproof bottoms over her sweatpants. Then she slips her feet into sturdy hiking boots and grabs her wool gloves on her way out.

"Good morning," a raspy voice says in Finnish as Jessica shuts the door of the barn. Jessica starts; there's a hunched figure next to the ashtray outside.

Jessica twists her mouth up into a smile and quickly replies: "Hi."

Considering the ascetic surroundings, the old woman leaning on a metal cane is overdressed. An expensive-looking wool coat covers her frail body, and a camel hair scarf is wrapped around her neck. The wrinkled mouth does not respond to Jessica's smile. Her face reminds Jessica of an eagle's: her slightly slanted, piercing eyes study Jessica disdainfully.

"Is your room comfortable?" the old woman asks drily, slowly making her way to Jessica's window. Jessica glances over. Luckily she closed the curtains; otherwise this woman would probably be tut-tutting over her unmade bed and the sea of clothes spreading across the floor. At least that's how it feels, as if the old woman has come to the barn to perform some sort of spot check.

"I've slept in this room for twenty-five years," the old woman continues, and Jessica sees her fingers clench around the cane's leather handle. "But this time they said it was reserved for you."

"I had no intention of taking your room."

Now the woman's lips curve up in a smile. "It's all Åke's fault. He supposedly came here to help his mother but always makes a mess of things," she growls, and gives the barn's stone foundation a sharp rap with her cane, as if testing its durability. She does not take her eyes off Jessica, as if the awkward conversation is just beginning.

"I understand you come to the island every year," Jessica says, shoving her hands into her coat pockets. For some reason, she doesn't want to leave the old woman snooping at her window. Who knows? Maybe she still has a key.

"Where do you get that impression?"

"*Twenty-five years, in this room*," Jessica says.

The old woman looks as if she's been caught in a lie, and then a malicious smile spreads across the stern face. "So you know everything already."

Jessica looks at her in confusion. "I'm not sure I understand."

The old woman shakes her head before nodding at the villa. "I'm sure that old parrot already told you everything. She's not very good at keeping confidences."

The old woman takes a few steps closer, her penetrating bright blue eyes fixed on Jessica. Her breath smells of peppermint. The braided knot of gray hair looks so thick and healthy that Jessica figures it must be a wig.

"So if you've brought any secrets to this island, I suggest you keep them to yourself," the old woman whispers, before she turns and walks purposefully to the villa.

11

JESSICA CROSSES THE yard and steps onto the low lip of stone between the boathouse and the dock. Three upside-down rowboats without their plugs have been tied up close to the water.

A few hundred meters out, a fishing boat passes the island. Its wake has already reached the shore and licks the granite at Jessica's feet. For the most part the sea is unfrozen, but treacherous-looking ice floes that probably wouldn't carry the weight of even a small animal, let alone a human, bob here and there. A patch of open sea is visible between the two closest islands, or at least that's what Jessica's untrained eye sees. In reality, she figures there must be room for a few of Ahvenanmaa's nearly seven thousand islands between the pair of islands and the horizon.

She tucks behind her ear a fluttering strand of hair that has escaped her beanie and she shuts her eyes. The fresh air seems to trigger a surge of endorphins in her body. The sudden bouts of nausea have been relatively mild since she arrived at Smörregård, so maybe things are as her late friend and boss Erne once put it: the archipelago heals body and soul better than the most skilled psychiatrist or most effective antibiotic.

The thought makes her smile. In her mind, she can hear the Estonian accent and see the sly, pockmarked face, the aggressively growing gray stubble that never fully succumbed to the razor and always grew back within a few hours. Since arriving at Smörregård, Jessica has thought a lot about Erne: it would soon be the anniversary of his death. The approaching milestone has made Jessica miss him more than ever. Erne was the beacon that helped her navigate any darkness. Or maybe the anchor that held Jessica's feet firmly on the ground, even when she was on the verge of losing touch with this reality. Erne was a father figure who never betrayed Jessica's trust. There's no doubt in her mind that he would have died for her if the need for such dramatic action had ever arisen.

Jessica isn't sure, however, if Erne was the right person to testify to the island's healing powers. The crusty old bugger had been born and raised in a small fishing village on the island of Saaremaa in Soviet Estonia, but his habits were anything but healthy. According to his own words, he'd been chain-smoking and drinking like a grown man by the time he was a teenager. In his twenties, Erne had moved north across the gulf for work, quickly received Finnish citizenship, and after a few twists and turns ended up on the police force. Erne had never lost his foreign accent—luckily, because it made the teddy bear of a man even more approachable. But his sensitivity took its toll: Erne's long drinking career was an open secret at police headquarters, but it had to be said in his favor that he was never drunk on the job and never let his problems impact his subordinates. Erne was a so-called functional alcoholic. And even amid all that, the kindest, most warmhearted person Jessica has ever met.

Erne had meant everything to Jessica, despite the fact that he could be patronizing and overprotective at times and drove her to the brink of fury. Ironically enough, after Erne's death she found herself most intently missing those traits and mannerisms that had irritated her the most when he was alive. The lung cancer that had spread to lymph nodes and other organs led him to his grave within a couple of months of diagnosis. Erne had been divorced and lived alone, and Jessica had taken him in, bathed and fed him.

Administered his medication and tucked him in. Clipped his nails and, when the end came, was at his side, stroking his hair. Erne's adult sons, who for whatever reason were not particularly close to their father, did remember to show up when the estate was being divided up. Jessica remembers leaving the meeting without shaking either's hand.

The Faithful Reader.

Jessica feels a lump in her throat when she thinks about the speech she wrote for Erne's memorial service. He had wanted to hear it before his death, and Jessica had obliged. When he heard the speech, Erne cried profusely and made Jessica swear to take care of herself. She had promised to. And yet here she is now, giving up.

"Excuse me!"

The voice behind Jessica brings her out of her reverie. She turns and sees Åke approaching in his red-and-black plaid coat, with one hand raised.

Damn it. Jessica dries her moist eyes on her sleeve.

Åke's step is brisk, and he smiles broadly as he walks toward Jessica. "I told Astrid," he says when he's no more than a few meters away. "Dang it, I knew it."

Jessica decides to cut off with a curt smile the rumors that are apparently spreading like wildfire.

"I just wanted to say that if you need anything . . . anything at all . . ." Still grinning, Åke shifts his weight from one foot to the other. "Oh man, Astrid really loves detective novels."

"OK," Jessica says, although she's not clear on what kind of help he could offer in writing a detective novel—a detective novel that doesn't actually exist and isn't even in the works.

"What I mean is . . . things happen here too. If you need stories for your book," Åke continues, glancing over his shoulder at the villa as if it is a bastion of great mysteries.

Jessica can't suppress a smile at Åke's words: *Things happen here too.* Having over the course of the past year investigated a murderous cult, a ruthless human trafficking ring, and the assassination of a business magnate in his own home, Jessica is pretty sure Åke can't have much more to add in terms of inspiration for a detective novel—if she were even writing one, that is.

She slides her hands into her parka pockets and, to rid herself of him, makes a gentle suggestion to Åke: "Do you suppose Astrid needs help with the early birds? Was that what those guests who just arrived call themselves?"

When Åke turns back to Jessica, he looks somehow enigmatic, as if mentioning the name of the party has crossed some invisible line.

"So Astrid told you . . . ," he says, and wipes his mouth on the back of his knobby work glove, then continues in a lower voice, "about the birds of spring."

"Not really. Just that they come every year."

"And did she tell you about the legend of Smörregård, the girl in the blue coat?"

Jessica shakes her head. An eager gleam has kindled in Åke's kind eyes. The broad smile reveals a row of uneven teeth, yellowed at the gumline by snuff.

"Now, that has the makings of a detective novel," he says.

At that instant, Astrid's voice carries over the blustering wind, calling her son by name.

"You'll come to dinner, won't you? The story's more exciting when it's told by firelight anyway," Åke says, then starts walking toward the villa.

"We'll see," Jessica calls out as she waves to Åke, who has already made it to the boathouses. That evening, she had planned on making a tour by headlamp of the northern shore, taking a hot shower, and eating a bowl of salmon soup alone in her room while she read a book. For dessert, she has benzos: depending on her mood, from a single pill to a whole vial.

But who knows? Maybe she could sit by the fire and listen to the local legend that made Åke's face beam with enthusiasm.

12

A LOW-HANGING SPRUCE branch scratches Jessica's cheek nastily, prompting a gasp of pain. There's a dirt road that winds its way across the island, but for a change of pace Jessica has decided to take a shortcut through the woods. The trees grow closely together, and the protruding eye-level branches are like bayonets just waiting for her to walk into them. Here and there the lush conifers form dark shadows where it's easy to imagine the dens and hideaways of animals.

Jessica looks up from the ground; before her rises a tall rock topped by gnarled pines bent horizontal by the wind; it would have been a hopeless habitat for the trees from the start. She keeps walking; cones squish under her hiking boots. A sappy, decaying smell rises from beneath the melting snow and ice, as do gases freed from the soil by the warming temperatures and borne aloft by the mist. The rock is slippery, and Jessica almost bites it more than once before she reaches the top.

During the occasional moment when her senses are being refreshed by the touch of pure nature, she has pondered the finality of her decision. Would it be possible to start over somewhere, in a different way and in a different place? Could she be happy alone in a small cottage somewhere in the archipelago, watching the sea grow blacker and more aggressive with the onset of autumn, until it eventually freezes and encases the shoreline rocks, the waves, the whitecaps? Might ascetic isolation soothe her restless spirit, or would it cast her into wholesale insanity?

She climbs down the steep rock and sees something farther off among the trees, something that breaks the soft harmony of the woods. A few minutes later, she pops out from the forest and finds herself at the edge of an overgrown dirt road, looking at a white building. Jessica walks closer, places her gloved hand against its uneven and in places sloughing plaster.

The building is beautiful in its austere way: it is low, only one story, but incredibly long. The foundation is laid with enormous blocks of granite. The place is like a whitewashed garrison. Four stone stairs lead to the wooden door. Two of the ten windowpanes on the front facade are broken, and the wind is whipping through the moldy curtains behind them. The place was clearly abandoned long ago, and at this point renovating it would not be the simplest of tasks. But there's something about the inhospitable property that sparks her interest. Maybe it's the view that opens from the building toward the dock and the open sea, the desolate monotony so very different from the view from the idyllic southern tip of the island.

Jessica could do it: buy a place like this.

She could do whatever she wanted.

She could build a new house, whatever kind she wants and wherever she wants.

The wind picks up and sets the scarf around her neck fluttering wildly. Beyond the scarf's billows, the building seems to come to life before Jessica's eyes. Or maybe it's more as if something were living inside the building. Suddenly Jessica feels as if someone is watching her from behind the shattered windows, from the depths of one of the dark rooms, and a shiver runs up her spine.

Jessica wraps the scarf more tightly around her neck and starts walking back. Even so, the gnawing at her stomach doesn't disappear, nor does the hateful sensation that she is not alone.

HOPE HAS STOPPED *eating. I bought bird food in town, but the picky little baby won't touch it. I don't get why he refuses to do his part in carrying out the simple plan that will save his life if it works. Maybe he wants worms, but they're still hiding under the frozen ground this time of year, and I can't just pluck them out of the dirt and feed them to him.*

Hope looks sick and weak, but his eyes are anything but discouraged. He stares at me with his little black beady eyes from the cardboard box as if I'm an imbecile. He sees through me. He knows I'm not in control of the situation. Maybe he's decided starvation is a better option than growing up under my care. I feel like punishing the ungrateful creature. Unlike in the past, tonight I turn off the light when I leave the shed. Maybe absolute darkness will bring him to his senses.

JESSICA PAUSES AT the door and takes in the room bathing in dim light. The long, occasionally protruding ceiling planks and the big beams supporting them. The blue, red, and white rag rugs on the dark red floor, at least five or six of them. The little red hearts taped to the windowpanes, apparently left in place to wait for next Christmas. Tonight white lace tablecloths have been laid to protect the round wooden tables, and a white candle popped into the mouth of a wine bottle flickers cozily on each one. A table at the rear of the room is occupied by three frail figures who appear to pay Jessica no mind. The elderly trio are dressed in their best: the man is wearing a dark suit; the women, evening gowns that went out of style decades ago. By all signs, the woman with her back to the door is the one Jessica met outside her window this morning.

If you've brought any secrets to this island, I suggest you keep them to yourself.

Something about the ambience makes Jessica regret coming: she really shouldn't have left her cozy little hole and dragged herself here. Just now a dinner laid on white tablecloths in the company of strangers is the last thing she wants.

But just as she is about to turn around, a hand falls to her shoulder, making her jump.

"So nice you came!"

Astrid's fingers squeeze the shoulder muscle the way Jessica's mother's bony ones did so many times in her sleep. Jessica feels a shiver run through her body.

"Yeah," Jessica manages to say. She sees Astrid's voice has drawn the attention of the "birds": the elderly people turn toward them and, with the exception of the man, who gives a thin smile, don't appear particularly delighted. Jessica nods at them in greeting, then turns away like a little child who's nervous about talking to adults she doesn't know.

"Sit, please," Astrid says, pulling out a chair from the table nearest the entrance and as far as possible from the birds. Luckily.

"Thank you," Jessica says, as Astrid politely slides the chair under her. As Astrid sets a menu on the table, she leans in and whispers to Jessica: "Let's let them reminisce for a moment. We'll put the tables together when it's time for dessert."

"Thank you," Jessica says again, even though she's relatively sure she won't be staying for dessert. Especially if eating it means social interaction with the eagle lady and her equally starchy friends.

Jessica sighs and eyes the menu, handwritten in a sloppy script on bone white card stock. Compared to those of the past few weeknights, this evening's options are clearly more elevated.

Vichyssoise with herb oil
&
Grilled Ahvenanmaa beef tenderloin with a mild cognac and pepper sauce
&
Burned sugar cake with vanilla buttercream, vanilla-marinated raspberries, and old-fashioned vanilla ice cream

Quite the upgrade for a Friday, Jessica thinks to herself. From salmon casserole to tenderloin.

Until now, the menu has consisted of straightforward home cooking that, Jessica must admit, has been delicious. Either the Friday-night menu always diverges from the norm, or—more likely—Astrid and Åke want to pamper the spring birds, who are dressed to the nines for the festive meal.

Astrid lowers a glass of water to the table along with a full pitcher and recommends a glass of the house white with the first course. Jessica hesitates, remembering what Tuula said about mixing alcohol and sleeping aids, but answers in the affirmative.

At that moment, the door to the dining room opens, and in step the fortyish couple from Sweden, who Jessica has overheard are from Kalmar and visiting the island for a few days before continuing to Helsinki—if the increasingly complicated situation with the pandemic allows, that is. Astrid seats them at a window table.

The man nods at Jessica, seats himself at the formally set table, and rolls up the sleeves of his dress shirt. As Astrid presents the evening's menu to them, Jessica finds her gaze wandering to the man. He has an angular jaw, gleaming gelled hair, and short stubble. The sinewy wrists and arms indicate a profession requiring physical labor, but his well-manicured hands mean he probably has a dull indoor job despite his muscular appearance. With her long blond hair, the woman is stunning, but the stiffness of her movements speaks of unease. It would appear that beneath the beautiful shell beats a timid and insecure heart. A handsome couple all in all, if not exactly exuding a passionate love for each other: they haven't glanced at each other a single time during the minutes that have passed since they took their seats. Apparently Jessica is witnessing the paradox of coupling up: the longer two people are together, the further apart they drift. Their eyes scan above and past the other parties, at their smartphone screens, to the view outside the window, when they ought to be stopping to look into each other's eyes. Maybe that's why it's never wise to get into a relationship with someone who is important to you. At best, the relationship could be a months- or even years-long trip to heaven, but eventually one has to fall back down to earth and get used to the fact that the first crush and falling in love, all the excitement of that initial infatuation, will never return in the same form. Is that what love is? Is that how things would be if she'd ever dared to say anything to Yusuf? If she'd understood that not speaking up would fill her with profound regret?

THE CLINK OF silverware against porcelain has stopped, and the room is utterly silent. Jessica hears Astrid sneeze in the kitchen and the dishwasher open with a bang.

Jessica tosses back the last of her wine and sets the glass down next to her empty plate.

She has spent nearly the entire dinner staring at her phone, even if she's barely been able to get the tabloids' news applications to work due to the lousiness of the network. Now and again, a bar appears at the top of her screen, allowing her to load a lone article, but that's it. She has yet to receive a single message. That being said, who would be texting her? At most maybe Hellu, who for some incomprehensible reason seemed genuinely concerned when they last met. The concern no doubt had more to do with the unit's reputation and Hellu's authority than with Jessica's health. In contrast, Yusuf sent a WhatsApp message before Jessica's departure, stressing his wishes for a peaceful trip and reminding her that the distance consciously placed between herself and her work and life in Helsinki won't have the desired effect if she is in any sort of contact with anyone back home. He himself promised not to be in touch unless she reached out first. And he has stuck to his word, damn it. Over the five days she has spent so far at Smörregård, there have been plenty of moments when Jessica has burned with the desire to tap out a message to Yusuf. Maybe even call. But what would she say? Ask what was going on without really wanting an honest response? Having to hear

Yusuf's awkward mumbling about Tanja and how they were looking at flights to Barcelona for next summer, when it would be possible to travel again? *That sounds amazing. I love all the beaches and restaurants there. Have fun. Remember to screw a lot.*

Jessica locks her phone, leans back in her chair, and lowers her hands to her stomach. The strange sensation gnawing at the pit of her belly will not leave her in peace. It's as if she is still hungry in spite of the generous portions.

"Would you care for dessert?" Astrid says, returning to the dining room and starting to collect the dirty dishes from Jessica's table. It's a tempting offer, but just now Jessica truly has no interest in sticking around to chat and get to know anyone new. She's grown accustomed to the silence during her sojourn on the island.

"Thanks, but I think I'll turn in," Jessica says, shooting a discreet glance at the table where the old people are sitting. They're talking in such soft voices that Jessica has a hard time hearing what they're talking about. And why should she be listening anyway? Has the guesthouse's owners' tendency to stick their noses into other people's business infected her? Didn't the eagle-beaked lady's comment this morning mean everyone ought to mind their own business, not anyone else's?

"Are you sure?" Astrid says, taking a seat across from Jessica. Jessica stares at her in bafflement. Incredible. Can't she enjoy one lousy meal without company being forced on her? Suddenly she wants to get back to Helsinki, to the bustle of the big city, where no one is ever alone and yet restaurants allow their customers to sit in peace without the staff constantly pestering them.

"I thought you might enjoy meeting our anniversary party. They have downright fascinating stories. The sort that might even impress a person such as yourself." Astrid tugs down the sleeve of her sweater as if to conceal the watch dangling at her wrist.

"A person such as myself?"

"Yes. A big-time detective."

Jessica shakes her head. "Thank you. I don't mean to be antisocial, but I guess . . . that's exactly what I am."

Astrid laughs. "Antisocial?"

"Yes," Jessica says. "I like being alone. Especially when I'm on vacation."

"I understand." Astrid rubs her wrinkled cheek. In the candlelight, the plump blue veins at the back of her hand look like worms trapped under the skin. Suddenly they seem to wriggle. Jessica turns away and wipes her hands on her napkin.

"Elisabeth told me you two met," Astrid then blurts out, as if desperate to keep the flame of conversation alive.

Jessica folds her napkin and sets it down on the plate in front of her before glancing past Astrid at the neck of the woman sitting at the far end of the room. "Elisabeth? Yes, I found her peeking in my window this morning. Not that she introduced herself."

Astrid doesn't look surprised.

"She's an eccentric woman," Astrid says, chuckling into her fist. "And exactly how you described yourself: a little antisocial. Quite literally. But very nice once you get to know her. I call her Diesel."

"Diesel?"

"Yes, because a diesel engine takes a while to warm up but—"

"I get it," Jessica says, then pinches her lips together. She could tell Astrid how that eccentric, antisocial diesel woman who's so nice after she warms up described Astrid in less flattering terms that morning. *An old parrot who will tell you everything.*

Jessica turns toward the entry hall, which has a view of the library beyond through a second open door. Åke is kneeling at the hearth. She thinks back to the conversation they had down at the shore and asks: "Who is the girl in the blue coat?"

Astrid's face darkens, and she takes a surreptitious peek at the old people's table as if to make sure she can't be heard.

"Just make-believe," Astrid says quietly, fingering the wine bottle holding the half-burned candle. "A local myth, a legend with no truth to it. The fishermen pass it down from generation to generation to amuse themselves."

"Does it have something to do with . . . ?" Jessica nods at the old people.

The old man coughs into his fist as if he is choking on his food, and Astrid quickly looks over to ensure no one is actually dying and waits for the fit to abate. Then she nods at Jessica. "In a way."

"In what way?" Jessica asks, surprising herself. Her professional curiosity has been piqued after having been extinguished for weeks.

Astrid looks at her as if she is a witness who doesn't want to reveal to the police what she knows. Then she places the wine and water glasses on the empty plate.

"Excuse me, Jessica. I have to serve the dessert now," Astrid says curtly. She rises from the table, dirty dishes in hand, and as she steps past Jessica, she briefly lowers her free hand to Jessica's shoulder before continuing to the kitchen.

Jessica turns to the open door and Åke, who seems to be admiring the fire he just started, and remembers what he said that morning: *The story's more exciting when it's told by firelight anyway.*

15

JESSICA TURNS ON the tap and looks at herself in the bathroom mirror. Then she dries her hands and returns the towel to the hook. The blue-tile walls are dense with art and old mostly black-and-white photographs of the archipelago, Villa Smörregård, and its shores and property. A slogan in Swedish has been embroidered into one fabric piece: *For men in a state of freedom had thatch for their shelter, while slavery dwells beneath marble and gold.—Seneca.* Jessica remembers the book on the coffee table in her room, the one she borrowed from the library here. Now that she thinks about it, it was written by Seneca too.

Jessica studies the pictures: in most she spots Astrid, whose narrow face, ramrod posture, and patch of darkened skin at the throat are recognizable regardless of when the photos were taken. In one, a young Astrid stands in front of the villa with a shovel slung over her shoulder like a rifle, fingers raised to her brow in a military salute. The caption at the bottom reads *Smörregård, summer 1958* in a beautiful hand. So the photo was taken over sixty years ago. *Exactly how old is this woman?* Jessica wonders to herself as she registers the sound of footsteps outside the door.

Jessica starts when someone tries the handle, and the loosely hung door starts to creak on its hinges.

"Just a second," Jessica says, taking one last look in the mirror.

But the handle is still jiggling; it rises and falls furiously, as if someone is trying to force their way in.

"I'm in here. I'll be right out," Jessica says, perplexed when the door handle still judders restlessly, with no sign of stopping. *What the hell?*

Jessica unlocks the door, and it immediately pops open. A wrinkled, suspicious-looking old woman is standing there in her finery. It's Elisabeth, eyeing Jessica as if she is cheap sausage.

For a fleeting moment, Jessica expects an apology, a contrite smile, or even a look of surprise. But all Elisabeth says is: "I need to get in there." Hatred emanates from her face.

Jessica steps out of the tiny room, making way for the old woman. "Of course."

She lets out an incredulous little laugh as Elisabeth pushes her way in and quickly shuts the door behind her.

What a strange person. Jessica has really dodged a bullet in turning down dessert and Astrid's attempts to generate conversation among the tables. How would that have turned out?

Jessica peers discreetly into the dining room, then continues to the library, where Åke is sweeping the floor in front of the fireplace. A fire crackles in the hearth; flames lick the thick, cross-stacked logs. A stuffed albatross and a few framed photographs hang on the stone chimney.

"Astrid said you like lighthouses," Jessica says from the doorway as she makes her way to the fire, arms folded across her chest. When she feels the warmth of the blaze on her skin, she realizes how cool it was in the dining room.

Åke turns with a start, as if Jessica has roused him from deep thoughts. Then the now-familiar friendly smile spreads across his bearded face. He nods and gestures for Jessica to take a seat at the fire.

"Would you care for a glass of Calvados? Or whisky?" he says, walking over to the opposite wall, where a glass cabinet abounds with brown bottles. "On the house."

Jessica nods and collapses into an armchair. "Sure. Something smoky, please," she says, thinking once more of Erne, who swore by peaty Islay whiskies and initiated Jessica into their mysteries once upon a time.

"Coming right up." Åke takes a green bottle with a big brown label from the cabinet. He pinches the cork out of the bottle's mouth, and Jessica hears two brief splashes as he pours.

A moment later, he hands a glass to Jessica and claims one of the three armchairs at the fire. Åke raises his glass and takes a sip. Grins pleasurably, in a way that speaks of either a love for the whisky's taste or simply the contact of ethanol with the mucous membranes in his mouth and its rapid effect on the central nervous system. Or both. Alcoholism and hedonism are not mutually exclusive traits. At least they weren't for Erne.

"Lighthouses," Åke says, lowering the glass into his lap. "For me they somehow symbolize peace of mind and tranquility. They stand there in lofty solitude, rising toward the sky. Always ready to guide others and receive the wrath of the world's seas."

"Poetic," Jessica says, and sips her whisky. The smoky tang immediately reaches her unaccustomed taste buds, and she gulps to clear her throat.

"I don't understand much about poetry, but peace of mind is key to Stoicism, which I deeply admire," Åke says.

Jessica unwittingly looks a little surprised, perhaps, and Åke grunts with the glass at his lips. "I know what you're thinking: what does the owner of a guesthouse know about philosophy?" he says. "But I can't help myself. Philosophy is my great love and passion; I taught it for decades in Sweden, at Umeå University."

"Really?"

Åke nods, eyes fixed on the flames licking the wood. His blue eyes are sad and in some way innocent, like a child's. "There's a season for everything. My passion turned into a rat race, and by the end I couldn't stop wondering whether a single student took away anything from the mandatory philosophy course I was teaching. I gradually began to agree with Arthur Schopenhauer, who had a cynical view of pedagogy. He once insightfully noted that if training and reprimands were of any use, there would be no way a student of Seneca's could have become the emperor Nero. A good teacher ought to be able to rid students of tendencies that harm others."

Jessica smiles, wishing the conversation would quickly move on to the girl in the blue coat. But she doesn't want to hurry Åke, who appears to be pondering matters of a very personal nature.

She hooks her thumb over her shoulder, toward the door. "I saw the Seneca quote in the bathroom. And there's a book here too . . ."

Åke chuckles. "Oh, there are a lot of them."

"*Letters from a Stoic*?" Jessica says. "I borrowed it from the bookshelf yesterday."

Åke looks at Jessica the way a proud teacher looks at a student. "If you have time to read while you're writing a book, I recommend a deep dive into it. A very inspiring work," he says, swirling the whisky around his glass.

"When did you return to Smörregård?"

Åke grunts, hides himself behind his glass for a moment. The flames play in the crystal, which reflects tiny golden rays onto his face.

"When I was approaching turning fifty, I finally gained an understanding of my own mortality, and I paused to reflect on whether I'd been living my life the way I wanted. Seneca presumably would have told me, the fewer days you have left, the more wisely they need to be spent. That makes them all the more precious." Åke takes another sip of whisky and lets out an unenthusiastic chuckle. "Either that, or I came home out of a sense of obligation."

Jessica eyes him quizzically.

"Dad died last summer, and Astrid is eighty-four . . . She doesn't have the energy to run the guesthouse on her own."

"My condolences."

Åke glances at Jessica as if he isn't grasping her meaning. Then he nods almost imperceptibly. "Thank you. He and I weren't close. I came home to help my mother. And I haven't regretted it a single minute. I suppose I never really left this place; I wasn't able to cut the apron strings. The archipelago is my home."

"I understand," Jessica says, glancing at her watch.

"Mom is a tough cookie and thinks she would have managed just fine without me. Did you know she was a doctor?"

"No," Jessica says, finding herself surprised yet again. For some reason she imagined mother and son had spent their entire existence living the simple island life in which the wave troughs were empty rooms, a bad raspberry harvest, or a plague that spoiled the autumn crayfish parties. Jessica is ashamed of her assumptions and suspects they lead back to her elitist childhood, when a sharp line was drawn between those who did academic work and those who performed physical labor.

"*The angel of life*—that's what they called Astrid at work. She worked at the Ahvenanmaa Central Hospital as an obstetrician until 1997, when she retired and started helping Dad with the guesthouse."

"That's inspiring," Jessica says. "A rolling stone gathers no moss."

"Exactly. There's a real model student of Stoicism for you."

Jessica could ask more about Astrid and her career as a doctor, something about Åke's father or Åke's life in Sweden, how he taught Philosophy 101 to indifferent university students. But she's tired and, after all the dithering, burning to learn what the story of the girl in the blue coat is all about.

"Speaking of lighthouses, Astrid mentioned you were familiar with the Söderskär case," Jessica says, crossing an ankle over the other knee. Might this be the segue that would finally lead them to the topic without her sounding too inquisitive?

Åke raises his glass and eyes the flames' glow through it. Then he nods and turns back to Jessica. A proud smile has spread across his face. "I recognized you right away."

"I had no idea the manga league case was in the news all the way out here."

Åke looks surprised. "It was in the news a lot. But as a matter of fact, I came to learn of the case when we had some young guests who were followers of that girl on social media . . . the girl who was later found dead. Since there was a picture of the Söderskär lighthouse in her social media accounts . . . It's in a class of its own when it comes to beauty. There was an exhibit of Tove Jansson's Moomintroll art there a few years ago," he continues.

"I wasn't aware of that." Jessica finds her body has relaxed in the warmth of the fire. But now they need to start gradually getting to the point, or her fatigue will beat out her curiosity.

Åke nods again and swirls the whisky in his glass. Jessica takes another sip. The taste takes her back to rainy evenings at the window table at Manala; Erne's cigarette-heavy breath; the chapped knuckles Jessica admonished him thousands of times to lotion, to no effect.

"This morning you said the story of the girl in the blue coat is more exciting in the firelight," Jessica says, to get away from the rapidly revived memory.

Åke grunts. "As a matter of fact, the story is exciting regardless of where it's told. Astrid thinks it's just a ghost story."

Jessica glances over her shoulder into the dining room, wondering whether Astrid can guess at the subject of this fireside conversation. "Is it?"

"You'll have to decide that for yourself."

"I'm all ears," Jessica says, then continues like a reporter on a scoop: "Who was the girl in the blue coat?"

Åke fiddles with the roaring lion's head carved into the wooden armrest of his chair. Finally he begins: "I'm sure during your walks you've come across the building at the northern end of the island and the old dock there."

Jessica nods.

"Unfortunately the building has fallen into disrepair in recent years, but as late as the mid-1980s, it was home to Ahvenanmaa's only orphanage. Since then, it has mostly stood empty. The municipality cut off the power to it ten or so years ago, and since then it's been allowed to decay in peace."

As she listens to Åke's words, Jessica watches the fire, hears the pops and sees the sparks shoot out like fireflies and disappear in the blink of an eye.

"But in order to understand the story of the girl in the blue coat, we have to go back a lot further, all the way to 1946."

"What happened then?"

"The birds of spring," Åke says, and suddenly there's sadness in his eyes. Now Jessica remembers that Astrid reluctantly admitted a link between the elderly guests and the story.

"I don't know how much you know about Finland's wartime history, but this is about the child evacuees. During the Winter and Continuation Wars, about eighty thousand Finnish children were sent abroad to safety. Most were placed in Sweden, the rest in Norway and Denmark."

"I'm more or less familiar with the episode," Jessica says, despite feeling a little ashamed of her deficient knowledge of history.

"When the war ended, most of the children returned to Finland, but a sizable percentage—as many as a quarter, it's estimated— stayed with their new families. Many of the children's parents had died during the war, and the children had no home to return to." Åke lowers his glass to the armrest and scratches his beard before continuing: "There is room for all sorts of fates among such a large cohort of children. Many were lucky; the luckiest made it from the remote forests of the Soviet border to luxurious Stockholm suburbs where swing played on the radio in the evenings and exotic fruit was eaten as a snack. Others of course had difficulty adjusting to their foster families, less advantageous circumstances, bullying, sometimes even violence—psychological or physical . . . Problems arose especially at the point when the children were to return to Finland, a place where suddenly everything might feel completely foreign, including one's biological parents and the language. Some of the children had to be brought back against their will. That must have been horrible for all parties involved."

"What do the birds of spring have to do with this?" Jessica says, ashamed of her impatience.

"The birds of spring were a group of nine kids who boarded a ship at the Stockholm free port in August 1946, over a year after the Lapland War came to an end. They sailed to Maarianhamina, where their parents were supposed to meet them. But the vessel their parents were on sank in stormy weather, drowning everyone aboard, including the crew. In other words, there was no one to meet the children when they arrived in Maarianhamina."

"How terrible," Jessica manages to say. Suddenly she feels cold. She thinks about the car accident that proved her family's fate, remembers herself as a badly injured little girl in a hospital bed. Orphaned. Alone.

"It wasn't possible to send all of them back to Sweden. It was a complicated situation. The decision was made in Maarianhamina that the children who didn't have any known close relatives in Finland would stay temporarily in Ahvenanmaa, until some sort of solution was found."

"And the children were brought to this island?"

"Initially they lived in an old warehouse at Fagerkulla, but there was a fire there at some point and they were moved here to Smörregård. A nurse named Monica Boman began to look after their affairs and later became the director of the orphanage. It was by no means an optimal solution, but the intent was to look after the children well."

Jessica sits up straighter. "The intent was to look after the children well?"

Åke empties his glass and looks at Jessica in confusion.

"It sounds like this noble plan didn't succeed for some reason," Jessica continues.

Åke sighs. "In the end, eight children between the ages of eight and thirteen were moved here, five girls and three boys. They killed time and waited to hear who would be picking them up and whether their journey would be continuing to Finland or perhaps back to Sweden. Folks started calling them the birds of spring, because everyone was sure they would fly off before winter. Three of those eight are still alive and sitting there in the dining room enjoying a delicious dessert you decided to pass up for some reason. Why, by the way?" Åke flashes a smile presumably intended to lighten the mood. "Astrid makes a melt-in-your-mouth sugar cake."

"The birds of spring," Jessica whispers, looking across the entryway and into the dining room.

Åke nods. "In a way, it was a time when they were all forced to grow up. And that's something that has brought them together ever since. What's happening in there is a class reunion of sorts. They come here every year and go pay their respects at the northern end of the island, where they lived for a few months seventy-four years ago."

"Months? So eventually all the children found new homes?"

"Seven of the children had been picked up from Smörregård by early December," Åke says.

"So all except one?"

Åke swirls the few drops left in his glass and purses his lips solemnly. "Maija Ruusunen. A nine-year-old girl whose wartime evacuation to a foreign country apparently traumatized her more seriously than the others. She had problems, difficult problems. She'd lost her mother before the war. Didn't exactly fit in, didn't play with the others. It was a nasty twist of fate that Maija was the last child at Smörregård."

Jessica swallows down the lump she feels in her throat. "What happened to her?"

"No one knows for sure. But what she did while she was on the island gave rise to a legend that still lives on to this day. It began when other children were still living at the orphanage," Åke says. "Maija would slip out of her room in the middle of the night and go stand at the end of the dock."

Jessica notices her arm hairs standing up. Suddenly the room feels cold.

"Maija was the girl in the blue coat," she whispers.

Åke nods. "And she still is, if you ask the local fishermen."

He stands and takes Jessica's glass. "Let's have another, and I'll tell you the rest of the story."

16

JESSICA LOOKS AT her empty glass in Åke's hand and is surprised to see the whisky somehow made its way down her throat. She has been so engrossed in Åke's story that she has been oblivious to her sipping.

"And it happened every night," Åke says, pouring more of the brown liquor into her glass. "Every night at two on the dot Maija would sneak out of her room, put on her coat, and go out and stand at the end of the dock, gazing intently out to sea."

"But why?"

Åke shrugs and sits back down in his armchair. "The belief was that she'd lost her mind among all the chaos. Think about how young children are viewed as being traumatized these days: they're not allowed to read Moomintroll books because the Groke is so damn scary, and wars and the Holocaust are taboo topics at school because it's assumed students will find them distressing," he grumbles into his glass. Then he reaches for a log from the wrought iron firewood holder and tosses it easily to the back of the fire. A few sharp pops ring out before the crackle rises again.

"Every night," Åke repeats in a soft voice, and suddenly his eyes look moist in the glow of the rekindled flame. "Maija would stand out there on the dock until the night watchman would go and fetch her and bring her back in by force."

"You said Maija was the last child. That all the others found new homes."

"Some returned to Sweden, to the families they'd lived with during the war, but there didn't seem to be anyone who would take Maija. The authorities began to arrange for her adoption, but there were hundreds if not thousands of such cases at the time, and the wheels of bureaucracy turn slowly. Besides . . ."

"Besides what?" Jessica says, as Åke holds a dramatic pause.

"It didn't help matters that Maija was viewed as mentally ill. Apparently Maija had a curious tendency to set things on fire. And to top it off, everyone thought what happened here at Smörregård—her going out to the dock in the middle of the night and standing there in the darkness—was really damn scary. I get shivers just telling this story." Åke laughs joylessly. "At the time, people had plenty of other problems as it was, and no one wanted to take in a crazy little girl. Damaged goods, as they say."

Jessica finds her grip around the glass tightening as the word "crazy" forms on Åke's lips. The fact that the girl repeated the same ritual every night doesn't give anyone the right to think of her as crazy. If anyone knows this, Jessica does. The world is not black and white. Jessica finds herself feeling sympathy for the Maija who once lived on this island, for the girl she feels she understands based on the little Åke has shared about events that happened over seven decades ago.

Suddenly voices can be heard singing in the dining room, and the melancholy tone clearly sets the melody apart from traditional Swedish drinking songs. Jessica glances at Åke, who grunts indulgently.

"That hymn is one of the traditions," Åke whispers. "A song they sang when they still lived on the island. Story has it that the director of the orphanage was a very religious woman. And it is a beautiful tune. Astrid used to sing it to me as a lullaby way back when."

Jessica lowers her empty glass to the table and listens to the wistful song. She doesn't recognize the melody, but it reminds her of "Sylvia's Christmas Song," a popular Finnish Christmas song and one of the saddest Jessica has ever heard.

"How does the story end?" Jessica says impatiently, as the birds of spring launch into the next verse.

"To my understanding, they eventually stopped trying to keep Maija from performing her curious ritual. As certainly as the sun rose every morning, that girl would be out there on the dock staring out to sea. Weeks passed, months. And then one night out of the blue, Maija vanished."

"Vanished?"

"One morning she was gone. And so was one of the rowboats." Åke coughs into his fist before continuing: "Story has it that the sea was calm that evening and the weather mild for December. But a ferocious gale blew in toward morning. So it's possible Maija managed to row out to open water and was caught in the storm's clutches. It's also possible the storm carried the boat off and Maija didn't have anything to do with it."

"And no one ever saw her . . ."

Åke shakes his head.

Jessica feels herself roiled by a wave of nausea. "Is it possible Maija didn't leave on her own? That someone came and got her?"

Åke eyes Jessica quizzically, then shrugs. "Considering the rowboat was gone and no one else was missing from the island . . . I guess no one really thought that was a plausible explanation. Besides, Maija didn't have anyone who would have come to fetch her. Do you want another drink?" he says abruptly, breaking the story's spell.

"No, thanks," Jessica promptly replies, and glances down at her wrist to check the time.

Åke looks like he means to stand but doesn't, as if telling the story has drained him of his strength.

"That's a really sad story," Jessica says, lowering her hands to her stomach. The white wine and whisky have made her drowsy.

"Part of me wants to believe Maija found her way to the mainland. And that she lived somewhere happily ever after."

"There's one thing I don't get," Jessica says.

"What?"

"Why does Astrid think it's a ghost story?"

"Because the story doesn't end with Maija's disappearance," Åke says enigmatically.

Jessica shifts in her seat and glances over her shoulder into the dining room, where the croaking choir is launching into the hymn's third verse. At the same time, Jessica sees through the window that the outdoor lights in front of the building have been activated; something or someone has tripped the sensor.

"After Maija disappeared, the building was empty for a few years, but then an orphanage was officially established there: Smörregård Children's Home. There were never huge numbers of children and adolescents on the island, but to my understanding the orphanage was still running until 1986, when it was finally shut down as redundant. Nevertheless, throughout its existence, the legend of the girl in the blue coat persisted tenaciously among the staff and the kids. No one else was ever assigned to room six; it was preserved as some sort of chamber of horrors. Not out of respect for Maija but because not a single child would sleep in it. The story of the girl at the end of the dock lived on for decades. Many residents of the orphanage claimed to have woken up in the middle of the night and seen the girl on the dock. And these sightings weren't limited to the children; fishermen and sailors also whispered about little Maija, said they'd seen a small figure standing on Smörregård's rocky shores in the middle of the night." Åke leans toward Jessica. "Sounds like a pretty classic story, right? The Loch Ness Monster, yeti, mermaids, Elvis alive and well at the supermarket, et cetera."

"It certainly does."

"It's as if the ghost of the little girl who died at sea came back again and again to haunt the dock," Åke says, pulling a puck of loose snuff and a metal dispenser from his pocket. "That's why Astrid called it a ghost story." He taps the tobacco into the dispenser, filling it with nicotine-impregnated crud, and shoots it under his mustached upper lip. "And then there's the—"

Åke is interrupted by a cough at the door. "Could you come give me a hand, Åke?" The voice is Astrid's.

Jessica turns toward Astrid and wonders how long she's been standing there, listening to her son's tale. There's a sour look on her face, as if she intentionally put an end to Åke's account.

Åke hoists himself to his feet. Now Jessica notices he's a little unsteady; he probably began drinking a good while before dinner.

"The end," Åke says, patting Jessica's shoulder as he passes her.

The smell of the wood burning in the hearth and the warmth radiating to her face feel comforting, but even they cannot conceal the fact that the story she just heard is still giving her goose bumps.

17

THE BEAM FROM the headlamp splits the near-perfect darkness as Jessica advances down the shoreline route. The walk from the guesthouse to the northern end of Smörregård is about two kilometers by road, and Jessica has made it in about twenty minutes despite a strong headwind.

She sticks her hand in her pocket, pinches her fingers among the pills at the bottom of it. For her they mean the possibility of freedom, a deep and endless sleep where her mind would finally be at rest. A journey to a place where the monsters wouldn't follow her. Death is a gossamer-thin opportunity to see the people she loves— those who have departed before her—one last time. If she wanted, Jessica could quit this hallucinatory solitude she's been trying to push away by investigating brutal murders, diving into the pitiless world of the wicked and their inhuman acts. She has been running from herself for ages, to a place where dread, despair, and cynicism know no limits. Jessica drifted into that world under Erne's guidance, because she wanted, she supposes, both to atone for her bloodshed and to do all she could to ensure that bad people couldn't freely walk the streets. To ensure that not a single young woman would be raped by a psychopath ever again, not on her watch.

But now the girl in the blue coat has piqued her interest and gnawed away some of her self-destructive thoughts, and Jessica isn't sure whether that's a good thing: she knows the relief is temporary and will serve only to put off the inevitable.

Between the stunted trees sprouting from the granite she sees the western end of the former orphanage, its shattered windows. The white building is easy to make out in the darkness. Jessica steps off the road and clambers up the rock rising next to it, admires the archipelago bathing in the moonlight. Unlike the view from the guest-house, which is dotted with dozens of inhabited islands, the seascape from Smörregård's northern end extends all the way to open water. There are smaller islands and islets at the edges of her field of vision, but they don't succeed in taming the open-water waves crashing into the cliffs. Whitecaps form in the restless roil, and the moon glowing behind clouds is trying to build a bridge across the water toward the next world.

At the time, people had plenty of other problems as it was, and no one wanted to take in a crazy little girl.

That's exactly the sort of girl I am, Jessica thinks to herself as she stares at the black sea, and her heart lurches at the thought. She's just as crazy as her mother was; it must have been outwardly evident even when she was a little girl. Aunt Tina must have known when she decided not to adopt Jessica. Luckily she'd had the Niemis, Dad's brother and his wife. They were brave enough to accept responsibility for her, despite the fact that if worse came to worst she might prove the same sort of walking time bomb as her mother: a person capable of killing her own family.

Jessica carefully descends the slippery rock and starts walking toward the building at the forest's edge; it stands about a hundred meters from the waterline. Power lines that once carried electricity extend from the dense trees.

Solid rock yields to softer soil underfoot as Jessica cuts between the trees toward the front of the building and through the overgrown sandy foreyard there. The drizzle that has been coming down for days sets the darkness glistening, as if nature is perspiring as it labors to call forth a new spring out of the frost. The black windows make the white building look threatening, like the skull of some beast. Jessica glances at the window she thought she caught movement at earlier that day, but now she sees nothing.

She turns from the building toward the T-shaped dock.

Why did you want to go to the dock, Maija? Why at two a.m. every night?

A derelict boathouse stands next to the pier; one of the shore-side corners has partially collapsed into the water. A slab of granite slopes up gently to the left of the ramshackle dock and undulates softly as it rises to a height of a few meters before being swallowed up by the woods.

A gust of wind rustles the treetops at the forest's edge. Nature is coming back to life on this black night in a place a normal person might, perhaps, call unpleasant. Forbidding. Eerie in some way. But Jessica finds all such things beautiful.

And then . . .

There she is. The girl is standing at the end of the dock, her back to the building, staring out to sea.

Jessica takes one step, then another.

Toward the dock, toward the girl who on this freezing night wears nothing but a beret and a thin blue coat over her pajamas. The light of the half-moon falls on the girl's hair; it's curly and the color of barley and dances in the wind.

What are you doing, sweetheart?

For a moment Jessica thinks she hears her mother's voice. *Sweetheart.* No one has called her that since her mother decided to disappear from her dreams.

Aren't you cold, sweetheart?

The questions feel like an invitation; they draw Jessica onward.

Maybe her mother has taken on a new form; maybe the girl standing on the dock isn't the Maija who vanished long ago, but Jessica's mother.

Jessica approaches the dock. Steps on rotted planks that give beneath her feet. A scream sounds from out at sea, and Jessica sees the silhouettes of birds against the dark blue horizon.

Sweetheart.

Jessica stops behind the girl. Expects to feel her mother's fingers on her shoulder, but nothing happens. She looks at the girl's light brown hair, which ripples from under the beret like stalks of grass in a meadow.

Jessica wipes the tears from her cheeks. Her lip has begun to quiver, and her throat tightens. Jessica isn't sure if she wants to see Maija's face, see what the girl who's been floating in the sea for decades looks like now. Then try to understand how someone so innocent could appear so hideous, how the world can let something like that happen.

And as if reading Jessica's thoughts, the girl slowly turns around.

But unlike Jessica has feared, Maija is not dead. Her face is whole, her gaze determined. Freckles cluster around her nose, and they look like a pale shadow in the gloom. Maija is beautiful—as a matter of fact, the most beautiful little girl Jessica has ever seen.

Don't cry, Mommy. Daddy will be here soon, Maija says.

She turns back to the sea.

And then it hits Jessica like a punch to the gut. She falls to her knees.

She experiences the truth as a pain in her breast.

Her mother is not coming back. Ever.

But Jessica called the girl sweetheart. And the girl called Jessica Mommy.

Something irreversible has happened. Or it is happening just now.

And a moment later, when Jessica's breathing has steadied and she raises her eyes from the planks of the derelict dock, the girl is gone. All that remains is the endless black expanse whose waves conceal an infinite number of secrets within.

18

WHEN SHE GOES to bed, Jessica does not take a single sleeping aid.

She drifts off without any trouble and has a dream in which she's looking at her reflection in a bathroom with walls of blue tile. In her dream, someone is jiggling the door handle insistently, again and again, and Jessica is afraid it's going to come off. She doesn't open the door, because she knows behind it there's an old woman whose wrinkled face is pale and whose eyes pierce like those of an eagle on the hunt. Then she hears the melancholy song the birds of spring are singing at the table, holding one another by the hand.

That hymn is one of their traditions, Åke's voice whispers. His bearded face is anything but gentle.

The sound of Astrid laughing carries from somewhere. Then the bathroom mirror turns into a window. Jessica sees Astrid outside in the pouring rain; she seems to be gliding across the yard. Astrid lowers the flag from the pole, rolls it up under her arm, and turns to look toward the window. She raises a finger to her lips. Jessica cranes her neck to look through the mirror, loses her balance, and falls into the shallows with all her weight. She sees a nightshirt and its wet hem, the white soles of feet under the water. She sees a red boat-house and a dock rocking on its pontoons. She hears lapping waves. Sees a scarf floating in the water.

Don't cry, Mommy. Daddy will be here soon.

Suddenly Jessica is back in the blue bathroom. The jiggling of the door handle grows more frantic. She hears the old woman hissing on the other side of the door. The song carrying from the dining room grows louder.

Has that old parrot told you everything again? Squawk squawk squawk.

Jessica prays someone will come and save her.

Then the door opens, and wrinkled hands appear at the crack. Jessica screams and huddles in the corner of the bathroom. But the hands stretch insistently toward her, grab at her hair. The old woman's black eyes flash with rage, and sharp teeth protrude from her open mouth and sink into Jessica's flesh.

My condolences, Jessica.

HOPE IS DEAD. *I found him lifeless this morning, curled up in the corner of the box. His tiny beak was open, as if he whispered his final words to the darkness of the toolshed last night. I feel guilty that I wasn't able to look after him better, that he lasted only a few pitiful days in my care. Would it have been better to leave him where I first found him? Maybe he wasn't an orphan after all, just momentarily separated from his parents.*

I look at the dead bird. His gaze is empty, and there's no sign of the disdain that emanated from the tiny eyes last night. I feel the urge to cry. But I can't. I don't want to. I've already cried enough. And never for myself.

Hope's life, which was cut short so soon, has clarified my thoughts; it has made everything easier.

It's time to bring all this to its conclusion.

Death has returned to Smörregård.

20

JESSICA WAKES WITH a start, and it takes her a moment to comprehend where she is. Her toes feel uncomfortably moist, and she's wearing wet shoes. She collapsed onto the bed fully dressed. She sits up; she's tired but not the least bit groggy.

The sun has risen, and gray-blue light is trying to push its way in through the curtained windows. Jessica rises to her feet and feels light; for the first time in a long time she feels so calm that it almost puts a smile on her face. She vividly remembers the events of the night before: Åke's engrossing story about little Maija and the girl who stood at the end of the dock.

This time Jessica's sensory delusion was controlled: it was something she had specifically sought out. But it hadn't provided a solution to the mystery of the girl in the blue coat. Of course not. How could Jessica have teased it out simply by visiting the site where the girl used to roam at night decades ago?

Suddenly Jessica is touched; she remembers how she called the girl sweetheart. And what was it the girl said to her?

Don't cry, Mommy. Daddy will be here soon.

Jessica rubs her eyes and takes off her wet shoes and socks. She understands her hallucinations don't really have anything to do with reality. Although they have offered her useful insights over the years, they are nevertheless merely products of the mind, and the words Jessica heard the previous evening were just sensory delusions colored by a sense of drama.

Jessica yawns and reaches for the book by Seneca that's on her nightstand. Åke is clearly captivated by its themes, judging not only by what he said but also by the countless excerpts that have been highlighted. *Difficulties strengthen the mind, as labor does the body* has been picked out in yellow and noted in the margin with an exclamation point. The same thing on the next page's *Why complain about the sea if you ride its waves again?* Jessica closes the book and wonders what would have become of her if she hadn't met Erne in Venice at the age of nineteen. Would she be a police officer? Or maybe a teacher, a business controller, or even a philosopher? Would she ever have worked for a living if she hadn't found her calling? Or would she have drunk or medicated herself into the grave, lonely and depressed amid her fortune and tormented by her demons? Considering the circumstances, this last possibility seems most likely.

Fuck my perfect life.

Jessica grabs her water bottle, tosses back the contents, and decides to eat a big breakfast.

WHEN SHE STEPS out she nearly collides with the Swedish man, who is standing outside the door of the converted barn, having a smoke in a heavy parka and flip-flops.

Jessica wishes him a subdued good morning and he returns the greeting. She glances at the flagpole; the Ahvenanmaa flag that was fluttering at the top the evening before has been lowered. With gray skies and frigid winds, the weather is downright bleak.

"Did you hear the news?"

"What news?" Jessica says, glancing at her reflection in the window.

"At the other side of the island," the man says, pointing northward with the cigarette hand. "A marine rescue crew is there. Apparently the police too."

"What happened?" The wind is nipping at Jessica's neck, and she pulls her coat tighter.

"Something unpleasant." The man takes a drag of his cigarette, then stubs it out in the ashtray. "Astrid and Åke are pretty upset. I'm not sure it's appropriate to go up there to gawk."

"Maybe they need help." Jessica tugs up her zipper and makes for the dirt road that leads through the woods.

JESSICA APPROACHES THE dock, and now she can see two medics in search-and-rescue coveralls. One is talking on the phone, and the other is speaking with Astrid and Åke. Their faces are grim. And then Jessica spots it: the human figure lying at the waterline, the soles of its feet sticking out from under a black tarp.

"What happened?" Jessica asks once she's closer, although the question seems pointless. There's clearly a dead body in the shallows, so she could have framed the question differently. All those present are, however, too focused or too upset to answer. After a moment, the medic who was speaking with Astrid and Åke lowers his eyes, apparently having said what he needed to say, and approaches Jessica.

"It's probably best if you head back to the guesthouse," he says. "The police are on their way."

"I'm a police officer," Jessica says. The medic doesn't seem to believe her words; maybe the mainland accent eats at her credibility. "From Helsinki," she continues, and peers behind the man to get a closer look at the body.

The medic shoots her a pointed look. He's about thirty years old and has a handsome face, a smooth-shaved chin, and a muscular build.

"Let's just wait for local law enforcement," he says as his female colleague ends the call. Obviously. Over the course of her career, Jessica has developed a look she uses to chase off nosy people hanging around the scene of an accident or a crime, and now she has become one herself.

"Of course," Jessica replies, unsure why she revealed that she was a police officer. Habit, she supposes. Besides, it would presumably come out anyway when the local police arrive or when Astrid and Åke open their mouths.

She takes a few steps backward and watches the tarp flap at the waterline. The sea that stretches as far as the eye can see seems distressed, as if nature is painfully aware of the tragedy that has taken place on the island.

Not long after, a blue and white police boat appears from behind a cliff; it slows as it approaches the shore. Jessica looks at the prow and the wake it creates, breaking up the sea into waves running off in opposite directions. The rocky shore, where the trees reach for the sky and its array of gray shades. The dock thrusting out over the water. Jessica's thoughts drift to the girl in the blue coat, who took fate into her own hands by rowing away from this island. Maybe she circled around the southern tip of Smörregård before continuing her voyage toward one of those hundreds of islands that fill the horizon in every direction except northward. But if that were the case, she would have turned up sooner or later . . .

"It's Elisabeth," Astrid's voice says, startling Jessica out of her reverie. The older woman has appeared at her side.

"Elisabeth?" Jessica repeats. Astrid's eyes are red; her gray hair hangs limp under her blue beanie. Whereas her youthfulness surprised Jessica earlier, right now she looks older than her age.

Astrid nods, reaches out her hands, and rubs Jessica's arm, as if to warm her up.

"One of the birds of spring," Astrid says.

Of course, Jessica thinks to herself. It has to be. There's presumably no one on the island aside from herself, the birds of spring, the proprietors of the guesthouse, and the Swedish couple.

"What happened?" she asks a moment later.

"No one knows," Astrid replies. "I found her in the water half an hour ago when . . ." She covers her mouth with her hand and shakes her head. "I don't understand what Elisabeth was . . . Why she would have come this far . . . alone."

"A sudden illness, maybe," Jessica suggests, even though she knows it's not an answer to what Astrid is pondering. A sudden illness would not explain why an old woman walked two kilometers across the island only to drown at the beach in front of an abandoned orphanage.

Jessica watches the police boat approach the dock, allows her eyes to slide across the rotted boathouse, the orphanage, and the sandy yard surrounding it. Suddenly Jessica is overwhelmed by the strange sensation that she knows more than she remembers, that she saw something despite her belief that she slept soundly through the night after her visit to the dock. Damn it; for the first time in ages, she's confusing reality with her imagination again. A long time has passed since this has happened, and it suddenly makes the surrounding world uncontrollable and frightening. She has got to start taking her medication again, despite the unpleasant side effects.

"I'm going back to the guesthouse," Jessica says. "Please let me know if there's anything I can do."

Astrid nods, and Jessica walks back toward the dirt road. As she passes the white building, Jessica sees the shattered windows and mildew-speckled curtains. She can picture Maija sitting in her room, staring at the sea that calls to her. And now, for the first time, the girl named Maija strikes Jessica as somehow frightening.

21

1946

THE RAYS OF the autumn evening sun stretch through the curtains and warm Maija's arms. Maija looks out the window, sees the gulls arcing and screaming over the dock, and smiles to herself. *You sillies never stop, do you?*

She adjusts the angle of the scissors in her fingers and rotates the magazine with her other hand for better access at the outlines of the paper doll.

"What the heck are you doing?" asks the tall girl who walks in. Beth's yellow tresses have been plaited into two braids with bows at the ends.

Maija glances over her shoulder but doesn't answer. Round-faced Elsa trails along in Beth's wake; her sole task seems to be following Beth. Ole and Axel: that's what Maija's father would probably have called them. The names come from a Danish movie she and her father went to see together before the Continuation War. Maija was five at the time and doesn't remember anything about the movie. But Dad wrote to her regularly when she was in Sweden, described in detail the things they'd done together before the war and that they'd do together when the war was finally over and he got his daughter back to Finland.

"You can also turn the scissors." Beth titters. "Then you won't have to turn the magazine."

Maija knows Beth is right; she usually is. Not always, but usually. Beth is thirteen and the oldest of the group. And unlike with the rest of them, her well-developed breasts and wide hips make Beth look more like a young woman than like a little girl. In contrast, at nine, Maija is the youngest child at the orphanage, now that Annikki, who was even younger, was fetched the week before by her new parents.

Even so, Maija has no intention of doing things a certain way just because someone else thinks it's better. Any way of killing time on the island is welcome. The island where the outdoors and the weather are growing harsher by the week; the leaves have fallen from the trees and turned into a wet, yellow mass that clumps on the soles of her shoes when she goes for walks in the woods. The wind blows so hard that sometimes it's difficult to hear what someone else is saying, even if the other person is shouting. And the sun that caressed their faces when they arrived at the island has gradually pulled on a gray disguise that has diluted its golden glory. That's the whole reason she climbed out of bed and moved over to the window to continue her crafts: because the sun is finally peering out from behind the clouds.

"Has she gone deaf?" Elsa says, sitting down on the windowsill. Maija watches the plump girl swing her legs in their wool socks. The left foot knocks against Maija's desk, and the steady tremor makes it harder to cut. Elsa isn't kicking the desk in spite of this but for this very reason.

"I don't know. Have you? *Mai-jaaa?*" Beth says, and Maija can feel the other girl's breath on her ear.

"Why don't you want to talk?" Elsa nags, and the kicks against the corner of the desk grow stronger.

Maija is overcome by the familiar gnawing sensation in the pit of her stomach. She wants to be left in peace, to sit there busying herself alone, out from under the others. Why won't the girls allow her that? Maija lowers the scissors to the desk and looks out the window.

"Why?" Beth says in a voice that sounds friendly but is anything but. The purpose of this examination is to boost the status of the tormentors, make them feel like masters of the moment.

Maija spent almost three years in Sweden, longer than any of the other children at the orphanage. She read and saved all her father's letters, answered them as best she could in writing, but just a couple months ago, when she was sent back home to Finland, she realized she hadn't spoken Finnish in years. It's still her mother tongue, but uttering the words feels hard. As if her mouth muscles resist whenever she considers trying or plans on saying something. Sometimes Maija tries speaking Finnish alone at night in her dark room: reads out loud from the Finnish magazines and adventure books the orphanage has brought over from the mainland. But she thinks she sounds stupid, like the deaf boy next door on Vikingagatan. The boy was nice but sounded like a seal. So it's better to keep quiet than give Beth and Beth's chubby henchman, whose feet keep knocking against the desk, a new reason to make fun of her.

"Suit yourself. You don't have to tell us," Beth says unexpectedly, then strokes Maija's tresses with her palm. "You have such beautiful hair, you know? Such a gorgeous color."

Elsa starts to giggle, but Beth silences her with a glare. "What are you laughing at, Hamhock?"

"No, I just thought—"

"I'm serious," Beth says. Now she takes Maija tenderly by the chin and slowly turns Maija's face toward her. "You have gorgeous hair. And a really cute face."

Maija wants to turn away, but Beth's firm fingers refuse to let go. Maija knows she could never squirm free of the other girl's grip in a way that wouldn't hurt.

"A pretty girl like you could have a lot of friends here," Beth says, and Maija can see from the corner of her eye that Elsa has lowered her gaze. Her feet have stopped kicking, as if Beth somehow wordlessly ordered her to stop. What the heck is going on? Maija has never heard Beth call Elsa Hamhock, even though everyone else does all the time.

"You and I," Beth says, finally letting go of Maija. "We could be friends too. Best friends. *Fattar du?*"

Maija nods even though she has no idea where the conversation is heading. She turns back to the paper swimsuit still attached to the page by a single corner. After snipping it, she could try all the outfits on the dolls from the centerfold.

"I heard you're not coming into town with the rest of us tomorrow."

Maija nods. No one is forced to go into Maarianhamina for the day, although all the children except Maija have always participated without grumbling. For the others, it's the highlight of the month.

"Then you probably don't need your allowance for anything," Beth says, and now Elsa looks up as if she finally grasps the point of Beth's grotesque little play. Maija feels a twinge in the pit of her stomach.

"I was thinking I could borrow some money from you again," Beth continues. Her mouth is twisted up in a smile, but her eyes are cold. "I'll pay you back soon, of course."

Yeah, right. Maija knows she would never see a penny of her money again. How could she? All the children are gradually going their own way. Would Beth supposedly look up Maija's new address and send the coins she borrowed by post? Fat chance.

Maija shakes her head. She realizes her hand is trembling and grabs the scissors to hide her fear.

"Because what do you need the money for if you're not going to do anything with it?" Beth laughs and then, fast as lightning, is serious. "Where's your piggy bank?"

A jubilant look spreads across Elsa's face. She gives Maija's desk one last healthy kick and jumps down from the windowsill. "Where is it, pretty girl?" Beth yawns and stretches her limbs, walks to the middle of Maija's room as Elsa continues: "Where—"

But Beth shakes her head, finger at her lips. "We're not robbers," she says from the doorway, gesturing for Elsa to follow. "Come on, Hamhock. And like I said, little Maija, I just want to *borrow* your allowance, not steal it. There's a big difference. So I expect you to bring your little pennies to my room voluntarily. In plenty of time before we leave tomorrow."

Elsa bursts out in laughter, and now she sounds like a pig, with her snorting chortles.

Maija feels an ire swelling within her.

"OK? I really want to buy a new lipstick, and if I don't get it . . . I'll be in a really bad mood. And when I get grumpy, I can be pretty mean. Right, Elsa?"

"Yeah, you turn into a total witch," Elsa concedes, giggling behind Beth's back.

Then the pair of them disappear into the corridor, leaving the door wide. Maija lowers her gaze to her book and sees she has snipped off one of the paper swimsuit's shoulder straps.

22

THAT NIGHT MAIJA has the same dream again. In it, the orphanage children are singing the song the matron always makes them
belt out in the evenings. Maija refuses to sing along, and the matron
grabs her by the hair. But Maija knows she's going to continue to
choose the matron's yelling and the blows from the map pointer
against her knuckles. The reprimands and threats. The hair tugs and
the knuckle thwacks. She's never going to sing that cursed hymn.

What Maija does instead is climb from her bed, glance out the
window, and eagerly rush outside. She races across the lawn toward
the lakeshore and feels the fresh morning dew on her bare feet.
Smoke is puffing from the sauna chimney; its cozy smell wafts everywhere. The sauna door creaks open as her father steps out onto the
sauna porch and wipes his hand on a dirty towel, as if doing so is any
use. His hands always look as grimy as the towel, and vice versa.

First swimming, then sauna.

Maija takes off her shirt and runs squealing into the water, even
though it will be a while before the sauna is hot. The bottom of the
lake is muddy, and her toes sink into the soft silt. Dragonflies drowse on
lily pads, and water bugs skate so lightly across the surface of the
water that they barely even wet their little feet. Maija refuses to wade
over toward the reeds; big fish splash there, and just the thought of
the touch of a slimy scale against her skin gives her the willies. Or
even worse: maybe a big fish would nibble at her just to make it clear
that the reedbed is its territory, not hers.

Watch out! There's a big pike! her father shouts, eliciting a shriek of terror from Maija. Maija quickly splashes back to shore, even though she's pretty sure Dad is just teasing.

Dad laughs, grabs a clean towel from the hook on the porch, squats, and wraps his arms around her.

The towel that looked like a little rag in her father's hands is big enough to envelop Maija's entire body.

Of course it is; after all, Maija is small, only five, and in her eyes her father, with his huge hands and broad shoulders, is a giant.

In that exact moment everything is fine, and Maija wishes the dream would never end.

Suddenly a low screech reaches Maija's ears, one that doesn't belong in her dream. She wakes with a start, opens her eyes, and looks around. She is no longer in the Kakskerta of her childhood but in a grim hellhole in the middle of the sea, where the wind rattles the metal roof. For a moment Maija is certain she just imagined the sound. That she has further embellished her repeated dream with a crane taking flight from the lake or . . .

"Keep your voice down."

"*No.*"

Maija sits up in bed, lowers the balls of her feet to the floor. Cranes don't talk, not even in the elaborate dreams her imagination sometimes conjures.

The voices are carrying through the door from the corridor, and they belong to a man and a woman. A boy and a girl.

Then Maija hears it again, the same screech, but this time she can tell it's a strange burst of laughter welling up from deep in someone's belly, as uncontrolled as an animal's shriek.

Maija stands and walks to the door. Cautiously presses her ear to it and hears the low, stifled laughter continue.

She cracks the door so slowly that it won't make the tiniest squeak, even by accident. The corridor is empty, but Maija catches movement in the watchman's cubicle across from the front door. Martin has been the night watchman for only a few weeks, and now a dark figure is pressed up against his body. On the desk there's a lamp that doesn't seem to really illuminate, at most adds yellowish tints to the surrounding darkness.

"Did you like your present?" Martin asks in a low voice.

"I love it. Come on."

"I can't."

"Let's go for a row," the woman's voice says. Blond hair swings from side to side as the woman tosses her head.

"I'm working, if you can't tell."

"That didn't seem to bother you last time." The woman turns her head. Now Maija can see her profile and immediately knows the woman isn't a woman but a girl. A long, thin arm wraps around Martin's neck, and they kiss long and hard. Elisabeth has undone her braid and brushed her hair: her curls dance across Martin's shoulders.

"What are you afraid of? Where are your little lambs going to run off to? We're on an island, Martin," Beth says as their lips pull apart.

"You're thirteen," Martin says. "I can get into trouble."

Beth doesn't immediately reply but pushes Martin so hard in the chest that he nearly loses his balance. Maija holds her breath. Reason tells her to shut the door and go back to bed, but her feet refuse to move. She has never seen anything like this before; she can almost smell the electricity in the air.

"You think I'm a kid?" Beth asks. "How old are you . . . twenty?"

"Nineteen."

"I'm sure at my age you were still playing with kids' toys, Martin," Beth says, lowering her voice so much that Maija has a hard time hearing her. Beth takes a step toward Martin, snatches his hand, and presses it firmly to her breasts. "Well?" she asks. "Do kids have these?"

Martin laughs like an insecure schoolboy.

"That's what I thought. Take me out rowing, Martin. Soon it's going to be too cold, and who knows? Maybe I won't even be here much longer. Then you'll be sorry."

The couple gives in to another passionate kiss. Maija's cheeks are burning. She shifts her weight, which makes the door move with an ominous squeak. Martin thrusts Beth off him and turns toward the sound. A cold wave washes over Maija, and she holds her breath. But luckily the hallway is dark, and Martin can't see her peering out her door.

For a moment it seems as if Martin is looking her straight in the eye. Maija stiffens in terror, but nothing happens.

"Did you hear that?" Martin says, but Beth just lowers her head to his chest.

"There's no one there," she says breathily.

Maija pulls the door shut as quietly as she can, creeps back to bed, and crawls under the covers. She expects to hear footfalls clomp against the corridor's stone floor, hear the door open, see the beam of Martin's periscope flashlight. *Who are you spying on, little girl?*

But nothing happens. The building has fallen into complete silence once again.

Before she falls asleep, Maija lies there for a long time, thinking about what a kiss like that must feel like.

23

THE NEXT MORNING, Maija wakes to a knock at the door. She quickly pulls up the covers. There are no locks on the doors in this building, either on the outside or on the inside. The children's home is no prison, and the adults must be able to access the rooms when the situation so demands. Neither Maija nor the other children have anything to complain about: it's a luxury in and of itself that they have their own rooms. At many orphanages (that's what Armas from the next room has called this place from the start) the children live in much closer quarters than they do here, and sleep in bunk beds in large dormitories. The matron has often said that the birds of spring are, despite their misfortunes, in a very privileged position. They have a roof over their heads and food to eat, and they don't even have to work for it. All they have to do is behave, keep their rooms tidy, and make their beds in the morning. And of course read the Bible and sing that dratted hymn.

Maija is just about to get out of bed when the door opens. The first things she sees are dark green wool socks, bare legs and knees, and a thigh-length white skirt. Then a short-sleeved floral blouse with a bow at the breast. Beth is incredibly beautiful, but the thing that makes the biggest impression on Maija is the dark red lipstick that makes Beth's mouth dazzle in the middle of her pale face.

"What do you think?" Beth says, shutting the door behind her. She puts her hands on her hips and twirls around like a model. The outfit is beautiful, but it has clearly adorned other beautiful girls before Beth. The white skirt has been mended in several places—not that anyone would pay any attention to that. The lipstick was not bought with Maija's money, which means Beth must have gotten it somewhere else, since the trip to Maarianhamina is happening today.

Maija smiles uncertainly and nods. She rubs her eyes and looks at the alarm clock on the nightstand. The time is five to seven. The clock is the only thing Maija has carried with her all these years, ever since she first left Finland. It was made in France and is apparently from a time before she was born. Aside from her father's letters, it's Maija's most prized possession, and recently, as Beth's behavior has grown increasingly threatening, Maija has begun to fear it will be stolen. It could probably be exchanged in town for a brand-new dress or shoes, and such a thought is no doubt tempting to a girl like Beth. The sort that thinks only about herself.

"Did you sleep well?" Beth walks over to Maija's bed and sits at the foot of it. The skirt looks amazingly good on tall Beth; the skin on her bare legs gleams like the hood of a just-waxed car. Her hair has been gathered on top of her head in a cloud of curls reminiscent of a poodle's coat. Sitting there at the foot of the bed, Beth looks surprisingly like Betty Grable, whom Maija just saw wearing high heels and the same sort of skirt and blouse in a big color photo. There are no pictures like that in Maija's magazines, but there are in the magazines the children found in a drawer in Martin's desk.

In any case, this morning Beth is so beautiful, Maija can't help but think she must have woken up at the crack of dawn so she'd have time to fix her hair before breakfast.

"Well?" Beth says, patting Maija's ankle. "Did you?"

Maija nods a second time and mumbles something in the affirmative.

Beth's eyes go wide, and a sly smile spreads across her face. "Wow. She can talk," she says, and Maija nods again. "Or at least almost."

For a moment, Maija considers saying something, uttering something in Finnish for the first time in ages. Real words, something other than "uh-huh," "yes," and "yeah." Something in Beth's ravishing appearance has emboldened Maija; with her long arms and legs, the older girl looks just like an adult. But as Maija opens her mouth, the smile that lingered on Beth's face for a moment vanishes, and the familiar frightening look appears in its place: the look that reminds Maija of a vicious, pitiless bird of prey.

"Because I have this feeling something kept you up last night," Beth continues, and Maija's heart skips a beat. Beth knows. Martin saw Maija at her door after all.

"Maybe you had to pee." Beth finds Maija's bare ankle under the blanket and gingerly takes hold of it. "Or maybe you wanted to get a peek at the things we grown-ups do in the middle of the night."

Maija gulps so loudly that Beth can't help but hear it. The word "grown-ups" strikes Maija as silly. Elisabeth might be tall, beautiful, and closer to womanhood than any of the other girls at the children's home, but she is most definitely not a grown-up, even if she looks like one. Nor will she be for many years.

"Either way, I came to make sure you're OK. And maybe it's a good thing I did, since you've started talking. Who knows what sort of stories you'll start making up if you really start running your mouth?"

Now Maija feels nails dig into her ankles. "Do you understand what I'm telling you, little Maija?"

The grip grows firmer, and Maija feels a sharp pain. Beth's nails are sinking into her flesh; it hurts terribly.

"Yes," Maija says quickly, and nods like a chicken running for its life. Tears well up in her eyes, and Maija wipes the corner of her eye just in case, so Beth won't notice. *Don't cry, Panda Bear.*

Suddenly Beth is smiling again, and the hold on Maija's ankle relents. Then she leans back and lets her head slowly drop back to the wall. Maija sees nearly imperceptible bruises at Beth's throat. She sees them because Beth wants her to see. Beth wants to show that she isn't a child anymore. Then Beth reaches into the waistband of her skirt and pulls out a little metal box containing a few cigarettes and a slim box of matches. She raises a finger to her lips, strikes one of the matches, and lights a cigarette.

Maija feels panic take over her entire body. Smoking is absolutely forbidden to the children, and along with drinking and lewd behavior is one of the things that result in a thrashing or worse. And now Beth is puffing in Maija's room and blowing the smoke toward the ceiling.

Beth lets the smoke drain slowly from her nostrils and shamelessly taps the ash to the floor. After a few theatrical drags, she stubs the cigarette out in the mortar between the bricks of the wall and stands. The half-smoked cigarette drops to the floor at her feet.

"Ooh. What's that?" Beth says as her hand is reaching for the door.

Maija's heart starts pounding even harder in her chest. She knows exactly what Beth is talking about, even though she doesn't immediately turn her gaze in the direction Beth is indicating. The metal box is usually hidden under the bed, but Maija forgot it on the edge of her desk after she read her letters by candlelight the evening before. The words are ready in her throat, but Maija can't get her mouth open. Beth must never be allowed to see the letters. Maija has a hard enough time fitting in as it is; she is already a freak no one sits next to in the dining room. But if Beth were to take a peek inside the box and find the letters her father has sent her over the years, as well as the diary Maija has been writing in particularly frequently over recent weeks, she would be labeled a complete idiot. Clinging to the past is not respected at the children's home. They're orphans, and such creatures do not make it through the world if they're crybabies. Crying is for childhood, the days before Sweden. In that sense, Beth is probably right. She's not a child anymore. None of them are.

Beth looks at the metal box, then at Maija. She opens the door.

"See? We all have secrets," Beth says with a wink, and disappears into the hallway.

Relief washes over Maija's entire body. She rushes over to open the window and flings out the smelly cigarette butt as far as possible.

24

THE DAY IS autumnal and cool, but the wind is not too keen and the sun is shining from the nearly clear sky. Maija pulls on her blue coat, the only one she has. It's not particularly warm, but when the Sundbergs sent her off on her return journey from Uppsala, they had no idea they ought to pack for cooler autumn weather and perhaps winter as well. Maija was to have been in Kakskerta with her father ages ago.

I'll come get you, Panda Bear.

Maija walks through the dense spruce woods, feels the soft soil underfoot, and hears the lichen, hard after a few days without rain, crunch under the soles of her shoes. She climbs up to the top of the rock rising in the woods: spindly pines cling to the mossy slope, their bark partly peeled off. Patterns bored by beetle larvae adorn the bald patches. Once she reaches the crown of the rock, Maija stops and turns westward to the shore and the archipelago opening up beyond. As she gazes, she sometimes imagines a similar horizon from her early years, the one that opened up a stone's throw from her childhood home. Maija can't be sure whether the memories formed later, whether they took shape from the detailed descriptions in her father's letters. In those letters, her father often mentioned Kakskerta Lake, where their house stood. Her father told her their home was special in that it was only a kilometer and a half from their lakeshore to the sea. That was the source of her father's saying: *The Ruusunen house stands where fresh water and salt water meet.* According to Dad, their whole life was crystallized in that sentence. Things weren't always easy, but the hard times would end someday.

Then we'll be together again, Panda Bear.

Dad had been wrong about that. Instead of everything turning out for the best in the end, things had only grown more complicated. Just thinking about it makes Maija's heart heavy with grief and rage: her father made it through the war alive and unharmed only to drown in a storm at a time of year when the sea is expected to treat those traveling on it with a tranquil hospitality.

Maija continues her walk through the woods until she arrives at a narrow dirt road. She has never come this far south before and isn't sure how much time has passed. She's supposed to be in her room before devotional and supper, which is served in the dining room at six thirty.

Maija advances along the edge of the road. The forest around her thins, and before long she can make out the shoreline and the necklace of islands beyond. The view is very different from the one that opens from the orphanage's windows. For a moment Maija thinks she'd rather live here, where she can see something aside from the wildly crashing sea outside her window. Something about the yellow trees on the island opposite calms her. If the ship that carried her father here from Turku had sunk in a place like this, maybe he would have had the strength to swim to the nearest island; maybe he would have survived.

Maija sees a red wall between trees; against the dark sky a chimney stands out, with smoke rising from it. When she ventures closer, she sees a villa in all its beauty, a lawn spreading out before it; berry bushes, apple trees, a huge barn, and wooden sheds on the shore. This place is a lot more comfortable than the one where the birds of spring have been living for the last few weeks.

Suddenly the door opens and someone appears on the steps.

Maija is startled, takes a step backward, and tumbles onto her back among the dry leaves. She quickly picks herself up and staggers away. As she runs, she hears a man shouting after her. She speeds up and doesn't stop until she makes it to the orphanage. The whole time, the words of the man who appeared on the porch have been hammering through Maija's head.

Don't be afraid, little girl.

25

As she crosses the yard, Maija sees someone is moving around her room. But the last rays of the evening sun are bouncing off the window, making it impossible for Maija to tell whether it's one of the children in her room or perhaps Matron Boman.

She sprints off, climbs the foundation-high stairs, and yanks open the heavy wooden door. Her left ankle aches; she twisted it running through the woods. She steps into the corridor and hears a door shut but doesn't see anyone. The legs of a chair scrape the floor behind the closed door to Armas' room.

Maija rushes to the end of the hall and glances in the watchman's cubicle; there's no one in there during the day. The watchman arrives every night at nine o'clock, when the children finish getting ready for bed and it's lights-out throughout the building.

Maija opens the door, but her room is empty. She can't help but notice the pungent reek of just-smoked tobacco and the still-smoldering cigarette in the middle of the floor. She stubs it out with the tip of her shoe, tosses the butt in the trash, and opens the window to let in fresh air.

Her hands are shaking from agitation. *What the heck does that dratted Beth want from me?* Maija gave her word she wouldn't tell anyone about Beth and the night watchman's after-hours shenanigans. Is Beth afraid she won't find a new home if people find out what she gets up to at night with that man? Or is the man the one who's afraid? Maija is sure the matron won't look on it kindly if he's caught fooling around with one of the children.

And then Maija remembers the letters.

Her heart skips a beat, and she lunges to the bed, drops to her belly, and reaches her hand way over to the wall. Her fingertips graze the box, and she lets out a sigh of relief. Then she wraps her fingers around the brass handle and pulls the box out from under the bed. She pops open the metal hasp and opens the lid. Dad's letters appear to be there, the same with the diary, thank God. But Maija knows Beth's tricks; there's no doubt she was there looking for the box. Maybe she ran out of time. Maija got lucky. But it's plain as day Beth won't give up until she finds what she's looking for. Something has to be done; she has to hide the box somewhere easy to retrieve it from when Beth finally clears out. Because for some reason, she's sure Beth is going to find a home before she does.

26

ONCE SILENCE HAS fallen over the orphanage, Maija opens her window and cranes her neck out. Although the building is only one story, it looks like a long drop to the ground. Maija lifts the box to the windowsill and opens it. She casts a final glance at the sheaf of dozens of handwritten letters. So much emotion fits on the yellowed sheets. Her father sent the first ones from Kakskerta, but later he wrote from the army and the front. Some include the place next to her father's signature; others read *Somewhere in the world*. The letters are saturated with love, sweat, and tears. Sometimes her father's hand is steady, but Maija thinks she can also spot the moments when her father was scared; her father never mentioned his fear to Maija, not a single time. His fear that they might never see each other again. But after reading the letters over and over, Maija understands her father wanted to protect her from the horrific truth. She presses her fingers to her lips and lowers a kiss to the topmost letter in the stack.

See you soon, Panda Bear.

Bye now, Dad.

As long as the letters exist, her father is with her.

Maija glances out the window again to make sure there's no one outside. The coast is clear.

She locks the box and wraps the thick twine she found in the kitchen around it. The box is heavy, and Maija is afraid the twine will snap, but she manages to lower her treasure undamaged from the window to the lawn surrounding the building. Then she backs out of the window and lowers her toes to the lip of the building's granite foundation. Her knees scrape against the uneven plaster, and Maija grimaces in pain as she lets go of the windowsill. Her boots hit the ground with a loud thud, and a nasty pain shoots through her sore ankle. She squats there, momentarily fearful that the lights will come on in the windows and the door will open, that Martin will rush up, shouting and pulling her hair. But nothing happens. Maija slips the box under her arm, turns on the flashlight she filched from the night watchman's drawer, and starts following the wall toward the forest beyond.

At the corner of the building, there's a tool rack; picks, a pitchfork, and a rusty shovel hang from it. She grabs the shovel and makes her way between two large rocks and into the forest. The wet, low-hanging spruce boughs sweep across her face as she steps deeper into the woods, toward the place where she knows the ground is soft. Her gaze comes to rest on a boulder with a surprisingly smooth surface; it reminds her of half an egg. Maija takes the shovel and sinks the tip into the ground. She is no stranger to digging holes; planting the yard at Uppsala was by and large her responsibility.

Besides, the box doesn't require a very big hole, and before long Maija is carefully lowering it into the ground.

I'll be back, Maija whispers so softly in Swedish that even the dark forest surrounding her cannot hear. She feels incredibly sad as she acknowledges that it will be a while before she can read the letters again.

"Hello? Maija?"

Maija's breath catches. A flashlight beam from the direction of the orphanage licks the roots of the trees. She quickly turns off her own flashlight and hurriedly scoops soil on top of the box. Her eyes haven't adjusted to the darkness and they see nothing but black.

"I can hear you!" the voice continues. It belongs to Martin, who must have noticed that Maija snuck out her window. Maija pats the ground and quickly kicks wet leaves over it. She knows she's going to be caught; it's inevitable, but it must not happen here. Martin cannot come upon her standing at her cache with a shovel in her fist. She grabs the shovel and starts running toward the shore. The darkness shows no mercy; Maija stumbles and the shovel handle hits her in the diaphragm, knocking the wind out of her. She holds back the tears and grits her teeth, picks herself up, and soon falls again. The flashlight drops from her grip, and her searching fingers do not find it.

"Get over here, goddamn it!"

Maija finally reaches the edge of the sandy yard. She steps out from the trees, and the beam of Martin's flashlight blinds her.

"Goddamn it, Maija!"

Martin stalks over to Maija; his frenzied footsteps crunch in the sand. Martin's fingers squeeze Maija's hand, and he starts dragging her toward the orphanage. As she stumbles along behind him, the shovel strikes her leg bone, and Maija squeals in pain.

"What the hell are you doing out here in the middle of the night? With a shovel?" Martin asks in agitation, at nearly a shout. Maija sees lights come on in the windows, first one, then another. The commotion has roused the other children.

"Answer me!" Martin shouts, then stops, yanks the shovel from her hands. He looks at the shovel, the fresh soil at its tip, and at Maija's dirty fingers. He's stupid, but not so stupid that he can't put two and two together. He turns to look at the woods.

"What were you doing out there?" Martin asks. "Were you digging something?"

Maija doesn't answer. Nor would she even if she could.

"Talk, you idiot!" Martin takes a step closer to Maija. Maija shuts her eyes. Maybe he's going to hit her, or at least slap her, just like the matron did the time Maija refused to sing. At Uppsala she sometimes wished her ears would be boxed properly; she wanted to feel like her new parents were interested enough to bother to discipline her. But all she got were bored looks, bulging eyes, and orders to get to work. *It's clear you're not a Sundberg—that's for sure.*

"*Jag vet om dig och Elisabeth,*" Maija says in Swedish, holding back the tears. *I know about you and Elisabeth.* She wants Martin to be angry, to hit her. He may as well kill her; she has no reason to live.

A few surprisingly slow seconds pass.

But Martin does not hit her. He glances over at the orphanage and takes a deep breath. His eyes are full of rage. "If you don't want any trouble, you'll keep your mouth shut," he says quietly in Swedish.

Maija shakes her head furiously. Her hands are trembling.

Martin grabs the back of Maija's nightshirt, hurls the shovel to the ground, and starts dragging Maija toward the building. Her nightshirt rips at the collar, and the fabric presses against her throat.

When they reach the door, Maija looks up at the window next to the kitchen. Beth has pressed her laughing face to the windowpane and is twirling her finger around her temple. Her mouth forms a word Maija has heard many times before in this place.

Crazy.

27

MAIJA WATCHES FROM the window as Eila walks toward the dock with the stout couple. Maija thinks the man and woman must have eaten someone else's food in addition to their own during the war to maintain their bulk.

Rumor has it that Eila's new home will be in Tammirinne, on the banks of the Vantaa River, in a place that's in the countryside but right next to the capital.

Maija wants to throw up. She feels her forehead. It's sweaty. Her head aches, and she's cold all the time, despite the wool socks and the two layers of clothing. Today is the fourth day in a row that Maija isn't participating in lessons and instead lies in bed, staring at the ceiling.

There's a knock at the door. A moment later, the door opens. Martin is standing there at the threshold. He's not wearing his faded military-style uniform but wide-legged trousers and a wrinkled shirt with an oil stain at the belly.

"Can I come in for a second?" Martin says calmly, and then enters without waiting for an answer. He steps over to Maija's desk and pulls out the chair. Maija feels her ears get hot; there's a lump in her throat. She's sure Martin has come to give her a thrashing. But in the daylight, he looks somehow shy and harmless. And on top of that, younger than his age. His curly blond hair falls over his eyes, and his cheeks are flushed, as if he ran all the way here.

"I, um," Martin says hesitantly, "I wanted to say I'm sorry for being so mean to you that one night. But you know you guys aren't allowed to sneak out your windows at night."

Maija nods uncertainly. She huddles against the wall and pulls the covers more tightly around herself.

"I'm responsible for you guys at night. That's why I lose my patience so quickly if someone breaks the rules. You get that, don't you, Maija?"

Maija nods again.

"Good," Martin says, and bites his bottom lip.

Maija waits for Martin to say something about Beth and what happened in the watchman's office, but instead he slaps his thighs and stands, as if there is nothing further to discuss.

"And hey," he says, reaching into his trousers pocket, "you got a letter."

Maija's heart skips a beat. A letter?

"Assuming, that is," Martin says with a playful frown, "that Your Highness is Princess Maija Ruusunen."

Maija's palms have begun to sweat. Martin hands her a white envelope with her name typed on it.

"OK, have a good day," Martin says. He opens the door and disappears into the corridor.

A moment passes before Maija ventures to look away from the door. She hears Martin's receding footsteps echo down the hall. Then the heavy front door closes. Maija pops out of bed and sees Martin walking toward the dock, where the boat that comes to the island three times a day bobs in the water.

Her heart is pounding, and she feels like her fever is getting worse.

Princess Maija Ruusunen.

There's only one person who calls her that. There's only one person who has sent her letters. But it's not possible. There's no way.

Maija grabs the scissors from her desk and slices open the envelope. The words typed on a sheet of bone white paper look blurry, and Maija has to focus her eyes to make them out.

The tremor in her hands makes the paper rustle. Maija reads the letter, looks down at the signature, which is soon blurred by her falling tears.

28

2020

IN THE VILLA'S front door there's a round window that evokes the porthole of a ship. On either side of the door, wide troughs have been bolted to the wall; Astrid no doubt plants them with flowers as soon as spring arrives. A little farther, closer to the toolshed at the corner of the villa, stands a barrel into which rainwater drains from the gutter.

Jessica steps inside and pauses in the entry hall, looks into the library through the open door. There's no fire in the hearth; the warm glow has been replaced by a cold gloom. Jessica stares at the empty fireplace; she can taste the smoky whisky on her tongue and hear Åke's words.

Astrid thinks it's just a ghost story.

How has this happened again? Death follows Jessica even when she's on vacation.

She enters the dining room and takes a seat at the window. Astrid has already laid the little buffet with the delicious foods she puts out every morning: cold cuts, fruit, cheeses, a half dozen types of fish, and a large pot of four-grain porridge topped with butter. But Jessica isn't hungry. She remembers her nocturnal walk to the north end of the island. The abandoned orphanage. The girl standing on the dock, her barley-colored hair escaping her white beret.

"It's Elisabeth," a hoarse voice says, and Jessica starts.

An old man has appeared at the doorway. He leans against the doorframe despite the wooden cane in his left hand. His furrowed face is narrow, his eyes peer from deep in their sockets, and his head is almost completely bald. He reminds Jessica of Edvard Munch's famous painting; the only thing missing is a scream coming from the open mouth.

"Excuse me?" Jessica says, although she knows what he's referring to.

The old man proceeds into the dining room, his cane hand extended before him as if the cane is in a hurry to move the man, not vice versa. His back is so hunched, it seems like he's reaching down to touch his toes.

"The circus has returned to Smörregård," he says. "And Elisabeth is at the heart of it. Yet again."

Jessica doesn't know what to say, so she just nods. She briefly considers whether she ought to help the old fellow sit; he seems to have quite a bit of trouble moving. And then she thinks of Erne, how he clung to his independence until the last. Jessica decides not to offer her assistance; the old man would ask for it if he needed it.

"Armas Pohjanpalo," he says, pulling out a chair at the next table and seating himself.

"Jessica Niemi. Nice to meet you."

"Hello, Jessica," Armas says mildly, then shakes his head and turns wistfully to the window. "I'm afraid a black cloud hangs over our first meeting."

"I believe you're right."

"Åke told me the sad news," Armas says. "But he didn't tell me what happened."

Jessica folds her arms across her chest and leans back, allows the old man to look past her and out the window. Considering the circumstances, Armas is behaving with a curious tranquility, despite the sadness coloring his face.

"Do you know what happened to her?"

"No," Jessica says, not completely sure why she feels the need to protect an adult from the truth. "Apparently she drowned."

Armas lowers his gaze to the table, gulps twice, then nods. "Isn't that something?"

Jessica eyes the old man's clothes: neat leather shoes, corduroy trousers, and a dark blue sweater with a white shirt collar underneath. He's not overdressed, but he is remarkably nicely dressed for a guesthouse breakfast. Maybe it's a generational thing. Jessica herself has been wearing loose, comfortable loungewear during her stay at Smörregård, because she simply doesn't have the energy to dedicate much attention to her appearance on an island where the locals dress like Norwegian whalers.

"My condolences," Jessica says.

"Thank you," Armas replies. He rises and heads toward the buffet. For a moment, Jessica has the impression that he crosses those few meters with less effort than he displayed just a moment ago. But once he reaches the food, he hunches over again.

The cuckoo clock calls out, indicating the half hour, but Armas pays it no mind. It's possible he's tired, but even so, there's something odd about his behavior. If Jessica's childhood friend were lying dead on the north shore, she would rush to the scene, even if she had to crawl. But Armas is shoveling cured whitefish onto his plate as if nothing has happened.

"When did you last see Elisabeth?" Jessica asks.

Armas stirs slightly. "What?" he says in a raspy voice. His brow furrows, and his breath rattles as he inhales. Then he returns to his table, plate in hand, and sits.

Jessica is surprised by her inquisitiveness; it's not her place to be asking such questions. As a matter of fact, she absolutely ought to keep her nose out of the whole business, quickly eat her breakfast, and go back to her room to wait for the police to knock at her door.

But for whatever reason, she persists: "I was just thinking . . . Do you remember whether she went to her room after dinner?"

Armas rubs his knuckles and appears to consider his response. Then he shakes his head.

"I was the first one to go upstairs. Almost immediately after dessert, around ten o'clock." Armas doesn't appear the least bit curious about why Jessica is asking him such questions. "The girls stayed downstairs to talk."

Jessica nods. So in theory it's possible Elisabeth never returned to her room, or at least didn't go to bed, before she died. But this would probably be easy to deduce based on what she was wearing when she was discovered. If Jessica could just get her hands on the police report . . .

No. No. No. Stop!

She shuts her eyes. She is not a police officer right now. It is not her business to find out whether the old woman was wearing her dinner dress or her nightshirt when she drowned.

"Astrid said you were a homicide detective," Armas suddenly remarks, as if he's been reading Jessica's mind.

Jessica gives him a joyless smile and feels a pang inside. Elisabeth was right: the proprietress of the guesthouse plainly cannot keep her mouth shut. Or did her promise of confidentiality apply only to Jessica's assumed writing project?

"In Helsinki, yes," Jessica says. "But not here."

Armas purses his lips and nods.

Jessica feels as if someone is pressing a finger into her belly; the smell of raw fish wafting from the buffet penetrates her nostrils. She stands, steps over to the fruit basket, and grabs an apple. Maybe eating something fresh will help the nausea dissipate.

"It's happening again."

Jessica starts and turns toward Armas. The fruit tongs fall to the floor with a clang. "What's happening again?"

Armas doesn't reply, just gazes at the sea. Apparently Armas Poh-janpalo is, in spite of all signs, upset; the words don't seem to mean anything.

"As I said, my condolences on your friend's passing," Jessica says. But as she walks by the old man's chair, she suddenly feels firm fingers around her wrist. She looks down to see an unyielding look in the old man's eyes; Armas has a surprisingly determined air about him.

"Listen," he says, and Jessica spies a tear in the corner of his eye. The fingers of the old man's free hand are trembling. "I saw it."

"Saw what?"

Armas gulps, and his voice fades to a whisper. "My room has a view of the entire yard, all the way down through the apple trees to the boathouses."

Jessica has the urge to wrench herself free of the old man's clutch; it would no doubt be easy, but the fingers wrapped around her wrist seem more like a desperate plea for help than an oppressive threat.

"What did you see?"

Now Armas licks away the tear that has rolled down to his mouth. His eyes are red as he reveals his ceramic dentures, and a grimace of horror accompanies his response. "Maija. Maija was standing in the middle of the yard last night. And I'm sure she killed Beth."

29

JESSICA RUSHES INTO her room, shuts the door behind her, and lunges into the bathroom. She lifts the lid of the toilet and drops to her knees in front of it. The pressure in her belly has intensified; her legs feel weak. But all that rises from her esophagus is air. Jessica coughs a couple times, considers sticking her fingers down her throat to stimulate retching.

Maija was standing in the middle of the yard last night. And I'm sure she killed Beth.

Jessica gives up. She lifts her head from the toilet, lets the saliva from the back of her throat collect, and spits it out. She collapses against the wall, pulls her knees up to her chest. Has the old man gone insane too? Or did he actually see Maija outside last night? And if he did, was what Jessica saw yesterday really a hallucination? Maybe there really was someone at the end of the dock. Someone who had something to do with Elisabeth's drowning.

Just then, there's a knock at the door. Jessica picks herself up off the floor.

She opens the door and finds herself looking at a man, about fifty, who is wearing a heavy dark blue sailing jacket. He has fleshy cheeks and a mouth that's somehow too small for them, as well as strikingly blue eyes. His face sprouts a few days' stubble.

"Good morning. I'm with the police," he says in Swedish. He has taken off his beanie, and his thick hair is pasted to his damp forehead.

"Good morning," Jessica says.

"I understand you speak Swedish," the police officer says, and Jessica nods. "My name is Johan Karlsson; I'm a detective," he continues, then falls silent as if he's forgotten something important. "Yes, so, apparently you already know what happened?"

Jessica nods again. She's getting hot; she hasn't taken off her coat yet. "Can we talk outside?"

Karlsson doesn't immediately reply, just eyes the room behind Jessica as if she is hiding something in there. Then he nods and leads the way across the small vestibule to the front door of the converted barn.

"A sorry business," Karlsson says, pulling a pen and a notepad from his breast pocket.

Jessica nods as they step into the mercy of the cutting wind. She folds her arms across her chest and looks at the flagpole, the villa, the apple branches dancing in the wind.

Karlsson asks Jessica for her name, address, and phone number. Jessica gives the address of her studio apartment on Töölönkatu.

"Purpose of your visit here?"

It's an idiotic question, and Jessica is about to give some smart answer about the annual seal conference at Smörregård.

"Vacation," she eventually says expressionlessly, out of respect for the gravity of the situation and the dead woman whose body has been loaded onto the police boat.

"I understand you're a police officer."

Once again, Jessica silently curses Astrid and her big mouth. "Word travels pretty fast around here."

"The boys from Search and Rescue told me," Karlsson quickly says, taking a pack of cigarettes from his breast pocket. But he doesn't pull a cigarette from the pack; instead, he appears to be counting them.

Jessica feels like a fool. Yes, for some reason she'd been in a hurry to divulge that she was a police officer, even though yesterday morning she did everything in her power to conceal this fact. Maybe she revealed her occupation out of a sheer sense of professional obligation, the way doctors do on flights if fellow passengers fall ill. Not that there was any benefit to speak of from her confession.

"Did you happen to see or hear anything out of the ordinary last night?" Karlsson says, putting the cigarettes in his back pocket.

Jessica shakes her head. She isn't sure what time she returned from her walk to the northern side of the island. Her memories of the previous evening are hazy; the last thing she remembers is seeing the girl in the blue coat on the dock. But she has no intention of telling Karlsson about that.

"Did you have any interactions with Mrs. Salmi yesterday?"

"We saw each other at dinner, but we didn't speak at that point . . ."

Karlsson looks up from his notebook. "You didn't speak at that point?"

Jessica stares at Karlsson. Although she has conducted dozens of difficult investigations over the course of her life, evidently the experience they imparted didn't equip her to make the leap to the other side of the table. But what difference does it make? This isn't an interrogation; it's simply a police officer asking a potential eyewitness some questions, and Jessica has nothing to hide. Why does the situation suddenly feel so oppressive?

"Yes, well . . . she came by here yesterday morning right after she arrived. She said she'd been used to staying in the room I'm staying in now," Jessica says. "As a matter of fact, we were standing right here. And then she went on her way."

Karlsson nods and jots something down. Jessica could report the old woman's strange behavior, her antipathy for Astrid and her son, and what Elisabeth told Jessica: *If you've brought any secrets to this island, I suggest you keep them to yourself.* But something inside Jessica tells her the matter is irrelevant—either that, or it's too relevant and will draw her into the case. Whichever it is, that conversation will remain between Elisabeth and Jessica, perhaps forever.

"What time did you go to bed?" Karlsson says.

Jessica narrows her eyes at the question. "Do you suspect a crime?"

Karlsson grunts drily. "Yes, you're a police officer. There's no doubt about that." He slides the pen into his pocket as if he's decided to commit the rest of the conversation to memory. "But I'd appreciate it if you'd answer the questions instead of asking them."

Jessica notices the warmth has vanished from Karlsson's eyes. "Of course," she says, and wonders if she ought to be completely forthright after all: tell Karlsson she went for a long walk to the other side of the island after dinner and returned to her room who knows when, in the middle of the dark night. Would the police find out about it anyway? Is there a game camera in the area? Maybe the Swedish couple staying in the next room saw or heard her return and checked the time. Or maybe someone else made the observation from the windows of the villa. Does it matter? There's no rule against walking around the island all night if she feels like it. But Jessica feels a pang in her gut when she realizes she truly does not remember anything about returning to her room. It could have been at any time at all, and in theory she could have wandered elsewhere, maybe bumped into someone. Maybe even Elisabeth.

"So?" Karlsson says, interrupting Jessica's thoughts.

Jessica lazily stretches her neck and closes her eyes. "I'm just trying to remember," she mumbles. The nausea intensifies again. "I went for a walk after dinner, but I have no idea what time I got back to my room. I'm sorry."

Karlsson looks around, as if to make sure they're on an island, and a pretty small one at that. "How long did you walk? Fifteen minutes? An hour?"

Jessica shrugs.

"Where did you go?"

Jessica knows she shouldn't allow herself to be provoked by the questions, but the way the detective is peppering her with them, it's as if he is trying to drive her into a corner and catch her in a lie. "Just around. Does it matter?"

"You know perfectly well it does, Detective," Karlsson says.

Jessica's head is hammering; she said she was a police officer but didn't mention anything about her job at the Helsinki Police VCU. That means Karlsson has checked her information somewhere. Jessica can't help but think he is also aware of the previous week's events. Maybe he's even seen that damn video and considers her suspicious because of it.

"I thought the old woman drowned," Jessica says, hoping Karlsson will tell her more.

"We'll see. Thank you. I'm going to have a word with the other guests too. Please let us know if you intend to leave Ahvenanmaa." Karlsson lowers his head in a way that presumably functions as a bow of sorts. He and Jessica step back into the building, Jessica opens her door, and then she hears the detective knock on the Swedish couple's door.

30

JESSICA THROWS HERSELF down on her bed and closes her eyes. She hears faint speech through the wall as Karlsson asks the Swedish couple all the same questions he just asked Jessica.

It suddenly occurs to her that it's downright strange that this is the first time she has heard any sounds from the other room. She has spent five days in this room, and she hasn't registered any noise at all. No thumps or speech, let alone sounds of lovemaking. Maybe she's been so lost in her own world, has slept under such heavy sedation, that she simply hasn't paid any attention to what's been taking place on the other side of the wall. Either that, or the Swedes in the next room are giving each other a world-class silent treatment. Judging by the signs, this isn't some honeymoon for them.

Jessica's eyes feel heavy, and she begins drifting toward sleep; she sees a distant reflection of herself on the surface film of dark green water. Smells the damp of Venice's narrow lanes, the stench of filthy water and sewers, the funk of fried fish wafting from kitchen windows. Feels powerful fingers gripping her buttocks. The man penetrating her, going deeper and deeper. Harder, faster, the fingers around her neck. The now-violent thrusts. The searing pain in her back. Jessica opens the balcony door and hears him rise from the bed and begin practicing his violin in the living room. Jessica's back aches; the pressure she feels in her crotch swells with every step she takes. Her fingers probe her swollen lip, which is still oozing blood. *How stupid can you be?* She should have known better than to disturb him when he was practicing.

There's a knock at the door.

Jessica wakes with a start.

Another knock. A third.

What the fuck does that B-grade Poirot want?

Jessica jumps up from the bed and marches to the door. But it's not the local detective standing there; it's Astrid Nordin, looking pale and grave.

"I'm sorry to bother you."

Jessica feels like slamming the door in the other woman's face, but after that morning's events, it is, she supposes, important to demonstrate some solidarity with the proprietress of the guest-house. She forces her mouth into a smile and reluctantly replies, "You're not bothering me."

"May I . . . come in?" Astrid pushes past Jessica before she can respond. "This is so awful, Jessica. So awful, terribly awful."

"It is," Jessica says, as Astrid plops herself down on the unmade bed and crosses her ankles beneath it.

"Apparently Elisabeth didn't drown this morning but sometime last night. She was wearing that black dress . . . and had a contusion on her forehead."

Jessica pulls her hair into a ponytail and seats herself on the wooden windowsill. She glances out over her shoulder. Åke is standing at the shore, hands on his hips, watching the search-and-rescue vessel pass by a couple hundred meters offshore and continue toward the channel marked between two islands.

"That's horrible," Jessica says, not even trying to pretend to be shocked.

"Do you understand how horrible?" Astrid continues. "If Elisabeth didn't injure herself in a fall, that means someone must have hurt her. And I suppose that someone has to be one of our guests."

"Please, Astrid," Jessica says. "Let's not get ahead of ourselves. In spite of everything, what happened to Elisabeth might have been an accident."

Astrid looks at Jessica in bewilderment. "So Åke didn't tell you?"

"Tell me what?" Jessica can hear the annoyance in her own voice. "Do you think this has something to do with that little girl who lived at the orphanage back in the 1940s? I thought you said it was a ghost story—"

"Listen, Jessica. It's not the first time something like this has happened."

"Something like what?"

"People have died on this island before. In the exact same way, near the orphanage dock." Astrid expels air between her lips like a pressure cooker. "It was a long time ago. But Elisabeth's death follows the same pattern."

"OK," Jessica says. "But you don't really think the girl in the blue coat—"

"Let's get one thing straight, Jessica," Astrid says firmly. "The story about the little girl who drowned and comes back to the dock over and over without ever aging a day is nonsense; there's no doubt about that. But the two deaths that took place in the early 1980s are as real as real can be. I saw them with my own eyes. Do you understand, Jessica? I remember them as if they happened yesterday. And what happened to Elisabeth echoes them in every regard."

Jessica climbs down from the windowsill and stands on the balls of her feet a few times to get some blood flow in her calves. Her knees pop from the movement. She looks at Astrid's panicked face and can't help but think her expression is exactly like the one on Armas' face a little while ago in the dining room. Should Jessica add fuel to the fire and tell Astrid what Armas claimed to have seen? It would be sure to send her over the edge, never mind the fact that Armas, who is at least eighty, was probably dreaming or simply imagining things.

"Listen up," Jessica says, sitting on a chair across from the bed. She takes Astrid gently by the hand and squeezes her fingers. "The police are investigating. I don't think there's any cause for concern. Why would anyone want to hurt Elisabeth?"

"I don't know," Astrid says seriously. Then her face brightens, and she grabs Jessica's wrist with her free hand. "But . . . you could . . . I'm sure you're better at solving cases like this than the local police; they have almost no experience with homicides."

Jessica now sees that Astrid isn't here to process her feelings but to ask for help. She shakes her head. "No."

Astrid's eyes plead with Jessica. There's something mournful about her gaze.

Suddenly Jessica hears in her ears a hum that swells so rapidly, it stabs at her temples like a lightning bolt. Jessica shuts her eyes, and when she opens them again, it's Elisabeth sitting there across from her on the bed. The old woman's eyes are anything but mournful; they are as pitiless as those of an eagle eyeing its prey.

Has that old parrot told you everything again?

"I know what's bothering you, Jessica."

Jessica still sees Elisabeth's face before her, but the voice belongs to Astrid.

"Excuse me," Jessica says, grimacing in pain. The throbbing travels from the back of her head all the way to her frontal lobe. She blinks a few times and feels Astrid's fingers knot through her own.

"Did you hear me, Jessica?"

"I want to be alone," Jessica says, pointing at the door. "Please. I'm not feeling very well."

"But—"

"Astrid! Please!" Jessica snaps. She stands, and the room around her starts to spin. "I want to be alone." She closes her eyes and staggers over to the bed.

Then she hears the door open and shut as Astrid exits the room.

I BURIED HOPE behind the barn last night.

I wasn't able to keep a little bird alive, but I can kill a human.

As a matter of fact, I'm surprised by the strength with which I pushed your drugged carcass into the water, forced you to breathe in the elixir of life. It never ceases to fascinate me that water is simultaneously necessary for life and lethal to it.

I no longer feel any pity. I enjoy killing more than I used to. I'd wanted to sink my fingers into your flesh, see the blood ooze from beneath your wrinkled skin. I'd wanted to bash your brains in, hear the blow of rock against bone. See the fear fade from your eyes and turn to utter emptiness as your cerebral cortex rips and all intellectual functions come to a sudden stop.

But a blow to the head is an overly fast exit from this world, and drowning is the most painful of all. So I refrain from giving my latest whims any purchase.

One more. Then I'll be done.

THE LIGHT DRIZZLE has transformed into a downpour that beats rhythmically against the barn's metal roof. Even without looking, it's easy to picture the way the rain forms irregular trickles on the window. All sounds are crisp, sharp; Jessica's senses are tuned to the extreme.

She feels a touch at her ankle.

Jessie.

Jessica forces her heavy eyelids open. A man is sitting at the foot of the bed, in the exact same position Astrid was sitting in a moment before.

What are you doing here?

At first all Jessica can see is his back, but then she catches a whiff of freshly smoked cigarette, the pungent smell there's no mistaking: Rumba-brand tobacco from Estonia.

Jessica sits up. The shift in position sets her temples pounding.

Erne looks around and shakes his head.

This place worries me, reminds me of Murano. Of that hotel room I came and got you from . . . all those years ago.

Jessica sighs dismissively, although she knows the stubborn old man is right.

Are you giving up?

"Are you serious?"

Erne nods, fist at his mouth; the words stick in his throat as a harsh coughing fit strikes.

"Maybe I am. And there's no one who should care anymore," Jessica says.

Erne looks back, hurt.

What about Yusuf? And Rasmus?

"They'll be fine without me."

You promised, Jessie. You promised to take care of yourself.

"I didn't lie. I was wrong." Jessica turns to the window to watch the rainstorm lash the windowpane.

What about Maija?

"What about Maija?"

Everything on this island is related to Maija. Including Elisabeth's death. And you know it, Jessie. You don't have to be the best homicide detective in Finland to understand that. Whether you like it or not.

"At the moment, I'm not anything."

Erne laboriously hauls himself up from the bed.

That's what you seem to keep telling yourself. But you'll always be an investigator. As long as you're alive.

"I'm not doing very well."

That's nothing new, Erne says with a good-natured chuckle. *Get some rest. And then go figure out what the hell's going on in this godforsaken place.*

Erne presses his kiss-moistened fingertips to her forehead.

Everything's going to be fine, Jessie.

Jessica can sense the smell of cigarettes fading, and when she opens her eyes a moment later, everything feels more complicated than before.

33

THE UPSTAIRS HALLWAY at the villa is narrower than one might expect from the building's exterior. The long rag rug that nearly covers all its surface feels lumpy underfoot, and the planks creak loudly with every footfall. A tall floor lamp, powered from an ancient outlet hanging loose at the floor, stands in front of the largish oil painting that dominates the space. The air up here is somehow stale, as if no one has opened the windows for a long time. Jessica walks the corridor wallpapered in beige anchor-patterned print and stops halfway down at a light blue door. She presses her knuckles to it, hesitates, and then gives it a light rap. At first there's no response; then shuffling footsteps can be heard from the other side—the cane taps sharply against the floor.

"Who's there?" a feeble voice says.

"Jessica," Jessica says, and when the old man doesn't immediately reply, she adds: "We spoke at breakfast."

A few seconds pass, and then the door opens, albeit no more than a crack, as if locked with an invisible chain.

Jessica unzips her coat and stands up straighter. "Do you have a moment?"

After considering briefly, the old man nods and lets her in.

Jessica notes that Armas' lodgings are smaller than hers. The stagnant air has an institutional whiff to it. The room is dim; the ceiling light isn't on. A housefly roused from its hibernation buzzes at the window frame, seeking a route to freedom. Some Swedish-language quiz show is blaring from the television; the host has orange skin and disturbingly white Hollywood teeth.

Jessica crosses to the window, swats the bumbling fly on its way, and cracks the white curtain. Just as Armas said, from the window she can see the entire yard and the shore, including the boathouses. From this vantage point, the branches of the apple trees that grow on either side of the building are no hindrance to visibility.

"Did the police come and talk to you?" Jessica asks, gaze still on the window.

"They did."

"I couldn't stop thinking about what you said this morning in the dining room." Jessica sighs and turns toward Armas. He stiffly lowers himself into the armchair and turns off the television. "That you saw Maija last night."

Armas nods emphatically and looks at the remote control as if it is bewitched. He is clearly shocked to hear the name uttered out loud.

"I'd like to hear what or who you meant by Maija," Jessica says, pulling a little notebook and a pen from her pocket. If she's going to conduct her own investigation, she may as well do it properly.

Armas looks offended, as if Jessica just accused him of lying. "What do you mean, who did I mean? I said it was Maija. Plain as day."

Jessica sighs and leans against the windowsill, hands folded across her chest. The man is old, his speech slightly slurred. But he is not senile: his eyes are sharp, and his words sound carefully considered.

"But we both know that's not possible," Jessica says calmly. Without meaning to, she must sound as if she doesn't believe Armas' mind is working at full capacity.

"Speak for yourself. I know what I saw." Armas grips the armrest of the armchair with the fingers of his right hand. His little mouth presses into a firm line. The Adam's apple beneath the wrinkled throat bounces up and down as he swallows.

"I'm not saying you were seeing things," Jessica says, grunting silently to herself. She's the last one to go around accusing anyone of having hallucinations. Or, now that she thinks about it, maybe after all these years she knows more about hallucinations than most people. "I believe you saw something that might resemble a child, but the little girl you're presumably talking about disappeared without a trace seventy-four years ago. You understand that, right?"

Armas pinches his narrow lips and wheezes softly, like a pug dog. "It was a child, damn it," he scoffs.

"In other words, you're sure you saw someone of small stature?"

Armas nods. "In a blue coat."

"And this child was standing in the yard?"

"Yes," Armas says. "I already told you."

"The police officer who was asking questions—Karlsson . . . Did you tell him all this?"

"No."

"Why not?"

Armas stares at Jessica as if the question is totally absurd, then twirls a finger around his temple. "Because they'd think I was crazy."

"If you'd mentioned Maija specifically to Karlsson, yes, *then* they would think you were crazy. But there shouldn't be anything strange at all about seeing a child—any random child." Jessica massages her forehead with her fingertips. "Even if it were the middle of the night and by all logic there shouldn't be anyone younger than me on the island."

Jessica takes a few steps closer and squats next to the old man's chair. The fact that his attitude toward the incident is so insistent raises questions about whether there's something other than a nocturnal sighting behind all this.

"Armas, please," she says, attempting eye contact with the old man. "This is about something more than a child in a blue coat, isn't it?"

"What do you mean?"

"There's something that makes you believe that Maija had to be here. Something that has you convinced it was Maija's ghost specifically that killed Elisabeth last night."

Armas shuts his eyes, and when he opens them again, Jessica can see a fierce blaze has been kindled in them.

34

MAIJA GLANCES AT her alarm clock. It's ten to two. She hasn't slept a wink, and she doesn't want to, because if she did so, she'd probably sleep through the night and not wake up until the morning. And then Dad would have come in vain. She hasn't dared to set her alarm clock, because the noise would be sure to wake the whole children's home. When she was alone, she tried to wrap it in a blanket and hide it under her pillow. She jammed cotton between the bells, but nothing worked: the clock is designed to rouse its owner under any circumstances. It's a fine clock; her father had the date and a dedication etched on the back.

Maija looks out the window and starts tugging on her boots. Maybe tonight will be the night. Dad didn't come to the shore the night before last. Or last night. But Maija's hopeful. You can never be impatient or give up. That's what her father said in the letter: *It may be a long wait, but your patience will be rewarded.*

She wraps her coat around her and pulls on her white beret, just like on the previous two nights. Maija quietly pushes the window open. The wood, swollen from the rain, chafes, but Maija has practiced opening the window so many times that the sound generated by the operation is almost nonexistent. She glances at her door and pricks up her ears to listen for footfalls carrying from the hallway. She would still have time to dive back into bed and claim she opened the window to air out her stale room. But she hears nothing. Maija climbs out the window and drops down, using the foundation as a toehold, just as she did on the previous nights, but this time she springs a little farther so the soles of her feet hit grass instead of the cobblestone embankment circling the building.

A damp, cold wind blows off the sea. Tonight dark clouds have eaten the moon. Maija starts walking toward the dock behind the tall boathouse. When her gaze finally reaches it, her throat constricts in disappointment. No, her father isn't there yet. But then again, it's only two on the dot.

As Maija steps onto the dock, a flock of waterbirds rises noisily from the reeds and makes for the forest, squawking loudly. Her heart pounds furiously. Hopefully the birds didn't wake anyone up. She steps forward, and the narrow dock rocks beneath the soft soles of her boots; the low thuds echo off the murky water.

Maija pulls her coat tighter. Her breath steams in the dark night. The waves that faithfully submit to the direction of the wind pass the dock in an endless ribbon. The water looks treacherous and cold. Maija wears a thick sweater beneath the coat because she got cold waiting for her father the past two nights. She's been through worse, she thinks to herself. Soon everything is going to be better, if she can just get away from this godforsaken place. Away from Beth and the others. Somewhere where she doesn't have to be afraid and she can be herself again. Maija isn't sure what sort of boat her father will be arriving in. Actually, Maija doesn't even know what her father looks like. Did he shave his thick beard or lose a lot of weight during all those years he spent at war? Her father has sent a lot of photos with his letters, but not a single one of himself. Maybe there's a reason. But if there is, Maija doesn't know what it is. Or why Dad has to come fetch her in the middle of the night. But that doesn't matter. The main thing is that he is coming.

Suddenly Maija hears someone calling her name. It's a man's

voice, but Maija can tell right away that it's not her father's. She remembers what her father's voice sounds like; at least she thinks she does. Dad's voice is warm, unlike the hoarse, drunken slurring calling her by name.

"What the hell are you doing out there?"

Maija turns toward the voice. A fat man in a black overcoat stands in the orphanage yard. It's Herman, one of the two alternating night watchmen.

He starts walking toward the dock. "Hey, did you hear me? What do you think you're doing outside in the middle of the night?"

Maija doesn't answer. She knows the man will grab her shoulder in a moment. Maybe tug her by the earlobe and drag her back inside. But before that happens, Maija turns back to the sea and stares at the dark swells and wishes she would catch even a tiny glimpse of her father, who has promised to come for her.

I'm sorry, Dad. I'll be back tomorrow.

35

ARMAS POHJANPALO FOLDS his shirt and his shorts, places them topmost in the little suitcase, and closes it. The potato soup they had for lunch has congealed under his breastbone, forming a warm lump. His palms are sweating, and a swarm of butterflies is buzzing around in his stomach. It's almost three o'clock, and someone from the children's home is going to be taking him to Maarianhamina, where they will be waiting for him.

They. Them. The Mönkkönens. A new family. A new mother, a new father. Four new siblings, including an adult brother. After all these weeks, he's finally getting a new home in Katinen, which according to Matron Boman is somewhere near Hämeenlinna. Although it's really all the same where his new home is located; the main thing is getting away from Smörregård. Armas sits on his bed and groans. His backside is still covered in painful bruises. Matron surprised Armas sneaking peeks at the girls when they were in the sauna, but instead of punishing Armas herself, she told Martin to do it, and Martin did not spare the rod.

Loud laughter echoes from the hallway. The girls from rooms 3 and 5 are fooling around out there: Beth and her faithful henchman, Hamhock. Armas had a crush on Beth but was badly disappointed when he realized that in Beth's eyes he's nothing but a scrawny twerp. *Keep dreaming, jerk. Do you think I'd really be interested in a runt like you?*

Beth looks and sounds like a grown-up but is incredibly childish and cruel. Not to mention her plump partner in crime, Elsa, whom everyone calls Hamhock without it seeming to bother her. The pair of girls sank their claws into Armas and then hung him out to dry after he did them a favor. Something Armas has no desire to remember anymore. And soon he won't have to.

The autumn day is bright, and Armas draws the curtain across the window. *My last day,* he thinks. Last hour. Then life will start again. A new life. No more hymns, no more Matron Boman's fingers in his hair; no Martin's whippings or being made to stand in the hall.

The girls' laughter rings through the corridor and eventually softens to a mumble as the pair make their way to Beth's room, which is right next to Armas'. Sometimes Armas lowers himself to the floor, pulls off a piece of the baseboard, scoops out damp masses of the sawdust insulation, and places his ear against the mouse-frittered wall. That way he can hear what the girls are whispering, especially if they're on Beth's bed, next to the wall. Armas once heard something from Beth's room he'd never dare tell anyone. Martin was in there with Beth, and the rhythmic creak of the bed, the heavy male breathing, and Beth's stifled moans carried from there.

Show me . . .

Armas hears Hamhock's voice and the giggle that follows.

On a whim, he lowers himself to the floor and performs the requisite procedures for eavesdropping, holds his breath to make out what the girls are saying one last time before he leaves this island.

"I can't, dummy. I don't have it; Maija does."

"No one has any idea why she's waiting out there. I was wondering too."

"Well, now you know."

"So you wrote the letter?"

"No . . . Martin has an old Remington at home in Listerby."

"How can that idiot think . . . Her dad is dead!"

"Shh!"

"*Still. She's stupid if she believes that letter. Where did you get the idea?*"

"*Well, I saw her letters . . . You can't tell anyone about this, Hamhock.*"

"*I know, of course not.*"

Armas can't hear any more of what the girls say; maybe they moved off the bed, or they just stopped gossiping. Armas waits a second to see if maybe the story will continue, and before long he notices his eyes have fallen shut. He's incredibly tired; he was so nervous about his imminent departure that he didn't sleep last night. Armas had walked over to the window to wait, watched one last time as Maija climbed out her window and stood on the dock for hours, the way she has for weeks now. As creepy as the ritual is, Armas is going to miss Maija. The crazy girl who never talks and whose hair is the color of barley.

Armas can smell the damp and mouse urine of the moldy wall. The sun peering through the curtains feels warm on his cheek. He quickly falls asleep.

36

ARMAS WAKES WITH a start when someone opens the door. It's Miss Boman, who immediately tears into him over the removed baseboard and the clumps of insulation on the floor.

"I'm sorry," Armas says, and rubs his eyes. "It was already broken . . ."

"What on earth do you think you're doing, Armas? You're fortunate you're expected . . . Otherwise you would have to work to pay off that damage," Miss Boman says. She takes him by the shoulder and orders him to get his suitcase, which waits by the window.

There's no clock in Armas' room, but the position of the sun in the sky indicates that he's slept at least a couple hours. He is still caught up in his jumbled and eventful dream, in which he was sailing toward America in an enormous sailboat with his father and mother and Maija and . . . Armas steps toward the suitcase and hears Miss Boman fussing over the broken baseboard.

Maija.

What Beth and Hamhock were talking about . . . Armas thinks and stops. *Dang it. That must be it. If it's true, then . . .*

Armas turns on his heel and bolts from the room, in the process dodging the grasping hand of Miss Boman, who is caught off guard by his sudden movement.

"Maija!" Armas shouts, passing Beth's room. He grabs the door of the next room and yanks it open.

"Maija!"

The room is empty.

"What on earth, Armas!"

Miss Boman's insistent voice echoes in the corridor as if from a megaphone.

Armas knows he won't get a second chance to talk to Maija. He already said his good-byes to the other children at breakfast, before they were told to clean their rooms. Armas dashes to the window and presses his forehead against it, tries to look for Maija.

He hears the door behind him open; Miss Boman's heavy breathing and low voice fill the room.

"Armas Pohjanpalo! Have you lost your mind?"

And now Armas sees Maija to the left of the boathouse. She's sitting right at the shore in her blue coat, staring out to sea. He quickly opens the window, climbs through, and drops wildly to the cobblestone embankment that surrounds the orphanage. His ankle twists as he falls, and Armas cries out in pain.

"Maija! I have to tell you something!" Armas shouts toward the shore, and now Maija turns toward him.

Armas starts limping across the yard toward the rock where Maija is sitting. A moment later he hears the front door of the orphanage open and Miss Boman shout after him, angrier than ever.

"Maija! It's Beth! And Hamhock!"

Pain spasms through his twisted ankle with every step he takes. But Maija makes no indication of rising or walking toward him. Miss Boman is on Armas' heels and sure to catch him before he makes it to Maija.

"And Martin! They're fooling you!" Armas now realizes he's speaking Finnish for the first time in ages. Maybe to make sure Maija really understands what he's saying, maybe because today is his time to go home.

Now Maija stands and looks at Armas as if his words didn't mean anything. Her face is void of expression. The breeze blows through her unbraided hair.

"Your dad isn't coming to the dock!" Armas cries.

In that instant, he feels rough fingertips pinch his earlobe. Their hold is firm, and Armas roars in pain as Miss Boman yanks him onward.

"What is the meaning of this, Armas Pohjanpalo?"

"They wrote a letter, Miss." Armas' eyes are still on Maija, who remains standing at the rock.

"What are you blathering about? What letter?"

"The night watchman. And Elisabeth."

Miss Boman releases Armas' ear. "I don't know what you're talking about, but right now you're trying my patience."

Armas is breathing heavily, can't get a word out. Miss Boman points at Martin, who's standing on the dirt road at the edge of the forest.

"Martin has kindly promised to take you to Maarianhamina," Miss Boman continues, then sighs. "I understand this is difficult. Leaving. It's difficult for all of us . . ." Miss Boman wipes the dandruff from Armas' sweater. "But it will only hurt for a little while."

After retrieving his suitcase, Armas casts one final glance at the shore but doesn't see Maija there anymore. Maybe he was able to get his message across after all. Warning Maija is the least he can do. Because through his own actions, Armas was the cause of the whole mess.

37

2020

JESSICA HAS A hard time admitting to herself that the smell wafting through Armas' room fills her with dread. It reminds her of the temporary nature of everything: of time's untiring labors, of old age and inevitable death. And how the mouth that told a little boy's story belongs to a man who's now more than eighty years old. About how life is something that is only on loan to all. And how even so, just last night she was sure she wanted to give it up voluntarily.

"It was a long time ago," Armas says, as if he's been reading Jessica's mind. "But I remember that day as if it were yesterday."

The words she heard on the dock come back to Jessica—*Don't cry, Mommy. Daddy will be here soon*—and a surreal feeling washes over her. "So Maija thought her father was going to pick her up from the dock in the middle of the night?"

Armas nods. Jessica isn't sure what to make of the old man's account. If it's true, if such a prank was played at the orphanage all those years ago, it was a terrible injustice. What now feels like the evilest treachery was only a cruel joke among children. Still, Jessica feels some sort of satisfaction that Elisabeth got what she deserved. The bully came to a shitty end.

The only problem is that there is no such thing as ghosts. Even Jessica—a psychiatric patient who has suffered from hallucinations for the entirety of her adult life—is perfectly aware of this.

It's only now that it occurs to Jessica that whoever murdered Elisabeth last night might be a danger to others too.

"What about Piggy?" Jessica says.

Armas looks at her in momentary confusion; then his eyes brighten. "Hamhock?"

"Right, Hamhock. Is she the third member of your party?" Jessica asks with a nod at the door.

Armas shakes his head. "Hamhock—I mean Elsa Lehtinen—died long ago. Twenty-five years ago . . . We had just started this tradition."

"How did she die?"

"She was seriously ill. I have the impression that before our first reunion here, she'd been undergoing some sort of cancer treatment. But unless I'm wrong, she died in an accident."

"Do you remember the details?"

"It happened somewhere abroad, Spain or France. But as I said, it was a long time ago, and she and I weren't close. I only saw Elsa once after the fall of 1946, and that was here at the guesthouse in the spring of 1994. Elsa passed away that summer."

"Does anything else come to mind about your reunion in 1994?" Jessica says, cracking her knuckles. It's what Yusuf would be doing now, she guesses, if only he were here.

"No . . . ," Armas says, then realizes he was being hasty. "Well, the fact that Astrid was running the place that weekend. Her husband, Hans-Peter, was away."

"Was that somehow unusual?"

"Back then, Hans-Peter ran the guesthouse with a couple staff members, and Astrid was working a lot at the hospital. Even on weekends. I don't think Astrid retired from being a doctor until 1997 or 1998, after which she began to help her husband and actually took over most of the responsibility for looking after the guests."

Jessica writes down *Astrid 1994* in her notebook, and beneath it *Elsa Lehtinen*.

One way or another, she ought to check Elsa's cause of death in 1994. Based on what Armas just told her, Elsa was almost as guilty for what happened as Elisabeth.

Armas hoists himself up from the chair and walks to the window. Jessica frowns. The cane the old man seems to rely on when in the presence of others has been left leaning against the armchair.

"Is the third member of your party involved in the story somehow?" Jessica asks, and notices she's nervous about Armas' response.

"No, I don't think so. Eila left the island for a new home before all that began, and I don't think she ever really had much to do with Beth or Hamhock."

Jessica studies Armas, then returns to her previous thought. "What about you? Do you have any reason to be concerned about your safety?"

Armas appears to ponder his answer, then shakes his head. "No. I tried to warn Maija."

"In other words," Jessica starts calmly, reminding herself that Armas, just like everyone else on the island, is a suspect until proven otherwise, "Maija would never feel it was necessary to hurt anyone else on this island?"

Armas looks at Jessica somehow gratefully, as if the mention of Maija's name means she believes he saw the girl in the blue coat. Then the old man's face darkens and he shrugs, as if what he is about to say is completely unimportant.

"The night watchman and Miss Boman are already dead, found just like Elisabeth," Armas says. "If there was anyone left who had to die, it was Beth."

38

JESSICA CLOSES ARMAS' door and lets her breathing steady. Now she understands why Astrid was so worked up about what happened: all those found dead at the orphanage waterfront played a central role in Maija's story. Assuming, of course, that Armas is telling the truth.

She has to find out what happened to Elsa Lehtinen in 1994.

It's perfectly possible, maybe even probable, that if there has been a series of homicides, there have been four murders instead of three. Jessica knows that, statistically speaking, homicides by serial killers are extremely rare, especially in the Nordic countries. But she has come across them on the job before. She has sat in on many courses facilitated by the National Bureau of Investigation and based on the teachings of legendary FBI profiler John E. Douglas. A serial killer— if that is who is responsible in this instance—usually doesn't stop until he dies or is imprisoned (if not necessarily for the murders he has committed). In rarer cases, the serial killer is driven by a need to eliminate certain people, and he can stop when the final victim is dead. That's why the most relevant question in investigating these cases is always whether there might be more victims.

Jessica considers knocking on the neighboring door, which is the door to Eila Kantelinen's room. But she feels a sudden pang of nausea and turns toward the stairs instead. When she gets down to the first floor, she sees Johan Karlsson sitting with Astrid and Åke at the rear of the dining room, at the table occupied the night before by the birds of spring.

Karlsson turns toward the staircase just as Jessica steps onto the lowest tread, and he casts a pointed glance her way. "Excuse me," he calls out, as Astrid pours him coffee from a copper pot. "It's Jessica, right? Could you come here for a moment?"

Jessica pauses between the dining room and library doors and glances at her watch, as if she has something better to be doing right now. In reality, all she needs is fresh air: perhaps a short walk would once again ease the unexpected bout of nausea.

"How can I help you?" Jessica says, hands deep in her coat pockets. She marches into the dining room, pulls out a chair from under the table, and takes a seat before anyone has time to invite her to.

Karlsson has removed his heavy coat. There's a poorly fitting black dress shirt beneath; a police ID hangs around his neck. He looks more agitated than he did earlier, and somehow bored. As a matter of fact, as he drinks his coffee there, Karlsson is surprisingly reminiscent of a Helsinki investigator who has seen so much shit on the job that he's no longer fazed by anything. Even so, Jessica has a hard time taking him very seriously.

"Did you speak with the people staying upstairs?" Karlsson asks calmly, coffee cup at his lips. His pinkie rises for a moment, but he quickly crooks it into hiding with the other fingers.

Astrid tries to interject: "Listen, Johan—"

But Karlsson silences her with a single raised finger. Jessica can't help but notice that the dynamic between them is oddly straightforward, as if they are well acquainted. Karlsson wipes his mouth on his napkin and assumes a more comfortable position. The look on his face is smug and self-satisfied. But Jessica is sure what she's seeing is an insecurity that Karlsson is trying to compensate for with his arrogant behavior.

"The owners of this establishment are, for good reason, concerned about their guests' comfort, but I'd still like you to answer my question," Karlsson says.

"Yes, I did."

"With both of them? Both Eila and . . ." Karlsson frowns, apparently at the taste of the coffee, and he lowers the cup to the table and pours in a generous amount of milk.

"Only with Armas."

"Why?" Karlsson asks, as Astrid and Åke exchange uncomfortable glances.

"You mean, why did I only talk to Armas?"

A smile flashes across Karlsson's face. "No, why did you talk to anyone?" He takes a teaspoon and shovels two spoonfuls of sugar into his coffee. Jessica can't help but reflect that by this point, the beverage has very little to do with coffee anymore.

Astrid raises a hand and is just about to say something when Karlsson gently taps the spoon against the rim of his coffee cup, as if about to give a toast. "I'm sorry; I didn't mean to be rude," he says. "But nevertheless, we apparently have a murder investigation on our hands, and I want to ensure that everyone, including potential eyewitnesses, understands the chain of command."

"I didn't realize we have a chain of command."

Karlsson raps his knuckles against the table. "My point exactly. In order for one to exist, you would have to have the authority to engage in law enforcement activities in Ahvenanmaa."

Jessica feels her fingertips tingle with rage. "In that case, I'd like to get back to what I've paid a sizable sum to do."

"And what might that be?"

"Vacation."

Karlsson chuckles, but all trace of goodwill has vanished from his face. "Be my guest."

Jessica draws her lips up into a fake smile. "I'm so sorry, Astrid. And Åke. This truly is a terrible situation." She stands and exits the room.

The drizzle is falling again. Jessica pulls up her hood and starts walking toward the barn.

After taking a few steps, she hears the door open behind her. Jessica is reminded of the events at her therapist's, of the bad breath of the overeager super, and steels herself to feel a man's hand on her shoulder. Her brain has already flipped into fight-or-flight mode.

"Niemi." Karlsson's voice comes from a few meters behind Jessica, and she stops.

Karlsson is standing, coatless, at the base of the front steps with a cigarette and matches. He strikes a match and successfully lights the cigarette on his first try, despite the strong gusts.

"You know, for some reason I've never liked being called by my last name," Jessica says.

Karlsson inhales, and the tip of the cigarette glows as the match in his fingers goes out. He takes a step closer to Jessica. "I'd like to apologize. We got off on the wrong foot here."

His face is lowered, which makes the reptilian part of Jessica's brain relax. She feels less threatened when the attention of the man isn't a hundred percent focused on her. The same goes for romantic encounters with men, situations in which she has met someone at the store, on the dance floor, ordering a drink at the bar. Overly intense and determined eye contact means danger. Jessica doesn't want to be a target. For her, eyes evaluating her face and body mean pain and have for a long time, ever since Venice.

"I shouldn't have ambushed you like that in there. In front of Astrid and Åke. My apologies," Karlsson continues, studying the cigarette between his fingers as if it is some foreign object. "It was unpleasant for them too."

"OK," Jessica says. She looks at the shore and sees the police boat chugging past the island opposite, headed toward the mainland. "Did you miss your ride?"

"They're coming back for me."

"So you're investigating this case now?"

Karlsson nods. "See, the thing that was bothering me in there was that Armas Pohjanpalo refused to talk to me."

"Maybe he didn't have anything to say."

Karlsson sneers even more mockingly than before, if possible. "Sure," he says, and blows out a nearly perfect smoke ring. "Except you spent a whole fifteen minutes in his room."

"Did Åke loan you his stopwatch?"

Karlsson chuckles. "Now I get it. You told jokes, and Armas laughed."

"Laughing makes you live longer."

"Unless it kills you. Like Elisabeth?"

"Is that what she died of?"

"If she did, you must be innocent."

"What exactly is it you want, Karlsson?"

The smile vanishes from his face, and his eyes narrow to slits. "When I tried to talk to Armas, the first thing he asked was whether I'd spoken with you."

Jessica feels a pang in her chest. Why the hell did the old man put a target on her back?

"Then you came and . . . I noticed you spent a pretty long time in there. So I don't have to be Helsinki's superstar detective Jessica Niemi to get a little suspicious," Karlsson says, cigarette in the corner of his mouth. "A locked-room mystery. A remote island. Eight people: two hosts, six guests. One of the guests dies and, judging by the injuries to the head, in a violent manner. The most famous investigator in the country just happens to be vacationing on the scene and for some reason wants to dig into things on her own. This is like a mishmash of the best Agatha Christie: *And Then There Were None* and Miss Marple, who just happens to be at the hotel when a murder takes place."

Karlsson shakes his head, the fingers holding the cigarette in front of his face. "What I find problematic is that the Miss Marple of this story spent so much time in Armas' room and I'm supposed to believe you two were watching *Wheel of Fortune*."

"I don't know; the channel selection is pretty limited out here in the islands."

"Did you eat a joke book for breakfast or something?"

"Maybe Armas needed some comfort."

"And in that case, you were doing valuable work, Niemi. Especially when you consider you didn't know the guy, and as a matter of fact you'd never exchanged so much as a single word with him."

Jessica shakes her head in amusement. "I thought you stepped out to apologize. Got off on the wrong foot et cetera, et cetera."

"I did. And to explain my behavior. Because I don't put the squeeze on anyone for no reason. Believe it or not, for an island hick like me, I have a perfectly good radar. It goes off anytime anyone is full of shit. And when the needle is showing red—the way it is right now—I don't always remember to be so nice."

"Great," Jessica says, then turns to walk away.

"We've been in touch with Helsinki," Karlsson says.

Jessica stops in her tracks. There's a painful stabbing in her frontal lobe, and she shuts her eyes. Goddamned busybody: now Hellu and the others are going to know where she is, if they didn't already.

"I know this vacation wasn't voluntary. You had to take it because you couldn't go in to work."

"What the hell is your problem, Karlsson? Your way of welcoming a criminal investigator from the capital to Ahvenanmaa isn't very collegial."

"We found something at the scene," Karlsson replies calmly. He drops his half-smoked cigarette to the gravel and grinds it out with the tip of his shoe. "Near Elisabeth. A scarf. I understand it's yours."

Jessica feels the pain in her forehead sharpen. Her brain is a blank. How could the scarf be at the scene, supposedly? Unless . . . it fell from her neck the previous night, when she saw Maija on the dock.

"Do you seriously think I . . . I killed that woman?" Jessica says softly, barely managing to stifle her rage.

Karlsson looks up at the sky as if he wants the gray cloud cover to fill his entire field of vision. "I don't know, Niemi. But there's something really damn weird going on here." He turns to go back inside. "Oh, and yes. It would be good for everyone to stay here on the island for now. Until we get a handle on things."

Karlsson gives her a quick salute and steps back into the villa.

39

JESSICA RETURNS TO her room and glances around restlessly. The scarf that has been hanging on a hook next to the door is gone. She sits down, reaches for the prescription vial on the coffee table, and pours the contents into her palm. Thirteen pills left. Out of a vial of a hundred. It takes her a moment to remember that most of them are still in her coat pocket. Just now, it feels absurd that the night before she brought a stockpile of the pills along, as if she were really considering killing herself on the orphanage dock. Maybe for a fleeting moment it felt like a realistic option: to sit down, lean against the wood, and close her eyes. To fall asleep to birdsong and the rustle of the wind.

But what if what Jessica thought was a dream is actually true? Maybe she has completely lost her grip on reality. She shuts her eyes, tries to remember even a sliver of what happened on the north shore after she encountered the girl in the blue coat. Some tiny detail that would reveal something about the passage of time, the order of events. But where the memories should be there is only darkness.

Jessica tries to breathe slowly and deeply. The silence is broken by a faint sobbing coming through the wall, the woman stifling tears. Then the man speaks in a calm voice, but Jessica can't make out the words. She thinks about Armas lying on the floor, ear pressed to the thin wall.

What was the last thing Armas said? *The night watchman and*

Miss Boman are already dead . . . If there was anyone left who had to die, it was Beth.

Jessica leans forward and sinks her fingertips into her hair. If less time had passed since the events at the orphanage, a year or even ten years, the connection might make some sense. But by now Maija would be eighty-three years old if she were alive. Which is theoretically possible, Jessica supposes, if unlikely, considering no one has seen her since she vanished from the dock—but that doesn't explain the child Armas saw the night before . . . Not to mention that an elderly woman hiding out on the island, killing people over ancient grudges, doesn't sound like a possible, let alone realistic, scenario.

When Jessica opens her eyes and sits up straight, she feels her stomach lurch. *What the hell is wrong with me?* she thinks. She's used to not being able to control her mind, to the fact that reality might be distorted anytime and anywhere. She is used to the agonizing—and often sudden-onset—neuropathy from the childhood car accident that crippled her entire body and put her in the hospital. In the past, the physical pain was often triggered by some psycho-emotionally taxing experience. But she doesn't recall ever feeling a nasty, churning nausea like this before.

Jessica pricks up her ears. The woman next door is still crying. She isn't wailing hysterically, which might rouse Jessica's suspicions—more inconsolably, perhaps.

Now Jessica remembers something: how she was moved to tears upon encountering the girl on the dock.

Don't cry, Mommy.

Jessica can still hear the girl's words but doesn't understand why they are weighing on her. Why was she so moved by what she saw and heard that she burst into tears? As if the moment was an inflection point, as if the simple act of setting foot on the dock had turned over a new leaf in her life.

Maybe it was fate. Maybe she really is Miss Marple and she's meant to solve not only the murder of the old woman named Elisabeth but also the connection between the deaths that took place in the 1980s and the mystery known locally as the legend of the girl in the blue coat.

Karlsson can go fuck himself.

Jessica draws a breath, jumps up, and opens her door.

40

Jessica stands outside the Swedish couple's door and listens. But the weeping has stopped, and no sounds come from the room. Jessica wonders whether the Swedes know last night's death is being investigated as a homicide. Either way, their vacation has taken a nasty turn too—assuming they weren't involved in last night's events one way or another. That's a possibility that cannot be dismissed, even though it's clear anyone could have landed on the island by boat in the night without being detected. This especially goes for the dock on the north shore, and why not also the guesthouse dock? But apparently in Karlsson's view that's not a very likely explanation.

Does Karlsson know something Jessica can't even imagine? And if Jessica is the primary suspect, based on the scarf found near the victim, the guy is barking up the wrong tree.

Jessica starts heading back to the villa. She knows she could leave the island if she wanted, that Karlsson doesn't actually have the clout to keep her from ordering a water taxi and discreetly leaving Smörregård. But Jessica doesn't want to run anymore. She already ran from Helsinki, which is why she is in this remote corner of the world, and she doesn't mean to run any more. She has nothing to lose, and she might just as well play what is usually her role—solving a fresh homicide—even if she is not presently on duty.

Jessica opens the front door of the villa and expects to be met with the critical gaze of her local colleague. But the entry hall is empty, as are the dining room and the library. The fragrance of dill wafts from the kitchen. She stops at the foot of the stairs leading to the second floor and hears people talking upstairs. She can make out Åke's voice, then Astrid's. When she hears Karlsson cough, she rushes past the stairs into the office on the other side of the dining room.

The door squeaks nastily, and Jessica doesn't hang around for any possible reactions from the group upstairs. She'll hear if someone comes down the stairs, and that will give her enough time to slip back into the entry hall without drawing attention to herself.

Jessica looks around. She sat across from Astrid's desk only a few days before, registering for her stay at the guesthouse, but was so tired and stressed upon her arrival that she paid no attention to the decor or other details of the room. The shelf behind the massive antique desk is filled with binders. A computer stands on the desk, along with office supplies. The walls are decorated with pastels and watercolors of the archipelago as well as a framed poster of Finland's lighthouses. Alongside the shelf there's a wooden rack; the guest room keys hang from it. Next to it is a largish metal cabinet with a red cross glued to it. Jessica fleetingly wonders what sorts of poison Astrid, as a former obstetrician, might be hiding in her medicine cabinet. Or does it contain only ibuprofen and gauze?

Jessica quickly eyes the desk, flips through papers, and opens the blue three-ring binder lying in front of the computer. *No, no, no*, she curses silently when she hears Karlsson call out something upstairs.

Jessica moves over to the folders on the shelf and lets her fingers slide along their spines. The bookkeeping since 1982 in tidy rows, insurance, invoices . . . *Nope, no* . . . Yes! Guest registrations, 1981–1984, in one binder; in another, equally fat, those from a longer period: 1985–1991. Judging by the amount of material the binder contains, business wasn't doing so hot at the time. A third binder contains 1992–1996 . . . Eventually, Jessica's eyes strike on a binder on the lowest shelf dedicated exclusively to 2020. She opens it, slides her fingers under the tab marked GUEST DOCUMENTS, and sees a photocopy of Elisabeth's passport right there on top. As she browses, she finds photocopies of the other two senior citizens' passports, then one of her own passport, and also personal information forms and copies of the Swedish couple's passports. Niklas and Pernilla Steiner.

Just then she hears noise in the corridor. Someone has started descending the wooden stairs. Someone heavy and, judging by the speed, relatively agile—no doubt Karlsson or Åke. *Damn it.* She might not get another chance. She pulls out her phone and takes pictures of the passport photocopies. Then she closes the binder, returns it to its place on the shelf, and tiptoes to the door. She hears somebody walk down the last few steps and stop at the foot of the staircase. Jessica presses herself up against the wall on the door's hinge side and holds her breath. A second passes, then another. Her eyes strike on a black-and-white photograph on the wall: it's of a little blond girl standing in front of the villa with her parents. Unlike the girl—who, judging by the skin on her neck, is Astrid—the father and mother have jet-black hair. At the bottom, text in cursive reads *Smörregård, May 1, 1948.*

The floor creaks ominously on the other side of the wall, as if whoever just came down the stairs is shifting his weight from one foot to the other—or creeping toward the door as quietly as possible. Jessica clenches her fists as if preparing for a fight. Her heart is hammering. Her palms are sweating.

Eventually she hears footsteps in the entryway, followed by the sound of the front door opening and shutting. To be safe, Jessica decides to wait a moment before leaving the room. But just as she's reaching for the door handle, she catches movement out of the corner of her eye: something outside the window. It's Karlsson, who has circled around the eastern end of the villa and is now standing next to the toolshed.

Jessica warily approaches the window and squats a couple feet away from it. Karlsson sucks on his cigarette, visibly agitated, and glances around. *Damn, the guy is on edge.* There's something odd about the way he's watching his back. He's acting like a teenager who snuck out for a smoke and doesn't want to get caught by his old man. Karlsson flicks the butt into the woods, then reaches up to the top of the shed's doorframe for something: presumably a hidden key, because a moment later he fiddles with the toolshed lock, and then the door opens effortlessly. Jessica can't see inside the toolshed without going right up to the window, and she doesn't dare do that right now. Karlsson vanishes inside the shed, and the door closes behind him.

Jessica stands there, wondering how suspicious she should consider the episode she just witnessed. Why did Karlsson seem so shifty? How did he know where the key was, and what exactly is he doing in the toolshed? Now that Jessica thinks about it, the little red building isn't necessarily a shed after all; she just decided it was one.

She decides to leave the office while the coast is still clear. But just as she starts tiptoeing toward the door, it opens, and Jessica sees Astrid's face, and on it a look of surprise that quickly shifts into stupefaction.

41

"WHAT ON EARTH are you doing in here?" Astrid says, turning on the lights. Jessica can't immediately think of an excuse but understands her creeping around in the dark has made the situation twice as suspicious.

"I'm sorry," she says, taking off her beanie.

Astrid eyes her from head to toe as if trying to think what Jessica might have stolen from the office.

"I came here looking for you," Jessica says, standing up straighter to seem credible.

"Where were you looking? Under my desk? And you shut the door behind you too," Astrid says, circling around behind her desk. She sits and kicks off her clogs beneath it. "Listen . . . I'm the one who ought to be apologizing. You're a guest here . . ." Astrid's voice is tired, and she lowers her head into her hands. "It has been a terrible morning, and I'm pretty upset. As I'm sure we all are."

"That goes without saying." Jessica seats herself on the worn leather armchair across from Astrid. The air between the upholstery and the cushioning escapes in one long hiss. Astrid turns the computer screen so they can see each other better. Her posture is surprisingly erect even now that she's sitting. Under other circumstances, Jessica might ask Astrid for her secret: how does she keep her spine so straight at her age? But would Jessica live long enough for the information to do her any good?

"Tell me what I can do for you," Astrid says, and when Jessica doesn't immediately grasp her meaning, she continues: "You said you were looking for me."

"Right. Um . . . I wanted to talk to you about Karlsson," she probes. "He's pretty feisty."

Astrid smiles woefully. "Yes, well, Johan is . . . Johan," she says, and Jessica thinks she catches a tear in the old woman's eye, but there's nothing there after she blinks. Astrid looks down at her hands, strokes one with the other. Jessica studies Astrid. So it's as Jessica suspected: Astrid and Karlsson were acquainted before this.

"Do you know him well?"

Astrid nods, gaze still on her hands, as if the conversation is about them, not Karlsson. "I've known Johan Karlsson since he was a little boy. He grew up not far from here. Was a detective since he was a whippersnapper." She chuckles and pulls a paper clip from a drawer, begins organizing the papers strewn across the desk. "He and Åke used to play here as children: point toy guns at people, take fingerprints, that sort of thing. Johan knows the villa and the whole island like the back of his hand. I'm sure he's taking Elisabeth's death very seriously."

"Why . . . I mean, did Johan know Elisabeth personally?"

"He might as well have, I suppose. Johan knows the story of the birds of spring. But I don't think they ever met, because after he grew up, Johan only visited us when Åke was at home. And maybe you've heard Åke visited here very rarely if at all before moving back last fall, after my husband, Hans-Peter's, death."

"But you said Johan was taking Elisabeth's death to heart."

"No, I said he's taking it *seriously*. Johan wants to solve the case because he has an emotional attachment to this place. I understand he might seem a little rude and officious, but I suppose it's his job to suspect everyone and everything; as a detective, you understand that."

"And *everyone* includes not only me but you and Åke too?"

Astrid laughs drily. "I suppose. Now that you say it out loud."

"Karlsson seems to believe there's no way the perpetrator could have been an outsider," Jessica says. "He was talking about a locked-room mystery and Miss Marple."

Astrid bursts into a guffaw that, under the circumstances, strikes Jessica as strange and for some reason sends shivers running up and down her spine.

"Well, as I said, Johan is Johan."

Jessica discreetly glances at the window, but from her chair it's impossible to see the toolshed door. When she turns back to Astrid, she is hunched over, studying her hands again. She strokes the plump veins on the back of the right hand that Jessica was staring at the night before.

"Look at that. An old woman's hand, veins like power cables. Did you know they look blue because they absorb red light instead of reflecting it?"

"I've never thought about it, to tell you the truth."

"Pale skin only serves to heighten the effect. That's why aristo-crats who avoided the sun and outdoor labor were called blue bloods," Astrid says. "The idiom lives on as a way of referring to royal lineage."

Jessica smiles as she imagines the moment she's going to be able to show off by using this bit of trivia on Yusuf. Then her thoughts lope onward to the question that's been burning in her mind for a while now.

"I'd like to ask about those earlier drownings," Jessica says.

Astrid's face darkens and she pauses before replying. "What about them?"

"I'm just trying to wrap my head around all this. You said two people have been found dead at the same spot where Elisabeth's body was found this morning. I heard from Armas that the victims were the director and the night watchman from the orphanage."

"That's true."

"Were those deaths investigated at all?"

"The first was considered an accidental drowning. But the police were interested in the second one, which is only natural, considering the victim was found in the exact same spot."

"Did the police have any suspects? Or any theories?"

Astrid shakes her head vigorously. "No. But there was talk that Maija had come back to take revenge on the watchman and the matron."

Jessica feels her pulse accelerate. "Take revenge for what?"

A look of amusement replaces the solemnity on Astrid's face. "I don't know, Jessica. I'm sure the orphanage wasn't the nicest place, but speculating about ancient history has never interested me, and I'm not going to start worrying about it now either."

Jessica sighs and stands. The toolshed door is closed. For a moment Jessica burns with the desire to ask Astrid what business Karlsson might have in the shed and if she knows he's snooping around in there. But it's not in her interests right now to draw attention to where she herself is headed: she's going to have to see with her own eyes what's inside the shed.

And then Astrid asks a question: "Why did they find your scarf at the shore?"

Jessica shifts her eyes from the window back to her proprietress.

"I was there when they found it," Astrid continues seriously. "Johan asked if I knew anyone who had a scarf like that. I couldn't start lying."

Jessica shrugs. "I went for a walk up there last night," she says, not bothering to register Astrid's reaction. Instead Jessica takes a step toward the window. She will wait until nightfall and investigate that damn toolshed when there is no one around to see. She should have no trouble locating the key, if the archipelago's very own Sherlock Holmes leaves it in the place where he found it a moment ago.

The only problem is the motion sensor that bathes the yard in light the second anyone approaches the villa.

"Thank you, Astrid. I think I'm going to go get some exercise."

"Fresh air is good in your condition," Astrid says as Jessica passes the desk on her way to the door.

"What do you mean?"

A warm glow emanates from Astrid's face. She stands and starts walking toward Jessica in her red wool socks. Up close, the scaly skin looks like it has been painfully burned, as if flames scorched her torso up to her throat and jawline. What sort of accident could have caused such damage?

"Or am I mistaken?" Astrid stops in front of Jessica, places her fingers tenderly on Jessica's belly. "No, no, I'm not. I have an eye for these things."

Jessica looks at the old woman's blue eyes and gray hair, then lowers her gaze to the veiny hands, the fingertips on her stomach. Feels the hum in her ears, the beat of her heart in her breast.

"What the hell—"

"Everything's fine, my dear child."

42

JESSICA PUSHES THE door open and heads toward the forest. She hears herself panting; her nose catches the dank sighs of spring from the surrounding forest. It feels like the moisture that lives in the trees' leafless branches has condensed on her skin in a cold compress.

Suddenly it all makes sense. Goddamn it all to hell!

The churning lump she feels in her belly in the mornings, the nauseous sensation that reaches up into her throat. Her senses sharpened to the extreme. The crippling exhaustion and the mood swings, and then her appetite, which has increased to a level she has never experienced before. And above all: Jessica understands that, deep down, she has known the whole time. That's why she called the girl on the dock sweetheart and the girl called her Mommy. That's why the night before she was overwhelmed by the experience that something profound was taking place, that she had just reached the biggest turning point in her life.

Jessica isn't sure whether Astrid called after her; all she hears is her pulse, her heavy breathing, and the twigs crunching underfoot as she steps from the road into the woods. She feels the soil squelch under her tennis shoes, dampening her socks. She pushes low-hanging boughs out of her way until eventually coming to a rest in a small glade split by a toppled tree. She's as short of breath as if she'd just gone for a long, sweaty run.

If it's true . . . No, it must be true. Of course it is. Jessica knows it's true and can't stop wondering how she wouldn't let herself admit it to herself earlier.

Tears well up in her eyes. She gropes at the trunk of the fallen tree for support; its stout boughs hold it a meter and a half above ground level. She seats herself on the trunk and lets the tears come. She doesn't want this; she never has. She wishes it weren't true but knows denying it is pointless.

The father is Frank. There has been no one but Frank.

Jessica sobs and lowers her face into her hands.

Frank, who pressed Jessica's service weapon to his temple in the elevator on Töölönkatu the night they made passionate love in her studio apartment. She never got to know Frank properly. Jessica thinks about the child, who will be born without a father. A father who was a former soldier, a sober small-time crook who blew his brains out against the elevator walls. The child whose mother will be a mentally ill, impulsive, cynical hermit who long ago stabbed a man to death with a serrated knife. The child who in all likelihood will inherent the schizophrenia that runs through the maternal line. The child whose mother tossed back schedule III sedatives by the fistful when she was pregnant and brooded over suicide on this accursed island, to which death inevitably found its way. Jessica roars out in pain.

She dries her eyes on the end of her sleeve and looks up at the sky. The tops of the trees bend lazily in time to the wind, and a bird sings somewhere in their shelter.

Jessica doesn't want a child. She's not one of those women who have dreamed of motherhood and want to dedicate themselves and their time to raising one.

But maybe the universe has made that decision for her.

If she decides to keep the child, everything will be much more difficult, no doubt, but perhaps also clearer.

And if that's the case, Jessica can no longer die on this island.

That option was a luxury that vanished instantly in the face of this new, earthshaking knowledge.

If she keeps the child.

She must leap into the unknown, without any chance to back out.

Amid the uncertainty and swelling panic, Jessica feels something she has never experienced before. It's a sort of clear conception of the future, of the opportunities and above all the responsibility fate has given her to bear.

She must leave this island tonight.

Suddenly Jessica feels a cold breath tickle her earlobe. She turns around and sees a little girl standing below the rock, at the roadside, walking slowly northward. Her blue coat flaps in the wind; her little boots are as wet as Jessica's shoes.

"Where are you going, sweetheart?" Jessica says softly.

Come with me, Mommy. I want to show it to you before you leave, the girl whispers, and then her contours dissipate in the wind. The bird that broke off to hear Maija's words bursts back into song.

"Show me what?"

My room, the voice says, even though the girl herself has vanished, becoming one with the gloomy conifers.

43

THE WHITE BUILDING rises, imposing, against the gray sky.

Jessica casts a rapid glance over at the dock, at the place where Elisabeth's body was found that morning. Three bodies in the exact same spot, even though nearly forty years have passed between the incidents. It's no wonder the locals are spooked.

Jessica advances toward the middle of the symmetrical building, where a few uneven stone stairs lead to a heavy-looking wooden door. Jessica climbs the stairs, reaches for the handle, and tries the door. It's locked and presumably very difficult to break down, even after all the years of being allowed to rot in peace.

Jessica takes a few steps backward and looks at the shattered windows, tinted gray by dust. The stone foundation is high enough that she can't see into the rooms, even on her tiptoes. But Maija lived in one of those rooms long ago. She can picture the girl climbing out of bed as the hour approaches two in the morning, opening the window, placing the ball of her little foot on the widest lip of the stone foundation, and then dropping the final meter to the strip of lawn that once surrounded the building. Maija must have known how to do it as quietly as a mouse, like an agile little cat whose comings and goings are undetected.

And if Maija managed to climb out the window and back in as a little girl, Jessica ought to be able to do so too, damn it. Jessica eyes the windows and decides the one just to the right of the entrance is the most badly damaged and perhaps the easiest place to break in without causing needless damage to the old building.

Jessica places the tip of her shoe on the stone foundation and springs up. She grabs the peeling window frame and, despite her precarious hold, maintains her balance. At the bottom of the windowpane there's a nearly perfectly triangular hole, and Jessica thrusts her wrist through to reach for the handle on the inside. She feels the moldy curtain, clammy from the damp, brush against the back of her hand, the rusty metal at her fingertips. The handle turns, and Jessica ducks out from under the window as it opens on its squeaking hinges. Then she presses her palms to the sill and heaves herself in.

Jessica pushes the curtains aside, lowers her feet to the desk under the window, and scans the room, which is maybe fifteen square meters in size. A faded landscape depicting broad fields hangs on the wall; there's a chair under the desk. A narrow metal bed stands to the right of the door. The rooms have no doubt been refurbished at least once since 1946, but an eerie timelessness marks Smörregård Children's Home. Jessica drops to the floor and stands there in the middle of the room. She thinks about Armas and how he said he had listened to Elisabeth and Hamhock with his ear to the floor. Jessica thrusts the bed aside; paint that has sloughed from the ceiling crunches underfoot. If there was once a hollow wall behind Armas' bed, it has now been filled, and a white wooden baseboard has been nailed in place. Presumably, or at least hopefully, the insulation has been updated.

Jessica opens the door to the corridor and warily steps out, allowing her feet to feel the way forward. The corridor is surprisingly wide and tall, at least compared with the impression made by the building's facade, and there are six doors on the side facing the sea and four on the side facing the woods. Each door bears a number. Instead of being identified by coldly bureaucratic figures, the rooms of an orphanage could, Jessica supposes, be labeled in a less institutional fashion—with, for instance, the children's names, or even animals: moose, bear, fox. Anything but numbers.

The bathroom door at the end of the hall is open. Across from the front entrance stands the staff cubicle, which at some point must have functioned as the night watchman's post. The general impression of the former orphanage's floor plan is one of an army barracks.

Jessica advances down the hall, passes room 5, which according to Armas' account was Elisabeth's. She continues to room 6, where the words STAFF ONLY have been screwed in at eye level. Jessica finds herself holding her breath, as if a booby trap is lurking on the other side, then opens the door and steps in.

Unlike in Armas' room, no attempt has been made to decorate this room with landscapes or flowered curtains. In its asceticism, it is surprisingly unhomey, and Jessica has a hard time understanding how anyone would have ever wanted to stay in it. Maija, or any other child after her.

I don't think anything has been done to it, the voice says, and Jessica feels a cold damp enter the room, accompanied by the girl's words.

"What do you mean?" Jessica asks, but then she understands. This was what Åke had said: *No one else was ever assigned to room six; it was preserved as some sort of chamber of horrors.*

Jessica clears her throat by coughing quietly into her fist and advances into the room. The more she thinks about it, the more obvious it is. The paint on the walls and ceiling is peeling badly; the whiff of mold is more pungent than in room 4. The room is presumably in the exact same condition as it was when Maija vanished. Jessica pulls the chair out from under the desk, tests it with her foot to make sure it can take her weight, and sits down to scan Maija's little cubbyhole as it bathes in wan natural light. There are mouse droppings on the floor; spiders have spun their webs in every corner. So much dust covers the surfaces that cleaning the room would demand determination and a powerful industrial vacuum.

Jessica turns to look out the dirty but unbroken window. From this vantage point, the dock is hidden behind the dilapidated boathouses. If Maija had really waited for her father, and if the boathouses stood there in the 1940s—which, based on their derelict state, they did—there was no way she would have seen her father's arrival from the room; she would have had to wait at the dock. Jessica feels a pang in her heart as she imagines the girl in this bleak room, standing watch at the window. Counting the hours. Climbing out the window hopefully, only to be disappointed again and again. Waking again the next morning in her grim cell.

"OK, I've seen it now," Jessica whispers, but for some reason she feels the need to linger. As if there is something more, something Maija wants to show her. "Or have I? What is it I'm not seeing, Maija?" Jessica asks, but the girl doesn't reply, although Jessica can still sense her presence in the room. Maija doesn't answer because she can't. Because Maija can't tell Jessica anything that Jessica doesn't already know.

Think, Jessica.

Jessica thinks about Elisabeth, Armas, and all the others who once lived at the orphanage. Now, sitting here in Maija's room, Jessica understands how incredible it is that Armas actually knew Maija back in the day. Just as it seems incredible that some elderly people once witnessed the Second World War. Ate sausage at the Helsinki Olympics. Met the legendary President Kekkonen.

In no time at all, Maija's story has captivated Jessica, and she's not the least bit surprised it has become a local legend. Maybe Armas can tell her more about the birds of spring and the letter Maija received. Jessica is sure she hasn't known to ask all the right questions.

Armas. Jessica silently repeats the name to herself and looks up at the ceiling. If the wall in Armas' room was hollow, maybe . . .

Jessica doesn't wait for the impulse to refine itself into a finished idea but moves the chair aside, walks over to Maija's bed, and pushes it a meter toward the window. The dragging sound echoes in the corridor, but there isn't a single guard or matron around to hear. Jessica kneels next to the wall, knocks at the base of it, and discovers it's hollow, or at least incredibly poorly insulated. The baseboard is loose; she pulls it off with one effortless yank. Her heart pounds as she thrusts a hand into the narrow gap between the plank floor and the wall. Nevertheless, her fingers don't strike on anything inside the wall, and her enthusiasm gradually turns to disbelieving disappointment.

Jessica rises to her feet and kicks at the wall plaster with the tip of her shoe. Motes of dust puff into the air, tickling her nose. She lies on her belly on the floor to explore the hole created by the tip of her shoe, but there's nothing hidden inside the wall. Damn it, she has made a mess of Maija's room for no reason, simply because she believed she would find something that might help her solve . . . Solve what? Maija's disappearance almost eight decades ago? Jessica feels ridiculous.

She's just pushing herself back up when she sees something on the wooden slats beneath the bed. She considers crawling under the bed, but then decides to stand and flip it over on its side.

Jessica pushes the bed onto its side in the middle of the room and kneels to read the writing on the bottom. The text is faded but still distinct on the brittle slats, which are white with mold.

Verinsuude veniaarteede venode velontade venatakade
vesässämetde venanmude veenmuotoisde vevenkide
vessävierede.

The handwriting is clearly a child's, although it's unclear how old it is. But if Jessica's intuition is right, if the room has been left untouched all these years, the words might well be Maija's.

Jessica stares at the writing. At first glance, it looks like some language related to Finnish, like Estonian or Sami, but all the words begin with "ve" and end with "de."

Vedekieli! Jessica remembers speaking and writing it herself as a child. It was pretty easy to get the hang of, and grown-ups often didn't have a clue how to decipher this simple code. Jessica pulls her notebook from her pocket, flips to a blank page, and writes down the words.

Verinsuude . . . How did it go again? Get rid of the "ve" and the "de" . . . *Rinsuu.* Reverse the order of the syllables: *suurin.* "Biggest." Jessica jots down the translated text, tongue lodged firmly in her cheek. *My treasure. My biggest treasure . . . is in the woods behind the orphanage next to the egg . . . shaped rock.* Jessica rushes out into the corridor, notebook in hand, and hurries to the front door. The door opens easily with a twist of the handle, and she steps back out into the fresh air; breathing it feels heavenly after the few minutes she spent in the moldy orphanage.

Jessica circles the building, spots a tool rack in the corner closest to the road, and on a whim grabs a badly rusted spade. She hugs the building toward the backyard. She sees a few battered trash cans, a metal barrel, rusted bicycles, and an ancient push mower. A jumble of things has been piled against the wall of the orphanage: fuel canisters, blue plastic crates, a chicken coop. The sagging gutters reach groundward, and the recent rain burbles along the stone foundation. The dense and surprisingly tall forest rustles ominously behind the building.

In the woods behind the orphanage next to the egg . . . shaped rock.

The old orphanage is tens of meters long, but for some reason

Jessica is certain Maija has hidden her treasure somewhere around the building's midpoint so it would be easy to find later. Jessica walks halfway down the building, then dives into the woods. She advances slowly so she won't miss the rock. In the end, she doesn't even know what size it is: maybe the stone is not only egg shaped but also egg sized. She hears a bird croak at the crown of a spruce, and then the air is split by the flap of wings. The heavy branches darken the sky. On this part of the island, nature feels desolate and unfriendly.

Jessica keeps going deeper into the woods, pushes aside branches, and is thinking there's no way the rock can be this far from the building when she suddenly notices a mossy, knee-high stone that truly resembles a bird's egg embedded in the ground. Jessica squats down next to it. There's a dip in the ground next to the rock. Without further ado, Jessica stands, strikes the spade through the moss and into the dirt: perhaps the frost that not long ago kept the soil captive has loosened its grip, and the shovel sinks relatively easily into the coarse substrate. Jessica digs the dirt out from around the rock, but all the tip of the spade hits is soil and gravel. Suddenly she's sure someone made it here before her. Of course. She was naive to think she would be the first explorer to find the treasure map and break the code revealing the location. That the coordinates of the treasure—whatever it is—would have remained hidden from other eyes over the course of the seventy-plus years the bed has stood in Maija's former room for any onlookers to gawk at.

Jessica wipes the sweat from her brow and becomes aware of a strange sensation. She is standing in the middle of a dense forest a hundred yards from the abandoned orphanage, and for some reason she has the distinct impression someone is watching her from behind the trees or from high up in them.

She releases the spade, and it drops at her feet. She has grown used to fearing unknown threats. But this time the fear is different.

Maybe that's because of the responsibility, because now she has to protect not only herself but also the new life growing inside her.

Jessica starts walking toward the southern shore.

She feels fear gnaw at her chest. Maybe no one found the coordinates on the bottom of Maija's bed after all.

Maybe Maija herself truly has come back to retrieve her treasure.

44

As Jessica hurries back to the villa, everything looks both the same and yet different. Something about the surrounding terrain, the dripping branches, and the leafless bushes sprouting from the ground has changed. Jessica smells, sees, and hears everything around her in a different way than before: it's as if she has replaced everything old and stale with something new and fresh, deep despair with pure curiosity. Everything is going to have to be different from this moment on.

When she reaches the guesthouse, Jessica sees Åke trudging from the shore to the villa, head hanging.

Åke doesn't notice Jessica until she's standing at the edge of the lawn. Then he raises a hand and starts slowly toddling toward her. The hems of his coat flap in the gusting wind.

"Did you have a nice walk?" he asks.

Jessica is used to seeing a light in his gentle eyes, but now his gaze is void of hope.

"I understand why you came back, Åke. There's something captivating about this island," Jessica says. "How are you?"

Åke shrugs. "First one of the guests dies under mysterious circumstances, and now Johan is going around harassing the ones who are still alive and trying to recover from their shock," he says, then looks as if he wishes he could immediately take it back. "Oh shit. I'm sorry. That sounded crazy. *Still* alive. That's not how I meant it."

Jessica has the sense that there's a lot of truth in Åke's slip of the tongue. "Do you believe someone else is in danger?" she asks.

Åke eyes Jessica for a moment, as if deciding whether it makes sense to answer the question. He must know about the scarf found at the shore and the fact that Jessica might, in theory, be the guilty party, just as much as anyone else who was on the island last night.

And then he pinches his lips together and shakes his head. The wind makes his reddish beard hairs shiver as if an electric current is running through them. "No, I don't think so. There's no need to pack your bags—"

"I don't think I could even if I wanted to," Jessica says.

Åke looks at her, then apparently gathers her meaning and nods apologetically. "Listen. Astrid decided that we're not going to charge you for your stay here."

"So I'd stay with you for three weeks for free?" Jessica says, although she knows she no longer will be staying that long, under any circumstances. Not even if Elisabeth's murder is solved today. Her personal situation has radically changed, and she can no longer just sit in place and wait.

"It's the least we—," Åke says, lips pursed.

But Jessica cuts him off. "Don't be silly."

Suddenly the photos she took earlier pop into her head. Now she has plenty of time to dig into the backgrounds of all the guests, see whether something interesting might turn up. She could get pretty far in her investigations by using the internet (if it worked, that is), but maybe if she dared ask Yusuf or Rasmus for help . . .

"What's your personal opinion?" Åke says, rubbing his neck. "You're a professional, so you must have some thoughts about what happened."

Jessica licks her lips and considers whether it's wise to speculate on the matter with Åke. But it probably can't do any harm, as long as no one gets the impression Jessica is conducting her own unofficial investigation here on the island.

"It's a pretty unusual case, I have to admit. I personally wouldn't exclude the possibility that some outsider came to the island last night." Jessica instinctively glances over her shoulder at the second-story window where she thought she caught a glimpse of someone the day before.

Åke looks doubtful; he clearly isn't convinced.

"You didn't tell me the whole story last night by the fire," Jessica says. "Astrid just filled in the blanks."

Åke sighs deeply and lowers his gaze to the tips of his shoes. "I didn't want to scare you," Åke says quietly, then briefly closes his mournful eyes. "The fact that people have died at that same spot before . . . It's really damn weird. Creepy."

"Do you remember those cases? Were you living on the island then?"

Åke nods. "Yes. And so was Johan. At the time of both the night watchman's and the orphanage director's deaths."

"How old—"

"Eleven when Martin Hedblom, the night watchman, was found dead in 1982. The second incident happened in 1985."

"Did the police talk to you at the—"

But just then Jessica sees Johan Karlsson open the front door of the villa and stand at the top of the stairs, hands on his hips, like the sheriff from some Sergio Leone Western.

"Enjoy the spring weather while you can," Karlsson calls out stonily. "There's going to be a big storm hitting this afternoon, and it's not going to pass right away."

"Let's talk more later," Jessica says to Åke, then walks toward the converted barn.

"Jessica," Åke calls after her, and Jessica turns around. "We'd like all the guests to come to the dining room at eleven thirty. We're going to be holding a little information session."

45

JESSICA STUDIES HER naked torso in the mirror: the small, round breasts, the stomach that appears to bulge the tiniest bit. She probes the area around her abdomen with her fingers, turns to the side, presses her palms to her belly. The more she looks at herself and her rounded stomach, the surer she is. How could Astrid have noticed something so intimate, something that hadn't even occurred to Jessica herself, despite the fact that it involves her own body and the life gradually developing inside it? Obviously, Astrid's eye is trained to detect such matters: for decades, it was her job to look after pregnant women, women giving birth. A slew of questions swarms through Jessica's mind. For instance, how the heavy medication of recent weeks has impacted the development of the fetus.

She sits down on the toilet, prescription vial in one hand and phone in the other. There's no indication of the 4G network, but it looks like there's one bar of signal strength. She brings up *Psychiatrist Tuula* from her address book and raises the phone to her ear. *The person you are trying to reach is currently unavailable.* Jessica presses the phone to her chest and considers other options. She has decided she can't stand the uncertainty a single minute longer.

Jessica selects another number from her address book, raises the phone to her ear, and as it rings a few times already regrets her decision.

Just as she is hanging up, a flat, emotionless female voice answers: "This is a surprise, Niemi."

Jessica hesitates before asking: "Do you have a minute?"

The line goes silent, and for a moment Jessica is afraid the call was dropped. "I suppose the question is more whether you do. I understand you've had a lot going on recently." The woman laughs drily, but there's no malice in the voice. Jessica has known Medical Examiner Sissi Sarvilinna for so many years that she has developed a sense of Sarvilinna's inner world and the black humor that tinges it.

"So you've seen it too," Jessica whispers.

"The video? Of course. But I know you don't go around kicking people for no reason. And when you take a closer look at that corpulent super, it's unlikely you did it out of love. You deserve better, Niemi."

"Can I ask you a question?"

"I've never heard you ask for permission before," Sarvilinna answers at the other end of the line.

"It's about benzodiazepines . . ."

"Wait a second. Does this have something to do with the Lindeman case? Because I understood for the time being you aren't—"

Jessica sighs deeply. "No, it doesn't. I'm asking in a personal capacity."

Jessica doesn't want to complicate things by lying. Telling the truth could not, she supposes, make things any more difficult than they already are. So she takes a deep breath and says: "I've been taking Xanor lately for anxiety and trouble sleeping—"

"Look, I don't know where this conversation is headed, but I have no intention of prescribing you drugs that work on the central nervous system. You'd better speak with the doctor who originally—"

"That's not what this is about."

A few seconds of absolute silence follow.

"What is it about, then?"

"I think I might be pregnant," Jessica says, then closes her eyes. It feels absurd that the pathologist with antipathetic tendencies is the first person Jessica is telling what is perhaps the biggest news of her life to date. It ought to be someone totally different. But for some reason, that someone is the last person in the world Jessica wants to tell right now.

"I see," Sarvilinna says. There's a metallic crash in the background.

"Is it possible the medication has harmed the fetus?" Jessica asks.

The silence at the other end of the line is so deafening that Jessica's palms start to sweat out of apprehension.

"How far along is the pregnancy?" Sarvilinna then asks.

"I'd say maybe sixteen, seventeen weeks." Another nerve-racking silence. "Hello?" Sarvilinna says something, but she's breaking up. "What? I didn't catch that."

"I don't believe any harm should have happened yet as long as you stop taking the medication immediately. If used regularly, benzodiazepinium salts are especially harmful during late pregnancy, because their use can lead to withdrawal symptoms in the newborn, or in the worst case to respiratory depression . . ."

"OK." Jessica wipes the tears from her cheeks. "So as long as I stop immediately, everything should be fine?"

"I would venture to say so," Sarvilinna says.

"Thank you. And please don't tell anyone about this," Jessica says, voice quivering. "About the drugs or the pregnancy."

"Wait a second," Sarvilinna says, and Jessica can hear her move away from the phone's microphone. "Hey, Risto. Jessica Niemi is pregnant. Right, the detective. Can you believe it?"

Jessica's heart skips a beat, and a moment later she hears Sarvilinna's voice.

"Sorry, Niemi. I just had to bare my heart to Risto here, who is lying on my table. But don't worry—he's dead. There was a stabbing in Munkkiniemi last night and—"

"You're a mess, Sarvilinna," Jessica says, and sighs. "But thanks."

THE WHITE PILLS swirl away into the depths of the sewer. Jessica closes the toilet lid and goes back into her room, where she sits on her bed and opens her laptop. The wireless internet promised on the Villa Smörregård website barely works, and even simple searches often end in a dropped connection. The internet is going to be of little to no use. Jessica zooms in on the photos she took with her phone in Astrid's office and makes a note of the other guests' information on the digital sticky note she opened at the edge of the screen.

Armas Kustaa Pohjanpalo, born 1936

Elisabeth Maria Theresa Salmi, born 1933

Eila Raili Sinikka Kantelinen, born 1935

Under them, she writes the name Elsa Lehtinen, aka Hamhock, who died in 1994, even though she knows nothing else about the woman.

Then it's the Swedish couple's turn:

Niklas Herbert Steiner, born 1969

Pernilla Steiner, born 1972

Checkout for the birds of spring has been noted as Sunday, March 22—in other words, tomorrow—while Niklas and Pernilla Steiner are not planning on moving on until Monday. Jessica shuts her eyes and tries to feel for any details about the Swedish couple. They appear to be a very ordinary middle-aged couple; Jessica has noted nothing strange about their behavior. The woman was crying inconsolably that morning, but is that so odd? After all, there was an unexpected death on the guesthouse property just a moment before. That alone would suffice to explain her emotional reaction, even though she didn't personally know the victim. Or did she? Unlikely. It would have come out somehow when they were all having dinner at the same time in the dining room. Of course, it's possible that after Jessica's exit, Astrid carried out her plan to combine tables and

Elisabeth managed to infuriate the couple so thoroughly that one of them decided to drown her that night. Hard to believe.

Armas Pohjanpalo. Jessica zooms in on the photocopy of his passport, studies the bony cheeks and furrowed brow. Is Armas' story credible? And if it is, why would he want to share his observations with Jessica and no one else? Furthermore, it's hard to understand why, after all these years, Armas has continued to participate in these annual reunions if he doesn't particularly care for his fellow orphans' company. Why has he wanted to pal around with his tormentors when he could have easily refused to be involved and lived his own life?

Jessica lifts her finger from the screen of her phone, and the photo returns to normal size. She swipes the screen a few times to browse through the photographs in case she missed something. The names of the guests are archived in the binder in reverse order of arrival: Pohjanpalo, Salmi, Kantelinen, Steiner, Steiner, Niemi . . .

And then Jessica's eyes strike on something: at the lower left corner of the shot of her photocopied passport and information, she can see another guest's documents. All that's visible is the bottom of an unknown passport and the right side of a completed form. The animals in the design indicate that the passport belongs to a Finn. The signature is impossible to decipher, and the name and the birth date are outside the edges of the picture. But whoever the guest is, they registered at the guesthouse the same day Jessica did—in other words, this past Monday, March 16.

Then Jessica remembers what she saw when she was standing outside yesterday: a curtain swaying at an upstairs window, and a dark figure moving behind it.

This whole time, a seventh guest has been staying at Smörregård.

46

Superintendent Helena Lappi, head of the Helsinki Police Violent Crimes Unit, is tapping her fingers against her desk and biting down firmly on her pencil, which has begun to resemble a beaver-gnawed log. But once again there is a weighty reason for this stress-releasing behavior. An hour earlier, the NBI office that works with the Ahvenanmaa authorities left a message requesting that she call them, which Hellu promptly did. A superintendent of the *Ålands Polismyndighet* named Maria Forsius came on the line, requesting information on a detective working in Helena Lappi's unit, a certain Jessica Niemi.

Helena's jaws' grip on the pencil tightens; her teeth sink more deeply into the wood, and then retract, seeking out a spot where there's something left to chew.

What the hell has Niemi gotten herself mixed up in this time? By Hellu's orders, Jessica was on a mandatory leave that would last at least until the preliminary investigation into the accusations of trespassing and assault was brought to its conclusion and delivered to the prosecutor. Based on the call that just ended, Niemi is in Ahvenanmaa, where she has apparently caused some sort of mess; there's no other reason those Swedes would be calling and asking about her! Damn Niemi.

Hellu can't help but berate herself: maybe she approached the whole matter too optimistically from the start, sweeping Jessica's problems under the rug and trying to square her unstable detective sergeant with a highly disciplined organization that lived and breathed rules and order. Hellu has been acting like a toddler who has decided to shove a star-shaped block through a round hole. Damn it! Yes, after a rough start, she learned to like Jessica and greatly appreciates her uncompromising professionalism. But the risks Hellu identified only a few months ago and decided in spite of everything to ignore have now been realized in perhaps the worst possible way. Jessica Niemi is clearly no longer in control of herself, and in recent months she has spiraled further and further into her shadowy personal reality, a place of horrors no outsider can even imagine.

No, Hellu doesn't know what has happened in Ahvenanmaa, but Jessica Niemi cannot be allowed to cause the unit further harm. The video spreading like wildfire on YouTube already means more than enough damage to the reputation of the entire institution, and if Niemi decided to beat up some intoxicated bum pincher in downtown Maarianhamina, Hellu hopes no one video-recorded her in the act.

Goddamn it. Hellu lets her head sink back against her chair and stares straight up at the ceiling so long that the glowing fluorescent lamps sear dark afterimages against her field of vision.

"You wanted to see me, Hellu?" The tall man's voice is low, his articulation clear.

Hellu blinks. "Thank you. Have a seat."

The man lets out a nervous whistle and does as ordered.

Detective Sergeant Jami Harjula, who is seating himself on the other side of her desk, is a tall, gangly man with analytical but uncertain eyes gazing out from the middle of his pointy face. Harjula is a good police officer but less popular among the detectives than, say, Jessica or Yusuf, both of whom have the kind of charisma and social instincts Harjula can only dream of. In many ways he is a bystander, and for the most part this is his own fault. Harjula is a better friend to the organization than are any of his colleagues and believes he's doing the right thing when the system and justice win. He is by no means a malicious or mean person, but he is a typical punctilious bureaucrat whose actions are directed by an invisible network of rules and regulations. Like Hellu herself, Harjula would probably be most in his element in some Cold War–era intelligence organization, the red rubber stamp in his hand rejecting travel document applications and informing on neighbors caught watching the movies of Kurt Maetzig. And it's exactly because of his apparent outsider status and unyielding convictions that Hellu has once more decided to use him as her personal periscope, through which she can, perhaps, peer over the fence to the other side.

"Is the Lindeman case ready for the prosecutor?" Hellu says, to warm up her subordinate before revealing her actual agenda.

"Yes," Harjula replies, then coughs into his fist, which looks like an oversized extension of his narrow and surprisingly long wrist. "Yusuf wants to continue questioning the girl, though."

"What for?" Hellu asks. "Isn't the case clear?"

Harjula shrugs.

"OK, I'll ask Yusuf myself," Hellu says.

Harjula nods, then lowers his hands to rest on the adjustable armrests of his chair.

"Listen, Harjula. I've been thinking I'd like to give you more responsibility from here on out. You've earned your stripes, and if you can just commit to continue training yourself, I believe a pretty nice path can gradually unfold for you here. There are going to be some jobs opening up in the autumn."

An almost embarrassed smile spreads across Harjula's face. "Thank you. I appreciate the—"

Hellu cuts him off. "I trust you. I know you're capable of handling things tactfully."

"What are we talking about now?"

"Niemi."

"Jessica?" Harjula asks. "Is this about that video?"

Hellu shakes her head. "No, but let's just say that because of that video I have to take action. You understand, don't you?"

"Maybe."

"I received a phone call today from the Ahvenanmaa police. They asked if Niemi is on duty, and I was forced to reveal how things stand. The woman I spoke to mentioned some active investigation but refused to divulge any details at this point. She promised to get back to me."

"What the—"

"Tell me about it. I tried to call Niemi, but . . . Well. I'm sure you can guess."

Harjula eyes Hellu and suddenly looks somehow enlightened. "You want me to find out what's going on?"

Hellu nods. "Discreetly."

"I guess calling Maarianhamina isn't very discreet." Jami Harjula stands and buttons his blazer.

"No," Hellu says, and shifts her gaze to the glass wall of her office and the corridor beyond. Yusuf and Rasmus are pulling on their coats at the door to the elevators. "But I'm pretty sure there's information to be had on Niemi's movements here at headquarters too. If you only know where to look."

47

YUSUF TAKES OFF his coat and scoots closer to the wall. The booth's high-backed benches are covered in crimson velvet, and music that can be interpreted as Nepalese blasts from the speakers as the mildly pungent smell of cumin wafts through the air. Yusuf looks at the fingers drumming nervously against the table, which belong to the unit's sole civilian investigator, Rasmus Susikoski. Between them stands the wooden cube etched with their order number that they received at the counter.

"Rasse, has it ever occurred to you that since they bring the food to the tables, they could probably take the orders at the tables too?" Yusuf says, shoving his wallet into his pocket.

"Yeah, well," Rasmus says, slowly lowering his hands under the table. "Staff is expensive."

"Yup. That busboy probably earns more than we do." Yusuf shakes his head. "We'll see if this place is still around by summer."

"Because of the COVID restrictions?"

Yusuf nods and looks up at the fat ventilation ducts running along the ceiling; no attempt has been made to disguise them. They make the place look like a space station and vaguely call to mind impressions of Sigourney Weaver running from a bloodthirsty creature. Despite this, the restaurant is cozy, and the energetic and friendly Nepalese staff provides good service. Unfortunately the place just opened a week ago—in other words, at the worst possible time, just as the nationwide restrictions on restaurants were coming into force.

"It's none of my business," Yusuf says after a moment's silence, then smiles tentatively. "But Tanja said you'd messaged her friend."

Rasmus' face flushes beet red, and he turns toward the clatter in the kitchen.

"Sorry, I'm not trying to be nosy. It's just . . . When you didn't show up for that date in February, I figured that was it."

"We've been texting," Rasmus says. His voice has become stuffy, as if he is allergic to the subject. And in a way, he probably is.

"Right on." Yusuf takes a big swig of the sugar-free lemon soda he was given at the counter when he ordered. He truly has no intention of teasing Rasmus about the subject; he brought it up to encourage Rasmus to keep on trucking. Until now, Rasmus has had pretty bad luck when it comes to anything even remotely involving the opposite sex, which is why his unexpectedly standing everyone up on the double date Yusuf and Tanja set up was so incomprehensible. Rasmus had his reasons, no doubt, but Yusuf knows Rasmus is his own worst enemy in this regard. Rasmus' social misfortunes are presumably some sort of cycle, emotional knot, or endless labyrinth that requires him to first clean the slate and start over in order to find his way out. Maybe that's exactly what he's done.

"How are you and Tanja doing?"

Yusuf swishes the soda around in his mouth and considers his answer.

Tanja is fun, smart, and cute, and everything works as it should in the bedroom. Even so, their dating, which appears to be slipping toward something more serious—exchanging keys, toothbrushes in bathrooms, shared Netflix log-ins, even deleting Tinder—somehow feels like a compromise to Yusuf. Since the most intense initial infatuation, Yusuf has started to wonder whether he's ready for a new relationship yet—despite the fact that after the split with Anna, he'd been thinking his next serious relationship would finally be the one that meant kids, a Labrador retriever, and a house in Sipoo. He knows it's not smart to put the cart before the horse, that things will roll along on their own momentum, but for some reason he doesn't see the future as rosily as one might expect from someone who has just fallen in love. He ought to be, he supposes, blinded by love, but he sees everything too clearly. He tries to picture himself growing old with Tanja, but the harder he does, the more unnatural the arrangement seems.

"Really well," Yusuf says, handing Rasmus a set of utensils wrapped in a napkin.

Their server appears at their table, sets metal platters down in front of them, wishes them a nice lunch, and vanishes into the kitchen with the wooden cube. The aroma rising from the butter chicken, fragrant rice, and naan is heavenly, and Yusuf decides right then and there that he will leave a tip when they're done eating.

Yusuf's thoughts are cut off by the sound of his phone ringing. When he sees who it is, he can feel excitement flare up inside him. He hasn't heard from Jessica in over a week, ever since she kissed him at her apartment and then ordered him to leave. But was something about that moment left unfinished? Yusuf notices his hands shaking, as if he's been waiting for Jessica to call this whole time.

Yusuf clears his throat and raises his phone to his ear.

48

THE WIND HAS finally abated. Rasmus Susikoski glances over his shoulder as he steps out of the restaurant and almost walks headfirst into the glass door slamming shut in Yusuf's wake.

"Dang, Yusuf," he says, despite managing to avoid hitting his forehead on the surprisingly nimbly moving door. For a total introvert like Rasmus, the reaction is unusually forceful; as someone who avoids conflicts until the last, he generally does not make a fuss over injustices he suffers.

"Huh?"

"No, I just thought you were holding the door open for me," Rasmus says as they walk up Kronqvistinkuja and past the bureaucratic apparition known as the Scandic Pasila Hotel. But Rasmus' colleague doesn't appear to be listening, let alone apologetic. Ever since answering the phone, Yusuf has been strangely quiet and unsure. Even so, he hasn't commented on the call in any way, hasn't said who it was or what it was about. And Rasmus hasn't probed.

"Is everything OK?" Rasmus now asks. A streetcar clanks up, then makes a slow dive between massive pillars and under the buildings. The tram line that runs through an apartment building has amused Rasmus since that day years ago when he first arrived at police headquarters by streetcar. As if the city's architects had run out of space and they'd had to run the tracks through someone's living room.

"Yeah." Yusuf starts striding across the street, but then slows down. He has shoved his hands deep in the pockets of his long leather coat, as if they would take over if left to hang free and would force a cigarette between his lips. Rasmus has never had a nicotine addiction, but he does know something about the challenges created by compulsions.

"That was Jessica," Yusuf says.

"Oh," Rasmus says, surprised. "Where is she?"

"I don't know. And it doesn't matter. She asked me to look into a couple of things."

"What?"

"To check the backgrounds of a couple people, see what the system says. That's all. Maybe you can help."

"But for which case? Jessica isn't assigned to—"

"Rasmus," Yusuf says firmly, coming to a stop on the sidewalk. A big semi crawls past. "I really don't know. And no, Jessica is not on the job right now. But if Jessica calls and asks me for a little favor, especially a kind that isn't going to cause anyone any trouble if I do it, I'll have her back, anytime, anywhere."

"Got it," Rasmus says as they cross Pasilanraitio. Yusuf's answers don't slake Rasmus' thirst for information, but it would appear as if Jessica truly hasn't divulged anything more to Yusuf. At the moment, the unit is working on a preliminary investigation into Rolf Lindeman, suspected of killing a male relative, a case that seems so straightforward that at most there's some fine-tuning to be done before it's turned over to the prosecutor on Tuesday. Rasmus can't help dreaming about something more complicated, a real puzzler that would require serious brain work to solve. Who knows? Maybe that's exactly what Jessica has just offered them.

"Meet you in the small conference room in five," Yusuf says as he opens the staff door with his key card. "And Rasse, not a word about this to anyone."

———

FIVE MINUTES LATER, Rasmus has filled his thermos with fresh coffee and is nervously sitting in the cramped conference room at the end of the hall, fingers at his laptop keyboard and ready for action. Three of the six fluorescent tubes on the ceiling are out and have been for months. The room is rarely in use, because its size makes it unsuitable for meetings of the whole investigative team. And that's what makes it the perfect retreat when the hecticness of the open-plan office gets to be too much. Or when there's a need to review evidence, have a private conversation, or, as is the case now, convene without any extraneous ears listening in.

The door opens, and Yusuf glances around before he enters and shuts it behind him. He sets his laptop down on the table and raises the screen.

"It feels stupid sneaking around like this, but the deputy prosecutor and some other people are in Hellu's office right now . . . ," Yusuf says, pulls a blister pack from his pocket, and pops out a few pieces of nicotine-infused chewing gum.

"Who are we looking for?" Rasmus asks, rubbing his sweaty palms against the thighs of his worn jeans.

"Here's the list of names Jessica asked us to check."

Yusuf pushes his phone across the table. The message from Jessica is on the screen: eight names total.

"Full Social Security numbers."

"Yup. Only for the first six, though, two of whom appear to be Swedes," Yusuf stresses as he starts tapping at his laptop. "I'll take the first four. You take the Swedes and the last two."

"Astrid and Åke Nordin," Rasmus mutters softly. "Place of residence Smörregård, Ahvenanmaa."

"Scroll down," Yusuf says. "The name of their company is there too."

"Smörregård Experiences Limited," Rasmus says, brings up Google, and taps the name into the search field. "Industry: hospitality, founded in 1955. CEO Hans-Peter Nordin . . ."

"Hmm . . . not on the list."

"But Astrid Nordin is chair of the board of directors."

"Is Hans-Peter the same person as Åke?" Yusuf asks without looking up from his laptop.

"No, I don't think so." Rasmus goes back to the search engine, types in Smörregård + Åland, and presses Enter. His eyes strike on the second to top result, which is a link to an article published only a few hours before in the newspaper *Ålandstidningen*.

Elderly Woman Drowns at Smörregård

"Yusuf," Rasmus says, scrolling down the article.

"Wait a sec—let me check . . ."

"Someone died this morning at Smörregård."

Yusuf seems to be roused from his thoughts; he jumps nimbly from his chair and circles around to Rasmus' side of the table. Rasmus has clicked on the link, and they read the online article, which at least for now is only a paragraph in length.

"It's in Swedish . . ."

"C'mon, Rasse; I'm from Sipoo," Yusuf says. "A Black Finn who speaks Swedish." He chuckles. "An Ethiopian triple agent—that's what someone said once. To the wrong guy, though. I was forced to correct him."

"Smörregård appears to be an island . . ."

". . . where there's a guesthouse . . . ," Yusuf continues.

". . . owned by these Nordins," Rasmus concludes.

"Bingo." Yusuf digs his fingers into Rasmus' shoulders and squeezes them like a trained sports masseur. "That's where Jessica must be.

She wanted peace and quiet, to go somewhere where no one would think to look for her. I encouraged her, actually. I said Dubai, though, not some damn Smörregård."

"So Jessica is at this Smörregård?"

"And now someone drowned there. It's no coincidence she's asking us to check the system for information on the other guests and the owners."

Rasmus leans forward, and Yusuf releases his shoulders. "Jessica got her hands on the guest registrations. That's how she has the personal ID numbers," Rasmus says.

"For the guests. But not for this . . . Elsa Lehtinen."

Rasmus cracks his knuckles. Yusuf breaks into the perfect white-toothed smile that compels women to let him get away with a lot and is the envy of many a male colleague.

"Jessica's investigating a homicide," Yusuf says.

"The drowning?"

"No, Rasse. You're not listening. A homicide."

"How do you know it's a homicide?"

"From the fact that Jessica is investigating it." Yusuf pats Rasmus on the shoulder and returns to his chair on the other side of the table.

"But that's the job of the local police."

"I doubt Jessica trusts those yokels."

"Do you think—"

Just then the door flies open so fast that it startles Rasmus and Yusuf. They see a tall man standing there in the corridor, his huge shovellike hands rising to his hips. The light current of air wafting into the room sets the corners of the documents on the table fluttering.

"What are you guys doing hiding out in here?" Jami Harjula asks, leaning his full frame against the doorjamb.

"Making moonshine. Planning a revolution. What the fuck do you care?" Yusuf says, turning his laptop so Harjula can't see it.

Harjula bursts into scornful laughter, then eyes his fingernails as if to make sure they're properly filed. That's what Harjula's like: a pompous pedant whose heightened self-righteousness is constantly giving his fellow investigators gray hair. His shiny blue dress shirt looks like it has been ironed that morning, but the sleeves of the wool blazer are far too short for his long limbs.

"You sure are touchy," he says. "All I meant was, if you guys are meeting about Lindeman, it would be polite to keep me up to date."

Harjula steps into the room, leaving the door open behind him. Rasmus can hear the clack of Hellu's high heels recede down the hall and can't help but think she has just fired a torpedo and is now making herself scarce.

"Susikoski, of the two of you, you're the worse liar, so you tell me," Harjula says, coming to a stop at Rasmus' side.

But Rasmus has had plenty of time to bring up the medical examiner's report pertinent to the Lindeman case. He takes a deep breath, looks first at Yusuf and then at Harjula, who is staring coercively at him. "Well, the fact is—"

"Rasse, you don't have to tell Harjula a thing—"

But Rasmus continues confidently: "Yusuf is helping me make a profile for a dating service."

Jami Harjula looks dumbfounded, but after taking a few seconds to digest this information, he says: "Great."

Yusuf looks at his colleagues, his jaw hanging, then nods to confirm Rasmus' words.

"It would probably do me good too. Romance isn't exactly blossoming on the home front."

In an instant, Harjula has lost his defiant self-confidence and looks as if he's just divulged too much about himself. His large, now-restless hands dig deep into his trouser pockets, and his eyes flash with sadness, perhaps a stifled despair. Rasmus remembers Harjula's revelations about the degraded state of his marriage and can't help but feel sorry for his colleague; he seems so lost.

"All right. I'll catch you guys later." And with that, Jami Harjula shambles out, closing the door behind him.

49

IT'S ELEVEN THIRTY, and the wind that has been buffeting Smör-regård all morning has picked up. The tarp over the tractor trailer parked in front of the villa balloons into a sail and then deflates, as if it is a breathing creature. Jessica enters the dining room and sees a pot on the buffet; she'd caught the aroma of salmon soup wafting from under its lid when she stepped in through the front door. In addition to Astrid and Åke, the last still-living birds of spring, Armas and Eila, are present, as are the Swedish couple and of course Johan Karlsson. Unlike everyone else in the room, he hasn't chosen a seat for himself but stands at the window, hands on his hips. Jessica steps in and can't help but reflect that one of the guests is absent from this convocation: the one staying upstairs in room 21.

Jessica looks at Astrid; the old woman is stroking the white table-cloth with her fingertips, lost in thought. She knows who the mystery guest is but hasn't said a blessed word about their existence. Maybe there's some natural explanation, but Jessica can't ask without revealing that she was snooping through the files in Astrid's office.

"It looks like everyone is here," Astrid says, and stands. Her proud bearing has not slumped despite the day's setbacks. "Please help yourselves to lunch whenever you want," she says. "As you all know, one of our guests, and the longtime friend of many, Elisabeth Salmi, passed away last night at the northern shore of Smör-regård. This is incredibly shocking, and I'm very sorry you've had to witness such a tragedy in a place where you came seeking revitalization and an escape from everyday concerns instead of more worries."

Astrid pauses briefly to take a swig of water. Jessica looks at Åke, who is sitting at the table, hands crossed as if he's praying he'll wake up from his worst nightmare.

"Unfortunately, the way things stand, the cause of Elisabeth's death is far from clear."

"What does that mean?" a male voice asks in Swedish.

The people in the room turn to look at the tanned, healthy-looking Swede who Jessica now knows is Niklas Steiner, fifty-one years old, from Kalmar. Steiner looks somehow different than he did the day before, perhaps because he has shaved off the stubble that had grown rather long.

Johan Karlsson hurries to intervene. "Well, it means that, considering Elisabeth's advanced age, unexplained head injury, and the fact that for as-yet-unknown reasons she ended up over two kilometers away from the guesthouse in the middle of the night, we have cause to suspect someone else may have played a role in what happened. As of now this is merely speculation, as the technical investigation is still underway."

Jessica feels a pang of hunger. No one has dared to approach the pot of soup yet, but she can't be bothered to wait. She makes her way to the buffet, takes a bowl, ladles in a generous helping of steaming salmon soup, and sprinkles chopped dill over it from a separate dish. She slices a hunk of baguette and fills a glass with kvass, which in all likelihood is as flat today as it has been every other day. All eyes are on her, and Karlsson waits for her to return to her seat with her food before he continues. "Which is why I'd like to ask all of you for your understanding and patience, as I'm going to have to conduct the necessary investigations and, in a manner of speaking, count each of you out from my calculations one by one."

"Wait a minute. Are you suggesting one of us . . . killed that woman?" Steiner snorts incredulously. "Why on earth . . . I mean, what damn reason would any of us have to do that?"

"As I said, I'm asking you for your understanding—"

"It could have been an accident; maybe she was sleepwalking. Or suicide! And if you're sure it was a crime, it could have been someone else, right? Boats travel up and down that channel all the time. It's mind-boggling that you would accuse us."

"That's not what—"

"Oh really? What did you mean, then? Come on, Nilla. Let's go pack," Steiner says in outrage, sending the legs of his chair screeching across the floor as he stands. The weepy-looking woman follows him to the door, and a moment later they're both gone.

Karlsson sighs and rubs the furrows that have appeared in his forehead. His eyes pinch shut as if he is suffering a sudden migraine, but within a few seconds he appears to have recovered.

The visibly anxious Astrid and Åke exchange glances.

"Well, that went well," Karlsson says, steps over to the buffet, and grabs a bowl.

Jessica tastes the soup and wonders whether the local detective has the authority to prevent the Swedes from leaving the island, especially since there's no probable cause to suspect their involvement. Not that Steiner's behavior a few moments ago wasn't the epitome of suspicious: Jessica has seen people lose their cool during interrogation dozens of times, and she knows it often happens when they actually have something to hide. Those guilty of crimes sometimes think it looks less questionable if they challenge the suspicions aimed at them. But it's doubtful that Niklas Steiner's behavior can be interpreted so straightforwardly: any tourist who has traveled abroad to escape everyday stresses would presumably lose their cool if they heard they might be suspected of a murder that took place at their hotel. Besides, before marching out, Steiner presented two valid facts: Elisabeth's death might have been an accident or suicide, and if a crime actually was involved, the perpetrator could well be someone else—someone who just landed on Smörregård in a boat and departed the same way. Or the someone who is lodging in the room upstairs—the someone Armas presumably mistook for Maija when looking out his window the night before last.

Jessica bites into a peppercorn and momentarily considers addressing the elephant in the room: asking Astrid directly about the mystery guest now that she and Karlsson are both present. But Jessica decides to proceed with caution in this matter, just as she means to with the toolshed. Take a look at her hand before she reveals it.

Jessica lowers her spoon to the lip of her bowl and turns toward the proprietress of the guesthouse. *Why are you protecting this person, Astrid?*

50

JESSICA DRAINS HER glass and sets it down next to her bowl on the table. Armas and Eila moved into the library a moment before, Astrid is washing dishes in the kitchen, and Åke has trudged down to the boathouses looking as if the world were coming to an end. Now, if ever, could be a good moment to sneak back into Astrid's office, but there's one thing standing in Jessica's way: Johan Karlsson, who is smacking his lips as he shovels salmon soup into his mouth at the neighboring table. The Ahvenanmaa police officer will not be letting Jessica out of his sight until one of them has left the island. His spoon clinks against the bowl a final time, and he wipes his mouth with a napkin. He and Jessica sit in the dining room without saying a word, intermittently glaring at each other as if this is the ominous moment just before pistols are drawn in a duel that will inevitably result in one or the other's death. Maybe Jessica and Karlsson aren't so different in the end. They're both police officers who investigate serious crimes for a living, even if the repertoire of murders and rapes in a place like Ahvenanmaa is narrower than in the capital. But that's as it should be. Maybe Karlsson is approaching the case with such gusto not only because he has a personal tie to the island and the Nordins but also because he doesn't usually get cases like this to investigate. This might well be the highlight of his threadbare career.

"I saw that video," Karlsson says, breaking the silence.

To her surprise, Jessica finds that his words don't succeed in shocking or even provoking her. She has assumed from the start that Karlsson sees her as something other than a squeaky-clean detective.

"Great," Jessica says. "I hope you remembered to give it a like."

Karlsson doesn't laugh or even smile. "I'm just wondering whether Astrid and Åke have seen it."

Jessica can't help but grin at the guy's brazenness. "Is that your next move? Show the video to everyone and convince them I'm a violent psychopath? And that's why I'm guilty of Elisabeth Salmi's death?"

Karlsson folds a napkin and places the corner under his bowl. Then he shakes his head and stands. "I don't have to convince anyone of anything. It's enough that I know what . . . you . . . ha . . ."

Suddenly his words slur into an unintelligible mumble. The self-satisfied smirk disappears from his face and is replaced by complete helplessness. Karlsson gasps for breath; his eyes fill with fear. Jessica registers the face that instantly lost all color and the gaze that sails aimlessly around the room, but she doesn't have time to react before Karlsson falls to his knees on the floor.

Jessica springs up from her table and rushes over. "Is everything OK?" she asks, although the question feels silly. Karlsson looks as if he's just suffered a severe concussion or maybe a stroke.

Karlsson doesn't shoo Jessica away as he focuses on breathing calmly. Gradually the color returns to his face, and Jessica helps him back into his chair. Based on the clink of dishes from the kitchen, it seems Astrid didn't notice the episode.

"Damn it," Karlsson says, burying his face in his hands as if he is too ashamed to reply.

The irritation Jessica felt toward her local colleague makes way for empathy. However, she has experienced too much to be a gullible fool, to allow a glimmer of humanity to influence her view of people who will show their true colors again once conditions become favorable for them to do so. She knows even the blackest souls are capable of playing vulnerable, or at least bringing forth their weaknesses if revealing them will provide the opportunity for a surprise attack. But Karlsson's face went white so suddenly that it couldn't have been a performance. There's no one who could regulate their body to such an extreme, under any circumstances.

"Does that happen often?"

Karlsson wipes his brow; the beads of sweat remind Jessica of water droplets on leaves after a rain. Then he reluctantly nods. "Occasionally."

Still kneeling at his side, Jessica catches a whiff of pungent sweat, which reminds her of headquarters and Rasmus. "I've had seizures of my own over the course of my life," she says, catching herself off guard with her openness. Now might be the perfect moment to get into the local police officer's good graces by revealing something personal.

Karlsson looks up from the floor and stares at Jessica long and hard, but the eyes don't look the least bit defiant. "I know it wasn't you, Niemi," he says, allowing his breathing to steady as some blender-type gadget blares out in the kitchen.

"So then why did you—"

"Because I want you to stay out of my way."

"I'm not following . . ."

Karlsson grimaces as if a bolt of lightning has just struck his head. Then he presses his fingers to his forehead. "There's this pressure here, damn it. It keeps shifting, makes everything harder until it finally goes away."

For a second, Jessica gets the impression that Karlsson is at least as crazy as she is. Then he smiles sadly. "Cancer," he whispers. "Inoperable."

"I'm sorry."

Karlsson shakes his head, and Jessica isn't sure if it's in answer to her condolences or if he is tentatively testing whether the movement will bring back the pain.

"No one knows yet," Karlsson says.

Jessica pulls over a chair from the neighboring table. "Not even Astrid?"

Karlsson shakes his head. "As a former doctor, Astrid's the one who sent me in for an MRI a few months ago. Said the cause of the symptoms had to be determined immediately, and then it turned out it was too late to do anything." Karlsson pours himself water from the pitcher on the table and empties the glass with his quivering hands. "Smörregård is my home too, in a way, Niemi. I spent my entire childhood here. What happened all those years ago . . . I'm afraid it's not over yet."

Jessica leans back in her chair, arms folded across her chest. "What if you let me help?"

"What do you mean?"

"I think my experience could be of use in solving the case."

Karlsson rubs his temples and lets out a deep sigh. "Fine," he eventually mumbles. "But I have two questions for you. First of all, why was your scarf found near the body?"

Jessica chews her bottom lip reflectively, and emerges from her reverie only when the noise in the kitchen stops. Astrid enters the dining room, bestows a grunt of surprise on the two detectives there, and continues on her way out the front door.

"It must have fallen from the dock into the water when I was out for a walk last night."

"What were you doing on the dock?"

"I was curious," Jessica says. "Åke told me about Maija, and I wanted to see the place with my own eyes. But before I answer your second question, I want you to answer mine."

Karlsson hesitates, then nods.

"What were you doing in the toolshed earlier today?"

Karlsson chuckles drily. "I thought I saw movement in Astrid's office," he says, gingerly rising to his feet. "I went in to check it out because Eila Kantelinen said she looked out her window last night and saw someone close the door to the shed."

Jessica gulps down the strange sensation in her throat. "Man or woman?"

"Kantelinen wasn't sure. For now at least, no one has admitted to entering the toolshed last night."

"So if everyone is telling the truth, whoever it was sneaking around the toolshed is presumably the same person who killed Elisabeth," Jessica says.

Karlsson nods, and Jessica feels the suspense spread from her gut to her fingertips. The adrenaline generated by an unsolved mystery is a drug she'll never be able to free herself of. Nor does she want to free herself of it. It's why she's continued doing police work all these years. Because the world can't offer her anything better than that feeling that comes from a convoluted crime that needs solving.

"My second question is, are you aware that there's a seventh guest registered at the guesthouse? In addition to me, the old folks, and the Steiners?"

Karlsson looks surprised. "What do you mean? Who?"

"Exactly," Jessica says. For a moment she considers whether she should tell Karlsson the whole truth: that she secretly photographed the guests' registration information. Right now she and Karlsson seem to be in sync, but it could just as easily be a ruse, some sort of carefully planned trap Jessica would step into by revealing too much. So: there's no point making unnecessary confessions. "When I registered at the guesthouse on Monday, I happened to see a document on the desk indicating someone else had arrived that same morning." Jessica is pleased with the white lie she came up with on the spot; it in no way changes the end result. She continues: "Besides, I caught a glimpse of someone in one of the upstairs windows facing the road—in room 21, which is supposed to be unoccupied. At first I thought it was Astrid or Åke, but based on today's events I'm not so sure anymore."

"Strange." Karlsson closes his eyes for a moment as if the pain has returned. "But now it's your turn to answer my second question: what did Armas Pohjanpalo tell you?"

"He . . . ," Jessica says, then hesitates. She isn't sure whether she's betraying Armas' trust by sharing what he saw with Karlsson, but the whole thing is too weird to keep to herself. Jessica can't solve the case on her own; the simple fact of the matter is, she doesn't even have the authority to investigate. She draws a breath as if gathering the courage to utter the words. "Armas said he saw a girl in a blue coat last night."

Karlsson laughs incredulously. "What?"

"Armas said he saw a girl standing outside in the rain. And that he's sure the girl was Maija Ruusunen."

"He's crazy."

Jessica taps the table with the nail of her forefinger. "And there it is."

"What?"

"That's exactly the reaction he was afraid he'd get from you. That's why he didn't want to tell you. Or anyone else."

"What reaction?"

"Being labeled crazy."

"And rightfully so," Karlsson says, unbuttoning the second to top button of his shirt. His hands are still shaking.

"I don't know what the old man really saw out there in the yard, but I don't believe he's making it up out of thin air. If Eila Kantelinen spotted someone at the toolshed in the middle of the night, it must be the same person Armas told me about earlier. Now, it's obvious it wasn't Maija standing out there, but maybe someone . . . small. Maybe a child?"

"Eila said she saw someone in the toolshed between one and two in the morning," Karlsson says softly. "Although she insisted this was just a rough estimate. She glanced at the time but wasn't sure if she did so when she got out of bed or at some other point in the night. She said she slept poorly and kept waking up."

The ever-rising gale sets the old house creaking at the seams, and Jessica shifts her gaze out the window.

"Listen, Niemi," Karlsson says. "I have a simple plan that won't require you to do anything illegal."

51

THE DOOR OF Astrid's office closes with a soft squeak. Jessica posts herself at the window to keep an eye out as Johan Karlsson goes through the guest registrations for the past week. They mean to make use of the pedantic Nordins' archives as well as discover the identities of those staying at Smörregård at the time of the murders in the 1980s. Just then, Jessica sees Åke making his way from a boathouse to the villa, drying his dirty hands on a chamois. The white flagpole in the middle of the lawn is wobbling ominously, as if it could snap in two at any moment.

Jessica rushes out the front door, opens it calmly, and walks up to Åke as unhurriedly as possible, so as not to arouse the slightest suspicion.

"Hey," she says.

"Hey," Åke replies, stopping in front of Jessica with his hands in his pockets. The breeze sets the curls visible under his beanie dancing. "This is starting to turn into a real-life detective novel," he finally says.

"Tell me about it."

"It must be hard to concentrate on writing. Or is it just the opposite?"

"A real death is never inspiring," Jessica says enigmatically, with a discreet glance at the villa's front door. Suddenly the whole diversion seems strange: as a police officer, couldn't Karlsson just tell Astrid he was going to have a look at the guest registrations in her office? Now that Jessica thinks about it, he also entered the toolshed clandestinely. Why is Karlsson operating in the shadows even though everyone knows he's officially investigating the case?

Åke draws his mouth up into a faint smile and is about to continue on to the villa, but Jessica delays him again to buy some time.

"You and Astrid are old friends of Johan Karlsson's?"

Åke turns back to Jessica. "We've known each other since we were kids."

Jessica shoots another glance at the villa. If only Karlsson would hurry up. "Then it's a good thing he was the one assigned to the case," she says when she can't come up with anything else.

Åke's reaction is completely unlike what she expected. He lowers his eyes and shakes his head, perhaps in amusement. "Assigned? I'm pretty sure Johan insisted he be allowed to investigate this particular incident."

"What do you mean?"

"Just that . . . I was kind of hoping the police would send someone else, someone who'd be able to look at the case objectively."

"Isn't Karlsson—"

Just then, the front door opens and Karlsson steps out onto the stairs. "Could you come with me, Niemi?" he says gruffly. Apparently he wants to communicate to those present that the cold war between him and Jessica is still raging. "I have a couple questions for you. Let's go down to the water to talk."

"I'm sorry," Åke says in a voice too low for Karlsson to hear. "About all this."

Jessica shrugs as Karlsson tromps past them, hands in his pockets, and on toward the rocks rising at the shore. Åke continues into the villa, and Jessica starts off after Karlsson.

"Well?" Jessica says, once the two of them have left the yard. "Did you find anything?"

"I took pictures of the guest registrations from September 'eighty-two and October 'eighty-five. At first glance it doesn't look like anyone was staying at Smörregård during either event."

"What about the person we're looking for who registered the same day I arrived?"

Karlsson stops, turns toward Jessica, and smacks his lips. "There wasn't anyone."

"What do you mean?" Jessica pulls her phone from her pocket. She shows Karlsson the photo she took of her own registration, in which the photocopy of the mystery guest's passport and registration form are visible under the corner of her own documentation.

Karlsson scratches his head helplessly.

"Someone removed it." Jessica takes a few steps toward the wildly churning sea and breathes in the damp air. "Very recently."

"Damn," Karlsson says. "Do you know what that means?"

"That whoever it is doesn't want to be found."

Karlsson nods, raises his chin, and draws the wind-borne smell of the sea into his nostrils. The sun that's barely visible beyond the clouds gives off no warmth; it's incredibly cold outside.

"You know what else? I grabbed the key for room twenty-one from the office and had a look. There was no one in there," Karlsson says.

"But—"

"The bed was made, and the room looks unoccupied."

Jessica glances at the window of room 21, the white lace curtain hanging there. Has the perpetrator left the island? Even if so, that doesn't explain why the documents are missing from the binder. And someone has also cleaned the room and changed the sheets. It's plain as day, then, that either Astrid or Åke or both know about the mystery guest and are covering that person's tracks.

Jessica's head is hammering. She turns toward the converted barn. Niklas Steiner is just stepping out in a T-shirt, no coat, and he lights a cigarette.

"Are you going to let them leave?"

"The Steiners? They can try and call a water taxi," Karlsson says, "but I doubt they'll find anyone willing to come out in this weather. So unless they want to swim to Alören . . ."

"They're stuck here," Jessica says. "What's your next move?"

"I need to go to the mainland."

Jessica glances at the dock, but all she sees are the rowboats turned over on the shore, their plugs presumably stored somewhere in the toolshed or a boathouse.

"Are you going to swim? Or is someone coming to pick you up?"

Karlsson laughs drily. "Well, to be completely honest . . . ," he begins, then turns to look at the dirt road running through the woods, where the overhanging branches revel in the ever-wilder wind. "I have a motorboat at the west dock."

52

JESSICA STANDS THERE, watching Johan Karlsson gradually disappear beneath the forest's eaves. Then she glances at the converted barn a hundred meters away, in front of which Niklas Steiner takes the last puffs of his cigarette; then he returns inside. The couple must be packing their bags. And no wonder; Karlsson managed to run the information session pretty clumsily, and since the couple has no part in the case, they understandably want to continue their trip somewhere where no one interrogates them as murder suspects while they're eating their salmon soup.

Jessica studies the now-deserted yard and feels a warm twinge in her heart. The place is a real island idyll. The lawn, neatly mowed in autumn and now yellow from winter; the flagpole surrounded by small ornamental stones, its wildly snapping flag raised to half-mast. The red and white villa and, fronting it, the bare gooseberry and red currant bushes, which will not be coming into leaf until summer. Built almost abutting the main building, the toolshed, faithful in appearance to the rest of the property despite being of clearly later vintage than the other buildings. Jessica chose this specific island as her hideaway at random, based only on the photos and positive reviews on Tripadvisor. But now a tragedy is being played out at the south end of tourist-beloved Smörregård, and Jessica has involuntarily ended up in the middle of it.

She has started making her way to one of the boathouses when her phone rings. It's Yusuf calling.

"Hi," Jessica says. Suddenly her throat feels dry.

For a second, all she hears is crackling on the line, and she's afraid the call will drop.

"You . . . on speaker." Yusuf's voice is breaking in and out. "Rasmus is also . . ."

Yusuf keeps talking, but his choppy words drown in the howl of the wind.

"Wait, Yusuf." Jessica picks up the pace to reach the boathouse more quickly. She hasn't ventured inside it yet, but she has seen Åke tromp in and out, which is how she knows the door isn't locked. She steps inside and shuts the door behind her, catches a powerful whiff of tarred wood mixed with the smell of the algae draping the structure's pilings.

"Sorry, there's a pretty big storm blowing in here," Jessica says. "I should be able to hear you better now."

"And when you say 'here,' you mean . . . Smörregård?" Yusuf asks.

"Does it matter?"

"I don't know. You're the one who called us."

Jessica switches the phone to her other ear and looks at the short flight of stairs leading down to the water. A largish rubber boat with an outboard motor hangs from the ceiling. Ever since she arrived on the island, she has wondered if Åke keeps a vessel in the boathouse and what sort it might be.

"I know. Thanks. What did you find out?" Jessica asks.

"Not much," Yusuf says. "There's almost nothing to speak of on Eila Kantelinen. Lives in Porvoo. Widow, four children, thirteen grandchildren, and six great-grandchildren. A big family. Sweet old lady. When the time comes, she'll have VIP access to heaven if it exists. Now, Armas Pohjanpalo, on the other hand, has lived a pretty eventful life."

"What do you mean?"

"He's got a long rap sheet: car thefts, burglaries, assaults, embezzlement. But the most recent sentence was in 1978, and Pohjan-palo hasn't been back to prison since 1980."

Jessica ponders Yusuf's words. At first hearing, it's hard to imag-ine such an extensive criminal background for the hunched, fearful old man, but considering the rough childhood he had, Armas was no doubt capable of all sorts of things in his prime.

"And when it comes to Elisabeth Salmi . . ." Yusuf holds a brief pause before continuing: "There's nothing really remarkable about her except that she signed up for private hospice care in early January."

"For a hospice?" Jessica says. The word calls to mind Erne, who could have likely been assigned a bed at a similar facility if Jessica hadn't firmly insisted he spend his final days at her home in Töölö.

"Which apparently means Elisabeth Salmi is terminally ill. But we don't have any way of looking more deeply into that without good cause."

Jessica shuts her eyes and hears the sea lap restlessly within the boat-house's walls. She remembers Elisabeth's pale, drawn face, the deep, wrinkled eye sockets. She'd been at a hospice, and the reunion at Smörregård was presumably meant to be her last. Intentionally or unintentionally, her murderer simply hastened the inevitable.

"Elsa Lehtinen was a tougher case, because we didn't have a date of birth, and there's a pretty big group of people with that name in Finland. There were five who were born in the 1930s and died in 1994."

"The Elsa Lehtinen I'm looking for was still alive in March 1994," Jessica says, because she remembered Armas' having seen her for the last time at Smörregård.

"OK. That makes it easier . . ." Jessica hears Yusuf tap at his com-puter in the background. "Now there are only two left."

"Can you check if either one died abroad? And if she died of nat-ural causes?"

"Wow," Yusuf says. "Sounds like you have something pretty sur-real going on."

Jessica is just about to say Yusuf doesn't know the half of it, but now Rasmus interjects.

"When it comes to the Steiners," his feeble voice begins, and Jessica says hello before he continues. "As you know, it's pretty hard for us to dig up information on Swedish citizens without asking for official assistance from our neighbors. So we don't really have anything more on these siblings except they're from Kalmar and they're both journalists—"

"Siblings?" Jessica says.

For a moment, there's total silence on the line. "Yes," Rasmus says. "What about it?"

Jessica walks down the steps to the water with the phone at her ear, presses the tip of her shoe into the water in a plastic tub on the bottom tread. Now that she thinks about it, Niklas and Pernilla Steiner haven't behaved in any way indicative of their being a married couple. As a matter of fact, just the opposite. Who knows? Maybe Jessica and Toffe would also vacation together if her little brother were still alive. Regardless, the thought of the siblings sharing a room as adults feels foreign to Jessica.

"I assumed they . . . Argh, it doesn't matter," Jessica mutters, and watches the sole of her shoe break the surface tension, sending tremors through the water in the tub.

"Pernilla Steiner has also played an active role in various demonstrations in Sweden. When she was younger, she was a member of an organization called Clean Earth and participated in protests that tested the bounds of legality," Rasmus says. "On top of that, in 2009 she appeared on a television morning show so out of it that they had to cut away in the middle of a live broadcast. Seems like a pretty radical type."

"Unlike her brother, who appears to be a respected journalist," Yusuf adds.

Jessica has seen Pernilla Steiner on only a few occasions, but she silently concludes that the facts tally with the woman's appearance.

"And as far as Åke and Astrid Nordin . . . ," Rasmus begins.

Yusuf hurries in to complete the sentence his colleague started: "Neither has a criminal record. Åke earned a master's degree in social sciences from Åbo Akademi in 1993 and has lived in Sweden since, first in Stockholm and later in Holmsund for an extended period. I found some information online indicating he worked at Umeå University from 2008 to 2019, mostly taught history of Western philosophy to first-year students."

Jessica switches the phone back to the other ear and gauges the roof structures of the boathouse. She already knew this about Åke.

"The guesthouse was established by Astrid Nordin's recently deceased husband, Hans-Peter Nordin, back in 1955. Astrid Nordin herself had an extensive career as an obstetrician over the period from 1964 to 1997, since which she has apparently worked at the Smörregård guesthouse with her husband."

"Was there anything else worth mentioning?" Jessica says, and immediately realizes how rude she sounds. After all, her colleagues have agreed to help her without asking for anything in return, not to mention the rebuke they risk from Hellu if they get caught—which is by no means impossible; any data or archive queries performed by police always leave trails in the system. And for some reason Jessica gets the sense that, despite her busyness, Hellu will make time to find out where the impetus for such searches came from.

"When I was looking through Astrid Nordin's old publications, I noticed she'd been profiled as an adoption advocate as early as the 1970s," Rasmus says. "Nordin spoke out on multiple occasions— sometimes she was even quoted in the mainland newspapers, like *Turun Sanomat* and *Kaleva*—claiming that Finland's slow and bureaucratic adoption process makes not only the children suffer but also involuntarily childless adults. Nordin said she'd brought dozens of babies into this world who would have deserved to start their lives in the care of someone other than their biological mothers."

Jessica presses her hand to her belly and can't help but reflect that Astrid might say this about her child. She looks at the boat hanging from three cargo straps. If she really wanted to be a good mother and think only about what was best for her unborn child, she would jump into the boat and speed off. Fly from Maarianhamina to Stockholm and on to who knows where from there. By nighttime she could be in Barcelona, Nice, or why not Rome?

"The articles also revealed," Rasmus continues, "that Astrid herself was adopted."

"Really?" Jessica says, coming out of her dreams of escape. She recalls the black-and-white photograph in Astrid's office and how the young Astrid in the picture looked different from the dark-haired adults standing at her side. Of course.

"Yup. And apparently she was involved in some accident, judging by the darker skin at her throat, which to my eye looks like a serious burn injury," Rasmus says. "But I couldn't find any information on that. Despite spending a lot of time in the public eye, Nordin has never spoken about her injury."

The wind pops against the boathouse door. A long-handled hook clanks against its nail on the wall.

"Nordin's husband, Hans-Peter, on the other hand, appears to have been quite the hustler and serial entrepreneur in the 1970s: he was registered on the boards of at least five limited companies and two associations in Ahvenanmaa. Until it all came to a screeching halt."

"What do you mean?"

"According to data from the Patent and Registration Office, Hans-Peter quietly resigned from all his board positions in March of 1983, with the exception of Smörregård Experiences Limited, the company that operated the guesthouse. He stayed on that board until his death."

"Why?"

"It's anyone's guess. We didn't find any information on any sort of scandal or judgment that would have forced him to resign from those companies and positions of trust."

"OK. Sounds weird."

The line is silent for a moment. During those few seconds, Jessica is able to conjure up the scent of Yusuf's new cologne, the way he tasted during those few seconds when their lips touched.

"Of course, we've just scratched the surface here, but if you give us something concrete and a few more hours—," Yusuf says, but Jessica emphatically cuts him off.

"You guys have already done a lot. Thanks. I do have one more request, though."

"You're investigating that old woman's death as a homicide, aren't you?" Yusuf says, and when Jessica doesn't reply, he raises his voice half playfully. "Huh? Come on—tell us."

"Maybe I am. And my other request involves two deaths that took place on Smörregård, one in 1982 and one in 1985."

"Do you have the victims' names?"

"One was Boman, I think," Jessica quickly replies. "Both of them worked at an orphanage that was here on the island, at least at some point over the course of their lives."

"OK, that might be a little trickier, considering almost forty years have passed since the incidents and the files probably won't be in our database."

"Do what you can. If you can. I get that you guys have other things going on."

"What are the local police there up to if you have to solve not only a recent murder but ancient homicides? Riding around in boats fishing for salmon?"

"There's one feisty local detective here, Johan Karlsson. Apparently he's been in touch with Pasila and asked about me. Has Hellu happened to mention anything about that?"

"No, but . . ."

"But what?"

"Harjula came by here a second ago . . . was oddly curious about what we were doing."

"Damn it," Jessica says. "So Hellu has set her hound after me."

In that instant, the door behind Jessica creaks. A slim beam of light falls over the gloomy space, and a dark, restlessly moving figure appears at the top of the stairs, startling Jessica. The phone slips from her fingers and bounces straight into the black water.

53

THE FIGURE STEPS back toward the open door, apparently groping for the light switch that Jessica didn't find a moment before.

"I didn't realize anyone was in here," Niklas Steiner says with a frown. The weak lamp casts a shadow over his chiseled face; the rain has pasted his curly hair to his forehead. Since Jessica last saw him, he has pulled on a flannel shirt and a hooded coat.

Jessica glares at him in agitation, draws a breath, and squats at the bottom of the stairs, where her phone fell into the water. "Goddamn it all to hell," she says when she realizes visibility to the bottom is nonexistent.

"Did you drop something?"

"My phone."

Steiner pulls a sympathetic face. "Sorry. I can help you look for it."

He stands at the top of the stairs, waiting for Jessica to let him pass. Jessica gladly makes room for him, and he takes off his coat, drops nimbly to his stomach on the lowest step, and thrusts his flannel-sleeved arm deep into the water.

"There's a perfectly seaworthy boat in here," Steiner says, raking his hand through the water. "And we supposedly can't find one to take us to the mainland."

"Are you guys really in such a rush to leave?" Jessica says.

Just then, Steiner's face breaks out in a jubilant smile. He pulls his hand out of the water and pushes himself up into a squat. He hands Jessica her phone; the home screen is lit. Apparently Yusuf wasn't interested in listening to the burble of water and hung up, but the important thing is that the phone works.

"Thanks."

"To be perfectly honest: this place is creepy," Steiner says. "But that came as no surprise."

"What do you mean?" Jessica says as Steiner pops to his feet and walks up the stairs. "Why didn't it come as a surprise?"

Steiner wrings out his sleeve over the plank floor and rolls it up to his elbow. Then he lowers his voice to no more than a whisper. "That story about the girl in the blue coat. Weird old people singing weird songs. Death at the dock."

Steiner reveals his teeth and grimaces; apparently the expression is supposed to convey horror. It feels strange to Jessica, standing in the cramped boathouse with a man she just got information on from her colleagues in Helsinki.

"Wait—how do you know about all that? I mean, the girl in the blue coat . . ."

Steiner bursts into nervous laughter. "Åke asked me to keep a low profile so I wouldn't make the other guests nervous. Which I suppose, now that it's low season, technically means you. Because those old folks definitely know the story better than well."

"Make me nervous how?"

"I guess at this point I can just go ahead and tell the truth. I don't suppose it makes any difference anymore. We didn't really come here to vacation. Pernilla and I are writing an article for *Barometern*, the local paper in Kalmar, about the birds of spring. Åke and I have known each other since we met in Stockholm about twenty years ago, and he recently hinted that these reunions of child evacuees could make for a poignant story. An in-depth profile that would touch on the war, orphans, and starting life over. Solidarity. The ability of children to adapt to any and all situations. There were plenty of angles. All I would have to do was pick one or more."

Jessica looks at him, stunned, and can't help but think her instincts about people have deteriorated dramatically in recent weeks. Until the call from Yusuf and Rasse, she'd assumed the Steiners were an alienated couple on vacation at Smörregård. Now she gets the sense that nothing at Smörregård is what it seems. And no one seems to tell the truth, at least at first.

Steiner rubs his little turned-up nose and looks around. Jessica smells the fresh aftershave that wafts out from under his collar as he turns his head.

"We were supposed to have a leisurely talk with the birds of spring today, but then one of them bit the dust and Karlsson started breathing down our necks. We want to go while the going's still good, although it looks to be a little late for that. There's a storm rolling in, as you can see and hear."

"So the birds of spring had agreed to be interviewed?"

"I assumed so. Åke said he'd handle everything, and as long as we let the old folks enjoy their dinner first and give them some time to catch up, we'd have all of the next day to talk to them for our story."

"But your article got a totally new angle this morning."

"There isn't going to be an article. It was supposed to be a true-to-life depiction of the realities of war and a neutral neighbor, and it was supposed to be told in the evacuees' own voices. The fact that a handful of orphans were stuck on this accursed island for months . . . There's something so ineffably tragic about it. And at the same time pretty beautiful." Steiner lowers his chin as if readying himself to be reprimanded. "But now . . . Now the story would be nothing more than a cheap, sensationalistic murder mystery that would require us to harass two fearful old zip lips. I'm not sure Åke even warned the three of them that they were going to be interviewed. It feels like the whole idea was a big flop."

Jessica takes a moment to digest this information, then points at the boat hanging from the ceiling. "So you came here looking for a boat?"

"Yup."

"Now you found one."

"I'm a journalist, not a thief. If Åke refuses to take us to the mainland, we'll have to spend another night here." Steiner shrugs his shoulders and opens the door with assistance from the wind. "I don't think I introduced myself earlier. Niklas."

"Jessica."

"OK, Jessica. Let's talk more soon if no one drowns us first," Niklas Steiner says, vanishing through the door.

54

JESSICA REMAINS SITTING on a blue crate in the dim boathouse. Rain lashes the roof. Her head aches, and the gnawing sensation in her stomach has intensified again. But knowledge of the sensation's source, or to be precise, its likely source, makes everything noticeably more tolerable. Jessica sighs and eyes the fishing nets and green, algae-stained buoys hanging on the wall. In the center of the wall, a wooden pole with a metal hook at one end rests on nails. Niklas Steiner was right when he said this place was creepy. Everyone is inconsistent somehow; no one's behavior seems to align with who they are or what they've once been. The case is bursting with weird facts and occurrences: Elisabeth's terminal illness, Armas Pohjanpalo's extensive criminal history. The old people's somehow peculiar demeanor the night before. Elisabeth's behavior in the bathroom, the terror on Armas' face. Åke's story about Maija. The adopted Astrid's career as an adoption advocate after being raised near an orphanage. Pernilla Steiner's inconsolable crying, which doesn't quite line up with the image of a journalist used to challenging the powers that be. The disappearance of the mystery guest's documents from the files in the office. The vacant room 21, where Jessica is nevertheless sure she saw someone.

Something about the story stinks, and stinks badly, but Jessica doesn't know what angle offers the best approach to the puzzle. She looks up at the boat again, sees herself lowering it into the water and piloting it along the shoreline all the way to Maarianhamina. If she could just successfully avoid the shoals, she could . . .

Suddenly everything turns into a hazy, blurry mosaic tinted by obscure shadows, as if Jessica is looking through a kaleidoscope.

Are you going somewhere? the man says in English. The accent is strong, and Jessica would recognize it even in her sleep. Logic tells her Colombano isn't there, that the dead speak to her only in her mind, but at the same time she can't be sure. She cannot escape the visions. Rational thought has no impact on them.

Besides, her mind is clear, and now, for the first time in weeks, she has the sense that things are somewhat under control, despite the fact that she hasn't touched her medications in two days.

Running is not an option, Zesika, the man says, and Jessica feels his warm breath at her ear. *You didn't run then, so why would you run now?*

The boathouse has grown almost pitch-black; the seawater that lapped at the bottom of the stairs just a moment ago has risen to her ankles. The water is not cold; it's lukewarm. Slimy eels writhe around her legs. The patter of the rain has slowed; the drops seem to pound the metal roof more selectively. The air in the boathouse is humid now, and it smells of polluted water, urine, and rotten fish. Jessica feels her bare back against the sweaty sheets, the man's thick hair between her legs. Her ribs ache, and when she turns her head, she notices they're bruised. Bruises are par for the course; they're a by-product of pleasure and love. There's no love without pain.

You should have had a child with me, Colombano whispers in her ear.

The water keeps rising.

"Is that what you wanted?" Jessica says as he comes. "You wanted a little monster?"

Rough fingers stroke the hair back from her head, and Jessica expects them to suddenly squeeze around her throat. Two hours of practice, a violent, brutal interlude, and then he would pick up his violin again and . . .

No, Colombano says. *No one would want a child with a whore like you. Maybe Frank understood the consequences of his actions and that's why he blew his brains out.*

"No," Jessica says, raising her chin. The warm water grazes her neck. She knows she will only drown if she keeps talking. "That's not why Frank killed himself," she whispers.

You are death, Colombano says. *Everything you touch dies before long. And it's going to happen to your child too, whether you like it or not . . .*

Now Jessica can feel the seawater filling her nostrils. It has risen so high she can no longer escape it; she and her troubles would drown in it for good. But suddenly the fingers release her neck, and Colombano's boozy breath recedes. The shrill wail of a newborn carries from somewhere.

You're a killer, Zesika. If anyone knows that, I do, Colombano says.

Jessica opens her eyes. Her phone has begun to ring, and she quickly raises it to her ear to get away from Colombano, the sweaty hotel's damp walls, and the stench of spoiled seafood. Dirty dishes, wet towels, an unmade bed. The critical eyes that follow her down the hotel corridors and at breakfast. *Filthy whore.*

"Jessica? Are you there?" Yusuf's voice says.

55

JESSICA GASPS FOR breath. The water has receded. Her clothes are dry. So are her shoes.

"Jessie?" Yusuf's voice says again.

The line crackles.

"Yes, Yusuf?"

"Hellu ordered us all into the conference room, and it might be a long meeting. I thought I'd call you real quick and tell you what we found."

Jessica takes a deep breath and closes her eyes. *Everything's fine.* She has to calm down. "Well?"

"I'm sure we'll find out more once we really get into it, but here's what a quick check turned up: the man who died at Smörregård in 1982 was named Martin Hedblom, fifty-five years old. Long-term night watchman at Smörregård Children's Home. Cause of death drowning, although the report also mentions the victim had other injuries, but not the sort that would have caused the police to suspect a crime. Three years later, at the exact same spot, Monica Boman died at the age of sixty-six. She had been director of the orphanage since its founding in 1951."

"But—"

"Note that's when Smörregård Children's Home was officially founded, but of course it's possible both Hedblom and Boman had the same or similar positions there in 1946."

"Was Monica Boman's cause of death ever determined?"

"Not really. Jessie, you need to consider that on such a short timetable and without a good reason we can't get our hands on any actual investigative material; this is all pretty much based on what we were able to dig up online and from the news archives. But by all indications, Boman's death was considered suspicious at the time as well. Not least because it was so similar in nature to Martin Hedblom's death three years earlier."

"OK." Jessica finds herself disappointed. The investigations her colleagues have conducted in Helsinki haven't brought anything new to the table.

"What about the old woman . . . Elsa Lehtinen?"

"Nothing yet."

Jessica hears a door open at the other end of the line, followed by a mumbled exchange.

"I gotta go, Jessie," Yusuf finally says softly. Chair legs scrape the floor in the background.

"OK."

Then Yusuf's voice drops to almost a whisper. "But we have a hook for you that might be of use."

"What's that?"

"According to the population register, police lieutenant Anna Berg, who investigated the deaths at Smörregård in the 1980s but has been retired for years, is alive and lives in Lövö, which is just four kilometers as the crow flies from the southern tip of Smörregård. We have a phone number here, but it's only a landline."

"OK," Jessica says, and glances at the boat. Despite the incoming weather, it could carry her to the former criminal investigator, if Berg would only agree to meet with Jessica. But why would Berg want to discuss old cases with a Helsinki police officer who's been temporarily shelved? Unless . . . Jessica feels her thoughts clearing:

unless the questions were posed by someone with good cause to dig into old cases. Someone who could disguise the request as an opportunity. Like, for instance, a veteran reporter from a respectable Swedish newspaper.

56

THE RAINDROPS HAVE lost their softness and now prick the skin like tiny, ice-cold needles. Jessica walks toward the converted barn, its roof tirelessly swept by the birch branches stretching from the edge of the forest. At first she thought she would wait for Johan Karlsson to return, but she decided there's no time if she means to make it back before the storm arrives. Besides, Johan Karlsson and Anna Berg must know each other, and going over the case among old acquaintances would not be very fruitful.

"Sorry to bother you," Jessica says when Niklas Steiner opens the door. Jessica can't see his sister, but she hears the toilet flush in the bathroom. There's an open suitcase on the floor, and a gym bag with folded clothes inside. Unlike Jessica's room with its queen bed, the Steiners' room has two narrow beds with a nightstand wedged between.

"You were just talking about a cheap murder mystery," Jessica begins, wiping her rain-dampened forehead on her sleeve. "I can guarantee you people love murder mysteries, and this is not a cheap one."

Steiner shoves his hands into his pockets and looks at her expectantly. Jessica has caught his attention; now she just needs to convince him.

"You don't have to leave the island empty-handed," she says.

Steiner pulls a pack of cigarettes from his breast pocket, glances in it, presumably to conduct some sort of rapid inventory. He still has on the flannel shirt; the rolled-up right sleeve is soaking wet.

He's wearing yellow-green ankle socks that clash with the rest of his attire.

"Come in," Steiner says, puts the cigarettes back into hiding, and walks into the room. "Your phone works, doesn't it? Sorry about that again . . ."

"It works," Jessica answers, and stands in the middle of the room with her hands on her hips. "They're designed to be waterproof, aren't they?"

"Maybe. Until they're a year old, and then suddenly they're nothing proof." Steiner knocks on the bathroom door. "Nilla, we have a visitor. Don't freak out when you come out."

"We can talk outside if—"

"No, no. It's fine," Steiner says quickly. "So, what's up?"

"I keep thinking about what you just told me. About the birds-of-spring story for *Barometern*. I'm sure it would be a nice article. But maybe not incredibly original."

Steiner laughs drily and seats himself in an armchair just like the one in Jessica's room. "Apparently we have an editor in chief here too," he says, drawing an invisible circle on the armrest with the nail of his forefinger.

"I'm thinking about it more from the reader's perspective. If you really want to write something memorable but also poignant, write a story about what everyone on the island is talking about: the girl in the blue coat." There is genuine enthusiasm in Jessica's voice.

Steiner doesn't look convinced. He grabs a bottle of mineral water from the coffee table, and there is a hiss as he untwists the cap. The pipes in the bathroom start to rumble again. "I don't know. Like I said, the whole thing strikes me as a sailor's ghost story and . . ."

"Everything is connected," Jessica says. "The girl in the blue coat, the orphanage, the drownings during the eighties, the night watchman, the director of the orphanage. Elisabeth Salmi's death. The child evacuees. As a matter of fact, you guys would be writing the exact story you were originally going to, but the headline would generate a lot more buzz."

Steiner takes a swig from the bottle. His finger comes to a stop on the armrest. He tilts his head back and eyes Jessica speculatively. Maybe intrigued, maybe not. Just now his face is remarkably blank.

"Do you think all journalists chase after buzz-generating headlines and fame?"

"As long as professional ethics are taken into consideration, I doubt fame is a problem for a single journalist out there."

Steiner looks out the window and raises his fist to his mouth.

"Give the story a chance," Jessica says.

"How?"

"Come with me to see a woman named Anna Berg. She investigated the drownings that took place here on this island in the eighties and might be able to tell how everything is related to the girl in the blue coat."

Niklas Steiner frowns, perplexed. "Why?"

Jessica can feel the momentum, and she isn't sure whether she's winning Steiner over to her side or if this is a total loss. He doesn't appear to have understood a word of what she just explained.

"So you can have the story of the century," Jessica says, faint agitation in her voice.

"No, why are you so interested in this series of events?"

Jessica looks Steiner in the eye and flashes a sly smile. "Because I'm writing a detective novel. And this would make a really damn good story."

"A detective novel, huh? When is it coming out?"

"Let's agree that it won't be until after your story has been printed and delivered to a hundred thousand mailboxes."

Niklas Steiner chuckles ambiguously and rises to his feet. He folds his arms across his chest and looks at Jessica; it's hard to tell from his expression which way he's leaning. Then he extends a hand. "Deal."

Jessica smiles broadly and shakes Steiner's hand. His palm is warm, his grip firm. Jessica feels against her skin the thick, smart ring he wears on his forefinger.

"Is the meeting with Anna Berg set up already?"

Jessica shakes her head. "Let's hope she's at home," she says, swiping her phone's touch screen. "It'd be better if you called her yourself. In the meantime, I'll go ask Åke if he can take us to Lövö."

57

JESSICA STEPS THROUGH the front door to the villa and wipes her wet shoes on the coarse doormat. She looks first into the library and then into the dining room, and there doesn't appear to be a soul downstairs. She knocks on the door to Astrid's office, and when there's no response, she tries the handle. The door is locked, which seems unusual considering it has been wide-open all week. Did Johan Karlsson perhaps lock the door behind him after he went snooping through the guesthouse's records? Or has Astrid realized the room has been accessed without her permission?

"Hello? Åke?" Jessica peers into the library again. With the exception of the hypnotic patter of the rain against the roof, the villa is absolutely still. Just as Jessica is about to set foot on the stairs, she catches sight of a gray electric panel in her peripheral vision; it's on the wall between the staircase and Astrid's office. On a whim, Jessica opens it. The circuit breakers have been neatly marked with tape, and one reads *motion detector (yard)*. Jessica flips it down.

She starts up the stairs. After a few steps, her eyes strike on a framed black-and-white photograph almost identical to the one Jessica saw in Astrid's office, although Astrid is perhaps a bit younger here. The bottom of the picture reads *Smörregård, July 1, 1947*. Jessica leans in for a closer look. The adoptive parents are a handsome couple. The father is a tall, strong-jawed man with thick whiskers and a goatee. The mother is wearing a pale summery dress and a sun hat. Astrid is easy to identify not only by the scar tissue at her throat but also by her erect bearing.

Jessica wraps her fingers around the wooden railing and continues climbing. Photographs of Smörregård are arranged in a neat row above the stairs. In one, the villa and its surroundings are seen from the dock; in another, a color shot, the barn is being converted for residential use. According to the caption, it was taken in 1980. In a third, two boys have a pike so huge that their four hands aren't enough to hold it up. *Do fish drink water? Åke & Johan 1981.*

In the picture, Åke is the spitting image of a young philosopher whose face emanates optimism and curiosity about the world around him. But Johan—who, based on what she has heard, Jessica presumes is the Johan Karlsson she met on the island today—is clearly more withdrawn. Over the course of her long career in law enforcement, Jessica has endlessly trained herself to read people's body language, micro-expressions, and mannerisms, all details useful in the profiling and interrogating of criminals. There's something about the face of the ten-year-old that might be interpreted as watchfulness or anxiety. And suddenly Jessica gets the sense that she made the right decision in not informing Karlsson that she means to consult Anna Berg. But now she needs to hurry and find Åke, and—

"Can I help you?"

The voice startles Jessica, and she looks up from the photograph. In the light of the window at the top of the stairs stands a man, and he may have been standing there for quite some time.

58

YUSUF AND RASMUS step into the conference room, where Hellu is sitting at the head of the long table, tapping her fingers against the tabletop. The room smells of cardamom buns, but there's no sign of a serving platter. There's only a crumpled brown paper bag, which aptly symbolizes the prevailing mood in the room. Apparently, today the stick is being served instead of the carrot.

"Let's get started," Hellu says as Rasmus and Yusuf pull out chairs for themselves.

"What about Harjula and Nina?"

"Out in the field."

Yusuf feels his stomach drop. It appears as if his intuition that he and Rasmus are in for a schooling was accurate.

"OK," Yusuf says, and bites into the surface of the nicotine gum he popped into his mouth. "I thought we would wrap up Lindeman—"

Hellu cuts him off: "Do you boys think I'm stupid? I know calling you boys isn't appropriate, but this time I can't help myself."

Yusuf senses a sneeze coming on and tries to stifle it by crinkling his nose.

"I've received two phone calls from Ahvenanmaa today," Hellu continues.

Yusuf and Rasmus exchange quick glances.

"The first time, they asked about Niemi. The second time, they informed me it wasn't possible to fulfill the information request on a detective named Karlsson and that the inquiries regarding Niemi involve a death that took place on the island of Smörregård this morning. That they're looking into the backgrounds of everyone on the island."

"OK."

"And I probably don't have to be some Amazing Kreskin to realize you two have spent the last couple hours of your work time digging into a case that has nothing to do with your jobs or even your purview."

"But—"

"What is it you two can't get through your heads? Niemi has turned her back on all of us," Hellu says, injured pride in her voice. "She's using you and your positions so she can play private investigator on some damn island. And why on earth would Jessica ask you to look into this man named Johan Karlsson? And how are you two such numbskulls that you actually pick up the phone and call Maarianhamina to ask about him?"

"Because . . ." Yusuf catches himself because he knows any excuses will make Hellu see red.

"Goddamn it, Yusuf Pepple, you had better come clean now or you will have the privilege of taking a long unpaid vacation yourself, in which case I won't give two hoots if you go to that same island where Niemi is stirring up trouble right now."

"Jessica didn't ask us to do anything . . . at least when it comes to this Karlsson. She just mentioned he's a police officer who called here and—"

"I haven't gotten a call from any Johan Karlsson," Hellu says, massaging her cheeks.

"Jessica said—"

"Jessica said. Jessica this, Jessica that. I am so damn fed up with the lack of discipline in this unit. I understand bonds inside the team, friendships and loyalties and so on . . . But if someone has been put on mandatory leave due to violent behavior and potential prosecution, then you will not take any further orders or instructions from her, so help me God."

"Requests."

"Exactly, and it's all the fucking same to me."

"Hellu, please," Yusuf says.

For a moment it looks as if Hellu is ready to keep upping the dial. But then she lets out a long breath and folds her arms across her chest. "Five seconds," she says.

Yusuf stands, circles around to the other side of the table, and leans across it. "Jessica is going to be coming back as soon as the dust settles. She's going to come back and we're going to be a team again. You don't hate her, Hellu. By now you understand why she's a good police officer and why everyone respects her and her competence."

"Three seconds, Yusuf."

"We need to look out for each other. Jessica has good instincts. If she says something shady is going on at Smörregård, Pasila, or even Honduras, then unfortunately she's right. Maybe not always, but usually. There's a pretty good chance. You don't deny that, do you?"

"Jessica is on mandatory leave."

"None of us is ever on leave. Remember how you said yourself that you collared a shoplifter in Málaga and held him down until the cops showed up?"

"Marbella."

"Same thing but different."

"Different but different. I was doing my duty as a citizen. I wasn't trying to force my way into meetings of the local investigative team," Hellu says drily. But she has clearly cooled off enough to ponder Yusuf's words.

Yusuf shrugs and slowly approaches Hellu. He isn't sure if he's been able to mollify the superintendent, or if he's just making things worse with a speech presumably influenced by the clever repartee of American legal dramas. "No one has done anything illegal except maybe wasted an hour's worth of mainland Finnish taxpayer money on solving Ahvenanmaa's problems."

"Presumed problems."

Yusuf nods emphatically; he has to let his boss have the last word on something. No one says anything for a few seconds, and Yusuf hears his stomach grumble. *Damned lentils.*

"OK. Tell me exactly what Jessica suspects," Hellu finally says.

"People have drowned on Smörregård before."

"A serial killer who drowns people?"

"Maybe."

"When did these previous—and note, I'm still not convinced—drownings take place?"

"In the 1980s."

Hellu bursts into laughter. "And immediately afterward, in 2020?"

"Yup."

Hellu drums the tabletop with her fingers, then glances at her watch. "A banana that tastes like a dick," she says in a serious voice.

"Excuse me?" Yusuf splutters, shooting Rasmus a questioning look. Rasmus stares at the table, looking shell-shocked.

"An invention as pointless as this theory of Niemi's. I'm giving you both a verbal warning."

Yusuf emits a soft whistle. The house of cards that he has carefully built in the conference room over the past few minutes has collapsed; Hellu blew it down with a single sentence.

"But—"

Hellu's fist slams against the table so hard that her empty plastic cup bounces to the floor. "No buts. I don't want to hear another word about Smörregård. The case is being investigated in Maarianhamina by a woman named Maria Forsius, and she's perfectly capable of drawing the necessary conclusions herself. You must both understand that Niemi isn't doing well, and she may be seeing bogeymen and mysteries in places where there's nothing to solve."

"Forsius?" Rasmus asks in his wheezy voice as Yusuf turns toward the door in protest.

Hellu gathers up the papers from the table in front of her and slips them into a red folder before she stands. "Yes, Forsius. What about her?"

"But what about Johan Karlsson?"

"He was fired from the force the year before last."

59

THE STAIRS CONTINUE to creak although Jessica has stopped in her tracks. The faces in the black-and-white photographs seem to be staring at her at least as intently as the man standing at the head of the stairs: Åke.

Åke descends a few stairs and stands there, waiting for Jessica's answer, the fingers of one hand gripping the railing.

"Is something wrong, Jessica?" Åke asks, a suspicious look on his face.

"Not really. Is Johan here?" Jessica asks as her right hand reaches for the railing.

If possible, Åke looks even more downcast than before. "I haven't seen him for a little while . . . Listen, Jessica. About Johan: he—"

"It doesn't matter. That's good, actually."

"Excuse me?"

"I'd like to ask you for a favor."

"What sort of favor?" Åke asks, then continues descending the stairs. In the end, he stops at the foot of the stairs, staring at the electrical panel as if he's noticed something is awry.

"I know you invited the Steiners to the island to write a story on the birds of spring," Jessica says quickly, to draw Åke's full attention to her. "Niklas told me."

Åke turns from the electrical panel to Jessica and suddenly looks as if he's seen a ghost, as if what Steiner has revealed might cause a major scandal.

"But—"

"Does Astrid know?" Jessica asks.

Åke glowers at Jessica. "No. I don't think she would be very excited about the idea," he eventually answers, scratching his beard.

"Why did you want him to write the story?"

Åke sighs deeply and shakes his head. "Because otherwise this place is going to die. We need more customers, Jessica. I reviewed the bookkeeping as soon as I got back and was shocked by the state of affairs."

"So you wanted the Steiners to write about the birds of spring so Villa Smörregård would get free advertising?"

"I've known Niklas for years. I presented the idea to him, and we agreed it would make for a touching story. And that if it were written correctly, it would be cited in other publications for years. This place could turn into a mythical travel destination. Maybe not Easter Island or Stonehenge, but at least . . ."

"So you didn't mention anything to Niklas about the murders at the beginning? Or the girl in the blue coat? Isn't Maija's story what makes this place mythical? A little girl who has come back to haunt the place and so on and so forth?"

Åke swats dismissively and walks over to the window next to the front door. Jessica descends the stairs and seats herself on the lowest step.

"I could tell right away that Niklas wasn't into the idea," Åke growls. "But I thought—or hoped, I guess—that if he came here and heard the whole story in its original setting, he would change his mind."

"And he did."

Åke turns to Jessica, and a flash of something she interprets as relief scuttles across his face. "What?"

"Niklas said he would write the story."

"He did? A second ago he was packing his bags and—"

"Let's just say I was able to change his mind," Jessica says, then glances at her phone. There's not a single bar at the top of the screen.

"But that's wonderful. Thank you, Jessica." Åke is clearly trying to conceal his enthusiasm, maybe because his spontaneous smile doesn't seem very appropriate in light of the events of the last twenty-four hours.

"Thank you, Åke."

"For what?"

"Right. This brings us to the favor I just mentioned."

60

THE RUBBER BOAT bounces over the waves; the cold spray hits Jessica in the face, perched as she is at the prow. She sweeps the wet hair out of her face and readies herself for the next wave by turning toward the stern, where Pernilla and Niklas Steiner are huddled side by side. For some reason the closeness between the siblings strikes Jessica as strange, foreign. As the air rushes in her ears and the archipelago seascape shifts with surprising speed, Jessica thinks back to her childhood and Toffe, her little brother who never made it to adulthood.

"There it is," Åke calls out, and Jessica hears the motor's revs drop as he eases up on the throttle.

Before them an empty beach appears with its ice-cream stand and changing booths. To the right of the beach, a forested rocky peninsula reaches out into the sea, and Åke steers the boat toward the dock floating behind it.

"Is this an island too?" Jessica asks.

Åke chuckles. "This is Ahvenanmaa. There's nothing here but islands. But seriously: this is the Ahvenanmaa mainland. From here it's an hour's drive, if that, by road to Maarianhamina."

Jessica nods in response, and Niklas Steiner points at the dock and says something to his sister. Jessica turns in the direction in which Niklas pointed and sees a light blue three-story wooden house built on a steepish slope; it has a red metal roof and a balcony supported by white wooden pillars. The woman standing on the balcony, no doubt Anna Berg, watches the boat make its approach. Åke guides the boat side first against the dock, and Pernilla Steiner is the first to jump out. Jessica watches her pull the rope taut and tie it to the cleats on the dock with a practiced hand. It's clearly not Pernilla's first time in a boat.

As THEY CLIMB the slope in the dusk, a beautiful view of the sea playing in tones of dark blue opens up; dozens if not hundreds of islands spread out in a blue and green quilt. To reach the house on the crest of the hill, Jessica, the Steiners, and Åke climb a long flight of steep wooden stairs with powerful outdoor lights embedded in them. The lawn facing the shore is abundantly planted with currant bushes, and apple trees stand here and there in less symmetrical formation, their branches no doubt providing an abundant harvest in the autumn.

Judging by everything, Anna Berg's house is quite old, but when Jessica steps in through the downstairs door she notes the smell of fresh paint and raw lumber, as if the interior has recently undergone a renovation.

Anna Berg greets the party and leads them up a spiral staircase.

"You have a beautiful home," Niklas Steiner says, apparently to break the silence once all five of them are seated at the round dining table. There's a contemporary open-plan kitchen at one end of the living room, the walls are covered in light blue wallpaper, and the floor is hardwood. A meter-tall cat tree rises behind the sofa set, but there's no sign of the cat itself. Maybe it's outside despite the stormy weather.

"Thank you," Anna Berg says. A deep blast carries in from outside, and a large man flashes past the kitchen window, carrying something in his hand. "Pelle is washing the car," Berg continues with a shake of her head. "As if the storm wouldn't take care of it for him."

The others chuckle good-naturedly and Berg pours coffee into the ladybug-themed mugs on the table. Jessica hears Berg's wheezing breath and can't help but silently compare her with Astrid, who is a couple decades older. The gray-haired, hunchbacked, and stout Anna Berg is the total opposite of the mistress of Villa Smörregård. "I understood there would be two reporters, but . . . Why the delegation? I'm starting to feel a little too important," Berg says, and the small mouth between the round cheeks turns up in a smile.

Jessica raises the automatic camera she borrowed from Niklas as a prop, and it seems to suffice as an answer.

Berg clicks a few artificial sweeteners into her coffee and turns to Åke. "And you I know, Åke Nordin. Do you remember me?"

Åke nods and suddenly looks embarrassed. "It's been a long time."

"True. You were just a boy back then," Berg continues, with a gentle smile. "I remember how excited you were—you and your friend—when we came to Smörregård to talk to the people from the orphanage. It must have been pretty thrilling at the time."

"Well, it's not like there was a whole lot going on there back then. Or since either."

Berg eyes Åke for a moment the way older people look at sweet children: a wistful affection in her eyes combined with the painful awareness of how fast time flies.

"I heard about your father. My condolences," she says, and Åke nods. For some reason, Jessica gets the impression that Berg's condolences and Åke's understated reaction are both somehow feigned. As if they are a matter of some unpleasant obligation that simply needs to be gotten out of the way.

"And you're here as the journalists' moral support?" Berg finally says.

"As a matter of fact," Åke says, and clears his throat, "to be perfectly honest . . . the article was my idea. Or, originally the angle was different, but Elisabeth's . . . I mean . . ."

"Åke suggested doing a story on the children evacuated during the war," Pernilla Steiner interjects calmly as Åke stumbles over his words. Jessica looks up from the table. This is the first time she has heard the other woman talk. "But now we have the makings of something much more exciting."

"So a person's death is exciting?" Berg says, her voice tinged with a reproach that reveals something about a former police officer's attitude toward reporters.

"I'm sure what Pernilla means is that now, if ever, is a good moment to highlight the island's history," Niklas Steiner hastens to say. "In light of the events of the last twenty-four hours, it would be downright contrary to journalistic ethics not to write about it. The truth, whatever it happens to be, has to come out."

Berg nods, then eyes each of them probingly in turn. She is clearly a police officer, even if years have passed since she hung up her badge. *It takes one to know one.*

"How exciting," Berg remarks laconically. "So, how can I help you ladies and gentlemen?"

Niklas Steiner opens his notebook, and Jessica sees the bullet points scribbled in a sloppy hand: these are the questions he and Jessica drafted before they left Smörregård.

"You were working for the Maarianhamina police in the early 1980s," Niklas Steiner begins as the metal roof pops ominously. The wind seems to be grabbing the house from below, setting its corners creaking.

"I was an officer until 1982, and after that I was a detective, yes. I was the unit's first and only woman until 1988, when I took officer training and was eventually able to choose my own subordinates."

"What do you mean?"

"I mean I started to hire women."

"I see. And so you moved over to investigations in . . . ," Pernilla Steiner leads, and Anna shuts her eyes to remember better.

"August."

"In other words, you'd just begun working as a detective when Martin Hedblom drowned at Smörregård in September 1982."

Berg nods. "Actually, the Hedblom case was the first death that came to me. My first real case, if professional relevance is measured in the loss of human life."

"Would you care to tell us a little about that?"

For a moment Berg looks like she doesn't understand the question, but then she draws a breath and starts to talk. "I remember it very vividly. I had just dropped off my daughter at day care when I received a call on my police radio that a man had been found dead in northeastern Ahvenanmaa. Drowned, they said. The chief told me to drive straight to Alören, where a search-and-rescue boat would be waiting for me. I remember swearing, because it was at least an hour's drive to Alören, and I used to get lost when I was driving alone. Well, in any case, I asked the desk if we couldn't just have the body brought to Doktorsvägen for examination. Why did I have to drag myself out there if no one had been shot or stabbed?"

"And what did they tell you?"

Berg looks reflective. "I guess the director of the orphanage thought there was something a little strange about the incident. It was unclear whether one of the children might have seen or heard something. And whether everyone was telling the truth."

Niklas Steiner shoots a look at Jessica. "Did the director suspect any of the children of being involved in Hedblom's death?" he asks.

"I don't think so. There was just something strange about it. The night watchman leaving his desk in the middle of the night, wandering down to the shore, and drowning in shallow water. Of course the first thing to come to mind was that he was drunk, but only a small amount of alcohol was found in his blood during the autopsy."

"So in the end the cause of death was drowning?" Niklas Steiner asks.

Berg nods. "And that's how it appears in the records: accidental drowning. But the incident nagged at me."

"Why?"

Berg lowers one hand on top of the other and lets it slowly slide from the wrist to the elbow. Jessica sees the white hairs on her skin stand up, as if Berg finds recalling the case somehow unpleasant.

"One of the children, a little boy about five or six years old," Berg says in a dry voice, and lubricates her throat by gulping twice, "said he'd seen a little girl outside that night."

Jessica feels her fingertips go numb.

"One of the children from the orphanage?" Niklas Steiner asks. Jessica is pleased he's so alert and she doesn't have to steer the conversation.

"No," Berg says firmly. "The boy was talking about Maija, or at least thought he was."

"The girl in the blue coat?" Pernilla Steiner asks, and Berg nods.

"Everyone knew the story. It was already a local legend back then, a story that was told around campfires and no one believed. So I didn't give much weight to the testimony, but it was still strange."

"That the boy saw a girl outside?"

"Yes, that and . . . The same boy said he also heard an alarm clock."

Jessica quickly clenches her fists to get the tingle in her fingers to stop.

"When?" Niklas Steiner says.

"At two a.m. on the dot. The boy was woken by an alarm clock, looked out the window, and saw the girl."

Niklas Steiner digests this information for a moment. "Did the alarm clock ever turn up?"

Berg takes two quick sips of her coffee, then shakes her head, the cup still in her fingers.

"There was only one old-fashioned alarm clock at the orphanage as far as anyone knew, the mechanical sort that works by clockwork and makes a loud noise." Then she looks out the window. "And that alarm clock had once belonged to Maija Ruusunen."

61

JESSICA SHIFTS HER weight in the streamlined but slightly uncomfortable designer chair and straightens her tired legs. The seascape indicates that the storm promised for that evening is not going to disappoint. The horizon has turned midnight blue, and as she was climbing the outdoor stairs a moment ago, Jessica sensed the electricity in the air, which she usually encounters only during thunderstorms triggered by high-summer hot spells.

"So you disregarded the boy's account?" Niklas Steiner blurts, and Jessica hopes Anna Berg won't take the words as an accusation. Berg could put a stop to the conversation at any moment, if she felt it was taking on interrogational tones.

"Yes. By all signs, the poor child had not only been seeing but also hearing things, as the alarm clock in Maija's room had not been set to go off at two. Why would it have been?"

The look on Niklas Steiner's face is pained; he also seems to have had his fill of the awkward chairs. He twists his torso from side to side and then says: "And the case continued to nag at you?"

To everyone's surprise, the retired detective shakes her head. "Actually, it didn't. Not at the time."

"But you just said . . ."

Berg raises her teaspoon and appears to be looking at her reflection in its concave surface.

"Please try to understand that at the time everything seemed crystal clear. But the case came back to mind when the long-term director of the orphanage, Monica Boman, suffered the same fate only three years later. Think about it: someone on the orphanage payroll is found dead and fully dressed in the shallows at dawn. The case was identical, down to the spot where the bodies were found: next to the dock, face and airways just barely under the surface, up against the rocks," Berg says, and Jessica thinks about Elisabeth, her frail body lying at the waterline.

"It was because of these similarities that a notably more comprehensive cause-of-death investigation was conducted in Boman's case. And this time something was found that indicated something truly odd was afoot. A rather considerable amount of sedatives was discovered in Boman's body."

"But in Boman's case as well, the cause of death was drowning?" Niklas Steiner asks.

Berg gives a barely perceptible nod. "The director had been at the orphanage late doing paperwork. She had intended on spending the night in her office—which she occasionally did—and then continuing her work first thing in the morning. According to the night watchman, who had just started his shift, she left her office and the building at around eight p.m. and never returned. When his shift was nearing its end and he realized that the director was not in her office, he had made a round of the vicinity and discovered the lifeless body at the waterline."

"Was the night watchman's account credible?"

"The children confirmed it. Several of them had seen Boman leave at around eight o'clock, and many said the night watchman hadn't left his desk all night. We were in a situation where the only thing that made the death suspicious was the similarity to the Hedblom incident. The way an insurance company only begins to suspect fraud when the barn burns down for the second time."

"Was the night watchman a suspect?" Pernilla Steiner asks.

"Of course that possibility was on the table, but there was no proof. Besides, the guard on duty the night of Boman's death was nowhere in the vicinity in 1982. We felt the similarity between the acts—if they were murders—meant it had been the same perpetrator both times."

"And the director didn't tell the night watchman why she left the orphanage at eight p.m. or where she was going?"

Berg shakes her head.

For a moment, all five at the table sit in silence, raising their coffee cups to their lips. The wind howls through the corners of the old house and rattles the windows. Suddenly the landline on the sideboard next to the kitchen door blasts out ringing. Berg hauls herself to her feet and makes her way over to the phone.

"Berg residence. Oh, hi. Sure. Right. We have visitors right now. We're going to be home all night. I'll call you later."

Jessica watches the woman lower the plastic receiver to its cradle and reflects that she hasn't seen anyone speak into such a device in almost a decade. Jessica shifts her gaze to the others sitting around the table, and something about Pernilla Steiner's alert demeanor catches Jessica's attention: presumably, the way Pernilla is frowning at the phone. Maybe a landline is an even greater rarity in her world.

"That was just Emma . . . My sister. Where were we?" Berg says as she returns to the table and folds her hands in front of her.

"Monica Boman's death," Niklas Steiner says. He licks his fingers and turns over a new page in his notebook, in which he has conscientiously made a note of everything Berg has told them so far. Pernilla, on the other hand, is still staring at the phone, eyes narrowed.

"Did anyone see Maija that night?" Jessica says, and Berg trains her eyes on her, as if flabbergasted that a photographer would insinuate herself into the conversation without permission.

"No," Berg replies nonetheless, pointedly raising a finger. "It's also worth noting that almost none of the children who were at the orphanage in 1982 were still there in 1985."

"Almost?" Jessica says, but before Berg can reply, Åke rises to his feet. His hands are shaking and his cheeks have gone pale. He agitatedly makes his way over to the window and stands there looking out to sea.

"Åke, is everything all right?" Jessica says.

Åke doesn't answer, just shakes his head. "I should have told you," he then says softly. "But I promised Johan . . ."

"Promised him what?" Jessica asks.

"I need some fresh air," Åke says, reaching a trembling hand for the door handle. He pulls the large sliding door aside and steps out onto the balcony.

"What the hell is going on?" Niklas Steiner says, trying to decide whom to look at in hopes of getting answers.

Out on the balcony, Åke leans against the railing, the wind ruffling his curls and long beard.

Berg takes hold of the coffee pot and pours herself another cup. "As I was saying," she continues calmly, "almost none of the children from 1982 were still there in 1985. But there was one boy who was living at the children's home at the time of both deaths."

Jessica turns from Åke back to Berg, who wraps her fingers around her coffee cup.

"It was someone Åke had made friends with."

62

JESSICA FEELS THE adrenaline surge into her veins and set her heart pumping faster. She looks at Anna Berg's broad cheeks, the jet-black mole sprouting under her right eye, and the crooked teeth visible between the thin lips. Berg just said something that hadn't even occurred to Jessica as a possibility and that Åke, who is out on the balcony airing his thoughts, had wanted to keep to himself for one reason or another. A sudden insight throbs at Jessica's temples. Johan Karlsson was on the island at the time of not only Martin Hedblom's and Monica Boman's deaths but also Elisabeth's. Karlsson is the mystery seventh guest, the unknown figure she saw in room 21, and that is why he wanted to enter Astrid's office alone and assured Jessica there was no one staying in the room upstairs. How damn stupid can she be? And Astrid and Åke have protected and hidden Karlsson because they've known him since childhood.

"What does . . . What I mean is, was Johan Karlsson suspected of being the perpetrator at any point?" Jessica asks.

But Berg seems to find the question more amusing than anything else. "In the first place, at the time of Hedblom's death Johan was only ten, and when Boman died he was thirteen. Besides, the night watchman would have noticed if Johan had snuck out and—"

Now it's Jessica's turn to snort incredulously. "Are you serious? Johan wouldn't have been the first child to jump out of his window without a guard noticing."

"In any event," Berg says coolly. She shoots the Steiners a questioning look, waits for a nod from Niklas, and then continues: "Johan Karlsson was just a boy, and the fact that he was around at the time of both deaths did not, simply put, suffice to arouse suspicions. By the same logic, we might have just as well suspected the guilty party was one of the Nordins, who lived on the island. All of them were also present when the deaths took place." Berg folds her arms across her chest, then nods at the balcony. "Just like this time."

"Johan was on the island when Elisabeth died," Jessica says, and now both Berg and the Steiners look surprised.

"What are you talking about? Karlsson didn't arrive until this morning, in the police boat," Niklas Steiner says.

But Jessica shakes her head. "No, he didn't. He arrived a lot earlier."

Jessica stands and marches over to the balcony, with the other three watching her. Jessica pulls the door shut behind herself so sharply that Åke's shoulders shake in fright.

Åke wipes his eyes before he dares reveal his sad face to Jessica. The storm wind carries the smell of smoke with it. The wind chime dancing above the patio table clinks eerily.

"What's going on here, Åke?" Jessica says as calmly as she can. The sound of Pelle's pressure washer carries faintly from the other side of the house.

"I'm sorry, Jessica," Åke says. "Johan is like a brother to me, and . . ."

"Did Johan do it? Did he kill Hedblom and Boman? And Elisabeth?"

Åke shakes his head. "I don't know. But part of me is afraid he did."

"But why? Johan was just a kid back then . . ."

"For the longest time I didn't think it was possible," Åke says, then sighs deeply. "That night in September 1982 when Martin Hedblom drowned next to the orphanage dock, Johan was spending the

night at Villa Smörregård with us. Boman would sometimes give
him permission to do so, because we'd become good friends and it
did Johan good to be in a different sort of environment from time to
time. We were almost the same age, and on top of it all, Astrid treated
him like her own son . . . She and Dad even considered adopting him,
I understand. And I guess they would have, except . . ."

"Except what?"

Åke looks like he's stopped to consider whether he's let slip something he ought to have kept to himself. "He was just such a damn
weird kid. That's it," he then says, and bites his lip.

"But if Johan had spent that night at your place, there's no way he
could have . . ."

"Right. It doesn't make any sense. Besides, how would a ten-year-
old boy even kill a big man like Martin Hedblom? A strong, unpredictable man with a vicious streak—that's what Johan always said."

"So then why are you afraid it was Johan?"

Something about the way Åke gazes at the gray sky and the dark
blue veil of clouds shifts. "Because it happened again just now when
Johan returned after all these years. You have to understand, Johan
has always been very eccentric, and that's presumably why no adoptive family was ever found for him. Some sort of obsession with
Smörregård gradually developed inside him . . . With me and Astrid. At some point it felt downright scary; Johan might spend the
night at our place, go back to the orphanage as agreed . . . and then
suddenly appear at our door again. He said he was coming home,
even though it wasn't really his home."

"Why did you two lie to me?"

"What do you mean?"

"Johan didn't arrive on the island this morning with the police
boat. He registered as a guest on Monday, only a few hours before
I did."

Åke lowers his head, and the regret seems to be crashing over him like a tidal wave. "Johan had told Astrid he needed to protect the birds of spring. That someone meant them harm and that he was the only one who could prevent it."

"So he was staying upstairs without the other guests' knowledge to protect the birds of spring? And in the end he wasn't able to protect Elisabeth, even though that was the specific reason why he had come to Smörregård."

"Like I said, Johan is a special case . . . The fact that he wants to protect someone might actually mean that he wants to hurt them. Besides . . ."

"Besides what?"

"He was let go from the police force some time ago."

Jessica slams her palm against the railing so hard that she hurts the base of her thumb. The trio at the dining table turn toward the sound.

"Goddamn it!" Jessica shouts so loudly that even Pelle must hear her cry, above the storm, the wind chime, and the pressure washer.

Åke strokes his reddish beard with his rough fingers; his little lips quiver as he searches for the words. "You have to understand, Jessica, that if you've grown up with a person like that . . . it's hard to be objective."

Jessica shuts her eyes and lets the storm wind lick her face. Then a new question occurs to her. "But if Johan isn't a police officer, who's investigating Elisabeth's death?"

"The men from Search and Rescue this morning decided Elisabeth had drowned. I guess they didn't immediately connect the death to the earlier incidents, which is no surprise: it's unlikely either of them had even been born when they took place. Mom and I didn't want to feed them any nonsensical theories; everyone was shocked enough as it was. And then a little later, Astrid was asked to send the police the information on everyone staying with us, so an autopsy will be performed in town and all options looked into. But it's unlikely anything is going to happen before tomorrow," Åke says, and Jessica has to admit to herself that there's sense to everything Åke says. In retrospect, it would have been a little strange if a criminal investigator had shown up on the first police patrol boat. Despite the fact that the island's statistics when it comes to strange deaths by drowning were already grim.

"So you let your old friend play policeman like this is some goddamn Shutter Island? Harass me and the other guests with his nosy questions and snarky comments? The guy has been fucking with me all morning. If I'd known he wasn't a police officer anymore—"

"I'm sorry. We tried to get him to stop. I told Astrid we needed to call in the police, but she told me not to intervene. She said Johan wouldn't hurt anyone. That he would calm down before long and be on his way, as he no doubt eventually will. The way he has before."

Jessica shuts her eyes and thinks about Johan Karlsson, his theatrical seizure, his surprisingly believable fib about a brain tumor, the west dock and the boat he arrived on and departed on earlier today to go to . . .

"Does Johan Karlsson have a brain tumor?"

Åke looks like he has the urge to laugh, but settles for a grunt and reluctantly says: "Johan has had every tumor and disease imaginable since he was a kid."

"Åke, is there a dock on the island's western shore?"

Jessica looks at Åke, his kind eyes and thick beard. His right eyelid twitches a few times, and then worry colors his face.

"Johan Karlsson didn't come to the island on his own boat, did he?" Jessica says. Her heart skips a beat.

"No, he came by water taxi on Monday. Just like you."

"So at this moment Johan is at Smörregård with Astrid and the birds of spring?"

It takes Åke a second to understand what Jessica is driving at. "He came to the island to protect—"

"What did you just say, Åke? In Johan's world, protecting can mean something totally different. Do you think Armas and Eila are safe? If Johan actually killed Elisabeth . . ."

Åke raises his hand to his mouth, breathes through his fingers for a moment, presumably weighing the gravity of the situation. Then he rushes past Jessica and yanks open the sliding door.

"We have to go. Now."

63

DURING THE INTERVIEW with Anna Berg, the swells grew so large that Åke, who has his phone at his ear, appears to be wondering whether making the trip in the small rubber boat is safe. He ends the call, wipes his forehead, which is wet from the rain that is now a horizontal shower, and turns to Jessica.

"Listen up," Åke begins in a loud voice, directing his words not only to Jessica but to the Steiners, standing behind her, as well. "I wasn't able to reach Astrid, or Johan either. You don't have to come with me. This is a mess we can sort out ourselves. Astrid, Johan, and I."

"What are you talking about?" Jessica says, stepping up to the edge of the dock.

"The sea isn't safe in this weather. At least if there are four of us . . . The storm caught up to us faster than I'd expected."

"We need to call the police and have them go out. Real police," Jessica says, and Niklas Steiner nods in support of the idea. But Åke doesn't seem to be listening; he unties the rope from the two cleats at the end of the dock. "Did you hear me, Åke?"

"No. No police," Åke says firmly, wrapping the rope around his fist. His wet beard shimmers in the gleam of the dock's lampposts. "If Johan really is behind all this, I want to clear it up myself."

Niklas Steiner protests: "Isn't it pretty clear that Johan is—"

But Åke stomps on the dock so violently, even Jessica is startled. For the first time, the man with the bovine temperament has shown he has a pulse. "Johan is like a brother to me, and . . . I'm going to make sure nothing bad happens to anyone. If Johan has done something wrong, I will bring him to the police myself. OK?"

After he has said his piece, Åke takes a deep breath and shakes his head. A flock of gulls shoots off into flight from the neighbors' dock. "I'm sorry about all this," he says, more calmly now, and steps into the boat, which rocks under his weight. "I can order you a taxi to Maarianhamina; there's usually room at the Savoy on Nygatan. You can send the bill to us; you'll get your bags first thing in the morning."

Jessica glances over her shoulder at the huddled Steiners, who are clearly considering the offer.

A moment later, Niklas Steiner appears next to Jessica. "Fine. Pernilla will take a taxi to Maarianhamina."

"So the boat will be lighter," Pernilla calls to them.

Åke nods in approval and pulls his phone from his pocket. "Great. I'll just call—"

"No need. I'll call myself, thanks," Pernilla says.

Åke shrugs. "Are you sure?"

"She is," Niklas Steiner says, and steps past Åke and into the boat, which rocks dangerously. "We need to get going."

"I'm not going to any Savoy on Nygatan," Jessica says.

Åke's mouth curves into a shy smile, as if he secretly hoped that Jessica would refuse the offer. He extends a hand to her, but she clambers into the boat without any assistance. Åke turns the ignition; there's a high-pitched signal, and the outboard motor rumbles to life.

Jessica seats herself at the prow again and grabs the plastic handles with both hands so she won't bounce over the edge at the first wave. Åke calmly steers the boat into the restlessly roiling swells, and Jessica glances one last time at Pernilla Steiner. She is still on the dock; her figure forms a black silhouette against the brightly burning lamps. The hems of her coat and the hair that has escaped from her beanie flutter in the wind. Standing there, Pernilla Steiner is like the spitting image of the girl in the blue coat: the war orphan Maija Ruusunen, who now is saying good-bye to her brother. Just for one night, or maybe forever if everything goes awry somehow. And as the boat gradually recedes from the shore, Jessica turns to Niklas Steiner, who has a remarkably placid look on his face considering the circumstances. Jessica is overcome by the sense that there's something predetermined about the entire situation: that the surface similarities actually form one controlled whole Jessica is unable to make sense of yet.

64

ANNA BERG SETS the wooden tray with the dirty mugs down on the counter. The howl of the wind carries in from outside, along with the low thumps at the metal roof that sound as if a giant is hopping on the house. She hopes this storm won't topple a single tree in the nearby woods, which has been on their property for a few years now. A storm that blew through last autumn knocked over not only the old oak but also a twenty-meter pine, the top of which was sawed into logs the next day in the greenhouse that had been ruined beyond repair.

She loads the dishwasher and feels an ache in her lower back as she straightens her carcass. She's a tractor engine that has seen better days, been driven into the ground, and cut out the second it was retired. Her only mementos of a substantial career in law enforcement are the diplomas and the silver medal of commendation hanging on the wall.

When her first marriage ended, Anna was a trim forty-year-old. Back then, Pelle—who was the maintenance man at the police station and didn't have much professional ambition to speak of but had an appreciation for all things of beauty—had fallen in love with not only her appearance but also her successful career as an officer of the law.

Anna yawns and glances at her watch. Yes, her career as a police officer was a successful one, but she never managed to solve the mystery of Smörregård. The visit from the journalists and the Nordin boy have opened old wounds, and she isn't sure giving the interview wasn't a mistake after all. Pelle had warned her: *Don't let them start digging into that, damn it.*

Anna starts the eco program and closes the dishwasher door with a click. She sees raindrops sliding down the windowpane, and now it occurs to her that the monotone sound of the pressure washer stopped some time ago. Where has that Pelle gone off to? It's unlikely he started doing yard work in this weather.

At that instant, there's a knock at the door.

Anna frowns, walks over to the balcony, and looks out. Åke Nordin's boat pulled away from the dock some time ago and is now a few hundred meters offshore, lurching toward the channel in the rough swells.

There's another knock at the door. The cat mewls in the bedroom.

"Pelle?" Anna calls out, even though she knows it's pointless. Her husband is outside. But why has he circled around to start banging on the downstairs door? The front door isn't even locked.

Anna starts descending the wooden spiral stairs and hears the knocking again; this time it's more insistent.

What on earth are you up to, Pelle?

Anna groans. Her back pain reminds her of its existence with every step she takes. Cursing softly, she passes the statue of a sleeping dog and yanks open the door.

It's not Pelle standing out there in the rain, though, but a soaking-wet woman whose black eyes are gleaming brightly.

"Did you forget something?" Anna says uncertainly, and can't help but wonder why the woman didn't board the boat she saw plowing through the waves just a moment ago.

"As a matter of fact, I did," Pernilla Steiner replies with a smile.

65

JESSICA GRIPS THE plastic handles more tightly and pictures the blood draining from her knuckles toward her fingers. The rubber boat rises to the crest of a big wave, and gravity presses Jessica toward the back of the boat and the windshield behind which Åke is turning the wheel. Jessica feels the rain on her face intermittently mingle with seawater. The water spraying up from under the boat is colder than the rain and tastes salty. She remembers how Erne took her to visit his childhood home years ago. Jessica remembers the smell of the catch, the drive through the endless coniferous forest to the harbor at Papissaare, where abandoned Soviet-era warehouses and the factory where Erne said his parents had worked were falling apart. Jessica remembers the sausage stand that sold Saku beer, the cracked concrete pier where the rebar visible under the ragged surface reminded her of human bones stripped of flesh. The moss covering the rock, and the wooden pilings supporting the pier, which had broken at the top; the sea had draped its slimy capes over them through the years. That was the dock where Erne had sat as a child, fishing for dinner for his family.

Jessica can hear his lighter click shut, and Erne's characteristic smell spreads everywhere.

What do you think? he asks. In the evening sun, his long shadow falls over Jessica and beyond, all the way to the water.

It's a bleak place and tastes of a hard life, stifled creativity, fear, and the presence of a foreign power. The waves licking the pier seem to be coming from somewhere very far away. They tell stories of a different sort of world, the kind where you can speak and think freely. Be yourself.

JESSICA CONSIDERS HOW to answer Erne tactfully. Everything at that shore is desolate and ugly and makes Jessica understand why Erne left it all behind and crossed the Gulf of Finland in search of a better life, which is why, in spite of everything, Jessica likes the place: because it's part of the life story of someone she loves.

I like it, Jessica answers, but Erne doesn't believe her. Cigarette smoke puffs from his mouth like dust from a rug that's being beaten. Jessica joins in his laughter.

Come on. Let's go eat, Erne says. *There's a place with tablecloths not too far away.*

Jessica emerges from her reverie when a big wave slams into the bottom of the boat.

She watches the waves gather their strength some distance ahead: they're preparing for their attack. Åke increases the revs. Jessica can't help but think that if she loosened her grip on the handles, if she turned her life over to fate and gave in to the mercy of the moment, she'd find herself in the frigid water as soon as the boat scaled those meters-high waves.

Stop, Jessica. Don't even think about it.

The spray forces Jessica to shut her eyes, and she can hear Erne's raspy voice again.

The alarm clock, Jessie. The boy heard an alarm clock in the middle of the night. And saw Maija. Do you believe what that boy said?

I don't know.

What if the person who killed three people isn't at Smörregård anymore?

What do you mean?

I think you know. I'm sure it occurred to you already.

Jessica opens her eyes just as the boat is plowing into a huge wave, and her fingers clench the handles even more tightly. When she wipes her wet face on her sleeve and realizes she's still sitting solidly at the prow of the boat, she understands something is terribly wrong.

66

ÅKE STEERS THE boat to the dock, and Jessica is the first to jump out. The nausea is churning in the pit of her stomach, and she feels weak. Lights burn in the windows of the villa, and there's movement in the dining room. Jessica isn't sure what Johan Karlsson is capable of or if he is perhaps armed. She can't help but think that over the last half hour she has made two mistakes. In the first place, she should have called the police from the boat regardless of whether Åke thought it was a good idea. Åke was convincing when he said he'd handle Johan, but if Johan has truly murdered three people, a police presence will be required sooner or later anyway. Why take unnecessary risks and delay the inevitable? Second, Jessica now thinks they shouldn't have left Pernilla Steiner at Lövö. Jessica isn't sure what it is about the setup that smells fishy to her, but in retrospect the rapidly developing situation seems strange. Why did Pernilla travel from Kalmar all the way to Ahvenanmaa only to jump ship when the adventure began?

Jessica waits for the men to catch up to her before they all make their way to the villa. The storm has toppled two medium-sized spruces at the edge of the woods. Their trunks lie partly across the dirt road; the branches seem to be waving at them in greeting.

"We should have called the police," Jessica says when Åke appears at her side.

"Trust me," Åke says. "Johan would never harm me or Astrid. I'll handle this."

Jessica, Åke, and Niklas Steiner approach the villa's front door. Jessica sneaks over to the dining room window and sees Astrid, Armas, and Eila sitting at a table. No food has been set out, and something about the trio's body language seems to indicate that not everything is as it should be. None of them are eating, drinking, or talking. It's almost as if they are sitting still because they have no choice.

"Dining room," Jessica whispers. "Astrid and the birds of spring. No sign of Johan."

Åke dries his face on his sleeve. "OK. I'm going in."

"Are you sure?"

"Wait here," Åke says, and starts climbing the steps that lead to the villa's front door. Jessica presses herself against the outside wall and gestures for Niklas Steiner to follow her example. She's not used to hanging back from action, but now she needs to do exactly as Åke said: trust him and his ability to resolve things by talking.

"Hello?" Åke's voice calls out; then the door thunks shut behind him, and all Jessica can hear is the bluster of the wind.

She glances at Steiner, who looks curiously calm, even excited. Maybe straight-up action is a welcome change for a journalist.

Suddenly a shout carries over the roar of the wind. Jessica rushes to the window and sees Johan backing up to the table where the old people are sitting. Åke is standing at the door to the dining room, saying something. Johan raises his hand, and Jessica sees he's holding a large kitchen knife.

"Goddamn it," Jessica whispers to herself. "Good thing we didn't call the police."

"What's happening in there?" Steiner asks, glancing uneasily at Jessica.

"Call the police. Now!"

She remembers the side door to the dining room; she has seen Astrid use it to carry the catch from Åke's fish trap straight into the kitchen. Jessica hunches over and runs to the corner of the building. She glances at the threshold to the toolshed, the wet sawdust pasted to the stone. The metal railing feels icy against her palm as she climbs the short flight of stairs leading to the side door of the villa. She tries the handle. It's unlocked.

Jessica opens the door, steps in, and now she can hear what the men are saying.

"Put away the knife, Johan."

"I don't take orders from you! I'm a police officer."

Jessica makes sure the door shutting behind her doesn't clunk the tiniest bit. She shakes off her wet boots, then crosses the small vestibule to the dining room in her stocking feet. Jessica hopes Åke's eyes won't give her away and that she can sneak up behind Johan without his noticing. There's also the risk that one of the old people at the table will say something when they see Jessica. If Karlsson registers her presence too soon and has time to lunge at her with the knife, Jessica's chances of emerging the victor from a struggle will be slim.

"You're not a policeman anymore, Johan. This can all still end well," Åke says.

"Johan, please listen to Åke," Astrid says.

Jessica can hear Johan sobbing inconsolably. "Please don't get involved, Astrid. I failed with Elisabeth, but I'm not going to fail again. It's going to happen again tonight . . . I know it."

Jessica approaches the doorway. She sees Karlsson's back, his restless movements, the knife slicing through the air.

"You don't know what happened in the cellar," Karlsson shouts at Astrid.

"What on earth are you talking about?" Astrid says. In that instant she spots Jessica, but she quickly shifts her gaze back to Johan. Luckily.

"Johan, my dear friend," Åke says conciliatorily, and takes a step backward. "We believe you."

Jessica grabs a broom leaning against the wall and raises it into the air. She inches her way over the threshold, but when her heel touches down on the wooden floor, the planks make a nasty creak.

Karlsson turns around and lets out an animal roar as the broomstick hits the wrist of his knife hand. It's a sharp blow and unexpected enough that he loses his grip on the weapon. Åke lunges from the doorway and manages to restrain Karlsson without any trouble. Jessica lets out a long sigh and watches him lying there on the dining room floor, with Åke's arms wrapped around him.

And then Astrid bursts into a flood of tears.

67

JESSICA TAKES A seat in the armchair and stares at the fire blazing in the hearth. Just a moment before, she and the others watched from the front of the guesthouse as the police boat carrying Johan Karlsson gradually disappeared into complete darkness. After that, Astrid vanished into the bowels of the villa without saying a word, and Åke quietly retreated to his room for the night too.

The floor creaks beneath the feet of whoever entered the room. Over the past week, Jessica has learned to identify from the sound alone whether footfalls belong to Åke or Astrid or someone else. Astrid's are light and steady, whereas Åke makes a more expansive sound.

It's Astrid, glass in hand. She lowers herself into the other armchair, the one where Åke sat the night before and told Jessica the story of the girl in the blue coat. Now, a mere twenty-four hours later, things have changed significantly: the murderer has been caught, even if the motive is anyone's guess. Jessica knows the glory does not belong to her: things would have fallen forward on the force of their own momentum and resolved themselves without her. For once. If only crimes would solve themselves in Helsinki too.

"Are you religious, Jessica?" Astrid says, swirling the whisky at the bottom of her glass.

"No," says Jessica. "Not at all."

"Me either," Astrid says. "So it would be hypocritical to pray on Johan's behalf?"

"I suppose," Jessica says. She studies Astrid's profile in the fire-light. The scar tissue visible at her open collar and up to her jaw looks painful in the glow of the warm flames, as if the heat is scorching the old injury. Maybe it really is a burn.

"I'm sorry we let it happen," Astrid says.

"What?"

"Elisabeth's death. Whatever it was Johan was trying to do in the dining room. Letting him harass you. Putting our guests in harm's way."

"You didn't believe Johan was capable of that?"

"Of course not."

Astrid sips her whisky, stares at it up close as if gauging the glass-distorted flames. Then she drains her glass.

"Johan was always an unusual boy. We hadn't seen him for ages when he appeared on the island early last week. He'd heard the birds of spring would be holding what might be their last gathering here, and he wanted to come. To protect them, in his own words."

"That's what Åke said," Jessica says. "But I don't really understand what that means. Protect them?"

Astrid shrugs and stares intently at the fire. Jessica is dying to ask if it was fire that damaged her skin, seared its eternal mark into it, but she doesn't have the nerve.

Instead, she asks: "What did Johan mean by the cellar thing?"

Astrid turns from the flames for the first time during the conversation. "Excuse me?"

"The cellar." Suddenly Jessica has the impulse to avoid Astrid's gaze, which has turned strangely penetrating. "Johan said you don't know what happened in the cellar."

"I haven't the faintest clue."

"Does it have something to do with Smörregård?"

"There's no cellar here," Astrid says, and lowers the glass to the tall table between the armchairs. "Johan is clearly delusional, Jessica dear."

Astrid stands with astonishing agility, then steps over to Jessica and lowers her hand to Jessica's shoulder, as she has done many times before. "I'm going to go to bed. I'll leave out the salmon soup; help yourself if you're hungry."

"Thank you," Jessica says as Astrid's light footfalls mingle with the crackling of the fire. The case seems clear, but the gnawing sensation in the pit of Jessica's stomach won't leave her in peace. She hears Astrid turn off the lights in the kitchen, close the office door, and climb the stairs.

A moment later, an oppressive silence falls over the villa.

68

NOW THUNDER RUMBLES right overhead. When Jessica glances over her shoulder, the orphanage is gone. Where a sturdy white building stood a moment ago there is only an undeveloped patch of land, and a long-handled spade struck into the sand. Jessica turns back to the sea but all she can see are endless rows of surging shorebound waves that crash into the rocks again and again.

Not tonight, Jessica whispers.

The wind blowing from the sea carries faint singing from another time and place.

> *When you take to wing, look back for a final glance.*
> *So you don't forget your home, so there's no chance.*
> *The journey is long, and you may lose your way*
> *But when spring returns, the northern dawn breaks gray.*

The long dock does not rock under her bare feet. Soon Jessica feels coarse gravel and wet grass on her toes. Only now does she understand how astonishingly desolate the site is, even without the grim building. The pitch-black forest looming behind the opening is like a gateway to another world; it signifies the boundary between death and life.

Suddenly someone emerges from the trees. A dark figure whose footfalls are somehow compulsive and unnaturally swift. The figure is like a marionette lurching in unskilled hands; it approaches

Jessica surprisingly fast. The despairing scream of a gull echoes from the sky.

The figure seems to be whispering something. Its head is tilted, the hands bounce from side to side, and the fingers move like a stenographer's.

Even so, Jessica isn't afraid. "What do you want?"

The figure stops abruptly in front of Jessica. It brings its shapeless face right down in front of hers. It's not a human face. Nor do the whispers come from a human mouth.

Anna Berg knows what happened in the cellar, it says. There are two black holes where the eyes should be.

"What?"

And now Jessica sees more figures emerging from the woods. The black creatures rush at her, all running in the same way. Nor is the glade completely unbuilt anymore; a small building stands in the center. It's a red toolshed.

The shrieks grow louder and louder; the figures approach Jessica and, before long, have covered her entire field of vision. Jessica hears a high-pitched screech and feels wet hands on her face. And then suddenly everything goes black and the shouting stops.

Jessica opens her eyes.

She's lying on her bed, fully dressed. The clock on the wall says it's midnight.

For a moment, the room bathing in darkness tries to feed her imagination, forms unpleasant creatures where they don't exist. The shadows seem to be alive; the corners continue their whispering. The shrill cry still throbs in Jessica's ears.

Anna Berg knows what happened in the cellar.

Jessica lowers her hands to her stomach, tries to sense the life growing there.

She should have checked before.

She takes her phone from the nightstand. Anna Berg and her

husband would no doubt be angry about being woken in the middle of the night by the sound of the phone, but Jessica can't shake the thought that Pernilla Steiner ought to have climbed into Åke's boat with them at the Lövö dock. Jessica brings up the Bergs' home number and holds the phone to her ear. She hears it ring once, twice. The Bergs will answer if they're all right; she's sure of it. Everyone answers their landline if it rings in the middle of the night. A third time, a fourth. Jessica anticipates hearing Anna's irritated voice, or maybe Pelle's, who has fallen asleep in front of the television. A fifth, a sixth. Nothing happens. Jessica listens to the phone ring for so long that there's no doubt.

She hangs up and presses her phone to her chin. Damn it. If Pernilla has harmed the Bergs, why is Niklas Steiner still here?

The toolshed.

Johan Karlsson went into the toolshed.

It must be related to all this somehow.

Jessica stands, glances out the window, and sees that the villa is dark.

69

THE DOWNPOUR THAT lashed the island earlier that night has settled into a calm drizzle. A half-moon peers through a tear in the veil of clouds, making it easier to operate in the dark.

Jessica arrives at the corner of the villa, from where it is only a few strides to the toolshed. She spots the motion detector she deactivated earlier that day, which under normal circumstances would have already turned the yard lights on. But now Jessica creeps from one building to the other without arousing the attention of anyone in the villa. She steps under the eaves of the toolshed and glances over her shoulder. The windows at the end of the building, where both Astrid's and Åke's bedrooms are located, are dark, as is the oval window upstairs. Jessica lowers her gaze to her shoes; wet sawdust clings to the soles.

Jessica gropes around the top of the doorframe for the key. But her fingers don't strike on anything, and Jessica is silently cursing Karlsson for taking the key with him when it suddenly drops at her feet. She turns on her headlamp and retrieves the key from the muddy ground.

She fits the key into the lock and twists. The door seems to slump from its hinges as she pulls it toward herself. A nostalgic smell wafts out: the creosote-treated wood and the moldy surface of the granite foundation remind her of her childhood summers in the Turku archipelago. Jessica thrusts her head in and casts a quick glance around the toolshed to make sure there's nothing dangerous or un-expected inside. Just as she suspected from the outside, both of the windows are covered with dark green tarps. The shelves covering the walls are full of supplies; a big black mud rug lies on the plank floor. A small car or tractor would easily fit in the shed, Jessica sup-poses, but the door is too narrow and there's no ramp leading up to it.

Jessica tentatively enters and shuts the door behind her. She re-moves her headlamp and holds it in her hand. Presumably the heavy tarps will prevent the light from being visible from the outside. *It's fine.* It's unlikely anyone is looking at the toolshed just now.

Jessica lets the beam of light slide across the wooden shelves and the miscellaneous items on them. She sees tools, and labeled glass jars containing screws and bolts. Screwdrivers, chisels, a pry bar. Painting supplies: brushes, turpentine, tins of paint. Lures, floats, rods, reels, a fish trap, fishing nets. A set of narrow rubber tires hanging from long nails, the highest of which is so high that to reach it Jessica would have to lift the ladder lying on the ground. But the more closely Jessica scans the toolshed, the more it starts to seem like exactly that: an ordinary shed where there's nothing to be found.

She aims the lamp into a brown cardboard box on a table: at the bottom there's a thick layer of sawdust, and two bowls. One has wa-ter in it, the other seeds. There are bloody feathers on the floor in front of the table.

Jessica stops in the middle of the floor and looks down at her feet. And the mud rug she's standing on. *The cellar.*

She pulls the rug aside and is disappointed to discover there's no hatch beneath. But when she lowers the headlamp right to the sur-face of the aged planks, she sees an empty space above them. She aims the light at the wall and realizes that some sort of support structure has been built under the floor, but at the center of the shed it seems to be missing.

The planks have been screwed into the framing. Jessica reaches for a Phillips-head screwdriver and gets to work.

Just then, she thinks she hears a creak and stops. She holds her breath and listens. The wind is snapping against the roof of the villa. But nothing happens, and Jessica keeps removing the screws.

Eventually she has unscrewed two wide planks. She carefully lifts them aside.

She trains the light into the hole revealed beneath and sees a short wooden ladder that drops down a couple of meters. Jessica briefly considers whether it makes any sense to climb down and crawl into a claustrophobic nightmare. The events of the previous autumn are still fresh in her mind: she can see herself, sledgehammer in hand, smashing newly laid brick in an apartment-building laundry room. Finding the decomposing bodies of a young woman and man inside the wall. She remembers the moment when she realized she had committed a huge error in judgment. And that error nearly cost Jessica her life. She would never let anyone catch her off guard again. Especially now that the stakes have multiplied many times over.

She stands and walks over to the window. She turns off the head-lamp, gives her eyes a moment to adjust to the darkness, and cracks the tarp that is stapled to the window frame. She looks at the villa bathing in the nighttime darkness; not a single window is lit, and there's no sign of movement anywhere. She grabs a bicycle lock from a shelf and loops it through the hasp on the doorjamb. Now she will at least have a moment to prepare if someone tries to enter the toolshed.

Jessica returns to the ladder and starts slowly descending. She feels the ever-increasing damp and mold and the intensifying smell of creosote. Eventually her feet touch solid ground. Now she sees that the space, which looked cramped from above, is simply a door-way to a larger room.

Jessica spots a light switch on the plastered concrete wall and presses it. A lamp struggling to shine from the depths of a metal shade flickers a few times before it turns on, and Jessica's heart skips a beat.

There she is. Maija. The girl is standing in the middle of the room, wearing her blue coat, her head tilted a little to the right, and golden-brown hair at her brow.

JESSICA'S HEART IS pounding in her chest. She takes a step forward. The situation feels surreal, but at the same time, she understands that the figure she sees now isn't just a mirage but that it actually exists.

"Maija," Jessica whispers softly, and when the girl doesn't react, Jessica surprises herself by continuing: "It's OK, sweetheart."

Jessica hears her own footfalls and the crunch of small stones underfoot. The cellar belowground is the same size as the toolshed above. Hunching, Jessica creeps toward the girl, whose face is hidden in deep shadow. Jessica's head grazes the lampshade hanging from the ceiling, which sends the weak light swinging from one wall to the other, as if it has woken up and is now frantically searching for a way out of this grim, nightmarish cellar.

"Maija," Jessica says once she is standing right in front of the girl. And now she sees it's not an innocent child's face peering out from under the hair but something cold and devoid of expression.

Jessica touches the girl's shoulder, feels something like thin bone under her fingertips. She holds her breath and squats in front of the girl. Raises the girl's chin with her fingers, feels something other than skin. The face is fabric. Irregular stitching circles an oval face stuffed with cotton or wool. Jessica cracks the coat and sees that the torso reminiscent of a girl's frame has been cobbled together from two planks nailed into a cross, on top of which slender branches are interwoven to give the figure a human shape. Two thick sticks jut under the trousers and have been solidly planted in a pair of boots. Now Jessica understands that what so many people over the years imagined was Maija is not a real child or even a small adult. All along it has been nothing but a cheap trick: a scarecrow that when seen from a distance is no doubt effective at arousing perplexity and fear, especially if the person seeing it is familiar with Maija's story. Johan Karlsson has gone to a lot of trouble moving the scarecrow around the island, especially with the risk of getting caught.

Jessica looks around. With its whitewashed walls, the cellar room is ascetic, and it clearly was not designed to serve as a storeroom. A little chair stands near one wall, and a thick rope lies on the floor before it. A few shelves have been bolted into the walls, and there's a metal box on one.

Jessica walks over to the shelf, takes hold of the metal box, and studies the lid. A name is engraved on the brass plate: Maija Ruusunen. She hesitates as if she is about to cross the bounds of propriety, get mixed up in something questionable. But it's too late to turn around and walk away now. She has to know, because Maija would surely want everyone to know the truth. Jessica opens the box; the tiny rusted hinges resist. She sees that a sheaf of handwritten letters have been cached inside. There are dozens of them. Jessica looks at the dates: *1944 . . . when the war is over, Panda Bear. Love from somewhere in the world.* Stickers and dried flowers are glued to some of the paper. *March 1945: we'll see each other soon. I hope everything's all right there. Your mom would be so proud of you, and I know she's looking down on you.* All the letters bear the same signature: *Dad.* Jessica feels her heart leap: the letters are so full of love and warmth that she understands why they were once Maija's most prized possessions. Apparently Maija kept every single letter she received from her father and stored the letters in the little box. But wherever it was that Maija vanished to on that sad, infamous night long ago, for some reason she did not bring the box along. She had buried it next to the egg-shaped rock, where Johan Karlsson later found it. So Maija must have been convinced she couldn't bring the letters along wherever she was going. But Maija had hoped the letters wouldn't be lost forever. That must have been why she wrote the coded clue under the bed and hoped someone would find it one day.

Jessica holds the letters in her hand. Their weight is a concrete reminder of how much life has been documented in them. She glances over her shoulder at the hunched scarecrow and feels grief wash over her entire body. She knows she's not looking at Maija, that the girl is somewhere far away, moved on to another world long ago. But right now, the scarecrow dressed in a blue coat represents the little girl's pain, the feeling of bottomless alienation that Jessica finds it incredibly easy to relate to.

Now Jessica spots something at the feet of the wooden Maija. She approaches the scarecrow warily. On the floor behind the heels of the boots is something that's hard to make out in the dim light. Jessica knows it would be smartest for her to leave the cellar and the toolshed as fast as possible. She could call the police right away and tell them what she has found. But her inquisitive nature drives her on. She crouches down next to "Maija" and takes hold of the effigy's wooden ankles to carefully move it aside.

There's a hunk of metal on the floor. It's an alarm clock with an inscription on the back.

FOR PANDA BEAR, CHRISTMAS 1940

She remembers Anna Berg's story about the boy who'd been woken by an alarm clock the night Martin Hedblom died. *The clock had once belonged to Maija Ruusunen.*

Jessica lowers the clock back to the floor and reaches for the book the clock had been standing on. *Diary, Maija Ruusunen*. Contrary to what might be expected, the book is not covered in dust. Apparently Karlsson has perused it recently.

Jessica cautiously opens the book, and the binding cracks ominously: the pages are yellowed and dry and struggle to free themselves from the ancient covers. Jessica looks up from the book and is overcome by the feeling that she doesn't have the right to open it, read the lines written there.

But she has to.

The first entries were written in March 1942, in the hand of a very young girl, maybe one who had just learned to write. Jessica flips a couple of pages forward: as time passes, the cursive letters find their shape, condense into tidy lines; periods and commas appear among the words. Jessica browses on, May 1945, September 1946 . . . Dozens of blank pages remain. And then something slips from between the diary's pages to the floor. Jessica picks it up and realizes it's a letter. It's addressed to Panda Bear and signed Dad. But for some reason this letter has been typed on a typewriter and did not end up in the metal box with the others. Jessica brings it closer to her face in order to decipher the tiny characters. As her eyes move from line to line, shivers run up her spine.

Dear Panda Bear

I'm sorry I didn't come get you from Maarianhamina even though I promised to. I wanted to come, I really did. But I couldn't. Because although everyone thinks the war is over, it really isn't, not yet.

I'm still fighting, but I don't have to fear the enemy's bullets or grenades anymore. This is something more secret, which is why I can't even write to you by hand, the way I always have in the past.

It would be too dangerous.

In the eyes of the enemy, I'm dead.

I have to let them believe I'm dead.

Even you couldn't be told the truth, because it would have put you in danger.

But now you're such a big girl that I dare to share all this with you.

I'm coming to get you.

Come to the dock at two in the morning, sharp.

If I can't make it the first night for some reason, I'll come the next night.

It may be a long wait, but your patience will be rewarded. Wait for me, Panda Bear. Don't ever give up.

Dad

Jessica swallows down the lump in her throat. She thinks back to the words Åke said by the fire when he was telling this story. *They eventually stopped trying to keep Maija from performing her curious ritual. As certainly as the sun rose every morning, that girl would be out there on the dock staring out to sea. Weeks passed, months.*

It's clear Maija's father really did die in August 1946, when the vessel carrying him and the other parents foundered in a storm. The typewritten letter is dated September. With their ghastly plot, Elisabeth and the others had no doubt played a role in Maija's losing her sanity. They committed a terrible wrong in giving the girl false hope. Thrust her time and again out into the cold, dark night, to wait for something that could never happen. Jessica feels herself fill with rage; she burns with a desire to crumple up the letter but restrains herself. Maybe it will prove useful when they finally get to the bottom of all that has happened on this island.

Jessica takes hold of the diary again, flips to the final entry.

At first I thought it was pain. That the pain I felt was because it wasn't you after all. That you're not alive after all. Not coming.

But in reality it was something else, the pain was from the betrayal. What they did is wrong, and it's really hard to forgive. But I guess I still have to, that's what you taught me. Maybe someone else will read this someday and know who can't be trusted. You behaved awfully, but I forgive you, Miss Boman, Martin, Beth, Hamhock & Armas.

Maija, November 24, 1946

Armas? How is Armas involved in this plot? Armas said he warned Maija . . .

And right at the very bottom of the page, Maija wrote a little more hastily, perhaps with trembling fingers:

Throw me to the wolves and I'll return to lead the pack.

In that instant, Jessica hears something. *Damn it.* Someone found her. Her heart pounds in her chest, and suddenly it feels as if all the oxygen has just been sucked out of the subterranean chamber. Jessica looks around, but of course there's no way out.

She creeps over to the light switch and flicks it off, even though she knows it might be too late. Jessica stands there in the pitch-black cellar, not even daring to turn on the light on her phone.

But all she hears in the empty space is the steady drumbeat of water dripping from the roof to the floor. The lamp has settled in place, and now that Jessica has stopped to listen, she realizes it was making a low hiss. Jessica folds the letter in two, then places it carefully in her coat pocket. There's nothing else she needs just now; the local police can come and conduct their own investigation. Johan Karlsson, who with probable cause will be suspected of at least three murders, truly has good reason to sleep poorly tonight.

The wind is still brisk enough to set the toolshed creaking ominously. Jessica closes her eyes and tries to pick out anything from among the sounds she hears. Anything at all. The tread of boots, the creak of a door. The murmur of speech. In the inky blackness it's impossible to see anything, but her other senses are sharpened. The smell of the cellar seems to have intensified, as have the noises of the gale raging outside: the dribble of water dripping from the gutter and the scrape of branches against the roof. Then she hears a noise that sounds like the hammer of a gun being cocked. And it's not coming from above but from behind her.

Jessica feels it. The touch on her shoulder.

It's like her mother's, but the fingers are smaller, their grip weaker.

Mommy, a girl's voice says.

Jessica's flesh is instantly covered in goose bumps. She slowly turns around, and even though the cellar is bathed in perfect darkness, she can make out the girl's pale face, the blue lips that form the words.

"What, sweetheart?"

You have to take me away from here, the girl says. Her head is still tilted to the right. Her barley-colored hair is wet, dripping water to the floor.

"But—"

It's dark in here. And Daddy's not coming. Ever.

Jessica wants to say something, to comfort the girl, but she cannot sink into her hallucinations, not now that she's sure she heard something outside the shed a moment ago. But then again, so what? Karlsson isn't on the island anymore. There's no one who means her any harm, right? She could just climb the ladder and . . .

I didn't use it.

"What?"

The alarm clock.

The girl raises the hand holding the alarm clock. The words emerge from her mouth a little hesitantly, as if she is speaking for the first time in a long time. There's a Swedish note to the Finnish words.

Jessica can hear the old clock's second hand move forward. The sound of the cocking hammer must have come when Maija wound up her old mechanical clock.

"I don't understand," Jessica whispers.

The boy they told you about . . .

"Yes?"

He was lying. He couldn't have heard the clock because it was broken. Beth broke it, the girl says, and turns on her heel. And then the girl slowly walks to the rear wall of the cellar and vanishes into the darkness that has wrapped everything else in its cloak.

71

JESSICA CLIMBS UP the short ladder and warily raises her head through the gap above it to make sure there's no one else in the toolshed. Everything looks the way it did a moment before. Jessica slides from the gap to the floor and brushes the sawdust and dust from her clothes.

The wind is humming in the roof of the toolshed and the tops of the trees. Jessica listens, but the only other thing breaking the silence is the patter of the rain. She steps over to the window facing the villa and cracks the tarp, confirms that there are no lights on in any of the windows.

But just then, someone flashes past the oval window in the second-story corridor. The obscure figure lingers for just a moment, then disappears as quickly as it appeared. Jessica can't help but think someone peered out the window to see what was happening in the toolshed. Might that someone have seen Jessica cracking the tarp? Jessica lowers the tarp back into place and then checks her phone for the time. It's twenty past one.

Jessica removes the bicycle lock and opens the door. A current of cold air snatches it, and Jessica grabs it just before it slams against the wall. She closes it behind her. She glances up, and the oval window is nothing but a mirror reflecting the night sky.

Jessica starts walking cautiously toward the villa. The wind ruffling the hair at her ears whispers ominously, and the wildly lurching branches of the apple trees scrape her face as if trying to hinder her advance.

Once she makes it under the eaves of the villa, Jessica nearly trips over her own feet and is forced to steady herself against the wall. For some reason, every step she takes feels fraught with danger, as if she is walking toward the inevitable destruction of herself and her unborn child. Why didn't she just go back to her room and call the police?

When the moon emerges briefly from behind cloud cover, Jessica sees someone step out of the converted barn across the lawn, carrying something in their arms. She squats behind a metal barrel filled with water. It's impossible to be sure in the darkness, but under the circumstances the figure must be Niklas Steiner. He looks around, then stands staring at the villa for a moment. For a split second Jessica is convinced he has spotted her behind the barrel. But then he starts off at a jog toward the dirt road that leads through the woods.

What the fuck is going on?

Jessica has seen someone wandering around upstairs in the villa in the middle of the night, and now the Swedish journalist spending his last night in the room next to hers has run off into the woods in the rain carrying something with him.

Jessica breaks into a sprint. She passes the villa as quietly as possible, then runs through the woods until she reaches the dirt road. She sees Steiner a hundred yards ahead, striding briskly northward with his gym bag under his arm.

She sees him briefly lift his phone to his ear but has no idea whom he is talking to, or if he has just unsuccessfully tried to call someone. Sneaking around there at the edge of the forest, Jessica can't help but think that there was something strange about the way the siblings looked at each other on Anna Berg's dock. That there on the dock, an odd flame kindled in the reserved woman who generally hid in her brother's shadow. Did Pernilla Steiner stay behind on the island because she had something to tell Berg? Something that wasn't meant for the others' ears? Or maybe it was something much worse, Jessica thinks, and hears the monotone ringtone she listened to not long before, when Berg didn't answer her landline. *Damn it,* Jessica curses silently. Has she perhaps offered the retired detective on a silver platter to a person she actually knows nothing about?

72

IN THE LIGHT of the moon peeking through the clouds, Niklas Steiner stands in the sandy yard, gazing at the building that was once the Smörregård Children's Home. Just now, the derelict structure truly does look like the setting for ghost stories. From behind a toppled tree, Jessica sees Steiner continue toward the dock. She waits for a moment, then starts crossing the yard in pursuit. But at that instant Steiner whirls around. Goddamn it. She followed the man across the entire island only to be spotted at the most critical moment.

"Who's there?" Steiner shouts, taking a step backward. His rear foot lowers to the wobbly dock.

Jessica curses her bad luck and momentarily considers dashing into the woods and remaining anonymous for now. But she has come to the north shore to see what Steiner is up to, and she has no intention of retreating even if she has made the amateurish mistake of being spotted by the man she has been shadowing.

A pair of rusted garden scissors hangs from a tool rack at the corner of the building. Jessica grabs the scissors, shoves them under her waistband at her lower back, and steps forward.

"It's me," she calls. "Jessica."

Steiner slowly retreats down the dock. "Don't come any closer!" he says, looking around, apparently for something to fight with. His tentative body language reveals that he isn't armed. He looks more like a cornered gazelle than like a hungry lion.

"What are you doing here in the middle of the night?" Jessica asks, approaching the dock.

"I just knocked on your door," Steiner says. "I was trying to warn you. Get you to come with me."

Jessica eyes him pointedly. There's no way she can be sure he's telling the truth. Her room has been empty for the last half hour, so it's perfectly possible that Steiner knocked on her door.

"What's going on?"

Steiner doesn't answer; he turns toward the sea, and now Jessica spies a small dot of light against the black background. It's gradually growing brighter: an approaching boat.

"Going somewhere?"

"Far away from here," Steiner says.

"What are you running from?"

"This island is sick. There's something wrong with these people," Steiner shouts, constantly looking over his shoulder as if that will make the boat get there faster.

Jessica stops at the head of the dock, far enough from Steiner in case he gets it into his head to do something stupid. She can't get the notion out of her mind that for some reason or other Steiner's sister has harmed Anna Berg, and now they mean to run off together. Brother and sister, whose dynamics have been strange since the start.

"What the hell are you talking about?" Jessica says. "Johan Karlsson was arrested."

"That won't do any good," Steiner says, and now Jessica realizes he's afraid. "I'm not going to spend another night here."

"What do you mean, it won't do any good?" Jessica asks, and when Steiner doesn't answer, she continues: "No one answered the phone at Anna Berg's house. Has something happened to her?"

Steiner looks flabbergasted. "What the hell are you implying?"

"Your sister stayed back in Lövö when the rest of us returned to Smörregård."

Steiner's expression shifts from frightened to amused. He laughs out loud, then for the first time takes a step closer to Jessica. The wobbly dock rocks under his feet, and Jessica fleetingly thinks he's going to tumble into the frigid sea.

"You think Pernilla stayed behind to harm Berg?"

"The Bergs didn't answer their phone even though they were supposed to be home all night."

"You don't get it, Jessica. But you can jump in the boat with me and get the hell out of here."

"What is it I don't get?"

Steiner turns back to the boat again as if to gauge how much time he has left. Then he takes a step closer, prompting Jessica to take a wary step backward.

Steiner chuckles. "See? This island is making all of us paranoid."

"I know about your sister's history."

Steiner's expression darkens. "Listen here, you snoop," he says, then wipes his mouth. He takes another step toward Jessica; no more than a couple meters remain between them. Jessica instinctively reaches for the handle of the scissors behind her back. "I'm going to ask again. Exactly what the fuck are you implying?"

Jessica opens her mouth to reply but doesn't know what to say. For the first time in her career, she's in a situation in which she's too tired and confused to grasp what's happening around her. Maybe Pernilla really has killed Berg and her husband. Maybe Berg's sister too, if she came to visit. But why Pernilla would have done so, and what this has to do with Smörregård and the girl in the blue coat, Jessica doesn't have the faintest clue.

Now she can make out more than just the headlights of the approaching vessel. The rumble of the outboard motor carries from the sea more and more distinctly.

"Anna Berg is supposedly a good detective," Steiner blurts out. "She spent enormous amounts of time and resources on investigating the deaths at Smörregård but didn't get anywhere. Yet solving the mystery would have required asking only one clarifying question of the only person who saw and heard something the night Martin Hedblom was murdered right there," Steiner says, pointing at the shore. Jessica has no trouble picturing Hedblom's corpse sprawling in the shallows.

"You remember what Berg told us today. One of the children said they'd heard an alarm clock ring. That he'd woken up to it."

"So?"

"The question is: what if the sound didn't come from an alarm clock?"

Light is falling on the back of Steiner's trouser legs. The boat is closer now.

"Jump ahead three years. It occurred to Pernilla that Monica Boman didn't go out for fresh air on a whim, but that there had to be some other reason for the walk."

"And?"

"Pernilla got the idea when Berg's phone rang. The idea that perhaps a telephone conversation had preceded the death. That someone had called the director of the children's home that evening and asked her to meet. Threatened or told her to come to a certain place at a certain time. Maybe someone set a trap for her."

"But that was long before mobile phones. That someone would have had to be . . ."

"Exactly." Steiner's expression, which had momentarily brightened, quickly darkens again. "The call would have had to be made early enough, or from sufficiently close proximity, that the perpetrator would have made it to the scene to perform the deed. Pernilla returned to Anna Berg's door this evening to ask if the children's home's telephone records for that evening had been reviewed."

"What did Berg say?"

"Of course they had. Because Boman's death was eerily similar to Hedblom's, it was immediately investigated as a crime. Anytime a homicide is suspected, protocol demands the police automatically take a look at telephone records. As a matter of fact, there was only one number at the children's home and two phones, one on the night watchman's desk and the other in the director's office," Steiner says.

Jessica doesn't say a word as she waits for him to continue and explain what the hell is going on.

"There was nothing suspicious in the phone records," Steiner continues. "But Pernilla suggested something that prompted them to drive to the station at Maarianhamina tonight. Evidently Berg's husband took the wheel, because Berg herself hates driving. That's the reason no one is answering the Bergs' phone right now. They're still in Maarianhamina."

Jessica eyes Steiner, his fearful face. She slowly releases her fingers from the scissors; now she understands where this is going. "Martin Hedblom's death was never investigated as thoroughly as Boman's," she says softly.

Steiner nods. "Berg had her suspicions. But the case was closed quickly and written off as an accident—death by drowning, to be exact—because there was no indication anyone else had been involved. Only a scared child's unreliable testimony of an alarm clock ringing in the middle of the night and a little girl standing outside."

"Which means no one checked the phone records back in 1982."

Steiner nods. "And no one thought to go back and check the 1982 records in 1985 either."

"And as you just said, if the sound wasn't from an alarm clock..."

"It must have come from a phone. Someone called the orphanage landline that night. And that's what Berg wanted to confirm immediately, tonight."

Now Jessica hears, over the howling wind, the captain of the wood-paneled motorboat turning the throttle into reverse, and the boat slows as it approaches the dock. The reek of burned diesel wafts through the air.

Steiner drops his gym bag to the dock and walks up to Jessica, hands deep in his coat pockets. "Pernilla called half an hour ago," he says. "Berg had managed to alert a former colleague who's still an investigator. And by some miracle they managed to get their hands on the call data from almost forty years ago."

The boat slowly glides up to the dock, and the man on deck straightens his leg to assist the fenders so the side of the boat won't crash against the dock. The captain calls out something in Swedish, but the roar of the engine drowns out his words.

"I'm leaving now, Jessica. The police will be here any minute," Steiner says, as if he means to leave the rest of the story untold.

"What did they find out from the telephone records?"

"That someone did call Smörregård Children's Home on September 29, 1982, at one fifty-eight a.m. And that call was made from the other phone number registered on the island." Jessica feels her heart start pounding faster before Steiner can even finish his thought: "The call came from Villa Smörregård."

"Right, but . . . Anna Berg said Johan had spent the night at Villa Smörregård."

"Exactly. But if we assume that the murder took place at two a.m. on the dot . . ."

"And the call was made from the other side of the island only two minutes before . . ."

Steiner nods. "If the call really was made by Karlsson, someone else must have drowned Martin Hedblom."

73

ARMAS POHJANPALO UNTWISTS the cork of the whisky bottle and takes a long swig. The worst of the storm has passed, but the surprisingly persistent rain continues to batter the windows, making his room feel like a giant aquarium. He senses the bottle mouth's jittery touch against his lips and knows it's because of his trembling hands. Armas glances at his watch: one forty-five a.m. He hasn't changed into his pajamas; as he sits in his armchair he's wearing the same cotton trousers and shirt he put on that morning. If only he had guessed the birds of spring would be meeting for the last time, he would have skipped the trip. On the other hand, deep down Armas knows Elisabeth deserved to die, that what they did all those years ago was incredibly wrong, and lifelong regret would not remove the fact that he and Beth were both culpable in Maija's disappearance. That through their actions, they'd driven the poor girl to the brink of insanity and to her radical resolution. Armas has always been a sensible man; he doesn't believe in God, let alone anything else supernatural. But he does believe his own eyes: he saw Maija Ruusunen, the little girl in the blue coat, standing out in the yard last night. As unbelievable as it seems, the legend of the girl in the blue coat is true. Maija's ghost returned to take vengeance, first on the night watchman and the director. Then on Hamhock. And now it was Elisabeth's turn. And next in line . . .

Armas hears someone walking down the corridor again. The footfalls are slow, dragging. He has been sure to lock his door. By morning the storm will have passed, and they will be fetched by boat from Villa Smörregård. But right now he isn't sure he'll see morning.

Armas told Jessica Niemi a story that's only halfway true. What he didn't say was that when Maija was gone, he was the one who rummaged through her room and found the letters, read Maija's diary. Armas had been madly in love with Elisabeth, still was to this day. He had gladly leaked the information to Beth, told her about Maija's father, Panda Bear, the home near the lake and the sea. Everything. Handed the girl the weapons with which she could carry out her malevolent plan. But in spite of his loyalty, Beth hadn't paid Armas the slightest attention, and instead had fooled around with the night watchman. During his final weeks at the orphanage, Armas had wallowed in heartache and tried to shut his eyes to what was going on around him. Besides, Martin Hedblom could be scary and short-tempered, and Armas hadn't wanted to end up on his bad side. It was only on the morning Armas was to leave for his new life in Finland, when there was nothing left to lose, that he had finally understood and dashed off to tell Maija the truth. Or at least tried. But Armas never discovered if his message had gotten through. According to what he'd heard, Maija continued her nocturnal excursions to the dock for several more weeks, until she disappeared, taking a rowboat with her. And Matron Boman had done nothing about it. Nothing, even though it would have been easy for her to discover the truth and bring the culprits to account for their actions. No, Monica Boman had wanted to avoid needless scandal at the orphanage she was in charge of and swept things under the rug. So she was just as guilty as the rest of them.

It all added up.

All of them had to suffer the same sort of death.

Armas hears a tap that rouses him from his reverie. Something has just hit his window. He tosses back the drop of whisky remaining at the bottom of the bottle and slowly stands. Another tap; a rock has hit the window. His hands are trembling; his legs feel unsteady. Memories spiral through his mind, and he can smell the freshly painted rooms at the orphanage, the apples that had fallen from the trees and lain on the grass for weeks. Feel the honed plank floor beneath his feet, the salt water condensing into droplets on his skin, dried by the sunshine that lessens with every day that passes. Hear the sound of the harmonium, Martin's shrill shout echoing down the corridor. The knuckle thwacks, hair pulling, and slaps. Beth's laughter, the sound of which makes his hormones go wild.

Armas emits a trembling sigh from his breast and cracks the curtain. He looks out into the yard and sees what he saw the night before. There she is: Maija Ruusunen in her blue coat. A tear rolls down Armas' cheek, because he knows tonight will be different. Tonight Maija has come back for Armas and Armas alone.

74

THE TIME IS coming up on two a.m. and the air in the interrogation room is humid and hot. Superintendent Maria Forsius of the Ålands Polismyndighet wraps a rubber band around her tight bun and inserts a small pillow of menthol snuff under her lip.

"You might as well tell us everything, Johan. We already know most of the story," she says, eyeing the man sitting across the table from her. He is cuffed at the wrists and ankles but right now looks surprisingly calm.

"I knew something bad would happen," Johan Karlsson says placidly. His thick hair is pasted to his sweaty forehead. On his cheek there's a wide scratch, which he got when Åke Nordin pushed him to the plank floor at Villa Smörregård and held him down.

"Tell me more," Forsius says, glancing at her watch. Thanks to Karlsson's arrest, she was forced to leave her daughter's eighteenth birthday party and come in to work—which, she had to admit, hadn't seemed to bother her daughter at all.

It's late enough that the middle-aged guests looked awkward on the dance floor. But several glasses of wine made their way down her throat over the course of the evening, and her head doesn't feel as sharp as might be best when conducting an interrogation.

"I didn't call Elisabeth Salmi. Or the others."

"But you were on the island during all three murders."

"So were a few other people."

"Are you taking your medications, Johan?" Forsius says, despite having already procured his epicrisis and a list of the drugs he has been prescribed. She has known Karlsson professionally for a long time but was not aware he suffered from bipolar disorder as well as borderline personality disorder. Separate medications have been prescribed for each. All Forsius knows is that the police long tried to intervene in his alcoholism, which eventually served as justification for letting him go a few years ago.

"Yes," Karlsson replies calmly.

"Why did you force those elderly people into the kitchen tonight and threaten them with a knife?"

"I wasn't threatening them; I was trying to get the situation under control."

Forsius looks at Karlsson; his face looks tired. "You've mentioned a cellar several times."

"That cellar is hell," Karlsson says, and a tear rolls down his round cheek.

"And where is this cellar?"

Karlsson looks around fearfully. "We grew up under the eyes of a monster. Åke and I."

"Who was the monster?"

"I should have arrested that monster," Karlsson says, lower lip quivering.

Forsius sighs and sits up straighter. Stretches her aching neck; she can still feel the numbing effect of the sparkling wine. "Why were high quantities of sedatives found in your blood?"

"I don't know."

"Why did you kill Elisabeth Salmi and the others?"

"It wasn't me. I've said it a thousand times, goddamn it."

"Why did you call Martin Hedblom in the middle of the night in 1982?"

"I didn't know where the phone call would lead."

Forsius has heard the story twice already. He tells it credibly and consistently. And yet she has a hard time taking the words Karlsson keeps repeating seriously:

"I thought it was just a joke."

75

FOR A MOMENT, everything around Jessica stops. The hiss of the reeds and the howl of the wind cease and are replaced by absolute silence. The landscape loses the little light there is, turns black. Jessica feels as if she is sinking into lukewarm water, deeper and deeper, until the pressure forming around her slowly drags her into eternal slumber. Suddenly everything takes on meaning: the little details that until now have only created a distracting background hum in Jessica's mind come together in a logical solution.

Throw me to the wolves and I'll return to lead the pack.

Jessica should have understood it before; the solution has been right in front of her the whole time.

"Did you hear me?" Niklas Steiner says as he steps into the boat. "From what I understood, the police are on their way. It's not safe here."

Jessica nods. She collects her thoughts and glances at her watch: fifteen to two. Her thoughts lope from wolves and packs to the last diary entry, where five people are listed at the end: Miss Boman, Martin, Beth, Hamhock, and Armas.

It's going to happen tonight. It has to happen tonight, because tomorrow the remaining birds of spring will leave the island and may never return. Tonight is Armas' time to die. And by all signs it's supposed to happen at two a.m. sharp. Armas isn't safe, because the person who is taking vengeance on Maija's behalf is not Johan Karlsson but someone he has known since childhood. Someone Johan has trusted.

"I need a ride to the south shore," Jessica calls to the captain. "Now. How long will it take if—"

"There's no way to dock a boat this big safely at the villa," the captain says as Steiner disappears into the boat.

"Why not?"

"Too shallow."

Jessica eyes the captain in a temper but knows arguing is no use.

"Niklas!" Jessica says sharply; he, however, makes no sign of climbing out of the boat. "It's going to happen in fifteen minutes!"

But Steiner isn't interested. Jessica glances at her watch again: thirteen to. Even if she ran as hard as she could, she wouldn't make it to the guesthouse before the clock struck the hour. Now Jessica knows who is behind everything. If she acts quickly, it will still be possible to prevent more deaths.

"Are you coming?" the captain asks.

"How long will it take to motor from here to Villa Smörregård?"

"I just said I can't dock—"

"How long? You don't have to go all the way to the dock."

The captain turns his gaze toward the southward shoreline. "Ten minutes, tops."

76

ARMAS SHUTS HIS eyes for a few seconds and hopes that when he opens them the girl standing out in the rain will have disappeared. But there she is, in the middle of the yard. Armas swallows to wet his dry throat and tastes salty tears at the corner of his mouth. *Forgive me, Maija. I didn't write that letter. I was just a little boy myself, a shy little boy who . . .*

But suddenly Armas sees something else too: a woman of erect bearing steps out of the guesthouse door and starts slowly approaching Maija. Her gait is oddly stiff and mechanical. The yard light is off, and everything is cast in gloom. Armas watches the woman cross the yard; her movements seem to slow with every step she takes.

"Astrid," Armas whispers softly, and hears his heart pounding in his ears.

Suddenly there's a knock at the door, and Armas jumps.

"Who is it?" Armas' hands have begun to shake again.

"Open the door, Armas!"

It's Åke's voice. Armas sees Astrid look up at his window, and Armas drops the curtain from his fingers, letting it swing in place.

He walks to the door, presses his forehead to it, waits, whispers: "What is it?"

"Something bad is about to happen," Åke says.

Then Armas hears the clink of a key ring, and suddenly the door opens. The bearded Åke is standing there, looking panicked and scanning around uneasily, as if there is something dangerous in the room itself.

"But—"

"I'm sorry . . . but there's no time now, Armas. We have to leave the house," Åke says. "And fast."

Armas thinks about Maija standing out in the yard and Astrid, who approached the ghost just a moment ago as if bewitched.

"But your mother . . . Astrid . . . She's in danger."

There's a pause in Åke's restless movements, and his facial muscles project a look of despair.

"No, Armas. My mother is the danger."

77

JESSICA FIXES HER gaze firmly on the shoreline flashing past to the right of the boat; she doesn't take her eyes off the coves opening up behind the forested headlands, but there's no sign of the red guest-house yet. She sticks her head under the roof of the boat, sees Niklas Steiner crouching helplessly on the bench, and grabs the captain's shoulder.

"Faster! Can you go faster?"

"Damn it. We're almost there."

"Punch it!" Jessica shouts, and the captain reluctantly obeys.

A moment later she sees the dock, the boathouses, the tall flag-pole, and the red wooden structures beyond. And some sort of ob-scure movement on the lawn, as if two people are standing there talking in the middle of the yard.

The captain eases off the throttle.

"Go toward shore," Jessica says.

"I said I can't dock—"

"Well, don't go up to the dock, then, goddamn it." Jessica casts a quick glance out to sea but doesn't see anything but the blue-black horizon and the black islands rising from it. If the police actually are on their way, it will be at least fifteen minutes before they arrive.

"Are you going to swim ashore?" Steiner asks.

Jessica gauges the distance to the dock; the gap is narrowing little by little as the boat approaches land. She briefly considers whether jumping into icy water can harm her child, but then she realizes there's no time to lose.

"Yes," Jessica says. "Get as close to shore as you dare."

The sea is still rough, and Jessica balances on the deck to avoid falling into the water too soon. The captain pops the gear into reverse to slow the boat, and eventually the boat stops about ten meters from the dock. Jessica looks down at the dark, rolling water and senses how cold it is. She turns toward the boathouses and sees that one of the people on the lawn facing them has turned and is walking toward the house. It's Astrid. And now that she takes a closer look, the remaining figure has the stature of a child and looks chillingly familiar. *Goddamn it. It's really happening.*

Jessica strips off her coat and lets it drop to the deck at her feet. She runs the length of the deck and springs feetfirst into the frigid water. She briefly sinks under the surface, feels the crushing cold around her. Her heart is pounding wildly, and the salt water fills her nostrils and ears. Then her head rises above the surface, and she draws a breath and swims toward the dock.

78

JESSICA GRABS THE swim ladder and climbs up onto the dock. Her soaking clothes drag her down and feel like they're freezing to her skin as the cold wind whips from the sea. She sees Astrid open the door and disappear inside the villa. Jessica glances back: both the captain and Niklas Steiner are standing on the deck of the boat, watching the strange drama unfold before them. Jessica sprints down the dock toward the shore and the villa. She passes the wooden Maija without stopping, and makes for the door Astrid entered just a moment ago.

"Astrid!" Jessica shouts as she closes in on the villa, but when she finally opens the door, the place is absolutely silent. The framing of the old wooden structure is creaking and embers smolder in the library hearth. Every corner of the weather-beaten building seems to be whispering something, as if every board and nail wants to divulge its dark secrets to Jessica.

"Hello?" Jessica says, her fingers fumbling for the garden scissors, which by some miracle are still there under her waistband, their tip having chafed painfully against the skin of her lower back. Jessica's clothes are dripping water, and she's shivering from the cold. But she doesn't have time to dry off now.

She glances at the scissors and decides they're a mediocre weapon at best.

The grandfather clock in the entryway shows one fifty-six a.m. If Jessica has read the situation correctly, she still has a few minutes to prevent another homicide, to save Armas' life. The police Steiner alerted won't be arriving for a long while yet, so Jessica is going to have to take matters into her own hands. She has been in this situation plenty of times before, leaped into the final battle against evil on her own and been close to losing her life. But this time it's not just her own life that's in jeopardy.

Jessica quickly glances into the dining room and Astrid's office, but there's no sign of anyone. Then she hears footfalls upstairs, followed by a heartbreaking shriek. Jessica knows her hesitation may have just cost a human life. She must act. She dashes to the stairs and starts climbing them, scissors in hand and at the ready.

ARMAS FEELS HIS frail ankles buckle on the soft dirt road as Åke urges him onward. Åke has helped him down the stairs, thrusting his arm through Armas', and led him out the back door, between the leafless apple trees toward the forest, and onward to the dirt road cutting through the thickets. Armas hears a bloodcurdling scream from somewhere—presumably the house—and glances back. But there's nothing there.

"Come on. We have to keep going," Åke says as the solid ground yields to soft, sinking moss under Armas' shoes.

Armas plants his cane firmly in its surface. "But . . . where?"

He is constantly on the verge of tripping at this speed, which is far too fast for his elderly physique. But Åke manages to keep Armas on his feet, just barely.

"Away from Astrid," Åke says, looking back. "Somewhere she won't find us."

JESSICA FEELS HER heart hammering in her chest. She strides up the stairs; her wet shoes squelch with every step she takes. Out of the corner of her eye she sees the black-and-white photographs of the century-old Villa Smörregård, the Nordins standing in front of it. Hans-Peter and Astrid. Their son, Åke, and the orphaned Johan. Older photos hang higher up the staircase, the ones in which the young Astrid stands on the same property with her parents. *The orphanage. Adoption. Maija.*

Jessica rises to the topmost stair; the cold clothes glued to her skin send shivers running up her spine. The hallway is unlit, but Jessica can see that the door to Armas' room is open.

"Astrid?" Jessica says, instinctively assuming a more solid stance, legs wide, her left hand rising to repel a potential attack, the hand holding the scissors falling back, ready to strike.

She has feared for her life plenty of times before, but never like this. This time her going rogue might have downright catastrophic consequences. And if something irreversible were to happen, if she now lost the child, she would never forgive herself. If that were to happen, she actually would rather die.

"Is anyone there?" Jessica calls out, even though she knows the question is pointless. She hears heavy breathing coming from Armas' room.

Suddenly the door at Jessica's side opens, and she flips the scissors so they're aimed that way. Eila Kantelinen's horrified face peers out of the gloom.

"What . . . What is going on out here . . . ?"

"Are you alone?" Jessica asks, and when the old woman nods, she continues: "Close the door and don't open it for anyone."

Jessica hears the door shut, and she slowly steps toward Armas' room. She could run, barrel in, but what was supposed to happen presumably already has.

Jessica steps up to the threshold.

She sees Astrid standing at the window, gazing out to sea. The old woman with the erect bearing is twitching strangely, as if she is possessed by some mystical force.

"Astrid?" Jessica says calmly. "Where's Armas?"

Now the old woman turns around slowly; her face is distorted by inconsolable weeping.

"You're too late, Jessica."

81

"I saw her . . . ," Armas says as his tired legs give and he lowers himself to sit on a rock. "Maija. It sounds unbelievable, but she was standing there at the shore."

Åke doesn't reply; he turns back toward the dirt road along which Astrid would in all likelihood be approaching to look for them.

"Not really," Åke says, squatting down in front of Armas.

Armas looks up from the tips of his shoes, senses his own tremulous breath. "Excuse me?"

"It doesn't sound unbelievable," Åke says. His reddish beard hairs shiver in the wind, but otherwise his face is still. It looks carved from stone, and the expression there is cold and calculating.

"Are you sick, Armas?"

"I don't understand."

"Cancer? Heart trouble? Do you have any reason to believe you won't live much longer?"

"What are you talking about, Åke—"

"Answer the question," Åke says, and he picks up a stout branch from the ground and snaps it effortlessly over his knee, as if to remind Armas how strong he is.

"Nothing like that . . ."

"But you're old. Eighty-five? A couple years younger than Beth."

"Yes, but—"

"Because I've always tried to live according to certain principles.

Even though I've never quite gotten a grasp on spirituality . . . Unlike Maija, who found strength in her faith in God."

Armas looks in confusion at Åke, and his fingers tighten around his cane. He feels his backside growing damp from the wet moss.

"But how could you know? We never talked to anyone about Maija," Armas says. "We agreed Maija was off-limits."

Åke grunts, then looks up at the sky, where the cloud cover has torn. "I know a thing or two about Maija. My guess is, even more than you do. Or the others, who made her life hell all those years ago."

Armas feels the panic slowly surge over his body. Suddenly he realizes he has made a huge mistake in going with this man, believing his words.

"Do you know anything about Roman philosophy, Armas?" Åke says calmly, as if the question is a completely logical continuation of the conversation. Armas can't get a word out.

"Seneca once wrote his father-in-law a letter in which he spoke wisely about time—or about cherishing and wasting time. He wrote that people only pay attention to the purpose for which time is demanded, not the time itself. It is requested and given as if it were nothing. Time is toyed with, although it is inarguably more precious than anything else in this world."

Armas feels the warm urine that wet the front of his trousers without his noticing drain to the cold earth. He has been trembling with fear ever since he saw Maija from his window, but now he is paralyzed with dread.

"For some reason, the ideas of Seneca specifically have made an indelible impression on me. He's one of those who somehow resolved many of life's paradoxes two thousand years before men more familiar to a wide audience . . . Kant, Nietzsche, Rousseau, Sartre. You see, Seneca understood stealing someone's time is the worst possible punishment for that person. Not life, but time. And I'm not talking about prison now, because in civilized societies that's almost synonymous with idleness. No, you have to take time away from people. Do you understand, Armas? I robbed Elisabeth of her final months in this world. If someone knows their end is imminent but still wants to live, isn't the taking of those seconds, hours, days, and weeks the worst possible punishment?"

When Armas doesn't seem to grasp what Åke is talking about, Åke laughs drily and shakes his head. "So you didn't know Elisabeth was terminally ill. My timing was perfect, actually, as in a month or two she would have probably been so sick, she would have prayed to be put out of her misery. But at this point she still valued her precious life so much that she begged me to spare it. And prior to that, she suffered her personal seventy-year purgatory."

"Take me back, Åke," Armas says, and lowers his palms to the ground to push himself up. But he can't manage it without help. Help that he is not likely to get from the man squatting before him. "Please."

"How does one live with something like that, Armas? How does one live a life knowing one destroyed a little person? You drove a girl to suicide. You wasted Maija's time, Armas."

"A day hasn't passed that I haven't—"

"Bullshit. That's what Hamhock said too."

"Did you kill . . . Did you kill Elsa?"

Åke chuckles joylessly. "What are you talking about, my dear Armas? Elsa drowned at a hotel beach in Nice in the 1990s. I happened to be staying at that same hotel, but so were a lot of other tourists."

"Åke . . ."

"I was here twenty-five years ago, the first time you arrived. Is it possible there were eight of you then? I remember thinking to myself that when you lived at the children's home you were all still children and that children cannot be punished the same way as the adults who allowed that to happen to little Maija. That I'd done my part in taking revenge on Hedblom and Boman. But you were sitting at the dining table of the guesthouse my father ran, laughing, singing, telling stories as if you owed nothing to the one missing from the group . . . It made me nauseous. Then and there I decided not a single one of the three of you whom Maija had named in her diary would experience the privilege of a peaceful death. That night in March 1994, I sat by the fire with Elsa—excuse me, Hamhock— and poured her a glass of whisky, conducted a sort of preliminary survey. I'd noticed she was wearing a wig, and she told me about her grave illness. But she also told me that despite everything, she was hopeful and wanted to live a long life. Hamhock said she had no intention of canceling the golf trip she had booked for France. That it was going to be an amazing experience and the Mediterranean climate would surely hasten her recovery.

"Note, Armas, that I hadn't prepared properly. There were a lot of people, and the thought of killing had popped into my head pretty spontaneously. By now nine years had passed since the previous oc- currence, so I was rusty. Astrid was coming to the end of her career, and there were no longer the same drugs and needles in the medi- cine cabinet that I'd used to sedate my earlier victims. I did manage to scare Hamhock; I know she saw the Maija I pulled out of the toolshed cellar after many years. But I couldn't lure her out . . . And when I was going to get her by force, I came across Astrid on the stairs and had to cancel my plans. I'm sure Mom understood some- thing strange was going on back then. So the one who was supposed to become the third person sentenced remained unpunished for the meantime. I considered Hamhock's illness both a threat and a possibility—there was always the risk that she would die before the next reunion of the birds of spring, or even worse: that her death would ultimately be a service to her. I couldn't wait too long, so I traveled to Nice in June 1994 to make sure that fat devil lost her final painless days the same way the rest of you did. By drowning. Just like Maija drowned long ago."

"How . . . ," Armas stammers through his tears. "How do you know Maija drowned?"

"As I said, I know Maija better than anyone else in this world. Despite the fact we never met."

"But . . . how?"

"Don't you understand, Armas? I found her letters and diary as a boy. Maija had even saved that grotesque contrivance that sent her spinning off the rails and ultimately prompted her to take her own life. I read the letters again, was moved and at the same time convinced how warm and loving the relationship between Maija and her father was. It was utterly unlike my relationship with my own father, that horrific monster. But I didn't feel envious of Maija; just the opposite. I was happy for her because she had at least one good thing in her life. Maija was always a victim. A victim of war, a victim of abuse, a victim of you goddamned bullies. And in the end, a victim of herself. The fact that there was always enormous love in the Ruusunen family despite the grief and death made an indelible impression on me."

82

TIME SEEMS TO have stopped in Armas' room. It still smells of old man, even though the man himself has vanished without a trace.

Jessica looks past Astrid into the yard, but all she sees is the rigid scarecrow standing there. She takes Astrid firmly by the shoulders. "Where did they go?"

"It's Åke," Astrid sobs. "It's been Åke this whole time."

"I know," Jessica says, scanning the shore. She sees no sign of the police boat she wished so fervently would come.

"How did you—"

"There's no time to explain now, Astrid. Do you know where Åke is taking Armas?"

"I'm afraid they're on their way to the orphanage dock."

Jessica feels a cold pang pierce her chest and make her heart beat even faster. Of course; what an idiot she has been. Apparently Åke has decided to take Armas where Jessica just returned from post-haste. She should have known that for the crime to take place at two on the dot, Åke would have to fetch Armas from his room much earlier. Walking with the old man would be laborious and slow regardless of whether Armas walked himself or Åke carried him on his back. Jessica could still catch up to them if she set out right away.

"Astrid, are there any guns in the house?"

Astrid looks at Jessica in shock, then exits the room. Jessica follows her into the big bedroom. Astrid opens an enormous closet and moves aside the men's coats hanging there, revealing a double-barreled shotgun behind them. Astrid hands the weapon to Jessica, but when Jessica takes hold of it, Astrid doesn't immediately release her grip.

Instead, she looks Jessica deep in the eye and says, lower lip quivering: "Åke is my son."

"Is the gun loaded?"

"What use would it be if it weren't?"

Jessica nods in a sign of silent mutual understanding and dashes from the room, shotgun in her hands.

Åke Nordin sits down at Armas' side, so close that their shoulders touch. The rain that has settled into a drizzle makes the terrain around them sigh soothingly.

"Are you awake, Armas?" Åke asks, and the old man grunts something in response.

"Actually, everything went just as it was supposed to. Your incomparable night watchman Martin Hedblom was already on his way to death. He was a fifty-five-year-old incurable alcoholic who surely knew the arc of his own pathetic life had reached its end. I was young and inexperienced that night, just a boy, and it happened so fast, he didn't have the chance to register what I'd done. The same thing happened with the orphanage director three years later; she was just about to retire."

"Åke, I don't know why you've taken it upon yourself to—"

"Because no one else did. Because those who do evil unto others must ultimately submit to the will of those they have tormented."

And then he hears something: the sound of rapid footfalls carrying from the dirt road.

JESSICA HAS WALKED this route many times and has committed the landmarks along the side of the road to memory. A moment earlier, she passed the fallen birch trunk propped up against a rock, where she saw a heron the day before yesterday. But everything looks different when she's running through the darkness. Jessica feels herself panting; the shotgun is heavy in her arms. The movement keeps her warm, even though she can feel the ice-cold air penetrate her wet clothes down to her skin. If she only makes it in time, she might be able to save Armas' life . . .

"Over here," a voice says, and Jessica's heart skips a beat. She stops and aims the shotgun in the direction of the voice. And now she sees two men slowly emerge from the trees: an old man trembling in fear and Åke, who holds the old man in front of him like a human shield.

"It's over, Åke," Jessica says. "Let Armas go."

"Did Astrid give you the gun?" Åke asks. "So you could shoot me, her only son?"

"No one has to die, Åke," Jessica says, quickly wiping the sweat from her brow.

Åke's mouth curves up into a sad smile. "How did you know it was me?"

"I found the cellar Johan was talking about."

Åke looks impressed. "So you read Maija's diary?"

"Yes."

Åke smiles and pulls Armas closer to him. "Armas is no better than the others, Jessica."

"Armas told me what happened. He tried to warn Maija. He's not guilty—"

Åke bursts out laughing. "Don't let an old man's sympathetic appearance fool you, Jessica. This man is a pathological fraud. If you'd read more of the diary, you'd understand why Armas is as guilty as the rest of them."

"Åke, you're not a judge."

"That's where you're wrong. I've been a judge since I dug up Maija's treasure in 1980. Someone had to bring these bastards to justice. But only after they've lived to the end of their miserable lives, regretting what they did every single day."

Jessica raises the shotgun so she can get a bead on Åke. But the distance is such that she cannot fire the weapon without injuring Armas too. Besides, Jessica isn't acting in the line of duty, so she doesn't have permission to use a firearm. The situation will have to be resolved by some other means.

"OK," Jessica says. "Tell me. What did Armas do?"

"He's the one who read the letters Maija's father sent. And told Elisabeth about them."

Jessica looks at the teary old man whom Åke has locked in his firm grip. Just now she has a hard time feeling sympathy for him, but even so, she has to save him from Åke's clutches. Whether or not he did wrong by Maija isn't relevant right now.

"I had a system, Jessica," Åke says. "I've just never been very good at this. Even though I grew up under a monster's eyes."

"What are you talking about?"

"But the main thing is finishing the job. I've never cared much about getting points for style."

Jessica is just about to reply when Armas' face twists up in a cry of agony. She tightens her grip on the shotgun; she doesn't understand what's happening. A soft rattle escapes Armas' lips. Jessica takes a step closer. Prepares to fire despite the risks.

Åke's grip on the old man fails, and Armas collapses to the ground face-first.

"No!" Jessica shouts, and tightens her grip on the trigger but immediately understands that shooting Åke will no longer do any good. Armas is lying dead on the wet dirt, a long kitchen knife thrust between his shoulder blades, no doubt all the way to his heart.

Jessica hears voices farther along the road, and the beams of flashlights flicker a few hundred meters away.

She eyes Åke through the scope; he stands there at the edge of the forest, hands at his sides, a numb look on his face.

"It's over now," Åke says. "Now Maija is finally free."

85

Superintendent Maria Forsius is a petite woman who has jet-black hair wrapped in a tight bun and thick eyebrows of the same shade. When she talks she raises them as if the movement is essential to her delivery, which is cryptic in other ways as well. The air-conditioning has been turned on so high in the glass-walled office on Maarianhamina's Strandgatan that Jessica is shivering in her T-shirt.

"There's one thing that still bothers me," Forsius says, folding her hands on the table for the umpteenth time. The ring finger of the left hand is adorned with a diamond so large that it borders on taste-less, which makes Jessica feel some sort of affinity with the other woman. Judging by the size of the rock, there's no need for Forsius to be a police officer, but she is one anyway.

"What's that?" Jessica lifts her water glass to her lips only to realize it's empty again.

"When Steiner told you about the phone call made to Martin Hedblom, how did you know it was Åke?"

"Who else would it have been? Astrid?" Jessica says.

"In a way, she was a more likely perpetrator in several aspects. Her advanced age argues against her culpability now, but especially with the cases from the 1980s it would have somehow been more logical."

"It's pretty simple," Jessica says. "Åke's interest in philosophy, particularly in Seneca, had its origins in a single sentence Maija wrote in her diary, her final entry. And which Åke adopted for the rest of his life."

"Are you referring to the diary now, or that one sentence?"

"Both," Jessica says, and Forsius grunts. "'Throw me to the wolves, and I'll return leading the pack,'" Jessica continues. "I read it in a book I borrowed from the library at Smörregård."

Forsius looks doubtful. "It wasn't very smart of Åke to leave books like that lying around the guesthouse for anyone to borrow."

"There was no way he could know I'd get my hands on Maija's diary," Jessica says.

"True." Forsius turns her attention to the papers spread out before her. She is perhaps a few years older than Jessica but very youthful, and if she has children (as Jessica has deduced from some earlier throwaway comment), her figure appears to have made a superb recovery.

"Is that everything?" Forsius asks, looking at Jessica in admiration.

"I heard yesterday that Åke had specifically arranged for a journalist to be on the scene to get publicity for his cause. At that point, I was still convinced his cause was Villa Smörregård. But in reality Åke wanted to tell Maija's story to the whole world."

"A noble mission. But at the same time really damn twisted," Forsius says. "And ultimately Åke Nordin's case is incredibly sad, to put it simply."

Jessica taps her fingers against the tabletop. *Sad?*

"I don't have anything else. I'd like to thank you on my own behalf for your alertness and otherwise exemplary action. You couldn't have prevented what happened to Armas Pohjanpalo. But you may have saved other lives. Åke Nordin may not have stopped at Armas."

"Thank you." Jessica closes her eyes and considers whether there's anything else about the equation she doesn't understand yet.

Forsius leans in toward Jessica, fingers still interlaced. "No: thank you. Now the girl in the blue coat that boaters have spotted on the shores of Smörregård for nearly eighty years can finally be put to rest. Maybe it could be burned, like the straw goat at Gävle."

Jessica grunts, although the idea sounds indecorous. It is of course nothing but a human effigy slapped together from boards, but even so, it represented little Maija in some way. The scarecrow is more deserving of a proper funeral, the kind Maija herself never had.

"What's going to happen to Johan Karlsson?"

"That's a little complicated. He's a problematic guy—in the minds of many, too strange and unstable from the start to be a police officer—but ultimately he isn't guilty of anything, except maybe aiding and abetting."

"For making a phone call to Martin Hedblom at Åke's request?" Jessica says.

"No, for protecting Åke all these years," Forsius says. "He was loyal to his childhood friend but genuinely wanted to prevent Åke from killing anyone else. Karlsson said he was horrified when he heard Åke was coming back. He had immediately understood one of the birds of spring would be in danger."

"I see."

"Åke put a large dose of sedatives in Johan's food Friday night so he'd be able to go about his business without any interruptions," Forsius says.

"Wow."

Forsius smiles; she seems to have caught hold of a fresh thought. "This Helena Lappi, your unit commander . . . Does she have something against you?"

"Is that what it sounded like on the phone?"

"Let's just say she was pretty taken aback by the praise you received from our *polismyndighet*. As if she'd expected just the opposite."

"I'm sure she did."

"Big-city life?"

"Something like that."

Forsius collects her papers and rises to her feet. Jessica is on the verge of excusing herself, but then she remembers something Forsius said just a moment ago. *That boaters have spotted on the shores of Smörregård . . .*

"Sorry, but I do have one more question," Jessica says.

Forsius stops, stands up straight, and raises her thick eyebrows. "Yes?"

"You said Maija had been seen on the shores for eighty years. But to my understanding, Åke only made the effigy after reading Maija's diary in 1980."

"I'm not sure how appropriate it is to discuss the details, but I can reveal that the effigy was not made by Åke; it was made by his father, Hans-Peter."

"But . . . why?"

"Hans-Peter Nordin married Astrid in 1956, and by that point he already had a vision of turning his in-laws' villa into a hotel. He was known as an opportunist and gold digger, but a resourceful one. By feeding the legend of the girl in the blue coat, he made Smörregård a popular tourist destination, and before long the guesthouse was flourishing. In order to keep the story alive, all he needed was a Maija boaters would see as they sailed past."

"But how did Åke . . ."

"He found it in the cellar," Forsius says. "Finding the doll inspired him to investigate more deeply. And just like you, he discovered the coordinates Maija had left in room six at the children's home. For Åke, Maija's diary became a Bible of sorts. And then he gradually adapted Seneca's philosophy for his own purposes. That has happened with other philosophers too, for instance Nietzsche, albeit those who have interpreted his teachings as they've seen fit have been much worse than Åke Nordin."

A sudden exhaustion washes over Jessica. Everything is clear and yet still doesn't add up. "How is it possible that Astrid Nordin didn't know about the cellar under the toolshed, despite having lived on the property her whole life? And that her husband hid a scarecrow in a blue coat down there?"

Forsius looks at Jessica like she is a toddler who has just asked something stupid. Or too difficult; her expression is impossible to read fully.

"I'm afraid we're moving toward a gray area, toward things unrelated to this case."

Jessica frowns. "What? What do you mean, unrelated?"

"Astrid Nordin was not aware of the existence of the cellar. I can confirm that. Unfortunately that's all I can tell you about it."

"But—"

"The car will take you to the Lövövägen ferry, so you can go retrieve your belongings from Smörregård." Maria Forsius extends a hand, which Jessica reluctantly shakes before exiting the room.

86

JESSICA ASKS THE taxi driver parked in front of the police station to wait a moment longer, claiming a sudden fit of nausea. It's a semi-legitimate excuse; Jessica truly does feel in the pit of her stomach a strange gnawing sensation that she doubts is from the pregnancy this time. She can't help but think that she has missed something very fundamental. Something Maria Forsius and the other locals already know. She closes her eyes and tries to connect the pieces hanging in the air, to form them into a clear image that will explain the bigger picture. What was it Åke said to her on Anna Berg's balcony the previous night? Jessica conjures up an image of the jovial, middle-aged man before her, his reddish beard shivering in the storm wind.

Astrid treated him like her own son . . . She had a tender spot when it came to orphans . . . She and Dad even considered adopting him, I understand. And I guess they would have, except . . .

Unless what? What else happened at Smörregård around the time of Hedblom's death? At least the life of Åke's father, Hans-Peter, had been roiled by some bigger development, since he resigned from all of his companies in March 1983, at the age of forty-six. Did it have something to do with what had made the cheerful, smiling Åke from the photographs retreat into his own world and develop an obsession with Maija's story, begin to take revenge on people he didn't know from Adam? And do it all on behalf of someone who had died years before he was born? Besides, it was somehow strange that Åke moved to Sweden when he reached adulthood and returned to Smörregård only after his father died. Now that Jessica thinks about it, she remembers that Armas said Hans-Peter wasn't at Smörregård the year of the first reunion of the orphans, in 1994. Åke and Hans-Peter Nordin may have never seen each other again after 1990.

Jessica glances at the taxi. The driver is sitting there with his window slightly cracked.

Last night, just before he stabbed Armas with the knife, Åke said something about growing up under the eyes of a monster. But he wasn't referring to Martin Hedblom or Monica Boman.

Jessica should have known right away.

Damn it! She strides briskly to the taxi and opens the back door.

"Lövövägen ferry?" the driver asks.

"No, but in that direction," Jessica replies, and shuts the door.

There is perhaps one person on this island who can tell her the truth.

87

FROM THE STREET, Anna and Pelle Berg's house looks less imposing than it does from the water. Whereas the seaside facade of the
hillside villa is three stories, from the other side it's barely two. A
gleaming, freshly waxed Nissan Pathfinder stands under the carport.

Jessica rings the doorbell, and a moment later the door is opened
by a broad-shouldered man of about sixty who has a surprisingly
heavy unibrow.

"Hi, I'm—"

Berg's voice from the living room cuts Jessica off. "Come in."

Jessica smiles politely and steps past the man.

"Would you like some coffee?" Berg says. She's sitting at the same
table where they conversed the previous evening. The living room
seems somehow smaller in the daylight.

"No, thanks. I won't stay long," Jessica says, taking a seat next to
Berg. She glances into the entryway, where Pelle is throwing on a
dark green hunting jacket. Then the door opens.

"Your husband is tactful."

"No, just indifferent," Berg says, and the little mouth between the
round cheeks turns up in a smile. She clicks two sweeteners into a
cup, pours in a splash of milk, then stirs the concoction with a spoon
and looks pointedly at Jessica.

"Where's your camera?"

"I'm not a photographer."

"I know. We have access to the internet," Berg replies, and sips her coffee. "You have quite a kick. Karate?"

"Savate." Jessica raises the cup set out for her. "Maybe I will have a little after all, please."

"What did that man do to you?" Berg asks as she pours the coffee.

"Put his hands on me. Just a little. But enough."

"Good for you, then. Damn it." They clink their mugs. "What can I do for you?"

Jessica lowers her cup to the table and leans back. The chair is still as uncomfortable as the previous evening, and she momentarily considers whether she has the nerve to suggest that they continue the conversation on the sofa set, which looks significantly cozier.

"I'm guessing, judging by everything, Smörregård has never been some idyllic little place," Jessica says. "But I didn't know the worst villain lived at the south shore."

"Åke?"

"No, the one who raised him."

Suddenly Anna Berg's expression is hard to interpret; it's simultaneously impressed and alarmed.

"Am I right?" Jessica asks.

"You are. Hans-Peter Nordin was not a nice man."

"Can you tell me about him?"

"Why do you want to know about him? The man is dead and buried. The mistakes of the past follow us throughout our lives, but Astrid doesn't need to know about them. Åke didn't want her to either. That's why he just left instead of telling his mother everything and breaking her heart."

"I want to understand what really happened on the island."

Berg stirs her coffee vigorously, apparently gathering up her courage.

"Fine," she eventually says, then sighs. "Hans-Peter Nordin was known in Maarianhamina in the fifties as a smart but penniless dandy who had his fingers in a lot of pies, and managed to do pretty well for himself, primarily because of his superb gift of gab. The marriage to Astrid gave him control over most of an island, and when they inherited it after Astrid's parents died, Hans-Peter came up with the idea of turning the place into a hotel. Oddly enough, it was a success despite its remote location, partly on account of the legend of the girl in the blue coat. The place attracted a lot of curious tourists; Hans-Peter had developed into a reputable marketer and salesman who was capable of selling sand to the Sahara and rocket launchers to pacifists. His reputation preceded him, and he had no trouble acquiring shares in various enterprises."

"Until something happened . . ."

"My father used to say that Hans-Peter Nordin was the nicest man he knew but he wouldn't trust him as far as he could throw him. That beneath the jovial shell there was something cold and soulless. You've probably come across criminals in your work who fit this description to a T."

"Psychopaths," Jessica says.

Berg nods. "I don't think Astrid ever saw her husband's dark side. She was so occupied with her work that she simply didn't have time to stop and look. But Åke was a different matter."

"What do you mean?"

Berg gulps twice, as if talking has suddenly grown difficult. "No one knows for sure. The police had their suspicions. And eventually, in 1983, the police were notified that Hans-Peter had been harassing the children from the orphanage. Inviting them into his home . . ."

"Are you saying he was a pedophile?"

"It was unclear. But one of the children mentioned a cellar where Hans-Peter had taken him sometimes and said strange things."

"Dear God Almighty." Now Jessica remembers the chair pushed up against the cellar wall and the thick rope on the floor. She hopes they have nothing to do with the story.

"The boy Nordin took to the cellar again and again was Johan Karlsson," Berg says, and a tear rolls down her cheek. "And even though the boy grew stranger and stranger by the day, what he said was disregarded because no cellar was ever found."

"So Hans-Peter was never officially suspected of sexual abuse of children? But the damage to his reputation was already done?"

"Efforts were made to quash the rumors. Behind closed doors it was agreed that Nordin would resign from all his positions of trust and the issue would be swept under the rug. It was a delicate situation, of course, because Nordin denied everything and felt it was a travesty of justice. But of course he didn't want word of the suspicions to spread."

"Why didn't Johan Karlsson tell anyone where the cellar was?"

"Evidently Hans-Peter took him down there blindfolded."

Jessica looks at Anna Berg in confusion. "But if Åke knew about the cellar, if he'd been down there himself . . . why didn't he ever say anything to anyone?"

"Didn't you hear what I just said? It was too late to save Johan. And Åke didn't want his mother to suffer. He was a young philosopher who didn't believe in pointless suffering."

JESSICA RELEASES HER grip on the suitcase handle and walks into the library. She stands in the middle of the room, hands in the pockets of her down parka, and looks at the old woman sitting at the fire; the fingers wrapped around the big steaming mug appear to be trembling.

Jessica coughs quietly into her fist, and it's only now that Astrid seems to notice her. She turns her face toward Jessica, but her eyes remain trained on the fire blazing in the hearth.

"So you're leaving now?"

Jessica nods and takes a step closer. "Are you sure you're going to be all right?"

Astrid lets out a brief sigh, which sounds more like a sharp exhalation. Then she nimbly stands. Jessica is still impressed by the way this woman over the age of eighty carries herself: she is blown away by Astrid's ramrod posture, inquisitive eyes, and firm chin. The sinewy shoulders that look like the wings of a bird about to spring into flight.

"'We islanders shall survive, we tenants of this wretched place. Barren land, grass and moss laid over a curve of endless rock,'" Astrid recites in Finnish, and a wistful smile flickers across her face.

"That's lovely," Jessica says. "Who wrote it?"

Astrid shrugs. "Simo Hietikko, a budding poet who stayed here with us years ago. I found a note in his room where the words were written in a beautiful hand. It's framed on the wall in my and

Hans-Peter's bedroom," Astrid says, and walks up to Jessica, hands on her hips. Hearing the man's name makes a shiver run through Jessica's body.

"You, on the other hand, were not writing a detective novel, Jessica. At any point."

Jessica shakes her head. "No."

Astrid laughs joylessly. "It was just a guess of Åke's," she says, and raises her hand to her mouth. "Little Åke." She shakes her head. "Am I ever going to see him again? My own son?"

"I'm sure you will," Jessica says.

Astrid wipes the tears from the corner of her eye. "Åke just did what he felt was right. He had his own view of morality . . . He was on Maija's side. Wanted justice for that little girl."

Jessica looks out the window, hears the flagpole line play its now-familiar ghostly accompaniment, the one with a single, wistful note. Jessica could say there was nothing right about what Åke did. That he murdered five people simply because he had an obsession with a girl who'd died over twenty years before he'd even been born. He was morbidly fixated on the mystery of the girl in the blue coat and dedicated his life to making sure the legend never died. To making sure no one would ever forget the story of Maija who once lived on Smörregård. That's why it needed to be written about in the papers. In a way Åke's moral compass—if a serial killer has one, that is—had been pointing the right way: the people who had tricked a little girl in an unforgivable fashion, especially the adults, should have been brought to account for their actions long before, but a death sentence was by no means appropriate. Whatever the right punishment might have been, there was no way it should have fallen on Åke's shoulders to carry it out.

"Maybe Maija's heart would be warmed by the thought that someone here on the island was on her side. Even if it wasn't until after her death," Jessica says.

Astrid nods and tries to pull herself together. Then she looks around, the room and its walls hung with art featuring her son's favorite motif, lighthouses.

"Maybe it's time to finally shut this place down," Astrid says. "I can't do this alone."

"Take your time and think about it," Jessica says, then pulls a folded piece of paper from her pocket and hands it to Astrid. "Wait," she says as Astrid starts to unfold it. "Don't read it until after I'm gone."

"OK," Astrid says, then places the paper on the table and looks at Jessica with an expression that's both sad and concerned. Then Jessica takes the initiative, steps forward, and hugs the other woman. She feels the dark red skin against her cheek, and Astrid seems to notice.

"Go ahead and ask," Astrid says when they pull apart.

"What?"

"You want to know why my throat looks like this."

But Jessica doesn't ask, because prying feels wrong.

"The sixth of February 1944," Astrid says. "The Soviet Union sent its greetings to the corner of Annankatu at seven fifteen p.m. My parents went up in smoke."

"I'm sorry," Jessica whispers.

They stand there, face-to-face, without saying a word. Then Astrid gently pushes Jessica away and whispers: "As a mother, all you can do is your best. No more. And then hope that everything will turn out for the best."

The words bring a tear to Jessica's eye. She can't help but think Astrid's biggest mistake with Åke was blindness. She looked away, ushered new life into the world when she ought to have been keeping her eyes on the one she herself created. Protecting him. Seeing the danger lurking nearby that drove the boy away as soon as he was of age.

"Remember: no one is capable of working miracles with children. Not even you," Astrid continues.

"But—"

Astrid raises her fingers in front of her lips and zips an imaginary zipper across her mouth, exactly the same way she did the morning before last in the dining room. And for some reason Jessica is sure that this matter will remain their secret, at least for as long as is necessary. Until Jessica is somewhere far away and it no longer makes a difference.

She looks Astrid in the eye, nods, and turns to leave. As she picks up the suitcase standing by the door, she glances over her shoulder one last time and sees that in the intervening few seconds, Astrid has stoked the fire and is back sitting in her armchair. Her bony fingers stroke the lion's head, slide into its open mouth, as if defying the hurts of life.

A remarkable woman, Jessica thinks to herself, and opens the door. Hopefully she'll be able to leave this world without knowing the whole crushing truth.

89

Yusuf Pepple tosses back the rest of his pint and stifles a belch
in his fist. An ambulance is parked outside the window of Manala;
someone over on the restaurant side suffered some sort of a mild
attack half an hour earlier.

Yusuf's friend and long-term colleague Nina Ruska returns from
the bathroom and sits down across from him. The biceps bulging
under her T-shirt and the veins snaking at their surface always make
for an impressive sight.

"Evidently they have it under control," Nina says, and takes a sip
of her nearly untouched drink.

"Great," Yusuf says.

Nina doesn't look convinced. "Is everything OK?" She taps Yusuf's empty pint glass with her fingernail. "How long did it take you
to down this, a full three minutes?"

"I was thinking I'd down at least three more."

"What's the happy occasion?"

"Anything but happy," Yusuf says. "I'm gathering up my courage."

"What for?"

Yusuf shifts his gaze from the ambulance to the all-night grill, to
the tree branches hanging above it, and then slowly back to Nina.

"I'm meeting Tanja at six."

Nina looks at Yusuf and now sees the pain he was able to conceal
just a moment ago.

"Jesus Christ, Yusuf."

"I've been thinking about it . . . for a while. It's just not really taking off. It never did."

"Tough stuff," Nina says, and presses a finger into the back of Yusuf's hand. "Really tough."

"How about you and the . . . banker?"

"Tom's a consultant. Fine. For now."

Yusuf nods, then looks back out the window. The medics exit the restaurant through the bar and jump into the ambulance. This time without a customer, fortunately.

"So, do you have someone else in mind?" Nina asks.

Yusuf gazes at the corner of Töölönkatu and Museokatu, at the beautifully plastered building standing where the streets meet, the top two floors of which belong to his best friend. He's been spending a lot of time at Manala lately, at this very table; the view seems to soothe him.

"I don't know," he says. "In a way. I always have."

"Are you going to do anything about it?"

Yusuf sighs and looks down at his empty glass. "I think it's too late."

"How do you know?"

"That woman's a mystery, Nina. Or she has been until now. But I think that I finally understand. I always thought she'd have a plan and that I just wasn't a part of it. But now it feels there never was a plan. And that I should have done something sooner and offered her one. Told her how I felt before she could shut me out."

90

JESSICA WALKS THE dirt road running through the woods to the north shore of Smörregård. The wheels of her suitcase are barely big enough to make pulling it along the dirt road possible. Most of the time, Jessica is just dragging it toward her destination, but it doesn't matter. She feels the mild breeze from the north on her face and inhales, filling her lungs with fresh air. It's a beautiful day: the sun is shining from the clear sky, and the birds are singing in the woods. A pair of squirrels still in their gray winter coats leap from tree to tree: it must be some sort of springtime mating ritual that will eventually lead to new life. The birth of a new, innocent creature into the world of tomorrow, which will be either a worse place or a better place than today. Presumably worse. Jessica has seen too much darkness over the course of her life to be optimistic, to believe the world can be a safe, good place to live. But lately, through therapy, she has realized that happiness is not being able to close one's eyes to the underbelly of life. Having a fairy-tale world supplied with all the creature comforts and surrounded by walls is not the answer. But neither is death: now Jessica knows with her whole heart that she wants to live. She has to live; she is responsible for something more important than she is. She can finally see the continuum alongside which the escalating pain of adult life and wrestling with one's own choices feels ridiculous and vain.

As she emerges from the woods, Jessica senses that the trees lower their boughs, send their pliable branches writhing toward her.

They wrap around her ankles, squeeze her waist, hold her firmly by the wrists. But when she continues striding purposefully toward the dock, the forest loses its grip. It could, she supposes, force her to stay, or at least try. But it's wiser than that. Jessica must leave.

The abandoned orphanage stands at the edge of the clearing. Before her spreads the sea that continues as far as the eye can see, its waves lapping tamely against the rock. The sunny day is as if custom-ordered for a voyage.

She walks across the yard toward the dock and the figure standing at the end of it. When she gets closer, she sees the motorboat moored there; it peers between the little boathouses built over the water. The driver of the water taxi is a small middle-aged man, surprisingly tan for the time of year, who has the long, curly hair of a rock guitarist.

"You have a suitcase," he calls in Swedish, and starts walking toward her. "I could have picked you up from Villa Smörregård."

"No. This was perfect," Jessica says, but doesn't refuse when the man offers to carry the suitcase into the boat.

"Be careful. The dock is in really bad shape," he says, taking a side step to maintain his balance.

"I know," Jessica mumbles, although he probably doesn't hear her. She casts a final glance over the dilapidated facade of the orphanage, its black, gaping, partially shattered windows. The stone stairs leading to the door and the curtainless window at the far end.

The face of a little girl appears at the windowpane.

Jessica raises a hand to wave, and the girl does the same.

Jessica feels pressure in the corner of her eye. She lowers her hand to her belly as the girl vanishes from the window.

As a mother, all you can do is your best. No more.

Maybe Jessica's mother did her best all those years ago, even though her mental illness ultimately caused irreparable destruction. And maybe Astrid, in uttering this adage, was not completely right.

Maybe parenthood demands something more: weighing whether doing one's own best is the same as doing what is best for the child.

Astrid tried to do her best with Åke. Even so, everything is over now. Astrid is alone. Of course the half million euros Jessica donated to the guesthouse would make it possible for Astrid to hire more staff or at least make her own life easier in some other way. Jessica would have wanted to stay in the room to watch Astrid unfold the note she had written. But this is classier. Making a donation is never completely altruistic, she supposes, but people's gratitude is often so naked, so tender and personal, there's no need to make a point of witnessing it. Sometimes financial help can even irritate the recipient. Who knows? Maybe Astrid will never withdraw the funds. Maybe she's too proud. But that's not Jessica's business.

"Where to?" the driver says, pulling on a red fisherman's beanie. Jessica glances at the boat outfitted with two large outboard motors: it could no doubt make it all the way to Stockholm, at least in this kind of weather. From there she could continue on to anywhere without leaving a trace. *They* could continue. She and the baby.

The man unlashes the rope from the mooring cleat and extends a hand to help Jessica into the boat. He's Erne's age and looks a little like him too. The furrows of a fully lived life are visible on his pockmarked face, and the whiskies tossed down his throat and the cigarettes he has smoked can be heard in his voice.

You'll do fine wherever you go, Jessie. I'm so proud of you.

Jessica exhales the air from her lungs and notices the quiver in her sigh: one chapter of her life has come to its inevitable end. She is lonely and rootless, but at the same time the meaning of life is clearer than ever before. She turns her back on the island knowing she will never return, just like the girl in the blue coat decided to do so long ago. The girl whose father loved her above all and called her Panda Bear.

"Somewhere far away, somewhere far from the sea," Jessica says, and takes the man's hand and steps into the boat.

91

1946

MAIJA RUUSUNEN CASTS a final glance at the stout stone building rising at the forest's edge, the place that has been her home for the past four months. She clumsily pushes the rowboat into the water. For a second she thinks the bottom is stuck on a rock, but then the boat moves. She quickly climbs in. The boat turns crosswise in the shallows; Maija takes the oars and turns the prow back toward open water. The evening is tranquil, but far out on the horizon, a gray mass of rain clouds looms over the sea. It takes Maija a moment to grow accustomed to the weight of the oars and get into the rhythm of rowing, but before long she can tell the boat is advancing steadily farther and farther from shore. She gazes at the gradually receding red boathouse and the rocks in front of it, where she and the others used to sit and dry off after swimming in the summer. It seems as if an eternity has passed since then. In the intervening time, summer has turned to dark fall, grief to hope and ultimately bitter disappointment.

Maija continues rowing determinedly; she looks at the orphanage that is slowly shrinking to the size of a scale model, at the black windows behind which the little rooms will be completely vacant after her departure. The only person sleeping inside those walls is the night watchman, who has been drinking all evening, who will wake up the next morning in an empty building. He will have his work cut out for him then, explaining what happened. Maybe he'll get the firing he deserves. On the other hand, after Maija leaves, there will be no one left to watch, and that means no watchman's job either.

HER SHOULDER MUSCLES ache, but she must keep going. Tiring out is not an option, not tonight. Not yet.

She closes her eyes for a moment and hears her own voice, the sentence she has been repeating to herself.

Dad isn't coming.

She has been telling herself the thought for a week now, simply to get used to it, to toughen herself up and prepare for the inevitable.

She is sure Dad had wanted to come, had tried his hardest. There's no doubt about that. He would have come if there were any way he could have.

Maija has waited patiently, hoped that any night would be the night.

But now she's positive the night will never come.

The bad people never succeeded in killing or capturing Dad, driving him to despair. The only one who'd been able to do that had been God, who had his own reasons for doing the things he did. No one could defy the power of nature, not even a strong, good, God-fearing man like her father.

And just like Dad, Maija is a survivor, who never bows before bad people.

Dad would understand her decision, even though thinking about it would make him sad. Dad would respect it, her courage and determination.

He would understand that Maija could not wait anymore, no matter how badly she wanted to. Maija couldn't stay a single day longer at Smörregård; it would have eaten her from the inside out, leaving behind only an empty shell, a pale girl they had started calling crazy long ago. A child no rational adult would adopt. Besides, Maija doesn't want that anymore anyway.

Maija has decided to take fate into her own hands. And that fate is going to be very different from Beth's, Hamhock's, Eila's, Armas', or that of those others who have boarded boats with their new parents and traveled to who knows where: Sweden, Denmark, or maybe back to war-torn Finland.

That's not the hand Maija was dealt.

When Dad said good-bye to Maija at the train station four years ago, he had hugged her with tears in his eyes, kissed her forehead, and said everyone's job is to do their best with the hand life had dealt them. Dad had said that so many times since too, in some of those dozens and dozens of letters he'd sent Maija in Uppsala. Unfortunately, Maija's hand wasn't very good to begin with. She'd merely been a motherless girl whose childhood was shadowed by ghostly air-raid sirens and the low rumble of bombers. War separated her from her father, sent her to a place where she never felt at home, even at the beginning. A place where circumstances stripped her of her childhood.

Maija thinks about her father's letters, which are lying in a single sheaf under the forest behind the orphanage. Maybe someone will find them someday and see that she, this crazy girl in a blue coat, was loved. And that her terrible life was separated from a perfect one by a single treacherous storm that buried her father at the bottom of the sea. How fragile are the threads everything hangs on.

Maija lifts the oars, feels the weight of the water in her shoulders and arms. Fifteen minutes go by, then another fifteen. She rows and rows and at some point she no longer knows how much time has passed or how far from shore she is in her boat. She can just barely make out the treetops of Smörregård in the darkness, there where the night-inked sea ends. The wind has picked up; the light raindrops it speeds along feel refreshing against her clammy skin. The fatigue in her limbs leads her thoughts away from her father and death.

Maija closes her eyes and inhales the scent of the sea. Her fingers are cramping, and her muscles are so tired that, now that she has stopped, she can't row a single meter more.

But that doesn't matter, because she has finally arrived.

A pale yellow moon peers out from behind the curtain of clouds, casting a beautiful bridge across the surface of the sea. Maija lets the boat come to a stop on the bridge's arch. It's the perfect spot.

She hoists the oars into the boat. Now she can see that the storm front that loomed far out to sea earlier will be overhead in just a moment.

It's all going the way it was supposed to. Dad would be proud of the determination Maija has demonstrated tonight. On the night that in a moment will strip off its mask and show its true face.

She calmly lowers herself to the bottom of the boat, pulls the blanket over her, and presses her arms to her chest. She has imagined this situation time and again, been afraid she would be too nervous when the moment finally came, would regret her decision. But now Maija notices to her satisfaction that she is completely calm. No fear, no regret, no hesitation. Just blue and yellow butterflies in her stomach.

Maija hears a bird cry, sees the gray silhouette of a gull arcing high against the ever-darkening sky.

She hears the soft rumble of the thunder overhead, closes her eyes, and smiles, content.

You'll be waiting for me, won't you, Dad?

THANK YOU SO MUCH

Pauliina, William & Lionel

My parents & brothers

Michelle Vega & the amazing team at Berkley

Elina Ahlbäck & the superstars at Ahlbäck Agency

Petra Maisonen & Tammi Publishers

Translator Kristian London

All the readers and friends of Jessica Niemi

GHOST
ISLAND

MAX SEECK

QUESTIONS FOR DISCUSSION

1. Jessica Niemi finds herself as the center of unwanted attention following the altercation near the beginning of the novel. How did you feel about her handling of the situation? Do you think her supervisor treated her fairly following the incident?

2. Jessica decides to isolate herself by taking a trip to a remote island. What do you think of her choice? Have you ever taken a solo trip?

3. The "birds of spring" have a fraught history with one another and with Åland. How do you think the courses of their lives were changed by what they experienced together? Do you have sympathy for any of them in particular? If so, why?

4. Astrid and Åke are very invested in the history of the islands and their inhabitants. How do you think history shaped who they are and what paths their lives have taken? Do you see any similarities between Åke's feelings regarding Maija and Jessica's relationship with her mother?

5. Bullying and how it affects the victim is a central theme of the novel. How do you feel about Maija's treatment? What do you think causes someone to become a bully? What are some ways that might help put an end to the bullying cycle?

6. The story of the girl in the blue coat is reminiscent of an urban legend. Were urban legends a part of your childhood growing up? Are there any you remember that scared you?

7. Jessica has several encounters with Maija. Do you think Maija really appears to her? Why do you think Jessica feels so drawn to her and is so invested in her plight?

8. Jessica has revealed a lot about herself to her coworker and friend Yusuf. How do you think Yusuf and Jessica's friendship has changed throughout the course of the books? How do you feel about the evolution of their relationship while Jessica is away from Helsinki?

9. The past plays an integral part in the lives of all the characters we meet in *Ghost Island*, including Jessica. What are the most important lessons you have learned from your experiences? Do you save relics from your past or keep a journal so you can look back on certain times in your life?

10. Jessica makes several significant decisions about her future in this book. Do you agree or disagree with her choices?

Photo by Marek Sabogal

International and *New York Times* bestselling author **Max Seeck** writes novels and screenplays full-time. His accolades include the Finnish Whodunnit Society's 2016 Debut Thriller of the Year Award and the Storytel audiobook award for best crime novel for *The Witch Hunter*, known internationally as *The Faithful Reader. The Last Grudge* won the 2023 Glass Key award for best Scandinavian crime novel. An avid reader of Nordic noir for personal pleasure, he listens to film scores as he writes. Max lives with his wife and children near Helsinki.

VISIT MAX SEECK ONLINE

MaxSeeck.com/books

 MaxSeeck

 MaxSeeck

 MaxSeeck

Ready to find
your next great read?

Let us help.

Visit prh.com/nextread

Penguin
Random
House